CAMP HELL
A PsyCop Novel

CAMP HELL

A PsyCop Novel

Jordan Castillo Price

JCP BOOKS

First published in the United States in 2009 by JCP Books.
www.jcpbooks.com

First Edition

ISBN: 978-0-9818752-6-2

"Written over the gate here are the words 'Leave every hope behind, ye who enter.' Only think what a relief that is! For what is hope? A form of moral responsibility. Here there is no hope, and consequently no duty, no work, nothing to be gained by praying, nothing to be lost by doing what you like. Hell, in short, is a place where you have nothing to do but amuse yourself."

—George Bernard Shaw, *Man and Superman*, 1903

✦ ONE ✦

"So. You're here to gloat over how you'll nail me with your civil suit." Roger Burke nailed *me* with the world's smuggest grin, and when I didn't accommodate him by being lured into some sort of argument, he added, "I'd just like to see you try."

My civil suit. I checked that phrase against the known phrases in my admittedly limited catalog of things-I-knew-about, and came up blank. I was coasting on the sweet spot of my Auracel and I didn't feel the immediate need to tell Burke that I had no idea what he was talking about, so I stared at him instead.

He'd been grinning at me. His smile faltered. "Don't give me that look."

I attempted to look even more like I currently did.

"Go ahead and sue me. I've got less than five thousand dollars in the bank. And believe me, I've got my countersuit all planned out. You could've given me a stroke by shooting me up in the neck. I'm prepared to testify that a long-time drug user like you would know that."

It had never even occurred to me to sue him. I pressed the heel of my hand into my right eye. It felt great, and then it hurt, and then I saw a flash of pretty colors. "Would you shut up for half a second?"

"Think you'd win over a jury? Maybe they'd sympathize with you on the drug angle if you did your 'boo-hoo, I'm a medium' routine. But once my attorneys parade in that big, smug, steroid-pumped gorilla you play house with...."

"I was planning on talking about a way we could avoid the courtroom, but keep running your mouth, and my next phone call is my lawyer."

Burke crossed his arms over his chest as far as his handcuffs would allow, and he glared. He had a hell of a glare. I'd never seen him use it during the time he'd been my partner at the Fifth Precinct. He'd spent over a month projecting a wholesome, helpful, non-threatening persona as the Stiff half of our PsyCop team, and I'd been totally sold on his good-cop act.

Now that I knew him for what he was, I had no idea how I ever could have seen him as harmless. His eyes, which once seemed unguarded and approachable—at least, for a homicide investigator—now looked so cold and calculating that I wondered why I'd ever thought it was safe to get into a car with him, let alone accept a drink he'd bought without my surveillance.

He sat across the plastic table from me in the visiting room, with his pale, reptilian eyes trained on me so hard that I felt like I needed to go take a shower under a water cannon to wash off the evil. There was a repeater in the corner, the ghost of a former inmate who'd died pounding on the two-way mirror, who continued to slam his fists into the glass long into the afterlife. I'd been spooked by him when I first came into the room and discovered I hadn't taken enough Auracel to block him. Now I found his presence almost comforting. It meant I wasn't alone with Roger Burke.

I controlled my revulsion toward him enough to plant my elbows on the table and lean forward. I'd been hoping to buy his information with Marlboros, but the guards wouldn't let me bring cigarettes into the visiting area. His hissy fit had given me an idea, though. "Here's the deal. I promise not to sue you, if you tell me what you know about Camp Hell."

I did my best not to look too full of myself, but I had to admit: a promise to refrain from any future lawsuits seemed a lot more valuable than a few packs of smokes.

Roger eased back into his chair. I wouldn't say he looked exactly comfortable, but he was interested enough to stay awhile, if only to taunt me about things that he knew, and I didn't. It was a start.

"I assume that you're not talking about the new Heliotrope Station. You want to know about the real deal. Where you trained."

In name only, Heliotrope Station lived on. It was now a series of night-school classes they held over at the Junior College. None of it was even remotely like the original Camp Hell—not the administration, not the staff, not the location. Hell, not even the textbooks. Still, even the old name made me start to sweat, and swallow convulsively.

Roger's smug grin was back. "You'd need to talk to me 'til my release date to find out everything I know about Camp Hell. And given that they haven't even set my sentence, who knows when that'll be?"

Posturing. That was good. It meant that he wanted to seem like he had something valuable to dangle over my head. Unfortunately, I already knew that he did. Lisa's *si-no* talent had told me that Roger could not only tell us why stories about Camp Hell had never made it to the Internet, but who'd managed to bury them.

"I'll be checking out what you say to make sure it's true," I warned him. "I smell bullshit, and I'll see you in court."

Roger smiled. There was some genuine pleasure in that smile, along with all the malice. My creeped-out meter ratcheted up to eleven. "April eighteenth," he said. "It's a mild fifty-five degrees outside. The subway tunnels are being drained from a freakish flood incident that occurred when an old access tunnel collapsed and the Chicago River poured in. And twenty-three-year-old Victor Bayne was transferred from the Cook County Mental Health Center to Heliotrope Station at approximately fourteen hundred hours. In a straightjacket."

My right eye throbbed. I jammed my thumb into the corner of it at the bridge of my nose, and reminded myself to breathe. "Big deal."

"Could anyone else have told you that story? Your co-workers? Your lover?"

He said the word *lover* like it was something rotten he'd found stuck between his teeth. "You know things about me," I said. I think my voice sounded normal. Maybe. "I'd be surprised if you didn't, since you and Doctor Chance schemed to kidnap me for, what, a year? Maybe two? That doesn't mean you know Camp Hell."

"West Fifty-Third Place, behind an industrial park that housed a small factory that manufactured dental posts and implants. No address. No signs. But a big, electrified, razorwire fence covered the whole perimeter. Been there lately? Seems like the whole building, all sixty-five hundred square feet of it, has just... disappeared. Kind of like the residents."

The front doors were black tinted glass. I blinked. Roger hadn't told me that. The fried remnants of my brain had cheerfully offered up the long-forgotten detail.

The gag reflex fluttered, deep down in my throat. How did I ever think I could hear about Camp Hell without shoving my keys into my ears and punching out my eardrums?

I stood. My cheap plastic chair tipped over.

"Am I wrong, Detective?"

"This was a dumb idea. Go back to your cafeteria food and your group showers."

"They didn't kill them all. Maybe half, give or take. But the ones who didn't pose any threat, or the ones they could use...." He spread his hands. His handcuffs clicked as the chain in the center hit its limit. "Well. They crop up every now and again. They might even be leading fairly normal lives. As long as they don't travel anywhere suspicious, like Afghanistan or Cuba, the FPMP is happy to let them go on thinking they're just plain, old, ordinary American citizens, just like you and me." He blinked in mock sincerity. "Although...come to think of it, neither one of us really does fit that description. I'm up on felony charges, and you're a class five medium—as far as they know, anyway."

"I tested at five a dozen times. That's no big secret. What's FPMP?"

Roger smiled.

Our little chat wasn't going anything like I'd planned. I was supposed to give him some smokes, and he would thank me for my present by telling me a name or an address, and that would be that. That's how it'd gone down inside my head, anyhow.

"A bunch of butch guys running around with letters sewn onto their windbreakers," I said, "right? Whatever. Look, I've got somewhere to be."

I went to the door and knocked. The guard opened it.

"You could always recant your statement, you know. Tell them it wasn't me holding you captive. I was just along for the ride."

Coffee I'd drank a couple of hours before burned at the back of my throat. I needed to get to a bathroom before I hurled. "Yeah. They'll believe that."

"Why wouldn't they? When you gave your testimony, you had traces of Amytal, psyactives and muscle relaxants in your system. You were confused." He stared me in the eye, and he'd finally stopped grinning. "C'mon, Bayne. I'd make it worth your while."

"Don't hold your breath."

"I can tell you about Camp Hell, but what's the point? You were there. A second point of view isn't going to change anything that happened. But the FPMP? The people who made it disappear? They're still around. Think about it. Can you really afford *not* to know?"

I was standing half-in, half-out of the room. The guard gave me an "are you through yet?" look. I took another step out the door.

"And...Detective?" He sounded so mild, so matter-of-fact, that I should have known a zinger was coming. But I couldn't stop myself from turning back around and taking one more look at Roger Burke's cold, pale eyes.

"What?"

Roger's grin reappeared, and spread like blood welling out of a deep papercut. "Happy birthday."

I lay in bed staring up at the tin ceiling, racking my brain and trying to figure out which was worse: knowing that Roger Burke would walk sooner, maybe even immediately, if I recanted my statement—or knowing that he could tell me everything I wanted to know about Camp Hell and then some, but that I was too gutless to pay the price he wanted for the information.

I heard Jacob come in and bound up the stairs. He's got energy to do things like that, because he eats right, exercises, and doesn't take questionable pills.

"Are you mad?" he said.

I glanced down from the ceiling. He stood in the bedroom doorway, loosening his tie.

"No. Why?"

"Me. Forgetting your birthday." He slipped out of his suitcoat and hung it in the closet. "Do you want to go out? It's not that late. I'll bet I can get us in at Villa Prego."

Villa Prego was fancy enough that I didn't think the staff would ruin my dinner by trooping out and singing me a half-hearted, cheesy birthday song. But they served fussy little portions of things that once crawled around on the bottoms of ponds. "Nah. Let's just get a pizza. I'm really not big into birthdays."

Jacob took off his holster and put it in a drawer. "How hungry are you?"

Thanks to my cozy alone-time with Roger Burke, my stomach felt like it'd been ripped out, switched with a giant wad of rotting trash, then stuffed back into my abdominal cavity. I shrugged.

Jacob flashed some skin while he pulled on a T-shirt and sweats, and even his unintentional strip tease wasn't enough to cheer me up. I was too busy mulling over just how much I hated Burke, and wishing that he wasn't the one who had the information I needed.

Jacob shut the closet door and looked at me hard enough to make him squint. "Something's wrong. Is it Lisa?"

"Lisa's fine. She sent me her e-mail address. Maybe one of these days she'll trust me with her phone number again."

He planted his hands on his hips and kept on staring. I felt myself scowl even harder. I know he was accustomed to teaming up with the Human Polygraph, but didn't he understand that sometimes people lied and minimized because they were wrestling with something too ugly to lay out there for everyone to see?

"You're mad that I borrowed your Auracel," he said, finally.

There—something I could hang my mood on. Thank you, Jacob. "Don't go through my pockets."

"I'm sorry."

Like I gave a damn that he'd slipped some of my meds to an astral rapist. It wasn't as if it was my last pill or anything. And it'd gone to a good cause. I did my best to scowl harder.

Jacob sat on the edge of the bed, pulled my foot into his lap and dug his thumb into the sole. I turned all to jelly inside, but I think my scowl didn't slip, much. "I'm truly sorry. I did what I thought was right at the time."

The nerves at the bottom of my foot seemed to be connected directly to my spine. I sagged into the mattress, and my eyes rolled up to stare at the ceiling again. Jacob swept his thumb over the ball of my foot, and I made a noise that I usually reserve for sex.

"Please don't be mad."

"I'm not mad," I said. "It's just been a rough couple of days."

✦ TWO ✦

A gunshot woke me.

Not inside the cannery or anything. Not as if someone was standing at the foot of my bed aiming a semi-automatic at us. A faraway gunshot, a few blocks away, at least. There weren't any followup shots, or screams, or sirens, either.

Typical noise. I'd been sleeping through it for years.

I looked at the alarm clock. Glowing green digits read 4:08. Jacob lay on his side with his hand nestled under his cheek, breathing deeply. He hadn't woken. Why had I?

I stared up at the ceiling and listened, but there was nothing more to hear. I struggled to remember which day it was, and almost had myself convinced that it was Friday. But then I remembered the guard escorting Roger Burke into the meeting room at Metropolitan Correctional Center, and I realized it was Monday, and I was faced with at least five days of work before I'd get to take it easy. I closed my eyes and told myself to go back to sleep and get two and a half more hours in. I'd be foggy and sore if I got up now. I needed to stay alert to see if I could determine who at the Fifth Precinct knew about the MP something something—whatever the fuck Burke had called it—and who were just the same old people I always thought they were.

I sighed. I'd need my wits about me to field a phone call from Stefan without sounding like a complete dumbass. He'd probably pick the least opportune time to call back, like when I was in the car with Zigler. I always suspected his talent told him when he could make someone squirm just for the fun of it, and he usually did, because that's how he is. Or was. It'd been over fourteen years. Maybe he'd outgrown his small sadistic pleasures.

I wondered what number I'd given. My cell, I would assume, since I didn't even know my new land line. And then it dawned on me. I hadn't left him any number at all. I'd totally forgotten to call him.

My eyes shot open and my adrenaline surged. What were his office hours? Nine to five? What if he came in early on a Monday morning to do some sort of clerical thing? It seemed unlikely, but it seemed even less likely that he'd carve out time on a Friday afternoon to do it.

Chances were one in eight million that if Stefan did come in early on Monday mornings to do his paperwork, he'd be doing it at four a.m. But I wasn't exactly thinking rationally.

I slipped out of bed, cracked my knee on the massive slab of furniture that served as a bedside table, and crept out of the room barefoot, praying that I wasn't going to discover a stray tack or chisel-edged staple the hard way.

I paused at the foot of the stairs. A streetlight shining through glass block windows provided enough illumination to see where the furniture was. I could make out the shapes of the doorways on the second floor, all three with their doors open. And even though Jacob could sleep through a hurricane or a gunshot, I decided that if I left the message now, he'd hear me and wake up.

I thought about locking myself in the downstairs bathroom, but then it occurred to me that Stefan would know. He always knew all kinds of weird things like that.

I decided it wouldn't be abnormal in any way to call from the kitchen. And also, that Jacob wouldn't be able to hear me if I did. I stubbed every toe on my right foot on the coffee table, swallowed down the word, "Fuckgoddamn," and slipped into the kitchenette.

I could see the room, kind of, by the glow of the microwave clock. There was a flashlight in my overcoat, but that was hanging in the entryway, and I figured I'd lose a limb if I tried to retrieve it. I could just turn on the light, but I was positive that Jacob would feel it shining through the bedroom floor, then come downstairs and demand to know what I was doing.

In a sudden burst of inspiration, I pulled open the refrigerator door...and was struck blind by the light thrown by the minuscule appliance bulb. I blinked away door-shaped afterimages as the coolness that'd been trapped inside the fridge settled around my bare toes, and I figured out what I was going to say to Stefan.

And then I checked the number on the sticky note that was plastered to my phone, flipped the phone open, and dialed.

I guess I'd expected Stefan's voice. He's got a deep baritone that would've made him the perfect host of a campy horror flick matinee. But it wasn't Stefan on the voice mail. It was a woman, maybe even a professional voice artist, by the sound of her.

"You've reached the office of Russeau and Kline, and we're pleased that with among all the empathic behavior-modification therapists available, you've selected us."

I forgot whatever it was I'd meant to say.

"We specialize in weight loss, smoking cessation, drug and alcohol counseling, and productivity in the workplace. If you have a goal, we can help you obtain it."

Did I have a goal? Shit. I drew a blank. A total blank.

"Office hours are Tuesday through Friday, ten to six. For a nominal convenience fee, limited after-hours sessions are available."

So it was possible Stefan was there now. Right now. If someone who needed therapy in the middle of the night had slipped him a big enough incentive. Think, I told myself, think. Be cool. It's just Stefan.

"Press one to make an appointment. Press two to leave a message for Lorraine Kline. Press three to leave a message for Steven Russeau. Press zero for more options. When you're finished, press pound for more options, or just hang up."

I pressed three. Three was Stefan's favorite number. I used to mock him relentlessly for having a favorite number. And then we'd steal a can of whipped cream from the cafeteria and inhale the propellant. And have sex.

A computer voice said, "Please leave a message for," and Stefan's deep voice, just the same as I remembered it, said, "Steven Russeau." Which wasn't his name. His name was Stefan Russell. Who'd convinced him to change his name, and how?

There was a beep. No time to wonder. "Uh, hey, Stefan. Steven. Uh, right, Steven now. It's Vic...Victor Bayne. I never changed my name. So, right, anyway...I was wondering if you want to meet. Just to talk. I mean, yeah. For coffee. Sometime." I said my phone number, probably too fast, and snapped my phone shut.

I told myself there was no reason to panic. It was just Stefan. If our younger selves could have seen me now, freaking out over leaving him a stupid message, we would've both laughed.

"Vic?"

The refrigerator door rattled as I gave it a spastic jerk. I threw my phone in the crisper and peeked over the top of the door. Jacob stood a few feet away from me, silhouetted in the archway that led to the cannery's main room.

"Are you looking for something?"

How long had I been standing there staring into the refrigerator—and how long had Jacob been watching me do it? I grabbed the first thing I saw, one of Jacob's protein shakes, and closed the door. "I was just, uh...hungry."

"Oh. You had such a strange look on your face, I was worried there were spirits in the leftovers." He came up beside me, pulled me against him with one arm, and re-opened the refrigerator door with the other. I stopped breathing as I wondered if he had a taste for lettuce, and if so, whether he'd wonder why the romaine was checking its messages.

Jacob pulled a half-empty quart of orange juice toward the edge of the shelf, coaxed open the top of the carton with one hand, then picked it up and drained it in one long, sensual swallow. He pitched the empty carton into the trash. "That's what you get for falling asleep without eating." He glanced down at the shake. "You like those? I'll buy more."

It had never occurred to me to drink one. I popped open the tab and took a swallow. It tasted like half & half spiked with kiddie vitamins, but mostly like the can. I shuddered. "I guess not."

Jacob took the shake out of my hand and put it back in the fridge. He shut the door, and then backed me into it. "I can think of something that tastes a whole lot better."

Magnets dug into my back as he went for my throat. His teeth grazed the marks left over from the previous week's encounters that had just healed.

"No biting," I said, and I tried to shrug him away, but there was probably fifty pounds more of him than there was of me, and he didn't budge. I struggled more, and his tongue touched my neck and moved lower, licks punctuated by small nips of his teeth. Enough to sting, but not enough to mark. I let my breath out carefully. The thought of him biting down on my collarbone made the slug of protein shake I'd just taken do an anticipatory cartwheel inside my stomach.

"I've been dying to get you alone, and awake. We've got a whole building to christen."

I'd never considered against-the-fridge to be one of the more appealing sexual positions, but it looked like Jacob was out to prove me wrong. He grabbed my hips, and even through my sweats, shocks of pain-tinged pleasure shot straight to my balls.

He let go of my hip to stretch the neck of my T-shirt. I heard thread snapping. His teeth closed on my shoulder, and my cock started to perk up. He followed with a long lick that led back to my throat, hinting at where he'd really like to bite down.

"You've been really hard on my clothes lately," I said. I pushed him away just enough to slip out of my T-shirt and drop it on the floor before he turned it into a stretched-out rag.

"I've been really hard...and your clothes are in my way." He raked his fingertips up my sides, my ribs, and I could feel the strength and the power in his hands. I got off on the thought that he'd tear through anything to get to me.

I cupped his face in my hands and pulled him up for a kiss. His tongue tasted sharp, like orange juice, and he stabbed it into my mouth. My cock twitched and nudged his leg. He groaned into my mouth and pressed his crotch against me. He really was hard. I let go of his face and crammed my hands down the waistband of his boxers. I squeezed a hand between us and grabbed his cock. Hot. Thick. Stiff. I grabbed his ass with my other hand.

Jacob broke the kiss and shoved my sweatpants down. While he was bent over, he clamped his mouth around my nipple and sucked hard. A shock ripped down my spine, and my cock gave another twitch. Jacob wrapped his hand around my balls and pressed his thumb between them. He tugged them as if he could draw the sensations right through my body.

"Fuck my ass," I said, because he loves it when I ask for it. He squeezed my balls together and slipped his other hand deeper between my legs so he could pet my hole with his fingertips. I had my arms wrapped around his head, and I breathed into his short, short hair. Deep, shuddering breaths. Breaths that wet his scalp. He pushed a finger into me and I gasped.

He let go of my nipple and latched onto the other one. He sucked so hard it stung, and his finger drilled higher. "Do it now," I said, because I was going to finish during the foreplay if he didn't.

He straightened up and continued to stroke his thumb over the cleft of my balls while he looked around. "Anything we can use? I don't want you getting bored while I go all the way upstairs to get the lube."

Lisa had unpacked the kitchen, not me. I had no idea where anything was, and I didn't feel like stopping to rifle through the cupboards. "Margarine?"

I regretted it the minute I said it. If the last thing I wanted Jacob to do was open the refrigerator, why'd I go and tell him to fuck me with the margarine?

He pressed his mouth against my ear. "I like the way you think." His voice was low and rough, more of a breath.

Damn. I couldn't take it back now. I shoved his chest to make enough room for me to turn around. "I'll get it." I opened the refrigerator door and was blinded again by the light bulb. I found the small yellow tub easily enough, on the door where we always keep it. I glanced down toward the crisper. I could make out the black shape of my cell phone through the glass of the lowest shelf. I moved a jar of pickles over to cover it and closed the door.

My eyes took a second to readjust to the nearly-dark kitchen. Jacob had stripped naked. He toyed with his nipple with one hand, stroked his thick, hard cock with the other—slowly, just watching me, and waiting. "You do it," he said.

I peeled off the lid and stuck my fingers in. Cold, but it would warm up soon enough. The fake-butter smell wafted up around me. I'd never noticed it before, not while I was making my toast. I scooped out two fingers' worth and sniffed it.

I figured I wouldn't feel so ridiculous if I wasn't facing him. I turned around and stepped the rest of the way out of my sweats so we were both naked, and I bent at the waist and pressed my forearm into the refrigerator door. I widened my stance and reached down between my legs.

I smeared the margarine over my hole. It was only cold for a second, and then I shoved two fingers in. I suspected I'd never look at the word *spread* on the label again without smirking. The buttery smell hit me again, strong. I could hear Jacob's hand working his cock.

I felt encouraged by the sound of him jerking off. I fucked myself deep with my own fingers, and he gave a low growl and dropped to his knees behind me.

Jacob grabbed my wrist, pulled my fingers out of my ass, and sucked them into his mouth, first one, then the other. My free hand clenched and unclenched next to my face as I pressed my forehead against my arm harder. I'd fallen on that arm and sprained it a few days ago, and the pain that throbbed in my elbow intensified everything else I was feeling. I closed my eyes, and lost myself to the slippery headiness of Jacob's tongue.

He went down on my fingers until he'd sucked all the margarine off, and then he took my ass in both of his big, strong hands and spread it wide open.

He sighed as he buried his face in my ass. His tongue slithered into my hole. "Damn, that's hot," I said.

Jacob grunted and kept fucking my buttery hole with his tongue. His lower teeth raked my taint, and my cock bobbed. I ran my hand over the shaft. Hard. I could bring myself off fast, if I wanted to. But I didn't. I wanted it to last.

Jacob trailed his tongue lower, and used his hand to push my balls into his mouth. He sucked one, then the other. I bit down on my lower lip. He kissed the inside of my thigh and stood, and I let out a breath I'd been holding. It shook.

I felt his cockhead slide over my hole. I spread my feet apart even more, tilted my ass up. He took my hip in one hand and his cock in the other, and he pushed in.

"Fuck, yeah." I arched my back, tried to get a feel for the angle. Jacob took the first few thrusts slowly. I wished we had a light. I wished we had a mirror. I would've loved to have seen him there, knees slightly bent, burying his cock deep inside my ass. I could hear it, though, squelching through the margarine I'd shoved inside myself.

He reached around, and I put my hand over his. "Not yet. Draw it out."

The fingers of his other hand dug deep into my hip, and he thrust hard. "Feels dirty," he said, and yeah, I knew what he meant. There was something a little too greasy about it. And then there was the smell. He pulled out and jammed his cock home again. "Real dirty."

Oh. He meant in a good way.

He let go of my cock and took my hips in both hands, pressing new finger-marks over my old, faded green ones. He started pounding me.

Pain jolted from my elbow and shot down toward my hips, and my ass felt like it was being split open. My breath huffed out of me, and I felt the warm slide of a bead of precome that rolled down my shaft. "Harder," I said.

He didn't just fuck me harder, he grabbed me harder too. I clenched up all over just trying to keep upright, and that made my ass tighten around his cock.

"I'm not gonna last," he said under his breath, so softly that the sound of our balls slapping and his cock squelching into me nearly drowned out the words.

"Do it," I said, and I took hold of my cock and stroked it. "Fuck my ass. Come inside me. Come hard."

I peaked in just a few strokes, and his cock slammed into me while I shot. My orgasm forced a wordless noise up from my throat, and Jacob fucked me harder still, grunting every time his cock slammed home.

I was reeling by the time he finished, so limp that his grasp on my hips was the only thing keeping me up off the floor. He slung an arm around my stomach and hugged me against his chest. He was sweating. His jiz crawled over the backside of my balls and ran down one leg. An aftershock rolled through him, and drew an answering shiver from me.

He kissed me gently between the shoulder blades, and his goatee tickled my spine. "I love you so much," he whispered. I felt his lips move against my back.

I made a noise in reply, something like "Mm," and I hugged his arm against me. My elbow ached, and my hips smarted, and now that I was no longer climbing toward the Big O, it felt less like kinky fun, and more like garden-variety pain. I turned so that we were facing each other and gave Jacob a slow, easy kiss.

The light beyond the glass block windows had paled, and I could see a little more of the kitchen now, and of Jacob. He held me against the fridge with his body and took his time trailing kisses over my jaw. "That wasn't too hard, was it?"

My ass felt like it was on fire. I'd be feeling it for days. "It was good."

"Maybe we need a code word—"

"No we don't. That's for serious kinkhounds in nipple clamps and horse costumes."

Jacob laughed—silently, but I felt his chest move against mine. "It doesn't have to be something silly. It's just...I wouldn't want to hurt you."

When we were in the thick of things, I loved the idea that Jacob had the strength to snap me in half. But talking about it afterward was a big wet blanket. "How about 'ow'?"

"You seem to enjoy it while it's happening."

"I do, okay? Do we really need to discuss it?"

Jacob didn't answer. He pressed his lips against my neck and stroked my hair. My bare foot touched something slimy on the floor, margarine or jiz, or maybe both. I wondered if Jacob was going to stand there and kiss me until we had to leave for work. I wanted him to leave so I could grab my cell phone. But the longer things coagulated on me, the more my attention wandered, and guarding the fridge took a back seat to parking myself under a hot shower.

✦ THREE ✦

I passed Betty's desk on the way to Sergeant Warwick's office. Betty kept about nine hundred pictures of her grandkids on her desk, and several of her cat, too. She had on a Pepto-Bismol pink sweater, as if she could make spring come early just by dressing brightly enough. Her smile was as bright as her sweater.

"Good morning, Detective!"

Betty had been distributing the confidentiality paperwork that everyone I knew had been strongly encouraged to sign. She'd never mentioned it to me. And yet, there she was, with her chirpy voice and her great big smile, and I couldn't bring myself to be a dick to her about it. She was just the middleman, after all. It wasn't as if she was a member of the F...what was it? The FPMP.

Bob Zigler cleared his throat behind me. I guess I'd been staring. "Hey, Betty, how's it going," I mumbled, and I squeezed my way into Warwick's office.

Now, Warwick? I could be mad at him.

I sat in one of the two chairs that faced his beat-up metal desk, and Zig sat in the other. I slouched a little, since I was feeling like a surly teenager, and I squinted at him.

Warwick didn't notice, but my attitude made me feel better.

Zigler covertly kicked the side of my shoe. Warwick was typing something on his computer, and since he hadn't bothered to look at either of us, he didn't notice that, either.

"I got a call from Sergeant Owens last night."

Jacob's sergeant. I squared my shoulders and eased out of my slouch.

"Seems his PsyCop team over at Rosewood was a little heavy on the Psy." He glanced up from his laptop and met my eye. "Good work. But you take it upon yourself to do something like that again, you clear it with me."

"Why? So you can arrange for my babysitters to be there?"

Zig made a weird noise in his throat. I could tell he wanted to give me another good kick, but since Warwick was now looking right at me, it wouldn't have been much of a warning. He probably would have enjoyed it, though.

Warwick didn't miss a beat. He must have been expecting me to figure it out for, what, years now. "I've got security on you. Is there a problem?"

Warwick was bigger, and older, and meaner than me, and he was accustomed to bossing hot-headed cops around. I swallowed. "I want to know. If it has to do with me, I want to know."

"I'm not at liberty to discuss it."

"So you're not really the one calling in the guards. It's someone else."

Zigler stomped on my foot.

Warwick's suitcoat strained around his broad back as he planted his elbows on his desk. He laced his fingers together, he looked at me over the tops of his bifocals, and he said, "I can't say."

All these years, I thought I'd been answering to Ted Warwick. I was sideswiped by the realization that I hadn't.

"Since you seemed comfortable enough to carry out an investigation at Rosewood Court," Warwick went on, as if nothing had just happened, "I've got some deaths at LaSalle Memorial Hospital that I'd like you to look into, see if we've got a Kevorkian on our hands, or if certain shifts are just really unlucky. Go down and take a look at the building, see if you're up to working in it."

Zig stood up and headed for the door. I stayed put and stared at Warwick. He'd already dismissed us by looking back down at his computer and starting to type. He had to know we were still there. How could he not?

Lisa had told me that he didn't actually know all that much, that Roger Burke was the one who could point fingers and name names. I wanted something more from Warwick, but it didn't seem like I would get it. Not now, not today.

"C'mon, Vic," said Zig. "They've got a pretty mean cherry turnover in the cafeteria at LaSalle."

Zig drove us over to the hospital. I was quiet and moody, and he was just quiet. The police scanner crackled with distorted words buried in a rise and fall of static. He parked as close as he could to the entrance without blocking an ambulance.

"Who d'you suppose is watching us?" I asked as Zigler killed the ignition.

Zig sighed, deflated, and slouched into his seat. "I don't know. I think we'll spot them eventually if we keep our eyes open."

"Back there in Warwick's office—why'd you keep trying to shut me up, anyway? What do you care if I ask him about all the extra security? Or did you sign something else that said you'd pretend nothing weird was happening?"

He cut his eyes to me. "Don't be a prick. Something weird's always happening." He stroked his cop-mustache for strength. "You looked too mad to get what you wanted out of it, that's all. Do I want you to know what's going on, who's authorizing which men, who's cranking out the next stack of papers to sign? Sure, if it'll give you some peace of mind. But I don't think you'll find anything out by going off half-cocked in Warwick's office."

I could've lightened the mood by asking him if he realized how many penis references were contained in his little tirade, but I decided against it. Mostly because he'd stopped me from acting pissy at Warwick because I was mad—and he'd probably been right in doing it. Also, Zigler and I don't joke about penises. Not with each other, anyway.

In the course of my day-to-day life, I'd driven by LaSalle General, but I'd never had any reason to go inside. Where the last medical institution I'd spent time at, Rosewood Court, was squared-off and horizontal in a sixties kind of way, LaSalle seemed to tower over us, five stories, huge and solid. The bricks were dark. The windows were small. And anywhere something had been added, changed or repaired, there was a patch of masonry that almost matched, but not quite.

The exterior doors and fittings were all brand new, huge sheets of plate glass that whisked open while we were still several steps away. Zigler went to the front desk and talked in low tones to the nurse on duty, who wore brightly colored scrubs that looked more like pajamas. When I was an inpatient at the Cook County Mental Health Center, the scrubs were all blue. Medium blue, navy, or sometimes teal, but always blue.

Times change.

I vaguely wondered what the staff wore at Camp Hell, and then I wondered why I didn't remember. My CCMHC memories were older, and soaked in Thorazine. So why couldn't I picture the wardrobe at Camp Hell?

Zigler handed me a plastic holder with an alligator clip and a piece of tagboard inside that read, "Security Level 2."

"Visitors have security levels?"

Zigler clipped an identical badge onto his lapel. "Looks that way. We can get into any of the public areas right now, and the guards will let us in to the pharmacy and admin sections whenever, but they'll need to assign a guide to us for Emergency and the ICU so that we don't get in their way."

I wasn't really looking forward to visiting any area of the building where people were wheeled around on creaky metal gurneys, anyhow. Although maybe things were done differently now. Maybe gurneys were made of plastic, and you couldn't hear them coming.

"You see something?"

Only in my own mind. I shook my head.

"So the lobby's clean."

I nodded.

"Are you...up for going in any farther?"

I blinked a few times. "Hm? Oh. Uh, yeah. How about the gift shop?"

We poked around for a few hours. There was a repeater in the gift shop, a repairman who kept spackling the same spot on the wall. He seemed old, and I kept losing parts of him in the balloon bouquet that framed him in a riot of color. The waiting room had a couple of ghosts sitting around looking spectral, some in physical chairs, and some floating around sitting positions without any furniture to prop them up. A transparent kid with a burnt face lingered by the elevator, her mouth wide open as if she was crying, or maybe screaming, but no sound came out. And a nasal voice near the information desk was threatening a medical malpractice suit.

"So, where do you want to grab lunch? I meant what I said about the cafeteria. It's not bad."

I could always trust Zig to make sure we didn't work through lunch. "Let's sweep it first. This whole building's thick with ghosts."

Zigler turned gray. "Sure. Or we could hit that pizzeria on Kedzie. They have a lunch buffet."

We climbed into an elevator with a guy carrying a potted plant that had a Mylar "get well" balloon sticking up of the center of it on a foot-long plastic straw, and a couple of nurses in wildly colored scrubs: flowers on one, starfish on the other. Zig's eyes darted from the doors to the numbers as we sank to the hospital's lowest level. That's what it was called—LL. I was pleased that they didn't call it the "basement."

"Y'know, I think I have a taste for pizza," he said.

"Don't worry. I'll tell you if there's anything in the cafeteria that would ruin your lunch—if you could see it."

The nurses strode out of the elevator with purpose—the balloon-guy, Zig and me, not so much. I looked around for ghosts, Zig watched me in case I was holding out on him, and the other guy rotated around to try to get his bearings.

Once the lost guy wandered away, Zig pulled out his cell phone and touched base with his wife, Nancy. He calls her without fail twice a day, at lunch and at five. I guess it reassures Nancy that nobody's shot him yet.

I'm not a big phone talker, so I don't usually bug Jacob unless I've got a question. And I trust him to do his best to not get shot at. I know that I do.

The sight of Zig on his phone did lead me to wonder whether Stefan had gotten my message yet, or if he didn't check his work messages on his day off. He was a therapist or something, right? He'd have to check his messages in case one of his alcoholic patients was on the verge of hitting the sauce. Wouldn't he? Or was that what the "other options" on his voice mail were for?

He probably checked his messages, I decided, because he never liked letting things build up. When I wanted to ignore something, a test or a paper or a big, nasty pill, he'd always tell me to stop agonizing over it and just get it over with as quickly as possible. So if he was going to return my call at all, I figured he'd do it sooner rather than later.

I patted my pocket to check and see if maybe he'd called me but my phone wasn't on, or the battery was run down. My phone wasn't there.

It was still in the fridge.

"Zig."

"Hold on, Nance." He looked at me.

"I need to stop at my house."

His eyebrows bunched up. He knew something was going on, but couldn't pinpoint exactly what.

"Then we'll hit that pizza place."

Zigler stared for a moment, and then nodded. If I was willing to entertain his contrived yen for pizza, then he'd need to be willing to drive me home for no good reason—none that I was willing to detail for him, at any rate.

He parked the Impala in the only empty spot on the block, the one by my walkway. "That's...different," he said. He was staring at the lotus shapes that bordered the slightly flared roofline.

"Yeah. It used to be a cannery." I could have invited him in. He might have even been hinting that he wanted to see the inside. But I was too worried about whether or not Jacob had found my phone on ice to remember if there was anything particularly gay laying around—anything that would put a strain on my relationship with Zigler if he ran into it. "I'll just be a second," I told him.

Some intrepid soul, or someone who didn't know the haunted history of the cannery, had left a plastic bag of Avon catalogs hanging on the front doorknob. Every time I got my key in the lock, it swung down and knocked the key away. I snapped it off, opened the door, and went in.

My phone was exactly where I'd left it. Which didn't really prove whether Jacob had seen it there or not. After all, he was probably wily enough to just leave it in the crisper and give me all the rope I needed to hang myself.

I could feel my pulse pounding in my temples as I flicked open the phone and checked my messages. The viewscreen fogged up, and I buffed it on my sleeve. Caller I.D. told me I'd only gotten a single message that morning. Russeau and Kline. I swallowed. My mouth had gone dry. I hit play and placed the phone to my ear. The receiver was really cold.

"Victor Bayne," Stefan began. His already-deep voice dropped half an octave when he said, "Bayne." Not good. "Now there's a name I haven't heard in a year or two. Or fourteen. My schedule's not quite as forgiving as it was back in the day, but I suppose I can fit you in tomorrow at three if you want to talk. Meet me at my office. You know where that is, don't you? I'm sure you'll be able to find it; according to the little 'I'm not here' message on your cell phone, you're working for the police now. Fifth Precinct? Detective. I'm sure the story behind *that* is simply *fascinating*."

I realized I hadn't been breathing. I took a few breaths and told myself to calm down. He said he'd see me. But the tone of his voice told me I shouldn't be expecting a balloon bouquet to be waiting for me when he did.

✦ FOUR ✦

Jacob had settled into our new kitchen by the time I got home. He chopped carrots on an imposing cutting board that most definitely had to have come from one of his boxes, since it never would have occurred to me to buy a kitchen accessory that I'd need to lift with both hands. At the sink, water ran through a colander full of lettuce. Good thing I'd swung by and grabbed my phone, otherwise I'd have some explaining to do.

Jacob leaned in for a kiss, then went back to his cutting board. I turned to go upstairs and ditch my suit. "You came home for lunch?"

I paused with my finger hooked over the knot of my tie. "Why would I?"

The sound of the knife clicking against the board stopped.

"Turn around."

Damn. I plastered on my best non-expression and faced Jacob. He stared into my eyes. I couldn't imagine how he'd caught me. Video cameras? Spies? Tracking device?

"Let's try that again. Hi, Vic, how was your day? You came home for lunch?"

"What difference does it make?"

Jacob turned off the water and wiped his hands on a kitchen towel. He looped his arm through mine and walked me into the other room. We sat on the couch. He pulled me into the crook of his arm and stroked my hair, and sighed. "It doesn't matter." He kissed the top of my head. "Tell me something else."

Way to make me feel like the world's biggest A-hole. "Fine. I stopped back home to get my phone. Is that what you wanted to know?"

"I was just curious." He kept his voice gentle and non-accusatory—as if he thought I'd cut and run if he cornered me.

"How'd you know?"

"There was a bag of catalogs on the hallway floor. That's all."

I sighed, and looked at our reflection in the dark television screen. "So, here's the deal. I tracked down someone from Camp Hell. I'm meeting up with him."

Jacob's arms tightened. He hugged my head to his chest. "Do you want me to come with you?"

"No. I trust him. We were...well, we were really close, actually. You know. Like that. But that's not why I don't want you to come with me. I mean, if you want to, I guess you can."

"Shh. It's okay." Jacob kissed my hair again. "Do what you need to do. Just remember that I'm here if you need me. Always."

Obviously, I didn't deserve Jacob. I pressed my ear against his chest and listened to the slow thumping of his heart, and felt like a jerk. I wondered if he'd known all along that I was planning an excursion. Maybe he'd seen my phone in the crisper while I was in the shower. Heck, maybe he'd seen me talking on it at four o'clock in the morning. I couldn't ask him without coming off like an even bigger dumbass, so instead I reached up and found his hand, and clasped it under my chin, and didn't say anything at all.

I'm not sure where I got the bright idea to have a yogurt in the cab on the way to Stefan's office. Maybe I was in the mood for blueberries. Maybe I thought it'd settle my stomach. Maybe I just wanted something to do, so I wouldn't have to think about the fact that I was actually nervous about seeing him again.

Anyway, that yogurt? I peeled up the foil, and it sprayed me with pinkish-purple flecks. Smooth.

I managed to rub in most of the yogurt before I got out of the cab, but it left my hands sticky and covered with black wool fiber. A revolving door led into the lobby, so I could push through with my upper arm. The elevator button was already pressed. If I could just make it to a bathroom, I'd be golden.

The high-rise housed a number of medical professionals, from dentists to acupuncturists to certified psychic healers—like Stefan and, I'm assuming, his business partner. It was bland in that way that all office buildings are bland, with everything done up in various tones of putty and beige.

Once I was on the elevator, I pressed the button with the one clean knuckle I had left, and rode up to the twenty-third floor. Thankfully, the men's room was right next to the elevators, so I didn't have to go into Stefan's office holding up my sticky hands so it was obvious that I'd just been slimed.

The bathroom was yards of even more shades of beige, granite or marble or some other kind of stone, expensive but unobtrusive. A big guy with a gray-streaked ponytail was washing his face at the beige-tiled basin. He wore a vest with a watch chain dangling from the pocket. I couldn't imagine the last time I'd seen someone in a vest. And I wondered if he'd had yogurt for lunch, too.

He reached back in my general direction while he knuckled soap out of his eye. "Hand me a paper towel, would you?"

It looked nothing like him...but, my God, there was no mistaking his voice. "Stefan?"

He straightened up slowly, pried one eye open, and squinted at my reflection in the bathroom mirror. "Figures." He wiggled his fingers at the paper towel dispenser. I pulled a couple out, being careful to handle them by the corner, and passed them over.

I sized him up while he groaned into the paper towels and blotted his face. He'd put on weight. And he'd stopped dyeing his hair—which was thinning on top. But there was something flashy and retro about his suit, like he'd just stepped out of an H. G. Wells novel. The suit was only part of his look. His facial hair was too edgy to let him blend in with the other corporate drones I'd seen in the building—a stripe of a beard down the center of his chin, and long, pointy sideburns that must've been a bitch to shave without screwing them up.

He sighed and lowered the wad of paper. He looked a lot older. But then again, so did I.

"You've still got most of your hair. I'll bet you still have a thirty-inch waist, too."

"I, uh...really need to wash my hands."

He stepped to the side and gestured toward the sink. I almost blanked out on the whole procedure. Water, check. Soap, check. Rub hands together—damn, did he really have to look at me so hard? Especially with that slightly curled lip. He used to look at the orderlies that way.

"So. Uh. This is your...building."

"I rent an office here. That remark you made, on your message, about me changing my name. What was that supposed to mean?"

Cripes. He could always argue circles around me, and now he had an arsenal of therapy-tactics to batter me with. "I just...I don't know. I couldn't find anybody—you, Big Larry, anyone else from Camp Hell. I couldn't find anything about the whole place."

I watched him in the mirror because it was easier than facing him. He'd been imposing in his twenties. Now, at forty-something, he looked like he could haul you down to the principal's office and give you a whack with a ruler that would sting for a week.

He tilted his head back and gave me his most imperious down-his-nose look, held it for a moment, then rolled his eyes and gave another long sigh. "Are you having a panic attack? Because I really want to be pissed at you, but it's kind of hard when you're peaking."

"What're you pissed at me about?"

"Earth to Victor. You were the one who left."

Left what? Oh, right. Camp Hell. We were talking about Camp Hell. And I left....

I left.

He was still there.

"Not that I blame you—I left the first chance I had, too. But you could have sent me a letter. A singing telegram. A cake with a file inside."

"Well, I just, um.... I mean...." I could have lied, said that I had written to him, and blamed Camp Hell admin for ditching my letters. But I hadn't written him, not once. I hadn't even thought of it. "How long?"

"Oh, a year," he said with fake breeziness, "maybe two."

"God." I held onto the beige sink. My knuckles were white.

"I'm not saying you should have stuck around and waited for me to get placed, of course. That wouldn't have made any sense. So what else could you have done?"

The sink was wet.

"I mean, aside from telling a reporter what was going on there. Or, how 'bout this, maybe someone at the Police Academy? Oops, did I say that out loud, or just think it?"

I grabbed a paper towel and dried my hands with it. I twisted too hard, and it started to shred.

Stefan stared at me. I couldn't see him. I couldn't see anything but the twisted pills of paper towel that fell onto the sink and stuck there in the water. But I could feel him.

"I'm going outside," he said. "I need a cigarette."

When Stefan said he needed a cigarette, I'd just assumed that he already had a pack, and he wanted to smoke one. Turns out he hadn't smoked in over ten years.

He scowled down his nose at the colorful, candy-like stacks of cigarettes behind the counter. "Almost six dollars a pack. I never would have started if it was this expensive."

"You don't need to start again now."

"It's not your business to tell me what I do or don't need." He couldn't decide which brand he wanted, and since both Camel and Marlboro had come out with new varieties since the last time he'd lit up, he decided he might as well try them all. He couldn't decide which color lighter he wanted, so he got a purple lighter and a red lighter, too.

The clerk, a bored Lebanese teenager, handed the bag to Stefan, along with a credit card slip to sign. "I think you missed something," I told him. "The fluorescent orange lighter, for instance. A pack of Virginia Slims. Cigarillos."

Stefan tilted his head back and aimed his disapproving look in my direction. I wondered if he'd flashed that expression once too often and his face had frozen that way.

We walked a few blocks to an alley between skyscrapers that was littered with cigarette butts. Stefan picked the plastic off a fancy black pack of Camels and lit up a cigarette. He took a drag and scowled. "This is disgusting." He dropped the smoke on the pavement and ground it out.

"Now that that's over, maybe we can go somewhere warm." I'd left my gloves in my car. My hands were jammed deep into my pockets, and the tips of my ears were freezing.

"No, I don't think so. Why don't you tell me whatever it is that you've been dying to say—after fourteen years?"

"Geez, would you cut me some slack? How was I supposed to find you? You changed your name."

He raised one eyebrow higher than the other and tilted his head. He shrugged.

"Can we start again? Hey, uh, Stef...Steven. You look great."

"No I don't. I'm retaining fluid."

I sighed. My breath streamed into the cold air in a big, white cloud, as if I'd been smoking one of those cigarettes from the fancy black pack.

"Okay, okay. How about this? I can't remember Camp Hell, and it's starting to freak me out. And now I can't find anything about it on the Internet, and nothing about me, or anyone else who's ever been inside."

"I can get you the number for Heliotrope Station. They're still training municipal Psychs there."

"Those pencil pushers at the community college? No, not them. They're not the real Camp Hell. They adopted the name, but none of the same people are running that program. I mean the real Camp Hell."

Stefan pulled out a red pack of smokes, picked it open, and lit one up. "Better," he said. He stared at it as it burned down, and I waited. When it was about half gone, he said, "I looked for you when I got out. I couldn't find you. I thought maybe you were dead." Stefan took another drag. He scrutinized the cigarette. Smoke curled from his nostrils. "Remember when you talked the nurses' aide into giving you half a pack of Newports so that you'd have something to give me for Kwanzaa?"

Kwanzaa rang a bell. I remembered Stefan's voice saying it seemed like a much cooler holiday than Christmas, and that he'd never read anything that said that white people couldn't celebrate it, too. But I didn't remember the Newports. "I just told you, I don't remember Camp Hell."

He stared at me so hard I thought I might wilt. His cigarette burned down some more. "Repressed memories are out of my league. But I might be able to help you out if, for instance, you want to gain some weight. I'm a licensed empathic hypnotherapist."

I shrugged. So few of my clothes fit me anyway. If I put on ten pounds, my favorite jeans would be too tight. "S'okay."

"What about work? Job productivity, that's the 'big thing' right now. I can charge lawyers and stockbrokers insane amounts of money to give them a business edge."

"I sense dead people. I don't want an edge. If anything, I'd want to dumb it down."

He frowned at his cigarette, which dangled from his fingers and continued to burn down. He fished the pack out of his pocket and offered it to me, but I shook my head. He shrugged and pocketed the smokes. Then he turned his hand to look at the lit end of his cigarette. "Remember that time we smoked a banana peel?"

"No."

"What do you mean, no?" He scowled even harder, and glared at me a little. "That fat slob of a janitor, A.J. or T.J. or B.J. or whatever he called himself.... He told us we could get high if we dried a banana peel and smoked it."

I shrugged.

"And so you snuck one out of the cafeteria in your pants, and I hid it in my room. I tried to dry it on the radiator, but it stuck there, and the whole room smelled like rotten bananas."

"I really don't...."

He talked over me, getting louder as he went on. "And then finally after about a week it was dry, all black and leathery and dry, and we made a bong out of a toilet paper roll and a piece of tin foil, and we hid in the corner of the smoking lounge."

I could hear the hurt in his voice, that he had this memory of something we'd done, together—and my half of it, the portion that I was supposed to cherish and protect? Gone.

"And we got Fat Judy to go stand by the door, keep the orderlies out...and the telepaths were all rooting for us to be the ones to discover some way we could entertain ourselves to keep from going crazy...?"

I shook my head. It sounded exactly like something we would do. I just didn't remember.

His cigarette had burned all the way down. He dropped the butt. "You got really sick," he added quietly.

I didn't remember.

"You vomited on my shoe. Not both of them. Just one. I threw it out. But I kept the good one."

"I remember...that the front doors were made of black glass." I felt sweat bead on my upper lip, then start to freeze in the winter air. I swiped it away with my sleeve.

Stefan sighed. "Good lord. You really are screwed up."

✦ FIVE ✦

I used to think The Clinic was creepy. Locked doors, fake windows, the fact that my last doctor was testing experimental psyactives on me. But standing in the middle of a regular hall in a regular hospital where I'd reported to work that morning, I was beginning to think that The Clinic was downright inviting.

"What was the approximate age at the time of death?" Zigler prompted.

I squinted at the apparition. Stick arms, stick legs, sunken cheeks, hospital gown. She pawed at the fire alarm, ran a few steps, and disappeared. Then she flickered back into being in front of the fire alarm again. "Uh...twenty-five to... forty?"

"That's quite a range." Zigler's pen squeaked.

"Look, it's really hard to say. She looks like a cancer patient or something."

"Communicative?"

"Nope. A repeater."

"Have you asked the patient her name? Out loud?"

Cripes. As if I didn't know a repeater when I saw one. "Hello, ma'am. I'm Detective Bayne, your friendly neighborhood medium. Care to identify yourself?"

The ghost's hand went through the fire alarm handle. She darted away, flickered, and disappeared.

"She didn't answer me."

"You don't have to talk down to them." More squeaking of the pen. A sigh. "Okay. Next?"

I pressed my temples between my thumb and forefinger. Zig had gone through a whole pad already, and we couldn't find anything that was willing to talk to us. And yet the repeaters were so thick I couldn't take two steps without walking into one.

The next ghost was a kid sitting against the wall. He was dusky-looking with glossy black hair, maybe Mexican or Middle Eastern. Hard to say with his hand cupped over his face. Blood oozed from between his fingers, ran down his arm. I closed my eyes to escape from the sight of him for a moment, but it didn't do much good. I opened my eyes again and crouched down.

"Hey," I said. "Kid. Can you hear me?"

He started to cry, and he kept on bleeding. I tried to coax something out of him, got nothing, described him to Zigler, and moved on to the next one.

"Ma'am?" I said. The ghost whisked by me, posture impeccable in her white A-line dress and low white shoes. "Ma'am?" I followed. She ducked into a patient's room. Zigler put his hand on my arm to stop me from following. He ducked in and asked the guy inside if we could take a look around, instructing him to be absolutely quiet.

"What are you, forensics or something?"

I peeked in and looked for the nurse. She seemed to be opening a window, except there was no window on the wall she was touching. Not anymore, at least.

"You're PsyCops, aren't you? Oh my God. Is that guy a telepath? Is he communicating with someone?"

"Sir," Zigler said. "What did I tell you?"

"Oh. Right."

The nurse was faint. I tried to shut out the psych-groupie's excitement and focus on the ghost. She stared at the wall for a moment, nodding as if she was rehearsing something in her head, and then she leapt into the wall and disappeared.

I touched the spot and felt a chill. It faded in a few seconds.

"What's he doing?" the patient stage-whispered.

My phone buzzed in my pocket before I could think of a sufficiently smart-ass comment to reply with. I gave Zigler the index-finger "just a second" gesture and went out into the hall to take Jacob's call.

"I am so, so sorry. I tried to wake you up when I got home last night, but you were dead to the world."

"Yeah, uh. I was..." zonked out of my mind on reds. "I took a sleeping pill."

"How was your meeting with Stefan?"

"I dunno. Okay. I guess. It wasn't exactly the warmest welcome I could've gotten. But he talked to me."

My call-waiting beeped. I couldn't tell who it was, not with Jacob on the line. But it occurred to me that maybe Stefan had cooled off a little overnight. Or warmed up. Or...whatever. "I got a call. I'll, uh...."

"It's fine. I'll see you later. Bye." Jacob had given me his sexy "bye," the one where his voice goes all low and smoky. I guess it was good for distracting me from ghostly nurses. I switched the call before I had a chance to get nervous.

"Hello?"

"You've thought about my offer?"

Sonofabitch. It wasn't Stefan—it was Roger Burke. I'd thought it was too much trouble to change my phone number after he checked in to Metropolitan Correctional. And he'd never called me...until now. "Uh, no. Not really. I just don't think it's, y'know...realistic...if I suddenly take everything back."

"Maybe you *can* come up with a better line to feed them—you've got your storytelling technique down pat. Here's the deal: my lawyer says I'm looking at six years, minimum. You get them to drop the kidnapping and assault charges, and the DA might not have anything to charge me with at all. For every year you get them to knock off, I'll give you a name. A good one, a living breathing person in the FPMP, complete with a job description. You get me off on time served? I'll give you everything."

He dropped his voice on the last word in a way that mirrored Jacob's patented "bye." I snapped my phone shut in a knee-jerk reaction, and stood there and gawked at the opposite wall for a good ten seconds before I realized that Zigler was standing beside me writing in his notepad.

"You okay?"

I closed my eyes and tried to calm down. "Yeah. Fine."

"If you want to knock off early...I really think we've seen our share of activity for the day. Besides, it'll take me hours to type this up."

I dropped my hand to my side and caressed the pocket of my blazer. I had two Auracel and a Seconal with me. I'd love the freaky high of the anti-psyactive, but I wouldn't be able to take it on a Wednesday afternoon, not if I planned to do any ghost hunting on Thursday. Years ago, if I did slip up and come to work in no condition to actually do my job, Maurice and I would have strolled around the neighborhoods for a few hours, hit a donut shop or a hot dog stand, and then called it a day. I was guessing Bob Zigler wouldn't be quite as understanding if I came to work psychically stunted.

"Sure. Let's get out of here."

Since parking in the Loop was more trouble than it was worth, I took the train to Stefan's office. There was a ghostly workman on the track at the station in my neighborhood, and a few see-through commuters at various other stops, but they weren't any more gruesome than the ghosts I had to drive through at the more dangerous intersections on the surface streets.

Even so, my heart was pounding by the time I got downtown.

I went through Stefan's lobby, and his elevator—beige, beige and more beige—and thank God for the bathroom, because I was sweating bullets by the time I got to his floor.

I washed my face and dried it and still felt clammy. I stuffed a wad of paper towels into my pocket, and went into Stefan's office.

A receptionist at a sleek granite-topped desk looked up at me. Young. Female. Black. I probably gawked at her. I don't know what I expected—that Stefan would just be standing in his office, all by himself, waiting for me to show up without calling?

"I need to speak to Mister Russell. Er...Russeau." At least my voice sounded calm.

"He's with a patient. Do you have an appointment, sir?"

A bead of sweat rolled down my side. "Detective. Victor Bayne."

Her dark eyes flicked down to her appointment book. "Should I interrupt him?"

I glanced down at the book, too. Not that I could read it upside down, from where I was standing. "No." I looked up at the clock. It was twenty to two. "How much longer will he be?"

"Five...ten more minutes? But then he has a three-o'-clock."

Shit. Why hadn't it occurred to me that Stefan had an actual job to do while he was at work? My hair was stuck to my forehead. I pulled a paper towel out of my pocket and blotted my face. Not very slick, but it beat dribbling sweat onto the granite desktop.

I turned and looked at one of the paintings on the wall. It was an architectural print of some kind, very detailed and a little warped, with too many stairways and whacked-out perspective. I was trying to figure out where one of the windows led when I heard a door open behind me.

"Carissa? Is Mister Mason here already...?" Stefan stood in the doorway to his private office. Another vest—bottle-green velvet today—and a startling white shirt with gigantic cufflinks. He looked at me as if he'd seen a ghost. Then he scowled, hopefully more in concentration than in anger. "See if you can reschedule Mister Mason, would you? I need to meet with Detective Bayne."

Stefan showed his current patient out, then shuttled me into the office and closed the door behind me. He pressed his back against it, and spoke to me in a whisper. "What's with you? I could feel you losing it through the wall."

"That's some trick." I laughed. It sounded forced.

"It's not funny. I'm worried about you."

I blotted my upper lip with the clammy paper towel. "You can get scrips, can't you? 'Cos some Valium would really hit the spot right about now."

"I'm not a doctor."

"But you're a therapist. You can get 'em—you've got some kind of connection. Right?"

He walked towards me. My body remembered him, even after all these years, and I didn't flinch back. He took me by the arm, and then I did cringe.

"It's...uh...I hurt it on duty. Sprained."

Stefan let go and took me by the shoulder instead, and steered me to the couch. "Sit."

I sat.

He eased himself into a thick, imposing chair across from me, placed his hands on the armrests, and stared. He was tapping into me, I knew, and maybe if he hadn't done it a thousand times before it would have sent me packing. But now I kind of wondered what it was that he'd see.

"I can get you Valium. But I won't. Not unless you let me train you to defuse the panic attacks."

"Christ. Is this one of those 'teach a man to fish' kinda things?"

"Do you enjoy being completely out of control?"

"Fuck you."

"Very mature. But my offer stands. We work on your triggers, or you stop wasting my time and crawl back into the fourteen-year-old hole you came from. It's your decision."

How nice of him to give me no choice at all, and then act like it was all up to me. I wondered how many people in my life had done that over the years. And then I realized for all his reputation for being ruthless in getting what he wanted, Jacob never did that. "What do you mean by a trigger?"

"Camp Hell, obviously, since you're repressing memories and self-medicating."

I opened up the wet paper towel, sat back on the couch, pressed the back of my skull into the cushion, and draped the damp paper over my face. "I know you're a professional and all, but I think there are some things that never go away."

"You won't know that until you try."

"I hate trying."

He laughed, a tiny sniff. He's a tough audience. I remembered when I did really get him going, he'd do these big, deep belly laughs—contagious, to the point where it hurt, and we still couldn't stop. It might have been the whipped cream propellant. But I like to think it was at least partially me.

"What?" he said.

"I remember...something. The whipped cream. When we huffed it."

"We did that dozens of times. Until they made the kitchen off-limits to us, anyway."

I searched for more detail, and then, miraculously, I remembered. "The time I was sucking the gas out, and you bent the nozzle and whipped cream came out my nose."

That got a little chuckle out of him. "You tasted it for days."

I breathed in the wood pulp smell of the paper towel. My heart rate slowed, until it almost felt normal.

✦ SIX ✦

"You are in a safe place. What happened in the past is only a memory now, and a memory can't hurt you. You're going to count back, from ten to one, and focus only on the sound of my voice...."

Stefan had a great voice for hypnosis. He should've been on those relaxation CDs they make. Seriously. He was that good. I missed him suddenly—which was lame, considering that we were in the same room together—but it sucked to think about all the years I'd lost where I could have known him again.

"Seven. Your eyelids are heavy. Your body is relaxed. Your arms are relaxed. Your legs are relaxed. Your fingers and toes are relaxed. Your tongue is relaxed...."

I'd left him. Funny, I'd never seen it that way. We'd go without seeing each other in Camp Hell for days on end sometimes, depending on who was in a focus group, or who was getting a...procedure.

"The past is only a memory. Memories have no power to hurt you. You are calm, and relaxed." Stefan's voice was louder, firmer, for a moment. I dropped my line of thinking and focused on him. "Four. Your arms feel very light, weightless. Your right arm is so light, so free, that it feels as if it could float right up out of your lap...."

They had set me up in the Police Academy right away, and no, I didn't try to contact Stefan. I didn't try to contact anybody. I was just barely treading water, and I was positive that one of the other cadets would figure out I liked dick, beat the crap out of me, and get me kicked off the force and back into the loving arms of Heliotrope Station.

"The past is only a memory. Memories have no power to hurt you."

"What?"

I blinked. Stefan raised a black, pointed eyebrow and gave me his most lofty eyeliner-focused look.

Eyeliner?

We stood in a hallway that was painted two shades of blue, navy on the bottom and robin's-egg blue on top. The horizontal line where the two paint colors met went all the way down the hall, which made it stretch and warp in forced perspective if I looked at it too hard.

"I think the hall's breathing," I said.

"What'd they give you?"

"I dunno."

He looped his arm through mine and I flinched, because my arm was sprained. Wait a minute, no it wasn't. Why did I think it was?

"Kitchen's this way," he said. "Don't dawdle in the hall. After that ridiculous 'no fraternization' line they fed us yesterday, I'm paranoid about getting caught."

We rounded a corner and collided with another resident—Movie Mike, Heliotrope Station's token telekinetic. "Gimme a cigarette," he told Stefan, "and I won't tell anyone I saw you two homos getting it on."

I might have been into other guys, but he was the one wearing a bright blue blazer with pushed up sleeves and a skinny tie with piano keys printed on it. Unfortunately, I was too high to argue about the various shades of meaning that could be attributed to the word *homo*. And I had no doubt that Stefan would be happy to wipe the floor with Movie Mike with no help at all from me.

Stefan countered with, "We're doing nothing more risqué than walking down the hall." So far, anyway. "You think anyone would even care?" Obviously, he was taunting Mike. And maybe tinkering around in his head, too—ferreting out his insecurity and self-doubt, and turning it a few notches higher. "Know what I found out after Show and Tell? I'm the best empath here. Level five. So what're you going to do to get admin's attention? Slide a penny across the table? I'm sure everyone will be so impressed."

Mike's cheeks colored. "No fraternization. They told me that when I went in for my talk."

"No smoking, either." Stefan gave him a glare that could wither a silk plant.

Movie Mike did his best to glare back. Stefan might wear more makeup than half the chicks in the program, but he was still the last guy anyone would want to hold a staring contest with. Mike caved first. He looked away, slouched beneath his shoulderpads and dodged around us. "Fucking fags."

"Asswipe." Stefan marched in the opposite direction, taking long steps now.

I stumbled along beside him. "I wouldn't have given him a cigarette even if I had any left."

Probably not, but Mike's threat to go tattle on us was nothing more than a bunch of hot air. Psychs were like nutjobs. They watched each others' backs. Mike was just trying to rattle Stefan's cage for form's sake. I don't know why he even bothered. Hopefully he wasn't angling for a three-way or anything. I didn't think so—Stefan probably would have called him on it if he had been, even subconsciously.

Stefan paused, and tugged my arm to stop me from meandering into the range of a rotating video camera. It swept the hall, red light blinking. When it focused on the courtyard door, he made for the kitchen, and towed me right along with him. He could move fast, for a big guy—especially when unlimited desserts and various institutional culinary propellants were there for the picking.

Stefan pulled a comb from his pocket, wedged the pointed end of the handle between the doors, gave it a twist, and clicked the door open. I slipped in, he followed, and he shut the door behind us. It was a crappy lock, obviously. It only locked from the outside. And you could pick it with a sharp comb if you knew where to press the bolt.

We snuck past a dozen tables with upside-down chairs on top. The industrial clock on the wall, lurking behind a steel cage as if one of us would go berserk and destroy it for no good reason, clunked as the second hand swept by the twelve. We had a good twenty minutes before the orderlies would herd us into the showers. Maybe more, but we always made it a point to be ten minutes early, at least. Especially now, with the creepy new orderlies on the payroll, I wasn't going to take any chances.

"Oh my God," Stefan cried from the kitchen. He sounded like he might be having an orgasm. "Brownies."

I tore open a cabinet and looked for something to sniff. Aerosol cooking spray. Yes.

"Do you think they'll notice if I eat one?" he asked.

"How likely is it you'll stop at one?"

"Good point. I'll need to be subtle. Help me." The brownies were pre-cut, so he'd need to shave a sliver off each one so that no one noticed a portion was missing.

"Just cut the biggest ones in half." I held the cooking spray upside down and sprayed until the oil cleared the tube, and I had access to the good stuff. I sprayed nitrous into a plastic food service glove and took a hit.

"So good." Stefan's voice was thick with chocolate. The walls inhaled.

I lowered the glove and the room dipped and swayed. "C'mon, do a whippit with me."

He stuffed a handful of brownie slivers into his mouth, then came over and pressed me into the stainless steel sink. I filled the glove with nitrous and he huffed it. Then he rested his forehead against my shoulder while he enjoyed the spinning.

"They put a dead body in there," I said.

Stefan tensed up, and spoke into my T-shirt. "What?"

"In the room with me."

He groaned, and pushed back. I stared at him in the greenish glow of the kitchen's after-hours lighting. He didn't need to see my eyes to feel what I was feeling, but I think it helped. "People should think twice before donating their bodies to science. You're strangely unperturbed. They must have given you some really tasty pills."

"I couldn't see the body itself.... The corpse. It was in a body bag."

Stefan shuddered.

"They gave me these pills and just left me there. Me and the body bag. It stunk. But I didn't notice right away. Once I did, the thought of how much of it I'd already inhaled made me sick."

"Have another hit," he said gently. "Want me to blow you while you're high?"

I sucked in a lungful of nitrous straight from the can and shook my head. It didn't feel safe; we were too exposed. I spoke as I let the nitrous out of my lungs. "Later on."

"What were they trying to do?" he asked.

"All I can figure was they were waiting for me to get a read on him. When he showed up, I described him, and they took my vitals and parked me in my room. Where d'you suppose the spirit was hiding for all those hours?"

Stefan ran his fingers over the stubbly sides of my head, then tweaked my Mohawk up in the middle. "Maybe it wasn't there. Maybe they gave you an enhancement, and then they got you to make a spirit show itself to you after it was already departed—call it back to the body or something."

I shook my head and the walls rippled. "No. They only give me enhancements in the green room. The one with lead walls, or Kryptonite or...whatever." I felt nauseated. I told myself it was a decent high. "I think it was something else. The opposite of an enhancement."

"There is no such thing." Stefan straightened my earrings. They were always getting tangled. I touched his black-dyed hair. It was crunchy with Aqua Net. He caught my hand, gave it a quick kiss, and then pulled away. If I wasn't going to drop trou, then stolen dessert trumped me. "Well, at least they only kept you in there for a few hours. Could've been worse."

I nodded, which was probably not the best idea, and then I upchucked into the sink. Nitrous must not mix well with whatever it was they'd had me swallow. Stefan tactfully ignored me and continued shaving pieces off the brownies.

I swished out my mouth and rinsed the puke down the drain. "I'll come visit you tonight," I said. I might not be fit for a blowjob at that very moment, but at two a.m., when the overnight orderlies jockeyed for their lunch breaks? Oh, yeah.

"Be careful. I don't like the looks of the new orderlies."

"I'm always careful."

Stefan glanced at the clock. "Come back now."

"What?" Was someone looking for us already? We'd only been gone a few minutes. "Do you feel someone coming? We gotta hide—or they'll catch us *fraternizing.*"

"Ten. You're focusing on the sound of my voice."

"Ten people? Fuck, they found out." If I rolled myself up into a ball, I could fit under the sink. But Stefan? No chance.

"Nine. You're breathing. You're relaxed."

I listened hard. I didn't hear a group of people.

"Eight. And the present begins to filter in. Focus on your right hand. And remember where it is, on the arm of the couch."

"I have no idea what the fuck you're talking about."

"Seven. I see you haven't lost your edge, after all. You're not in Camp Hell, Victor. You're in my office. Sitting. On the couch."

I was sitting? No I wasn't. I glanced back at the sink, and a wave of disorientation hit me. I was sitting. At least, that's what it felt like.

"...Three. Focus on the palm of your hand, make a fist, and open it again. That's right. You're very calm, and very relaxed."

"Stefan?"

The room spun, and I realized the dimly-lit kitchen was actually a dimly-lit office—Stefan's office. His face filled my field of vision, and my God, he was so old. I glanced down at my permanent press slacks, my standard-issue plainclothes dress shoes. So was I.

"...you awaken totally refreshed, and you remember everything you've seen." He watched me. I blinked. Was I really there with him? I could have sworn we were in the kitchen. I could have sworn I was twenty-three. It all seemed so real.

"You feel calm," he said, in his regular voice. Not his hypnosis voice.

"Yeah. I do."

"You went deep, fast. I was worried you might not be a good candidate for hypnosis. Good thing I didn't mention that and bias you against it. So—want to talk about it?"

His eyes were the same. Hazel. Shrewd. He'd stopped plucking his eyebrows and penciling them into sharp peaks, but they still looked groomed. My guess was that he still combed them into shape. His nose was...oh, there was a tiny dot, the size of a pore, where he'd used to have a silver nose ring. His mouth was the same.

I'd loved him so much.

"Or maybe you need to process it."

I nodded. I'd never told him. Not once. And then I just left him in that fucking...place.

"What's wrong?"

I shook my head. I wasn't up for waterworks.

He watched me for a moment, and then stood up. "Sit for a few minutes. Or lie down if you want. It's a decent couch. I've got to make some notes."

There was a clock within view of the couch. It was almost five. He'd knocked out his last two appointments for me. I hoped they weren't suicidal or anything. I tried to ground myself in the present. Beige wall. Berber carpets. Textured ceiling. I let my breath out slowly.

Stefan had to have heard it, but he continued to write without looking up. Just like he'd heard me ralph in the sink, but had kept right on pilfering brownie crumbs. "I remembered one of the times we raided the kitchen," I said.

"Thought so. You wanted me to huff your glove."

"Oh God. I was talking and moving and stuff?"

He dismissed my embarrassment with a flick of his hand. "Don't worry about it. I've seen worse."

✦ SEVEN ✦

I hung my coat in the hall and followed the smell of something better than I deserved for dinner into the kitchen. Sloppy joes, or spaghetti sauce, or...I lifted the lid and peeked. Chili.

Jacob came up out the basement in a T-shirt and jeans. There were cobwebs in his hair. He opened his mouth to say something, I'm guessing something a normal person might say, like hello. And I blurted out, "I just saw Stefan. And he hypnotized me, and I remembered something about Camp Hell."

He came over and stood in front of me, reading my body language. He was probably trying to see if I wanted to be touched, or if he should leave me alone. I hoped he'd figure right. I couldn't tell, myself.

My elbow twinged when he ran his hands up my arms, but I ignored it. I leaned toward him, and he clasped me against his chest. He was so big. And maybe I'd been wrong, when I figured he wasn't really my type, that I was into flashy guys. Because Stefan was all about the rock-star look, but he was also big and solid, and patient and smart. I settled my cheek against Jacob's shoulder, and focused on the places our bodies touched. They were all solid muscle. "You feel amazing."

"Are you okay?"

I nodded. "Yeah. I, uh...." Actually, realizing that I'd left Stefan at Camp Hell to rot was bothering me a hell of a lot more than the scene he'd helped me dredge up. "I realized that they tested Neurozamine on me. Back before it was on the market. Way back. Before it was even called that."

Jacob turned his face toward me and kissed the side of my head. He slid both hands up my back and wove his fingers through my hair. "Neurozamine's side effects are a lot milder than Auracel's."

That was true. "It metabolizes faster, too. Just a couple of hours."

He stroked my scalp with his fingertips. I closed my eyes. The smell. I'd smelled it plenty, since I'd worked homicide. But those first few times really stick with you.

"They figured that out by locking me in a room with a dead body and timing how long it took me to get a read on the spirit."

His fingers went still on my scalp for a moment. He reached down to steady himself on the countertop with one hand. And then his other hand began stroking again, gentle, patient, as if I hadn't just told him about the corpse.

I opened my eyes.

Jacob was squeezing the countertop so hard, his knuckles were white.

"I'm gonna ditch my suit," I said. I brushed a kiss over his jaw as I pulled back, and I wondered if a real wool blazer would have felt less clammy than the SaverPlus special with the man-made lining. I slipped it off, and my shirt was still damp beneath my holster. "Um...I'm thinking it shouldn't go back in the closet."

Jacob stepped up behind me, and his hand closed over mine. "I'll take it to the cleaners." He wrapped his other hand around me and loosened my tie. "The back of your shirt is stained with sweat."

"Nice."

"Let me take care of you." He dropped my jacket on the couch, then my gun and holster, and then he led me to the bathroom.

Our downstairs bathroom was big and brand spanking new, since the original owner died before she'd even finished installing it. In the eighties. I didn't mind the pastel tiles or the whitewashed cabinets. They were the closest thing to white we had in the whole loft.

Jacob parked my ass against the sink, turned on the shower, and peeled off my shirt. I avoided looking at it too hard. At Jacob, too. He'd seen me naked for months. But tonight it felt different, somehow. Vulnerable.

I stared at a spot in the center of his chest where a partial spider skeleton had caught on his T-shirt while he was rooting around in the basement. If I looked hard, I could see how each tiny leg had been jointed.

Jacob slipped my belt off, undid my fly. My dress pants dropped. He pushed down my boxers, and I shoved down my socks, stepped out of everything in one big wad of fabric and shoes. The bathroom was hazy with steam. Jacob slipped out of his clothes, let them mingle with mine, the whole mess of it fit to be thrown out on the street, except that I really liked the way his jeans hugged his package, so maybe those could stay, spider parts or not.

Jacob climbed into the shower first, then held a hand out to me. It was a far cry from my old shower stall, which had been molded all in one piece in a factory somewhere, and shipped by the dozens to every apartment rehab in the Midwest. No, this beauty was floor to ceiling tile, bizarre shades of salmon and ecru, seafoam and wedgewood. I knew Jacob hated it. But its condition was pristine, and neither of us had the time or inclination to have it ripped out and replaced with something less weird.

I ran a fingertip over the grout between a pale green and pale pink tile. "I can get a lawnchair," Jacob said. He put his hand on my hip and thumbed my hipbone as he said it. "That way, you can sit back and...."

Whatever he was going to offer, no doubt it would've been totally hot. Only my mind shifted to something completely else. Not like a cosmic hand was channel-surfing in my brain or anything. I still knew who I was, where I was, and with whom. It was more like picture-in-picture, a super vivid flash of Camp Hell.

The orderlies.

The showers.

Movie Mike, back from one course too many of experimental drugs.

Mike in a wheelchair, with his head bobbing around and weird-assed noises coming out of his throat.

A plastic chair, lying on its side on the grungy blue tiles. Water beaded on the arms, puddling under the seat. Or maybe urine.

"I can't," I told Jacob. I'd been aiming for a firm delivery, but I'd overshot the firmness aspect and ended up snapping.

Jacob caressed my cheek with his knuckles. "What is it?"

We all thought Movie Mike would snap out of it once the drugs ran their course. I always bounced back. So did Stefan. But Mike never did. The orderlies would strap him into this plastic chair and hose him down.

"Camp Hell. The showers." I shook my head. "No chair."

"Okay. We don't need a chair. I'll hold you up." He eased my back against the ridiculous tiles and pushed my wet hair out of my eyes. I really needed a haircut. Jacob never mentioned it. Because he never rode me about all the little things, the shit that didn't really matter.

He touched my shoulder. I looked down. A pattern of pale hickeys stretched along my collarbone from sternum to shoulder. Giant purple-red love bites covered my stomach where he'd sucked me hard. And my hips were dusted with smudgy green fingermarks. If I didn't know where all the decorations had come from, I would think I'd picked up leprosy somewhere.

Jacob pressed his mouth against a hickey, and kissed it. The shower pelted him in the back. He moved to the next mark, and kissed that, too.

He moved across my chest, and placed a slow, deliberate kiss on each mark he'd made, each place he'd left me a souvenir of the fun we'd had together. He pressed firmly enough to keep it from tickling me, and yet I felt jumpy, as if I'd shove him off any second and chafe gooseflesh off my arms. I even flinched a time or two, but Jacob ignored the motion, until he'd kissed his way across my neck and shoulders, and had to kneel down to press his lips against my belly.

Water droplets bounced off my chest, and my skin flushed from the heat. I looked down at Jacob's head. There was no Camp Hell flashback that could overlay what he was doing. It was too different, too new. He thumbed a bruise on my hip, and shook his head. I wondered if he'd be worried about breaking me now that I'd opened myself up to the brittle memories of Camp Hell. "Hey. I was having a good time. Remember?"

He glanced up. Fine water droplets beaded his hair.

I touched his brow. "A really good time," I said, emphasis on the *really*.

His mouth closed over the crest of my hipbone. He lavished a slow, wet kiss over one finger-shaped bruise, and then the next, then the next. My nipples stiffened in the shower spray, and my cock started to swell. I decided his tongue and lips weren't making me feel ticklish after all.

I leaned into the tile and rested my hands on his shoulders, and watched the top of his head. His hair had a mean swirl at the back, as if the hand that'd made him had finished him off there with a tweak. I touched the cowlick, and he murmured against the skin beneath my belly button. I didn't have a bruise there. But I guess he wanted to be thorough.

His beard grazed my shaft, and he worked his way across to my other hip. One by one, he kissed each and every mark on my body. I was hard by the time he finished.

Jacob coaxed my legs apart, then wedged one of his shoulders between them. I slung a leg over him. I figured I could get away with it; I was stone-cold sober and I had two tiled walls holding me up. The water that ran down the front of me was hot, but his mouth was hotter as it closed over my balls. He wasn't sucking and tonguing like usual, though. He was kissing.

My cock pointed toward my navel. I let my breath out slowly and determined that I wouldn't drown in the shower spray as long as I kept my face tilted down. Better to watch Jacob that way, anyhow.

Jacob's whiskers brushed my inner thigh, and then his lips, and the touch of his tongue. No bruises there that I knew of. But that was okay. He swirled his tongue behind my balls. I squeezed his shoulders, made a noise that told him if he wanted to pursue the tongue action, that'd be fine by me.

He kissed my taint. Sucked it. Kissed it again. I did my best not to breathe water.

I ran my fingers over the back of Jacob's head. Water sprayed off his short hair. He burrowed deeper, reached around to spread my ass open with his hands. I slumped against the shower wall, tilted my hips. His lower lip brushed my ass. My breath caught.

He kissed me there, tender and wet, and then followed with a long lick, and another kiss.

"Feels good," I said, which was the understatement of the year, and I think he knew, anyway. He kept on going—kissing, licking, sucking—and the leg that held me up started to tremble, but I just walked it out wide, flexed my hips toward him more so it was easier for him to devour my quivering hole.

I felt flushed from my knees to my ribs, and everything throbbed in time with the beat of my heart and the slow, steady swipes of Jacob's lips and tongue. There was a delicious ache in my cock. I touched it, and his tongue fluttered on my ass. I groaned, and stroked myself. Jacob layered kisses over kisses, and between them, slipped his tongue inside me. I started beating off, hard.

My leg shook, and he held my ass firmly. No bruises, not tonight, just enough to steady me against the shower wall. I made a sex noise, swallowed water, remembered to tuck my chin. My wet hair tickled the bridge of my nose. The spray had gone tepid. I didn't care. The peak was in sight.

Jacob drove his tongue in deeper, and I grabbed his head to steady myself, jerked off against the short, wet bristle of his hair. He sucked at my ass, tongue-fucked it. The water was cold now, sharp on my nipples. Jacob groaned—I felt it rumble behind my balls, and then I stiffened up all over, squeezed my eyes shut and held my breath. I shot my load, hot over my fist, then cold again as the water rinsed it away. The tip of Jacob's tongue traced my ass, and his hot breath made me shiver. I milked another bead of come from myself, and my stomach twitched.

I opened one eye and looked at the top of Jacob's head. He had to be freezing.

I got my leg under me again and Jacob turned off the shower. I was going to make a remark about the capacity of our hot water heater, but Jacob flattened me against the shower wall, chest to chest, and pressed his face into my neck. More tender kisses, as if he couldn't find enough places on me to put them.

✦ EIGHT ✦

I signed off on a stack of reports that Zig had typed up. Ghost count at LaSalle was up to seventeen, none of them willing to talk, most of them probably repeaters. I was supposed to be checking Zig's work for accuracy, but hell. I could tell after the first two or three that he'd written down everything I'd said, exactly how I'd said it. I stared at the paper and let the words blur until I figured enough time had passed that I'd look like I had actually read it, and I penned my forgettable signature on the bottom. And then I moved on to the next page.

Zig sat across from me, busy at work transcribing even more notes. We'd been at LaSalle for the better part of the week, and had zero to show for it. I don't think I'd ever had that many ghosts give me so little information.

My cell phone rang. Caller ID said *Metro Cor Cen*. Crap. I didn't want to talk to Roger Burke, but I was worried that I'd miss something and regret it later if I didn't. "Bayne. Hold on a second." I muted the phone. "I'll take this outside," I told Zigler. He nodded without looking up from his computer screen.

Outside was about five below. I headed toward my car, and then realized that it was possible that my car was bugged. Probable? Maybe not. But possible? Yeah. After everything I'd seen lately, yeah.

And, for that matter, my cell phone could have been monitored, too. "I don't think you should be calling me," I told him.

"I talked to my lawyer. He hasn't heard from you yet."

"It's only been a few days."

"I'm an ex-cop in prison. Every day is Russian roulette."

Shit. Probably so. I tried another excuse. "I think I can get the same information out of Warwick if I catch him on the right day."

"Hardly. He thinks he knows, but the FPMP only shows him what they want him to see. Now, me? How do you think I know so much?"

I sighed into the phone, hard. "I'm sure you can't wait to tell me."

"Because I was one of them."

I felt a cold jab somewhere behind my sternum. It would explain how he knew all that he knew about Camp Hell. About me. "What's it stand for?"

"The Federal Psychic Monitoring Program. They don't have a website or an ad in the Yellow Pages, but they exist. I'll even do you one better, since you're such a skeptic, and I'm dying to get out of this fucking metal box. I'll give you a name."

My heart thundered inside my ribcage. I held my breath. I fumbled in my pocket for something to write on. "Hold on."

"I've got thirty seconds. Twenty-nine. Twenty-eight...."

Damn prison and its fucking rules. I found a silver gum wrapper. I could use the back—if I had a pen. No pen. Fuck. Fuck.

"Twenty-four...."

I flashed back to Stefan's office, all low lights and soporific beige. And then farther, to a blue and blue room that smelled like antiseptic and fear. A light shining in my eye.

"Stop counting." The only thing that stopped me from throwing my phone on the ground and grinding it into the road salt and ice was the fact that I'd have to account for it later.

A pair of patrolmen veered around me on the way to their cruiser. I recognized the senior officer, but not the rookie. "Hey...borrow your pen?"

The officers stopped, and the older one—Monroe? Montroy—handed his pen to me.

"Okay, go."

"Constantine Dreyfuss. He's quite a character. He doesn't know much about Camp Hell, but he'd be able to tell you all about who's been keeping tabs on you lately."

That was probably more important. I could find out more about Camp Hell from talking to Stefan. It would all be stuff I already knew, of course, but at the same time, it'd be news to me. I didn't mention that to Burke. I couldn't have him thinking I was grateful or anything.

I tried to hand the pen back to Montroy, but he was already heading off toward his cruiser. He gave me a, "No, keep it," kind of wave. I couldn't tell if he was being friendly, or he didn't want to touch it once I'd handled it.

I looked up at the sky. It was gray on gray. Nearly March. Where it'd turn to rain on gray. Which would produce ice, and accidents, and still more ghosts.

Was the whole world eventually going to end up like LaSalle, thick with repeaters, or ghosts so busy blubbering into their own blood that they *wouldn't* communicate with me even though they *could*?

I knuckled my eye and wondered if my Valium had come through yet, and then I noticed that the new cop, the rookie, was watching me through his sideview mirror.

Not the kind of look I get from psych groupies, like that guy in the hospital bed. And not the kind I get from the forensics techs who hate me. This was a really calm stare, like the ones I got from the mystery cops who had doubled and tripled every time I blinked when I was helping Jacob track the astral rapist at the nursing home.

I found another scrap of paper in my pocket: this one a grocery list on a sticky note that said *coffee, milk, dish soap, bread (not white), O. J.* in Jacob's handwriting. I turned it over, pulled out my new pen and jotted down my cell number, then jogged over to the cruiser before it had a chance to pull away.

The cop who'd been watching me rolled down his window. He looked expectant. Or maybe mildly alarmed. I handed him the note. "Give that to Constantine for me, wouldja?"

I got on the beige elevator and rode to the beige twenty-third floor. I stopped off at the beige bathroom, as usual. Because, as usual, I was sweating buckets.

Good thing I hadn't decided to deal with my panic attacks during the summer.

Stefan's secretary was gone, and the light in the waiting room was dim. His office door was open a crack. I knocked on the doorjamb and he motioned for me to come in. Today's vest was black moiré, and he had arm garters on his white shirtsleeves like a Wild West bank teller. His office smelled like incense and pot.

"You get high in here?"

"Not during business hours."

He held the joint out to me and I shook my head. "All the good drugs act like psyactives for me."

"Really?" He took a hit, then licked his finger and tamped out the joint, which he propped in an ash tray. He spoke on the exhale, in that croaky way that pot-smokers do. "So how's the memory?"

I looked for somewhere to sit. There was the hypnosis chair. And the couch. And the chair across the desk from Stefan that would make me feel like I'd been sent to the principal's office again. I went to the window, pried the miniblinds open with my forefinger and looked out. The windows in the skyscraper across the street glowed yellow and white. "Memory's there. Parts of it, anyway. I was thinking about Movie Mike."

Stefan made a Stefan-sound of disgust. The same one he'd made every time they served pork roast for dinner. Which he'd claimed was actually made of dog. "At least what happened to him didn't happen to someone...nicer."

"Or me or you."

"That's right."

"Since we're talking about drugs...what do you think it was that did that to him?"

Stefan stood up and walked toward me with his hands tucked behind his back. He positioned himself so that he could see through the window over my shoulder. "My guess? They pumped him full of heavy psyactives to see how far they could open up his talent, they overtaxed him and he suffered some sort of aneurysm."

"God."

"It could've just as easily happened to one of us while we were doing nitrous. It's all one big game of Russian roulette."

How was it I could go for years without hearing the phrase *Russian roulette*, and then have it uttered twice in the same day? I reminded myself that he was a high-level empath. Maybe he'd somehow felt the words reverberating in my high-strung brain.

"I think I had some sort of seizure once when they tried psyactives on me."

Gurney.

Wrist restraints.

"Didn't we all? Lord, I remember that I couldn't tell who I was for days. I was such a mess—crying, laughing, screaming...complete meltdown. I think the orderlies drew straws to see who'd have to deal with the empaths and telepaths. They saved their special hate for us because we could see how dead they were inside."

Stefan strolled away, hands still clasped at his back. I turned and watched him pace. He could come right out and talk about what had happened to him. Did it help?

Then again, so far I could handle all the horrors of Camp Hell that had resurfaced. It was the things I had done—or hadn't—that really ate away at me.

"I'm really sorry."

"For what?"

"I should have done something different...back then."

"We do the best we can with what we've got, Victor. Now stop wallowing."

I turned back toward the window and tried to determine if I was wallowing.

"Do you want to try another hypnotic regression?"

What I wanted was for someone to tell me what to do about Roger Burke. "No. Not today. I just came by to pick up that Valium."

Stefan set a white paper pharmacy bag on the corner of his desk. I picked it up and looked at the prescription sticker. "Who's Fernando?"

"A sweet Mexican boy who needs a new pair of shoes."

I pulled out my wallet. "What's that mean in English?"

"A hundred fifty will do it."

It was steep, but I wasn't one to argue with a month's supply of ten-milligram tablets. I put a stack of twenties and tens on the desk and pocketed the pills. "Be sure to thank Fernando for me."

"Oh, I will."

He said it in the tone of voice he normally reserved for brownies.

My phone rang, and at first I thought it was the FPMP getting back to me. The sick feeling of panic in my gut told me that giving my number to that cop wasn't the smartest thing I could've done. I was just mad. And since Zigler wasn't in the loop, he couldn't have stomped me in the foot and told me to cool off before I did something stupid.

But the phone started to vibrate, too, and I realized it was Jacob. And I felt vaguely guilty that he was calling me while I was scoring pills. But only vaguely. "I've got to take this," I told Stefan. "Hello?"

"Are you still at work?"

"No. I'm at Stefan's office. But we're just finishing up."

"Perfect. Carolyn and I are at the courthouse. I can pick you up."

How coincidental. Or maybe not. They'd been in and out of court all week. I never went, myself, because "no court, no jail," had been the only clause I insisted upon when I negotiated my contract. But Jacob and Carolyn were regulars.

I gave Jacob the address, which I suspected he already knew, and he took it down to be polite. "Be there in ten. Bye." He used the sexy *bye*.

"That was, uh, my boyfriend."

"You're dating?"

"Yeah, we just bought a building, actually."

"You're dating seriously. Interesting." Stefan pulled a can of air freshener from his desk drawer and doused the room, then he tucked away his ash tray. "So what've you got to be nervous about?"

Was I nervous? My gut was clenched and my hands felt clammy, but that was nothing new. But Stefan would know. He'd tapped me a million times before.

"What's the worst case scenario?" he said.

I've never been very good at making things up, but I closed my eyes, and I thought. "That you see us together, him and me, and you think I'm a sellout for joining the force."

"And seeing you with your lover would lead me to that conclusion because...?"

"He's a PsyCop, too. It's more obvious when we're in a group." Otherwise, I just look like a used car salesman. So I've been told.

"I promise, I'll be nice. And I can't believe you just used the word *sellout.*"

Both Jacob and Carolyn came up to get me. I would've thought Carolyn would stay in the car to keep it from getting towed by an overzealous truck that didn't notice the police plates. Was she just curious, or did Jacob invite her up because he thought there'd be some conversation that required her professional opinion?

We met them out in the reception area of Stefan's office, which smelled slightly less like air freshener and pot. "Steven Russeau," I'd almost slipped and called him Stefan Russell, "Detectives Carolyn Brinkman and Jacob Marks." Everyone shook hands. Jacob and Stefan stared at each other hard.

"Victor knows you from Heliotrope Station?" Carolyn asked. Or maybe stated.

"That's right."

She walked over to the print with the funky perspective, tilted her head and looked puzzled. "Do you have an online presence? Victor seems to think the lack of information about him on the Internet is something he should be concerned about."

"Geez," I said, "Your small-talk skills are worse than mine."

"My practice has a website. Of course, my name isn't my name. What's your talent, if you don't mind my asking?"

"Telepath Two."

"Mm. I've always had a soft spot for telepaths." He looked at Jacob. "And you?"

"NP." That's short for non-psychic. Giving those two initials was probably just as difficult for Jacob as spelling it all out.

"I thought you were a PsyCop."

"I am. One Psych, one Stiff on each team."

Stefan's unreadable gaze lingered on Jacob. "If you say so."

"Are you doing anything for dinner?" Jacob asked. "You're welcome to join us."

Now what was he up to?

"Maybe next time. Fernando would never forgive me if I stood him up."

"Bring him along."

"Thanks, but no. Theater tickets."

"Ah."

Given that Carolyn didn't have anything to say about that, Stefan's excuse must have been legitimate. Then again, he didn't actually say he *had* theater tickets. I hadn't told him anything about Carolyn's talent—but maybe I didn't have to. Stefan was the strongest empath I'd ever met. Maybe he already knew.

✦ NINE ✦

Carolyn nabbed the back seat of the Crown Vic before I could take it. I briefly considered sitting in back alongside her, leaving Jacob up front by his lonesome. But that would've been weird.

"It's good to see a Psych in private practice," she said. As if the atmosphere in the car wasn't thick enough to cut with a dull plastic knife.

"I...guess." Stefan and I had never talked about what we wanted to be when we grew up. Maybe we never thought we'd make it out of Camp Hell fit for anything but Medicaid.

"I hope he takes us up on our offer," Jacob said.

"Our offer? You mean, your offer."

Jacob was busy navigating a packed on-ramp. He gave me a quick glance in reply. "Would you prefer I don't get to know him?"

"I don't care if you...that's not the point." I checked myself to see if I was being truthful. I was, as far as I could tell. "I just...I'm dealing with Heliotrope Station right now."

His hand landed on my knee. "I know."

I jiggled my opposite knee. "Look, I know you wanna be there for me...and stuff. But I...." I had no idea. I sighed, and I slumped back into the car seat.

"I don't suppose this conversation could wait until you dropped me off," Carolyn said.

Jacob squeezed my knee. "You shouldn't have to face this alone. We've got each other."

I snorted. "You just wanted to make sure Stefan and I didn't pick up where we left off."

"Of course not."

"Yes you did," said Carolyn, from the back seat.

Whoa. Slipping up and telling a flat-out lie, right in front of the Human Polygraph? Jacob shook his head. It served him right for bringing her along. He could've sprung for her to take a cab back to the Twelfth.

"Seriously? You're worried about what I'm gonna do? That's some nerve, after you spent all that time hanging out with Crash behind my back."

"I've met Stefan now. He strikes me as a decent person. I'm not worried."

I wouldn't go so far as to label Stefan as a "decent person," whatever that means. He'd just scored me under-the-table Valium. How decent could he be? But he clearly wasn't interested in sleeping with me anymore. I suspected that's what Jacob really meant, whether he knew it or not.

Jacob pulled up in the parking lot of the Twelfth and let Carolyn out of the car. If any of the men in blue moving among the parked cruisers were FPMP plants, I couldn't tell. Then again, I don't think the FPMP was watching Carolyn very hard. She was good at what she did, but her ability was so narrow and specific that it only ranked as a medium on the Richter scale of psychic ability.

The parking spot by the cannery was open, as usual. I'd need to make sure that no one knew our building wasn't haunted any longer, at least until the snow drifts melted from the dirt patch off the alleyway that passed for our backyard.

I helped with dinner. I'm reasonably good at chopping things up, especially if Jacob is very specific about what size everything should be. It takes me ten times longer to do it than it does him, but at least I can feel like I'm contributing to the food cause.

Jacob, meanwhile, was measuring, sautéing, and bringing water to a boil, all at the same time. Showoff. "You know I'm crazy about you," he said. "I can't help but want to know who you're spending time with, whether I need to be worried or not."

"I know you're crazy," I said. It really was hard to stay mad at him. He gave me his big-eyed look that was the best approximation of innocent that he could muster, and mostly it just looked hot.

"Stefan says I've got some problems with, uh, anxiety."

Jacob didn't disagree.

I fished my new prescription out of my pocket. "I'm taking a Valium."

No opposition.

"And, uh, it's not through The Clinic."

Jacob pressed himself against my back and mashed me into the kitchen counter. He rested his chin on my shoulder and looked at the bag. "So Fernando does exist."

"I imagine Carolyn would have mentioned it if he didn't."

"I'm all for you getting better. Take the Valium. We'll rent a movie and relax."

The rest of the night was surprisingly mild. I probably could've drilled home the fact that I was annoyed that Jacob had been keeping tabs on me, but I wasn't really annoyed, not anymore.

My prescription probably had something to do with my mood. The Valium was sweet, even better than Seconal, and I suspected that there was something to be said for getting a prescription from a real, live American pharmacy, even if the name on that prescription was *Fernando*.

I fell asleep halfway through a car chase and slept like a baby, and when Zig and I headed over to LaSalle the next morning, I felt both mellow and alert, all at the same time. If not for the dry mouth, it would've been the best I'd felt in ages.

The aftereffects of the drug didn't seem to affect my talent one way or the other. Ghosts were still thick, but they didn't seem as freaky-making when I waded through them.

I felt so gregarious that I almost told Zigler I was considering changing my name to Fernando. But then I figured he probably wouldn't be as excited about my new prescription as I was.

"Where do you want to start," he asked me. "Second floor, cardiac unit?"

"Wasn't there a snack machine downstairs?"

"On the lower level?"

"Yeah. The basement." I tried the word out. No willies. Amazing.

I think Zig noticed. He stared at me over that thick carpet-pile strip of mustache for a second, then shrugged. "Okay."

We rode the elevator down with a nurse wearing scrubs covered in bright blue and neon green seahorses. "Excuse me," I said. "What's the deal with all those crazy patterns? I thought scrubs used to come in solid colors."

She glanced at me. Her eyes were sunken, like she hadn't slept in about four days. "I dunno. I guess they're easier to keep clean."

The elevator dinged open and she headed for the cafeteria. "She must mean it's harder to see the blood stains." I stepped off the car and Zigler followed. He stood next to me and stared. "What?"

"Nothing."

Sheesh, couldn't I make a simple observation?

There were cafeteria smells in the corridor, coffee and fried things, and some form of meat. Underlying it all was the smell of disinfectant. It smelled similar to Heliotrope Station. Not exactly the same, as if maybe the formulation of the disinfectant had changed over the years, and perhaps the menu was more varied. But it was similar. I noticed the similarity. And I felt okay about it.

Zigler had his pad out and his pen poised. I must have been giving "the look."

I shook my head and he lowered the pen. "Let's find the vending machines," I said. I was dying for a piece of gum.

A ghost in a custodian's uniform passed by, but he disappeared through a wall before I got a good look at him. "This place could use a good cleaning," I said.

Zig squinted at the floor. "Seems reasonably clean to me."

"Ghosts, I mean. Why so many?"

His eyebrows bunched together. "Obvious reasons."

"Yeah, but..." I shrugged. It didn't seem like it necessarily had to be that way. I'd just spent a week in a nursing home where I could go hours without seeing any spirit activity. Heck, plenty of fresh ghosts had "gone to the light" right before my eyes.

"What do you think makes someone a repeater?"

Zigler fed a dollar into the machine and ordered up a plastic-wrapped brick of peanut butter crackers. "If you haven't figured it out, I don't think anyone knows for sure."

I dropped some quarters in and pressed a button, watched with fascination as the giant chrome corkscrew turned and turned, and my gum inched closer, closer, teetered on the edge, and then finally, when I thought it might end up stuck in that limbo between paid-for and mine, it fell.

"I know my antenna picks up more signals," I said. I stripped the wrapper from a stick of gum. It folded like an accordion when I jammed it into my mouth. "But there's gotta be some other medium around who's better at putting words to this stuff. Maybe someone who's more intellectual about the whole... deal."

Zig brushed orange crumbs from the front of his blazer. "You ever met another medium?"

"Sure, I..." I stopped short and drew a blank, had to really dig for a second to remember. Yes. Two. There were two other mediums at Camp Hell. Which meant that mediumship as a talent was sorely underrepresented in the larger pool of Psychs. "They were kinda..." I shrugged. "One of 'em was dumb as a bag of rocks." We'd called him Einstein. His actual name was Richard. His I.Q. was eighty on a good testing day, which was borderline retarded, depending on which charts and tables you look at.

Faun Windsong was the other, and despite the fact that we never called anyone by their real name, we did indeed call her Faun. Probably because we all knew it wasn't the name on her birth certificate. She'd changed it when she turned eighteen, in an attempt to embrace her Menominee heritage. I think she was something like one-sixteenth Indian.

Maybe one sixteenth is all you need. Faun didn't just accept her talent. She reveled in it. Thought she was some kind of big deal for being able to "speak to the ancestors." Except she couldn't really speak to them. She got vague impressions.

Cold spots were her specialty. She was usually standing right in the middle of someone when she "sensed" one. I never mentioned it—in retrospect, I'm not sure why. She was so full of herself that I would've loved to have taken her down a few pegs. But now that I thought about it, I never piped up when I saw them on our graveyard outings.

In fact, I agreed with Faun a lot of the time. It was as if I had a string you could pull, and I'd repeat a stock phrase. "I do sense a cold spot," or, "The energy feels male," or, "Someone is trying to make contact, but I just can't make the connection."

"Vic?"

I blinked.

"You want to tell me what's going on?" Zig was scowling at me, which I interpreted as "concerned."

My gum had lost some of its flavor. I spit it in the garbage and started a new piece. "I'm seeing a therapist."

Zig's eyes widened. "Oh." He held up his hand. "Say no more."

He'd been seeing someone for a couple of months now. He had a hard time wrapping his head around the idea that a dead body could be made to move around, given some herbs, incantations and ingenuity.

I ran a hand through my hair. Zig might not want me to talk about it, but I felt the need to explain, so that maybe I could understand, too. "I'm remembering...stuff." I nodded. "A lot of stuff."

"Is that good?"

"So far? It's okay."

He nodded. "I'm going to get some coffee."

I watched him plod down the hall toward the cafeteria, and I realized that I actually liked Zig—in a wow-he-never-hassles-me kind of way. Maybe I needed to hang out with straight guys more often.

My phone gave off its generic ringtone, and I realized I should probably put Stefan's number in my memory dial. It wasn't as if I didn't have enough open slots.

I wondered if he was calling me to talk about Jacob. I was sure he'd have something to say, I just couldn't tell what it would be, given the all-purpose raised eyebrow he'd maintained through the entire encounter.

"Hello?"

"Detective." It was a female voice on the other end of the line, which threw me for a loop. I scanned through my mental Rolodex of women I knew who would address me as "Detective" and came up empty-handed.

And I'd been so positive it was Stefan that I hadn't even answered with my work-greeting, my last name. "Yes?"

"I'm calling for Constantine Dreyfuss," said the woman's voice. "He wonders if you'd care to join him for a cup of coffee."

✦ TEN ✦

I coasted through the rest of the day at LaSalle. Sure, I saw ghosts and I described what they looked like, what they were doing, to Zigler—but most of my attention was on the diner I planned to stop at on my way home. And not for a club sandwich.

The smell of fries and scorched hamburger belted me when I walked into Uwanna Burger, but my usual response—uncontrolled salivation—was markedly absent. My mouth was bone dry. I swallowed, and wondered if I'd taken a Valium without realizing it. I hadn't. In fact, I wanted to make sure I was wound up and jumpy when I met my guy from the FPMP. I wanted to keep my edge.

I scanned the place, and looked for someone in a suit. A scattering of people were in various stages of finishing their meals, and none of them looked like a "Constantine" to me. I ordered a coffee but didn't bother putting any cream or sugar in it. I'd only gotten it so I could sit without anyone looking at me sideways. I didn't think I could actually swallow it.

The only clean booth was by the plate glass window in front. My head would be right behind the giant U if I chose to sit there—a perfect sniper target. I chose to bus one of the dirty tables toward the back of the diner, and sit there with someone else's salt scattered on the tabletop all around me instead.

I kept my eye trained on the front door and I made designs in my Styrofoam cup with my thumbnail. And I wished Jacob was there, because he'd know what to say and do.

A long-haired, middle-aged guy in a big navy parka paused at my table on his way back from the bathroom. "Weed?"

Jesus. Why did someone always try to sell me drugs when I was having a panic attack? I shook my head and glared harder at the front door.

"Seriously, it's good stuff." He made to slide into the booth with me.

"What the fuck? I said no."

He was undeterred. He parked himself across from me and looked very earnest. "You won't find anything better. North Side's totally dry lately...except for my source."

Very seldom do I get the urge to hit people. But I wanted to flatten him. "Look, asshole, I'm a cop—and I'll give you three seconds to get the fuck out of my face."

He held his hands up in surrender, though I noted that he made no effort to get up. "Okay, okay. I had to do that, double-check your reaction. I didn't think you'd be so hostile. Whoever wrote up your personality profile did a pretty lousy job of it. Can we start over again?"

I did my best not to gawk. "Who are you?"

"Con Dreyfuss. Constantine, actually, but everyone calls me Con. I'd of-fer to shake, but you look like you'd just as soon bite my hand off. Hard day at work?"

Now I really wanted to punch him. "You tell me. You're the one keeping tabs on me."

"Oh, touché." He swept salt into a pile with the side of his hand. I saw that he bit his nails. "I've gotta tell you, my organization's not some kind of George Orwell trip, you know? It might sound like it, with all the hush-hush and the non-disclosure clauses. But if you had to deal directly with the public? Trust me, Detective, you wouldn't like it. Not at all."

He swept the salt over the side of the table. "That old folks' home almost got ugly, you running around drunk, all those witnesses. We'll need to hire more agents if you keep up the high profile."

"Why did Roger Burke give me your name?"

He looked surprised. "Oh, so that's how you spotted us. Most Psychs either tune in to us within the first year, or they never notice. Depends on the talent, I guess. It's really hard to tail a precog, for instance."

"So you've been on me since I got out of the academy."

"Not me, personally. I made the Midwest Regional Director five years ago. Before that, I was in Florida."

"Didn't a level-four medium buy it in Florida last year?"

He looked pleased. "I'll bet they're sorry I transferred."

I tried to determine if "Con" was anything like he appeared to be, or if he was just another Roger Burke—someone who came off like a normal guy, but had the soul of a scorpion inside. Stefan would be able to tell me. Jacob, too—he'd known at first sight that something didn't add up with Burke. But I wasn't willing to hold up either of them to FPMP scrutiny, not until I figured out just how dangerous it was to be in the know.

"I know your name," I said. "I've seen your face. So, now what?"

"I'm relieved that I don't have to break the ice. See, empaths and telepaths? They're everywhere. But mediums are few and far between." Dreyfuss wiped some salt off his parka sleeve. "I'm gonna put this out there—and don't answer me, not now. Just think about it. But I could really use someone like you on my team."

I've never liked the word *team*. I've always equated it with being picked last and getting nailed in the groin with a dodgeball.

"Ah-ah." Dreyfuss held up his raggedly-cuticled forefinger. "Like I said, don't answer me now. I'm not asking you to quit your day job. The whole thing would be totally discreet, and I'd make it worth your while." He stared at me hard. "Really...worth your while."

I wondered what that meant, exactly. I must have looked like I was considering his offer.

"Cash? Or...Seconal. I really can hook you up."

I held my arm tight to my side, because I could practically feel my knuckles sinking into his face.

"Or new stuff that's not even on the market yet, something that'll blow Auracel out of the water."

"Didn't your files tell you that I'm a shitty guinea pig? The last time one of you slipped me a new psy-drug, he ended up in prison."

"That wasn't us. Roger Burke thought of that little scheme without any help from the FPMP. And besides, that was a psyactive. I'm talking anti-psyactive. One that doesn't come with a headache and an upset stomach. But I'm getting ahead of myself. I've got other things to offer, too. You want to catch up with some of your old friends from Heliotrope Station? I can find out where they are."

"The ones who are still alive."

"Or not. That's never stopped you from talking to anyone. Has it?"

The thought of the FPMP following me around had me so spooked that I didn't trust my cell. I swung by a battered payphone covered with stick-on tags that read *Hello, My Name Is...* with blocky, illegible, tagger-looking scribbles in the name slots beneath. I dug a quarter out of my pocket and made a call. To kill some time, I drove around for a while, then picked up my de-sweated suit from the dry cleaners.

Once it seemed like I'd dawdled enough, I stopped at SaverPlus. I walked through the whole store, from activewear to home and garden, and tried to figure out which of the other shoppers was watching me. Before I met Dreyfuss, I would've been looking for men who looked like cops. But now I was open to the possibility that the ninety-year-old woman with the walker or the obese guy with the pop-bottle glasses could've been working for the FPMP, too.

It was a couple hours until store closing, but the portrait studio was dark. I slipped past the fake tree background and down a narrow hallway, to the old bathrooms that were too dingy to even consider using unless you were in severe intestinal distress.

I ducked into the men's room. Crash was perched on the countertop beside the sink. His eyes locked onto mine. He hopped down and walked toward me, hands on hips. He wore a scuffed biker's jacket, tight jeans, and combat boots spray-painted purple. His green hair had faded a few shades since the last time I'd seen him.

I looked over my shoulder at the door. There was no lock, but there was a rubber wedge on the floor that could be used to hold the door open—or shut. I crammed it underneath.

Crash was right up against me when I turned back around. "This cloak-and-dagger act gives me a hard-on like nobody's business," he said. "I can't believe you touched a payphone. Who knows where that handset has been?"

"Would you quit it?" I edged past him, even though there was really nowhere to go. "I need to talk."

"Your mouth says no, but your guts say yes. 'Cos if *no* really meant no, I'd stop trying."

"Stop thinking with your dick for ten seconds and tell me if you've ever heard of the FPMP."

He backed up, hitched his thumbs into his pockets and rocked on the balls of his feet. "Sounds alphabetical. What do they call themselves for short, F-Pimp?"

I leaned against the wall, closed my eyes, and tried to go to a happy place. I was out of practice. "It's not funny."

I heard the countertop creak as Crash launched himself back up beside the rust-stained sink. "Apparently not." I opened my eyes. His feet were dangling. He stared at me and swung them. "Sorry. Doesn't ring any bells. Want me to look it up online?"

"Maybe you shouldn't. They're the Federal Psychic Monitoring Program. They're the ones who keep me off the Internet."

Crash's eyes widened. "Oh, shit. Be careful."

"Why do you think I asked you to meet me *here*?"

He raked his tongue barbell over his lower teeth, and leered.

"Look," I told him. "I don't know what to do. They offered me a job."

He picked at a few threads that were starting to unravel over his knee where the denim had worn thin. "Might be a good idea. Keep your friends close and your enemies closer. But I take it you're not here for my blessing."

"You could tell if they were lying. Right?"

"Whoa, whoa. You want me to put myself on the radar of the psychic CIA?"

"So you can't? You're always walking around with your hand on your stomach like you're getting a read off anything that breathes. I just thought...."

"Nice try, but I'm enough of an empath to know when you're baiting me."

Damn. I'd been hoping Crash would jump at the chance to do something subversive. And I guess I *had* been baiting him. "Maybe you could do it over the phone. I can get a new cell, one of those pay-as-you-go things...."

"No can do. Not on the phone. It doesn't work that way."

"But you can tell. When someone's lying."

He took his cigarette pack out of his pocket and turned it around longingly. "Not like Carolyn. She's a telepath—she hears people's mental process in words."

"But...?"

He unfolded the foil, touched the edges of the filters, then folded the foil back down and tucked his cigarettes away. "Yeah. If I tune in to that part of my head, I get an impression. I can usually tell."

"Seriously. I don't know what to do. I wish I could ignore them and they'd just go away, but I don't see it happening. If I don't go along with them, is that gonna put me on their shit list? And what about my friends? What about Jacob?"

"What *about* Jacob? I'm guessing you haven't told him, or he'd be all over this."

I stared hard at the ugly brown floor tile.

"Going behind Mister Perfect's back. That's fucking hilarious. You guys think you're so virtuous because you both fall into the same bed every night, but I'll bet you haven't had a single conversation that was a hundred percent honest. You know what? You two deserve each other."

What could I say? That was probably true.

✦ ELEVEN ✦

There was a note on the fridge for me when I got home that read, "I'm at the gym—really." Given that I was the one who'd just snuck off to see Crash and I hadn't run into Jacob, I believed it.

I was dying to ask Lisa if the cannery was bugged, but I didn't trust that either my e-mail or my phone was secure. What could I do, write her a letter? For all I knew, the FPMP had access to our mail, too.

I was sitting on the bed, staring at the wall, when Jacob got home. Either he didn't think I looked too crazy, or that's pretty much how I always look. "What's up?" he said.

"C'mere. Lay down with me a sec." I flipped the TV on and hit the DVD. It picked up where we'd left off—in the middle of a four-way blowjob chain that took place in a motel room with furniture worse than the stuff in my old apartment. I raised the volume.

Jacob peeled off his sweatshirt and started to undo his jeans. "Leave that," I said. "C'mere."

He climbed into bed and grabbed me by the head. I turned my mouth away from his kiss and spoke directly in his ear. "I have to tell you something. But I think they're listening." Which sounded incredibly paranoid, I realized, but only after I'd said it.

Jacob covered my mouth with his, then kissed his way along my jaw until his lips were against my ear. "Who?"

"The Federal Psychic Monitoring Program. They're real. They've got guys at the Fifth. And I talked to one of the head honchos today." I thought that's what Dreyfuss was, anyway. Regional...something. Damn.

"All right." Jacob's voice was just a breath. And above it, someone on the

TV yelled, *Hoo yeah, suck it, suck it good.* Three other guys moaned in reply. "What is it?"

"They asked me to do some kind of job for them. But I think it's really a test."

Jacob took the remote and cranked it to the max. The one guy who didn't have a dick in his mouth went, "Oh yeah, oh yeah, oh yeah," in a really nasal and repetitive way, but at least it covered up our conversation.

Jacob covered my body with his and pressed a kiss to the side of my neck. Damn. I'm such a sucker for the neck. I shifted and tried to shake off the creep of arousal. And failed. The sound of three dicks getting sucked and one guy moaning and groaning wasn't helping.

"How dangerous is this job?" Jacob whispered.

"Dunno."

"And what if you say no?"

"Don't know that either...but they're everywhere. I don't think ignoring them is an option."

I felt Jacob's cock against my thigh. Stiff. Crash was right, we did deserve each other.

Jacob slipped a hand under my T-shirt and brushed his fingers over my nipple. I gasped, but the sound was drowned out by a couple of guys encouraging one guy kneeling between them to suck them off at the same time while the fourth guy kept up the yeah-yeah business. "Do what you need to do," Jacob said against my ear.

I eased my hand between us and snuck it down the waistband of his jeans. I had no idea what I needed to do with the FPMP. But I knew how I could stop thinking about them, if only for a few minutes.

Jacob pushed himself off me and undid his fly. I struggled to get my T-shirt over my head while I was flat on my back. Jacob shoved the shirt up around my neck and dove for one of my nipples while I was tangled up in it. He sucked, hard, and my back arched. I made a sound that was nothing like the hypnotic *uhn-uhn-uhn* noises on the DVD, something desperate and raw that he'd coaxed from deep in my throat.

When I finally tugged my shirt off, Jacob trailed a long lick up my neck. I made another guttural noise. He pressed his mouth to my ear. "Can they see us?"

"Dunno."

Jacob sat back, unsnapped my fly and pulled off my jeans, then his. His cock stood away from his body. It bulged with veins—but so did the rest of him, his arms, his neck, his thighs—fresh from the gym and looking as if his skin could hardly contain him.

He grabbed my leg and pushed my knee to my chest. His mouth covered my ass and he teased me with his tongue.

"Fuck yeah," I said. It was lost among all the theatrical grunting on the TV.

He pushed his thumb inside me and engulfed my balls in the furnace of his mouth. I held my cock against my stomach, gave it a few absent strokes. Mostly I reveled in the heat and the wetness, and the feel of Jacob going at me like he was starving.

He shoved my leg up harder. My knee was buried in the pillow beside my head, my ass pointed up toward the ceiling, and I struggled to breathe. Fingers, tongue—he stroked and licked and fingered me until I was giddy from lack of air.

"Jacob, I'm gonna...."

He raked his teeth over my taint, tongued my ass.

"Fuck...." My body tried to uncoil itself, but Jacob held me there with my ass in the air and I couldn't have moved if I'd wanted to. I got off on it too, the idea that my ass was his and there wasn't a damn thing I could do about it. I clenched up all over and made a strangled noise, and felt the hot spatter of jiz on my neck and face.

Jacob's tongue invaded my ass in time with my spurts, so hot and so wet, and I wondered if I might pass out from lack of air and I didn't give a damn, because the strangle factor had made for such a sweet, throbbing orgasm.

But then Jacob did let up, and my back protested as I unrolled. But only as far as his veiny slab of cock.

I felt his knuckles as he lined himself up. Then his cockhead. I dropped my knees open and focused on the feel of him pushing in. I was used to the girth of him by now, but like this, with nothing but spit between us, he felt twice as big. He paused with just the head in me, ran his palms over my heaving belly. I had to have enough air in my lungs by now—maybe I was hyperventilating. It felt awesome, like I was flying.

He eased in another couple of inches. I felt like his cock was gonna split me in half. I flexed my back and tried to bury him deeper. He fit his hands over my hipbones, and his fingers covered the marks he'd made on me before, the last time we'd had sex, or the time before that, or the time before that.

And there was something so amazing about that, being with someone, night after night, trusting him like that. Or maybe it was the lack of air. But it felt incredible.

I reached under my ass and cradled Jacob's balls. He sank in deeper and then pulled out. He spat into his cupped hand, gave his cock a once-over, then prodded it in again. "Yeah," I said, loud, so he could hear me over the dull roar of the repetitively enthusiastic kids on the DVD. "Feels good."

He chewed his upper lip for a second, then twitched himself in deeper still. I panted and winced—God, it burned—and pulled on his balls to urge him to sink it all the way in.

He moved slow and steady, deeper with each thrust. His balls shifted in his scrotum, and the skin wrinkled against my fingertips. The kids on the DVD whooped—it was the part where the one on his knees took three loads to the face. I always liked that part, and I usually backed up and watched it a few times in a row just for the hell of it.

Jacob reached for my face and thumbed my jiz off my cheek. He sank his thumb into his mouth, his glistening, wet mouth, and sucked it clean.

He had me hard again. I grabbed my cock and started pumping.

Jacob hitched his hand under my knee and pulled one of my legs up and over his shoulder. He turned his head and tongued the sinew behind my knee. His goatee scraped my bare, wet skin. His other hand roamed my stomach and chest, traced glistening trails in the come I'd already shot.

Credits rolled on the DVD, and under the lettering, outtakes where the guys stopped acting porno and talked and laughed while they polished each others' rods. I liked that, too, seeing them being normal guys together.

And I wondered if Jacob and I were performing for someone who might be listening, even watching. Or if we were just us.

Jacob's thrusts grew steady, faster, and the muscles in his stomach hardened.

His body arched and he threw his head back. His neck was a column of muscle and vein, and his whole body seemed to pulse and throb. He pulled out, trailing wet come, and shot part of his load on my balls. I felt a thread of spit and semen trickle out of my ass, and stroked myself off until I came again. Just a couple of deep, heaving twitches, and a new spatter of jiz on my belly.

My leg dropped from Jacob's shoulder. My belly heaved as I sucked air. I felt like I was totally covered in spunk, like the kid who'd been shot on by three other guys. My ass was raw.

Jacob planted his hands on either side of my head and lowered himself over me. He could probably hold that push-up position for hours without breaking a sweat. His lips barely touched mine. "Wake me up early," he said, his breath hot against my mouth. "We'll go for a walk."

He held my gaze. He didn't look very happy, for someone who'd just come on my balls. He stared at me hard, and I couldn't keep the eye contact. I started to turn on my side, but I was covered in semen. I reached over the side of the bed, and grabbed his sweatshirt. I wiped myself off. Jacob turned out the light. I rolled over, and he fit himself against my back. Somehow, in the dark, the idea that someone else could've been watching us, could still be listening, seemed even scarier than it had while we were having sex. I didn't say anything, and either did he. Eventually, Jacob fell asleep. I watched the clock until eleven, then twelve. I guess I fell asleep before one.

Even so, I woke up before Jacob did. I turned on the coffee then came back upstairs and shook him. His eyebrows drew down, as if he'd been free of me as he slept, but now that he'd woken up, he had to settle back in to this life the two of us had created. He opened a drawer on his bedside table, and rummaged around inside. He came up with the stub of a pencil and an old receipt. He wrote so small I could hardly see it.

Separate cars. Horner Park.

He crumpled up the note, pulled on some clothes, and left.

Was it paranoid of him to write that down? Or was it smart? Maybe I should look up some of my paranoid compadres from the nuthouse. The super-paranoid ones—the real schizophrenics who actually looked crazy, the ones with facial tics who did weird things with their tongues, who hoarded moldy food under their beds and wore a dozen layers of clothes whether the temperature was nine degrees or ninety. They would be able to tell me how to watch my ass.

I got dressed, filled up my travel mug, and left. It was just after five, and there was almost no traffic. I saw Jacob's car in a lot and kept driving halfway around the block, where I parked near the baseball diamond. Snow covered the field, and there were old tracks that led to the dugout, which was surrounded by beer cans and cigarette butts, and if I got close enough to see more details, probably used condoms. I followed the sidewalk around the park with my hands stuffed in my pockets and my breath streaming out behind me. I walked until I came to a concession stand that was boarded up for the winter, and I slipped around back.

Jacob leaned against the back of the stand in his black leather jacket with his hands in his pockets. "These people. You really think they can hear us in our house?"

"Maybe."

He let his breath out slowly. It traveled away from him in a stream of vapor. "I don't like it. But other than going along with them, I don't see what else you can do. It's not like there's anyone you can tell. And it's not like there's anywhere we can go."

"I'm sorry."

Jacob shot me a heavy-duty look. "Why are you sorry? What could you have done differently?"

I didn't know. But I was too chickenshit to volunteer that not only had I initiated the contact, but I'd gotten the tipoff from Roger Burke.

"So this guy at the Fifth, the one you spotted—what's his name? What shift does he work?"

"Jesus. You're not going to...."

Jacob turned away and scowled at the snow. He was itching to do something, that much was obvious. To grab someone and wring some answers out of him. Physically, if need be.

"If I do this FPMP job," I said, "it's because I'm trying to get on the inside and figure out more about them—see who they are and what they know. You can't charge in and put the thumbscrews on one of their guys."

Jacob mulled that over, then nodded grudgingly. "I could arrange to meet him some other way. Get to know him. Hang out where he drinks. Join his gym."

"I hate to break it to you, but you don't do subtlety very well. If he's straight, which he probably is, you'll creep him out. And if he's queer, he'll think you're cruising him. Anyway, I didn't get his name."

Jacob scowled even harder. "I'm getting us some new phones."

"Okay." Chances were slim to none that I'd remember my new phone number, but it seemed like a good idea anyway. "I'm sure there's a way we can block out what we're saying at home. Power tools, a blender, something that makes a lot of noise."

"Or porn." Jacob's lips had turned up at the corner, but I wouldn't have called his expression happy by any stretch of the imagination.

I pulled my hand from my pocket and reached out to him. He did the same, gave my fingers a quick squeeze, then turned and walked back toward his car.

Jacob's patience wouldn't last forever. I had to figure out how deep the FPMP had their hooks in me. And how to live with it, or tear myself free, once and for all. There had to be *some* way. I was psychic, after all, and so were dozens of my acquaintances and colleagues. If I didn't know anyone who could find me a loophole, then I wasn't worth the paper my fifth-level certification was printed on.

✦ TWELVE ✦

I met Zig in the records room at LaSalle, which, unfortunately, was located in the basement.

"Aren't these things on the computer?" I asked him.

He planted his hands on his hips and looked at the long rows of banker boxes. "They digitized everything back to 1985."

"Okay. So why do you want to look here?"

"It was something you said to one of the nurses that got me thinking. You asked her about the patterns on her outfit. But you told me that you were accustomed to seeing everyone in blue, and that would be, what? Mid-eighties?"

I shrugged.

"And yet this nurse you saw, the outfit you described—white, right? All white. Down to the shoes."

"...yeah?" I couldn't imagine why it would matter.

"What if the place is thick with old activity? Everyone you've described is wearing a hospital gown. How would you know—without their hair done up, or makeup, or shoes—if they're current, or fifty years old?"

I stared down a row of faded boxes. The boiler room was next door, which made the file room warm and uncomfortably humid, and the old cardboard smelled faintly of mildew.

"If something did happen fifty years ago," I said, "what good will it do to piece it back together?" My phone rang and I checked the Caller I.D.—Stefan's office, returning the call I'd left before anyone was actually there. "I gotta take this," I said, and I made my way down an aisle of floor-to-ceiling shelves of cardboard boxes. "Hello?" Just a few feet in, the sound of my voice was muted, and my footsteps practically disappeared, as the cardboard absorbed the noise along with all the moisture in the air.

"So that call you left with my service this morning," said Stefan. "Is your big emergency an actual emergency?"

I'd been a little twitchy when I'd spoken to the guy who'd answered the phone. "You mean...?"

"Medical, psychological, what? Should I be referring you to the Emergency Room?"

I stared up at the ceiling and tried to determine if I'd end up in Admissions if I rose up through the stained acoustical tiles. "I really have to talk to you. In person. Today."

Stefan informed me that unless I was either experiencing acute psychosis or dying, he wasn't willing to come in on a Saturday for me.

"I wouldn't have called your service if it wasn't important," I said. I hoped I sounded earnest.

Stefan sighed so long I thought it would go on forever. "Oh, all right. I'll meet you there."

Zig didn't look very happy about sorting through all those boxes alone, but he didn't seem to want to know where I needed to go so urgently, either. I drove downtown and parked in a tall ramp with a twenty-dollar price tag, and ended up wishing I'd just taken the train. When I got to Stefan's office, I motioned for a piece of paper, and wrote a note that we'd have to go outside. Stefan went along with me, but not without looking at me like maybe I really was having a psychotic break after all.

"I'm not paranoid," I said. We walked fast and whispered, and a block away, the El rumbled by. I couldn't imagine how the FPMP could hear us. Unless I had a chip in me. Oh God. "There's this thing called the Federal Psychic Monitoring Program, and they send agents to watch me when I'm at work. I think they have my phone tapped and they can read my e-mails."

"That's absurd. You can't just tap someone's phone...."

"Whoever told you to change your name after Camp Hell? I think it's them. They're probably watching you, too."

Stefan paused, and whoever was walking behind us had to do some fancy maneuvering to keep from ramming into his back. At first, I thought it was an agent, maybe one with a listening device, some sort of amplifier that only *looked* like a cell phone. But if it was one of the FPMP, he was doing a damn good impression of a Foot Locker employee trying to order some lunch.

"I took the money and I changed my name. That was years ago. What makes you think they're still watching me?"

"Why wouldn't they? Why wouldn't they keep tabs on you to make sure you didn't slip up and tell someone about Camp Hell? They've been watching me for, what, fourteen years? If you did fall off their radar, you're back on it now that you're seeing me as a patient."

"Everything's under the table. You're not on the books. I've never even created a record for you in my database."

"It doesn't matter. They follow me."

People streamed past us—a woman in a business suit and sneakers. A delivery boy with bags of sandwiches and a tray of steaming coffee. A guy in lycra pants, powerwalking. Stefan watched them walk past, his expression unreadable. "What proof do you have?"

I leaned into him. "I met one of them," I said in his ear. "He wants me to do a job for him."

"What're you going to do?" Stefan said carefully.

"Play along. I have to do it. What else can I do?"

"Maybe you can get something out of it." He peeled away from me, pushed his hands deep into his huge overcoat, stared out at a line of yellow taxis, and sighed. "I wasn't thrilled about changing my name. But look what I can show for it—my practice. My career. I like what I do. I'm good at it. But without seed money, to go to school, to get the business off the ground, I never would've been able to do it. Who would loan money to someone like me? Back then, I mean, when the best I could hope for was a full one-hitter and an apartment door without an eviction notice on it?"

"I don't need money." Which wasn't strictly true, now that I had a mortgage to pay that was three times the rent on my old apartment, and I was hoping we could have a shower installed in the upstairs bathroom. Who wouldn't want more money? But I wasn't destitute.

Stefan gave a bleak smile. "Everyone needs something. Work with them. It's not the end of the world."

A bike messenger had a near miss with a taxi, which resulted in a deafening blitz of car horns and cursing. However fucked-up I thought my life was, at least I wasn't a bike messenger in subfreezing weather.

"I remembered some more Camp Hell," I told him. "Einstein. And Faun Windsong."

Stefan's gaze turned inward as he thought back. "And Dead Darla."

"What?"

He looked at me with his eyebrows raised.

Damn. Just when I thought my memory was there, only rusty and neglected, flabby from inactivity, there'd be a nugget of something that seemed like I should recognize it—but whatever it was, it simply wasn't there, no matter how hard I reached.

"I want to do a regression."

Stefan reached into a gap in his overcoat and pulled out his pocket watch—with the satisfaction of someone who actually gets to use his pocket watch in the company of someone else who notices. "You really are bound and determined to talk me into working on a Saturday."

"I won't do it in your office, though." I looked around for somewhere we could go. There were benches in Grant Park, but I doubted I'd be very receptive to hypnosis with the wind skimming across the lake and belting me with ice crystals. "We'll go in my car."

"What's wrong with my office?"

"You're not there 24-7. Someone could've come in, installed cameras, microphones. Have you lifted up the drop ceiling lately, looked underneath?"

"If you think my office is bugged, who's to say your car isn't?"

He had a good point. I'd need to take it to the dealership and have it combed over. "It's the best place I can think of right now. Will you do it, or not?"

Stefan made a face. Disgusted, but resigned. "If you don't go into trance in five minutes or less, I'm not going to keep going. I haven't eaten lunch yet, and my blood sugar gets really low when I skip meals."

"Don't worry. I have a granola bar in my glove compartment."

Stefan followed me to the parking ramp. We didn't speak as we climbed the stairs—neither of us was in good enough shape to spare the breath.

"That's your car?"

"Uh, yeah."

"How do you fit your massive muscle-man into it?"

I felt my cheeks flush. It was the first time he'd mentioned Jacob. "We usually take his Crown Vic if we're going anywhere...together."

"Good lord, I thought you'd at least have a mid-sized sedan." Stefan unbuttoned his overcoat and made a big show of adjusting all his layers before he got in.

My granola bar was long gone. I had nothing to offer but a starlight mint—which Stefan accepted, but with very little enthusiasm. He chewed it up and swallowed it, sighed dramatically, cranked the passenger seat all the way back, and began to speak in that deep, slow, hypnotic way of his. "Close your eyes. You're going to count back, from ten to one, and focus only on the sound of my voice...."

"Nice Mohawk."

I squinted at the pale chick with the humongous dyed-red hair. She was wearing too much pancake makeup. I had to fight off the urge to drag my fingernail down her cheek and see what was underneath. I'd been heading for the smokers' lounge, not because I smoked, but because I was high with the novelty of being able to go where I wanted, when I wanted, for the first time since I was nineteen. "So," she said. "You're a medium?"

I couldn't tell if she was challenging me or making conversation. I'd been told that other people at Heliotrope Station could see and hear things, too. And unlike me and the other jerks at the CCMHC, we might even agree on what those things were, so I didn't shift into full-on asshole mode when I answered. "That's what they tell me."

"I'm a medium too," she said. "A strong level four. My name's Darla. They call me Dead Darla." She smiled, an evil smile that she'd probably practiced in her makeup mirror. "I don't mind. I kind of like it."

"Vic Bayne...."

"Cool name. So, what's your level?"

"I, uh...they haven't tested me yet." Supposedly I still had Thorazine in my system, so they'd held off on the "testing" that seemed to be the ultimate placement exam of the psychic world.

Darla slipped her hand through my arm and pressed herself against me. She was as wide as I was tall, and hard to say for sure, but I think I felt her tits against my arm. Damn. If I told her I was queer, she'd know that I knew she was flirting with me, and she'd be embarrassed. I figured I'd just do my oblivious act. And eventually someone would find me and another male resident with our pants down, and everyone would whisper about it in the cafeteria, give me a few nasty looks, and after that I wouldn't have to worry about the unwelcome female attention anymore.

But for now, Darla was soft and pillowy against my arm. She pulled on me, and stood on her tippytoes like she had something good to tell me. I leaned over.

"I can give you some hints," she whispered. "The better you score, the higher paying job you'll get once training's over."

"Okay," I said. Because I was busy trying to figure out how to take my arm back without pissing off Dead Darla, and it seemed to me that if I made an enemy out of her, I'd be really, really sorry.

She pressed my arm into her softness. It couldn't have all been tits. Really difficult to tell, with the big, oversized black sweater she had on. She pulled me away from the smokers' lounge and down toward the pop machines. "First, the tester will give you an item that belongs to a dead person and try to get you to tell them who it belonged to. They switch that every time, so I can't help you with that, but I think maybe that's more to see if you've got any precog tendencies or not."

"Precog?"

"Precognitive. Knowing something without seeing or hearing it directly. Knowing the future."

"I'll bomb that for sure." If I had any kind of precog edge, I wouldn't have landed myself in the nuthouse by telling Mister Lubowski, my homeroom teacher, about the accident I saw that no one else could see...and then insisting I was right until they shot me up with sedatives and put me away. Fucking field trip. I would've cut class that day and cruised Boystown instead if I'd been precognitive.

Or at least I would've taken it all back sooner, everything I'd described, maybe said I was just making it up for attention. But no. I laid it all out there, everything I'd seen, down to the last spurting compound fracture. And before I knew it there was a straightjacket with my name on it.

"Don't worry about it," said Darla. "I just made stuff up, whatever came into my head, and I still scored high. See, if you really are a medium, you'll be able to tell them about the dead lady."

We slipped past the pop machines and down a dim flight of stairs that smelled like urine. "They never use this part of the building for anything else." She wrinkled her nose. "Maybe they're scared they'll clean the ghost out if they hose it down."

"Can that...happen?"

"A few physical things affect ghosts, but mostly salt, I think. Some Voodoo-based rituals use substances like soap and ammonia, though, so I think they're gonna keep playing it safe. Because what'll they do if they scare off the testing ghost? Kill someone just to make a new one?"

She smiled her evil smile at me. Too bad she wanted to do more than just pal around together. She seemed to know a lot about the way things worked.

The stairwell let out into a dingy hall with a few old offices on either side, a drinking fountain at the end, a red fire extinguisher in a rusted box, and a pair of restrooms. Dead Darla opened the ladies' room door. I hung back like a vampire that hadn't been invited across the threshold. "Come on." She flashed her wicked grin over her shoulder. "No one will know."

I took a step forward. The reluctance to enter a ladies' room gave way to the realization that if we were as completely alone as she said we were, she might want to do it. I prepared a lie. Crabs? No, genital warts. That would cool her off.

Darla walked toward a hole in the wall where a sink used to be with her arms spread wide. "Right here," she said, "is a cold spot."

✦ THIRTEEN ✦

I blinked. Dead Darla stood in the middle of a fucked-up film loop of a woman falling and cracking her head on the sink that wasn't there anymore. I couldn't see the sink. But I saw the blood.

Darla closed her eyes and held her hands out to each side, palm up, as if she was trying to catch raindrops. "It feels like a woman, to me. That's what I told them. And it's sudden. An accident."

Slip. Crack. Bleed.

Yeah, it looked like an accident to me.

I rubbed my upper arms and my teeth started to chatter. I expected to see my own breath, but I didn't. "It's freezing in here."

"You feel it too?" Darla opened her eyes and beamed at me. "What about the details? Are you getting any of them?"

"The details, that's where they'll get you."

I swung around. A man stepped out of one of the stalls, transparent, gaunt. His arms hung before him, wrists slashed vertically from elbow to palm. Suicide Charlie at CCMHC had told me that was the proper way to cut yourself if you really meant business.

The guy who'd spoken had been successful, judging by the fact that he was now transparent.

"Vic?"

I glanced at Darla. The woman she was standing in fell and split her head. Again.

"I told 'em what I saw," said the guy with the slit wrists. "Everything. That was my mistake."

"I don't like it in here," I told Darla. I backed toward the door.

"This isn't a malicious spirit," she said. "She won't hurt you."

"That's right," said the bleeder. "It's the head honchos around here you've gotta look out for. And the Feds. See, they tell you to do your best. And when you do...?"

Most ghosts just died over and over, but this one was talking to me. If Darla hadn't been there, I might have even been able to ask it a few questions. But I was glad she was there, because the fact that it saw me, was talking to me, scared me shitless. I felt like I was going to spew, but there was a ghost between me and the nearest toilet. I staggered out into the hall and prayed that the drinking fountain still worked. The knob was gone. I darted across to the men's room and locked the door behind me.

"Vic?" Dead Darla tapped on the door.

"I need a minute." I went to the sink and tried the taps. Water chugged out, reluctantly at first. I splashed water on my face and looked at the paper towel dispenser. It was empty. I dried my face with the hem of my T-shirt. A few deep breaths, and my breathing seemed to be under control. Good. I unlocked the door and looked out. There was Darla, fluttering her mascara-tarred eyelashes. "Hey," I said. "I'm, uh, chock full o' meds right now. I think I just wanna hang out down here. Alone. For a little while."

She tried to figure out what I meant—whether I was trying to snoop around and augment my test scores, or whether I had diarrhea, or whether I was just weird. Whatever the case, I wanted to be alone, and that was the last thing she wanted to hear. But I'm guessing she was reluctant to burn any bridges, either. "Oh, okay. I have a Sixth Sensory Skills workshop after dinner. Are you in that workshop? Maybe we can hang out afterward."

"I'm not sure. I might. I'll, uh, see if I see you."

"Well, all right, then." I think she might've hugged me, but I had the door open in such a way that only a six-inch strip of me showed. She was still smiling at me when I closed the door, locked it, slumped against it and let my breath out in a long, slow hiss.

"Shit," I said, out loud. Darla had felt a cold spot? Sensed a female presence? I could've told her what kind of earrings the ghost was wearing, which tile exactly she'd slid on, and how far her blood had spread.

And then there was the slit-wrist guy. I'd heard him, clear as if he'd been in the room with me. I guess that, technically, he was.

I had no idea what to make of the stuff he'd said about testing too high. I didn't know if ghosts could lie or not. But even if he could, why would he? He had nothing to gain by making me score badly on a psychic abilities test.

I didn't even know what I was supposed to be afraid of—but whatever it was, it was bad enough that he chose to buy his way out with a razor blade. Either that, or someone else had helped him do it, just to make it look like a suicide. I supposed I could go in there and ask him. Yeah, right.

The thought that I might've taken that test without first talking to Dead Darla—or her very dead friend—made my institutional lunch threaten to repeat. I'd have to dumb it down. Say I "sensed" stuff rather than saw or heard it. Maybe even get some details wrong, the age, the gender. Point to the wrong spot.

According to my preliminary Psych tests, it really was ghosts that I was seeing, and not schizophrenic hallucinations.

Damn. Good thing the Thorazine had done the talking for the first round. I'd pointed out which morgue vaults had movement in them, but I was too zonked out to follow the crazy stories the inhabitants were going on about well enough to repeat them.

I splashed more water on myself, tweaked my 'hawk into place, untangled my safety pin earrings, then pressed my cheek against the coolness of the old tile wall and wondered if it might have been safer for me to stay in the nuthouse.

Time passed, a lot of it, and I figured I'd better be somewhere findable unless I wanted to turn up on the scrutiny end of a search party.

I'd been hoping to sneak back to my floor unnoticed, but no such luck. There was a teased-haired Art School Punk in a black Nehru jacket at the top of the stairs. His back was to me, and he was busy beating up the pop machine. He stopped shaking the thing and looked at me over his shoulder. His eyeliner was perfect. "It ate my quarter," he said. His voice was as smooth and deep as a radio announcer's.

"You won't get anything by shaking it," I told him. "They're built to hold on to the cans that way." I was familiar with the make and model. We'd had one at the loony bin; it was a good source of extra income for me. A thirsty schizophrenic will do anything for some pop.

I knelt down and pressed open the chute. If I angled myself just right, I could sneak an arm up into the works and coax one of the cans out of its track. It wasn't easy. I practically had to twist my shoulder out of its socket, and it was cold in there, as cold as you could get without freezing. But it was about the only parlor trick I could do. That, and talking to dead people.

I reached, and strained, and finally, finally, I poked and prodded hard enough to make something give way. There was a thunk and a roll (Slip. Crack. Bleed. Don't think about it...) and a frosty can of ginger ale rolled out of the chute. I pulled my frozen arm out and handed the can to the eyeliner guy.

"I like a man who knows how to use his hands," he said. He had a very naughty smile. "Come back."

"Okay."

"We're in your car."

"What car?" Me? Owning a car? That was hilarious. I didn't even own a Walkman.

"I'll count again, from ten to one. And this time, you *will* come back."

No, that's not what he was going to say. What he had said? He'd told me I needed a reward. He took my frozen hand between his, so big and warm, and breathed on it. That was the sexiest thing anyone had ever done to me. And then....

"Ten, you begin to be aware of the sounds and feelings of the present. We're in your car. Your very small car."

I don't have a car. If we go in the stairwell, no one will see us. No one uses that stairwell. It smells like piss, and we think it's funny.

"Seven, you're aware of your body, the way it rests against the seat. The trash bag overflowing with fast food napkins under your right hand...."

We think it's...funny. Damn. It felt so good to laugh with him.

"Three, you think that maybe it would be a good idea if you came back so that I can eat something before I faint...."

I opened my eyes. My windshield was foggy. The digital clock on my dash read 2:46. That couldn't be right. It was ten after twelve.

"Two, you're breathing, you're relaxed."

"Holy fuck."

"And one. Please don't make me count down again."

I gawked at Stefan. He was so old. "What time is it?"

"Almost three. Look, we're not going to do this on the spur of the moment anymore. We can't. You've got to allot enough time if you're going to be diving in that deep, that fast. Call my office before you come. Give me a chance to juggle my schedule."

"Dead Darla. I met Dead Darla again. I remember her. She used to like me. Before...."

"Before she realized we were fucking each other. I remember full well the force of her loathing when she caught us coming out of the stairwell and she told me my pants were on inside-out." He smiled. "It was pretty funny. When you think about it."

No kidding. I'd never expected so much gratitude for a lousy can of pop.

"Don't look at me like that," Stefan snapped. "My schedule's all screwed up and I'm starving. And it's not as if you're hurting for company."

Shit. I hadn't been giving him a "look." Had I? I was just confused. Five minutes ago, I'd been a young kid who was busy showing off for a psych with a come-hither smile and perfect eyeliner.

Stefan had been a middle-aged guy fantasizing about a cheeseburger.

"Besides," he said. "You're not even my type anymore."

"I wasn't looking at you like...I mean, I don't want to...I'm not trying to...."

"And that lover of yours will skin me alive if I so much as linger too long over a handshake with you. So no funny stuff."

"You picked that up? From Jacob?" He hadn't acted like he was jealous of Stefan, not once they'd met. But who was I to differentiate the way people felt from the things they chose to say?

"Not...per se."

In other words, Stefan wasn't planning to elaborate on what he meant. I wished I could miraculously produce a granola bar from thin air; maybe I could use it to bribe a straight answer out of him. "Don't worry about Jacob. He's fine. And I'm not flirting with you. This regression stuff...it's just confusing."

Stefan pushed his feet against the passenger-side floor and pressed his neck into the headrest. He stared up at the ceiling. "No kidding."

It was after four by the time I got back to the north side. Zigler's Impala was still in one of the special doctor spaces in the parking lot at LaSalle. I took the other one. And I congratulated myself on owning a car that was small enough to fit in a tight parking spot.

I found Zig in the records room with a stack of boxes on either side of him and a printout full of checkmarks and Xs front and center.

"How's it going?" I said.

He looked up. His eyes were puffier than usual, probably from all the dust. "It's not. You didn't give me any names to work with, just physical descriptions—and even those are vague. The files are all names and stats. It's not like comparing apples to oranges. It's like apples to...."

"Ginger ale?" I suggested.

Zig didn't think I was very amusing. "You've gotta find one that's willing to communicate with you."

"Right. Okay." I didn't mean to leave Zig with all the gruntwork, but I was kind of busy trying to figure out what had happened to me at Camp Hell to worry about some people who died before I was even born. Big chunks of time were needed if I wanted to do these regressions, I was expected to be at my actual job during work hours, and moonlighting for Constantine Dreyfuss seemed inevitable. Maybe I should switch from benzos to speed.

"Zig, you're up on all the latest in the world of Psy. How many sixes or sevens are there?"

He looked up from his dead-end list. "What?"

"Sixes. Or sevens. Other than Marie Saint Savon. I know about her."

"Yoshihiro Harimoto, level six medium just outside Tokyo. He's a channel, speaks in the voices of the dead. But only in Japanese, so interest in him is limited to the Japanese-speaking part of the world."

"But what about the U.S.?" Somewhere the FPMP could get their hooks in someone.

"The Joneses."

I rolled my eyes. The Joneses were the running joke of the psychic world. No one knew their first names. Met in training, married, and went on to a seedy career in second-tier Vegas theme shows in which Mrs. Jones dug through the purses of the women in the audience and Mr. Jones announced the lipstick shades and prescription bottles from the stage a hundred feet away. "Seriously."

"I am serious. There's some speculation that they're telepath six. Both of 'em. And so tuned in to one another that they function as one mind. If they hadn't gone into show business, who knows what they could've done with their talent?"

Telepath six? Did tests even go up that high? My stomach sank.

"I told 'em what I saw. Everything. That was my mistake."

The words were as fresh as if I'd just heard them earlier that day; at two forty-five, to be precise. Damn. Maybe the Joneses weren't as drippy as everyone thought. Maybe they'd made a huge, frivolous, sequin-spangled spectacle of themselves so that if they disappeared, someone would notice.

And here I was, seeing ghosts. There was no way to fabricate a Vegas act around that, not without pissing off practically every religion on the planet. Then I'd have to worry about both the zealots *and* the FPMP.

"If you could narrow this down to a single year, I might have a chance at figuring out who all these 'repeaters' are."

"And then what?"

Zig scowled. I'd stumped him.

"This isn't a Vegas act," I said. "They won't disappear in an explosion of sparkles and confetti if we figure out who they are, and name them."

"Do you see another lead we should be looking at? Because I don't."

I planted my hands on my hips and stared at the rows and rows of boxes.

"What you need here is a precog, not a medium. Someone to tell you where to focus."

Zigler started packing up for the day. "I can't use what I don't have."

✦ FOURTEEN ✦

When I got home, I found a black SUV parked in front of the cannery. It was the first time since we'd bought the place that someone other than Jacob or me had taken that spot. I stared at it for a good minute or two before it occurred to me that I'd need to park my car. I found a space down the block.

I trudged up the salty sidewalks to my walkway and approached the building. And then I noticed the second strange thing. Music, coming from our house, audible through the closed door.

If this was some kind of belated birthday party, I was really not in the mood for it.

The vestibule looked like its normal self, except for some extra winter coats hanging from the pegs and a couple of black nylon bags leaned up against the wall. I steeled myself for the festivities and walked into the main room.

There was a buff guy who looked like he was using a metal detector on our sofa. And another one on his knees, unscrewing the plate on an electrical outlet.

"Hello?"

The muscle guys both turned and made a "sh" motion at me. A hand dropped onto my shoulder and I jumped. Just Jacob. The music had been loud enough to cover his approach from the kitchen. He steered me toward the downstairs bathroom, hustled me inside, and closed the door behind us.

"You sure throw a weird party," I said. "Who are those guys?"

"Keith and Manny, from the gym. Keith's a private investigator. If someone's eavesdropping, he'll find them. But until they give us the all-clear, if we need to talk about anything sensitive, we do it in here. With the radio on."

I wanted a pair of musclebound P.I.s combing through my house even less than I wanted strippers and a stale birthday cake.

"That cell phone idea won't work," Jacob said. "Keith says they transmit like karaoke machine microphones, and anyone within range who's got the equipment will receive the signal whether it's a new phone or not."

I felt exhausted. There was nowhere to sit. I flipped down the toilet seat lid, planted myself on it, and pressed the heels of my hands into my closed eyes. "How long are they gonna be here?"

"Until they're done checking the place out."

I could see that arguing with Jacob would be like fighting a brick wall. And besides, it was his place, too. If he wanted his gym monkeys pawing through all of our stuff, who was I to say they couldn't?

Back in the main room, I watched Keith—or Manny, who knows?—hook a very complicated-looking device full of blinking LEDs to a disassembled outlet. He took some readings and then moved on to the next one.

Once I'd decided that watching him work would be as much fun as helping Zigler with his files, I wandered into the kitchen, stood next to the sink and ate a bowl of cereal for dinner. Miraculously, nothing landed on my suit—which I was dying to get out of, but the thought of being naked with all that judgmental, muscular bulk in my house made me uneasy, like maybe I'd get a dodgeball to the groin if I dared take off my pants.

I went upstairs and sat on the bed, and tried to pretend that I didn't hear music coming up through the floorboards, and that there weren't a couple of strangers scanning all of my stuff, and that there wasn't any reason for me to worry about someone keeping tabs on me. But I've never been all that great at Let's Pretend.

Eventually, the music cut. When Jacob came upstairs to find me, I'd taken off my jacket and gun, but I was still in my dress shirt and slacks, lying on the bed and staring up at the tin ceiling.

"They're done. They didn't find anything."

"Okay. I'm really glad that you took me seriously and all, but here's the thing. You could've let me know about the sweep."

"And how would I do that? Call you on your cell phone?"

"It's just...I feel like I don't have any privacy."

"Because of the sweep? This is all about your privacy. I'm trying to make sure that no one hears what we're saying but us."

Supposedly the FPMP was all about my privacy too, but after the journey in time I'd taken to the women's bathroom in the empty wing of Camp Hell, I had my doubts as to the real reasons any super-secret organization would keep an eye on high-level psychics.

Jacob showed no signs of heading toward bed when I took a Valium and turned in early. I felt bad, in a vague and nebulous way. It wasn't so much that I wanted sex—after all, I could still feel our encounter from the night before. I just didn't want him to be pissed off that some government acronym was following me around, and because he'd moved in with me, their scrutiny was his problem now, too. Because if I was being honest with myself, that's the way things looked to me.

I woke up before Jacob did, which was nothing new, but after I'd made some coffee and eaten two bites of a hard-boiled egg that turned out to have a sickly green yolk, I decided not to wake him. The electrical outlet plates and couch cushions were all back where they were supposed to be, but I couldn't shake the image of a couple of strangers going through my shit.

And what was worse than that? The legions of much scarier strangers who likely had being going through my shit ever since the Police Academy.

I put my coat on, wrapped a long scarf around my neck, and went for a walk. Which turned into a ride, once I came across an El station. The route is incredibly convoluted on Sundays, which I figured out when the train turned around and started heading back north instead of going all the way downtown. Evidently, I was supposed to transfer to another line at Belmont. But it was fine. There was no one spectral on the train car, and I wasn't in a hurry.

The streets in the Loop were starting to look familiar from my visits to Stefan's office, but they felt different on a Sunday than they had on other days—quieter, less bustling and more stately. The main Sunday crowd consisted of shoppers rather than office workers, and they carried a different energy with them, a certain excitement that made them seem as if they didn't take the immense feel of the skyscrapers for granted.

Hunger didn't motivate me, so much as the dull, acidic rumble of my empty gut. I stopped at McDonald's and ate a couple of perfectly round breakfast sandwiches, popped an Auracel, and walked to the South Loop slowly enough to ensure the drug hit my system before I hit the prison.

A pair of older ladies whose arms bristled with Macy's bags brushed by me. I tried to imagine myself coming downtown for something other than visiting hours at the federal penitentiary or hypnotic stabs at my buried memories. That I might just go shopping, or visit the aquarium, or ride the Ferris wheel on Navy Pier. I couldn't visualize it.

I had no gun, no cigarettes to surrender at the prison. My biggest collateral was my willingness to recant my testimony. When Burke had first asked me to do it, I'd thought there was no possible way he could convince me. And now I was sitting on the fence.

The guard put me in a different attorney visiting room this time. It didn't have a repeater pounding on the security mirror, but it did smell like a combo of disinfectant and piss. It reminded me of CCMHC, which wasn't my favorite residence, but at least I'd never repressed the years I spent there.

The Auracel had me waxing philosophical about the parallel of my brain and the Internet, seeing the nuthouse plain as day but needing to be searched long and hard for traces of Camp Hell, when Roger Burke joined me in his shackles and orange jumpsuit. I think I may have even been smiling just a little.

"So you checked out Dreyfuss and found out he's legit?"

I felt my smile wither. "We talked."

"You talked to him." Roger shifted in his chair, and his shackles clanked. "That was really smart, letting him know you knew about him. *Really* smart."

"What did you say he did, again?"

"I didn't. But don't let his hippie-guy act fool you. He's high up. They're all like that, anyone who's higher than those grunts in uniforms who sprout up at your crime scenes. You'd never pick 'em out of a crowd. Like Jen."

"Who?"

He looked at me like I couldn't have been more of an idiot. "Doctor Chance. She played you like nobody's business. And she didn't even have to flash her tits to do it. Although, she probably would have. She had a thing for you."

This was nowhere near the direction I'd wanted our conversation to go. What I'd actually wanted was to get a bead on whether or not I should agree to work with Dreyfuss, because even though it seemed like I really didn't have any other option, I figured I could get some insight from Burke. Not that I could come right out and ask him for his advice. But I could gauge his reaction.

"This job that Dreyfuss wants me to do...."

"What?"

"I don't know if I should take it. Sure, it'll get me closer to him, give me an in. But it works both ways. He'll get to know me, too."

"He offered you a job." Burke's lip curled. "Bullshit. Don't think that you'll climb into bed with the FPMP and you'll be safe. That's not how it works over there. Dreyfuss thinks he's the head of his department—maybe he is—but believe you me, someone's watching him."

"I can't exactly refuse."

"Sure you can. It's not as if they can take you out for saying no. Marks would figure it out, and he's too high-profile to pick off."

True, Jacob did have his face splashed across the Tribune and the five o'clock news periodically, often enough that total strangers stopped him at the bank or the gas station just to say hello—and to be able to tell their friends, yeah, he looks even better in person. But if the FPMP was as super-stealth as all that, I was sure they could kill two PsyCops with one stone and get both Jacob and me at the same time, with a gas leak, or a housefire, or a dash of arsenic in our Korean takeout.

"So...you're saying I shouldn't work with Dreyfuss."

"Oh, no. By all means. Let Con work a con on you, make you think that you're all 'in the know' while he's probing into every last aspect of your life to see what you can be manipulated with. I won't stop you."

Burke's reverse psychology left a lot to be desired if even I could see through it. Or did it? Maybe he was right. Maybe I should figure out how to walk away.

"The name I gave you panned out. So you can't deny that I know what I'm talking about. Recant, and I'll give you more names. And better yet, I'll tell you how they keep tabs on all the high-level Psychs."

Damn it. Maybe Burke was psychic himself if he could figure out exactly what I wanted to know, and dangle it right there in front of my nose.

"What's the problem, Bayne? Are you worried that your reputation's going to suffer if you tell the Feds that you made a mistake, you were confused, exhausted? I've got news for you. The rest of the force avoids you for a reason, and not just because you're on the Spook Squad. You're a wreck, a disaster waiting to happen, and only someone as reckless and arrogant as Marks would chain himself to a sinking ship like you."

Was I supposed to be insulted? Cripes, I didn't know what to think. Or how he'd pegged Jacob so well. The two of them seemed to have each other's number at first eye contact.

I stood up and stretched my arms to call attention to the fact that he was the one in shackles and day-glo orange, not me. "You keep sweet-talking like that, you're gonna spoil me."

"You think I don't know how they follow people? I told you, I was one of them."

I did my best to look expressionless. "No. I don't think you do. Back in Buffalo, I think you were one of those fake cops who looks like a patrolman, but cashes a paycheck from the FPMP. You picked up one name—Dreyfuss—and you're using it to make yourself look smart. But that doesn't mean you really know anything."

"Good guess. That might be how I got my foot in the door. But don't forget, I didn't stay a beat cop. I made detective. And I moved up the ranks of the FPMP, too."

Holy shit, I'd guessed right? Too bad it was illegal for me to buy a lottery ticket, or I'd hit a jackpot and buy my own little island somewhere that the

FPMP couldn't follow. I decided to press my luck with Burke. The more I could force him to reveal, the less likely it was that I'd have to call up the Feds and feed them a big, fat, steaming pile of lies. I might not have much of a reputation, but that didn't mean I wanted it to get any worse than it already was. "I've been talking on my cell phone. I might as well have been e-mailing my agenda straight to the FPMP."

Roger frowned hard. Hot damn. I'd found another angle all by myself. With the help of Jacob. And his gym buddies.

I didn't have to fake the feeling of elation I had as I turned to knock on the door and summon the prison guard. I was proud of myself. I'd read someone right, and I'd outmaneuvered him. What a great feeling.

"That's not the only way they'll track you," he said.

My heart sank. I should've known it wouldn't be that easy. I knocked on the door anyway. I didn't feel like giving Roger the satisfaction of looking at him.

The guard opened the door.

"Two words for you, Bayne. Remote viewer."

No.

I froze. Probably just for half a second. But I felt a sickening lurch, like vertigo, like hypnosis, like a bad combination of pills hitting my bloodstream all at once.

If they had a remote viewer looking at me, a fucking psych who could see and hear through walls from any distance, then all the anti-surveillance technology in the world wasn't worth shit.

✦ FIFTEEN ✦

The map of the transit system should've been easy to read. I knew where I was, and I knew where I was going. The routes were even color-coded. But there was that transfer thing, and the special Sunday turnaround, and every time I thought I had a handle on which train station I should go to, the route dissolved in my mind and I was left gazing at the big map and starting over again at "you are here."

I was tracing the transfer point at Jackson and State with my forefinger when my phone rang. I flipped it open. Crash. "Hello?" I said cautiously.

"Lisa says that when she left, she gave you my MP3 player to give back to me. You holding it for ransom, or what?"

I touched the breast pocket of my overcoat. The MP3 player was still there. Along with a week-old parking ramp receipt, a Milky Way wrapper, and a bunch of change that would accumulate until the weight of it unbalanced the coat, and I had to empty it out.

"I'll drop it off some other time. I'm kind of downtown right now. Without my car."

"The blue line lets off two blocks from the store."

I looked at the map. There was the blue line, plain as day. An easy ride with no transfers and no reversible routes. "Did Lisa say anything else?"

"Like what?"

Like anything about remote viewers spying on me. Why would she, unless I asked her about it directly? And I'd promised to give the *si-no* a rest. Besides, I shouldn't be talking about it on a cell phone. "Never mind. You gonna be around? I'll bring it by."

I went underground for the train that let off in Crash's neck of the woods.

The air down there felt moist, and smelled like minerals, bleach and piss. The cavernous space was thick with gray industrial paint where the graffiti had been covered, and covered again, and it seemed like it would be the perfect place for spirit activity. But I was on Auracel. Not only would I not be able to see most ghosts, I'd need all my concentration to make sure I didn't end up riding in the wrong direction, nodding off, and finding myself in a strange neighborhood with my wallet and shoes missing.

The train was short—only three cars, since it was Sunday. I picked the middle car. A young, artsy-looking couple got on at Washington and proceeded to get into a screaming match in something that sounded like Russian. Or maybe Polish. They were a lot more fun to watch than repeaters.

Sleet belted me when I emerged from the subway station by Sticks and Stones. Shitty driving weather. I patted my pocket. The MP3 player was still there. I trudged two blocks and up the stairs, and opened the door. The room was hazy with cigarette smoke and incense.

And there were people there. Shopping.

I stood there in the doorway and gawked. A woman who looked like someone's mom was cruising the crystals. A shabby white kid with dreadlocks studied the Wicca paraphernalia. And a very serious teenaged girl browsed the Voodoo aisle with her hands clasped protectively around her middle and a scowl on her young face.

Crash rang up the purchase of a glowering Asian woman, tucked a sale flyer that was printed on bright pink paper into her bag, and gave her an especially syrupy, "Have a *great* day." Then he looked up at me, batted his eyelashes, and ran his tongue-barbell over his lower teeth. "How now, brown cow. What happened to your car?"

"It's, um...at home."

"Deceptive. Cryptic. Color me intrigued."

I made my way up the crowded aisles so we wouldn't have to keep shouting at one another across the store. Crash had one eye on me and the other on the teenaged girl, who kept glancing up and tucking her long, straight hair behind her ear. "Psy-groupie?" I asked quietly.

"No. Shoplifter. She never takes anything worth more than a buck or two. But I'm trying to make sure it doesn't escalate."

"You want me to go say something? I have my badge."

Crash snorted out a stifled laugh, knuckled his nose, and turned the noise into a cough. "Let her be, she's a fucking kid."

"Stealing from your store."

"Jealous that she's taking the same five-finger discount as you with that

High John the other day?"

"That's different. I forgot to pay you." I pulled out my wallet and put a ten on the counter. Instead of ringing it up on the cash register and giving me change, he folded up the bill and slipped it into his pocket.

I moved over to make room for the dreadlocked Wiccan. Crash rang up his stuff without any small talk. The lack of upselling seemed odd to me. Crash struck me as a natural salesman. But maybe his attitude was based more on what his gut told him, that the Wiccan wanted to get his stuff and get out without being harassed, than with the urge to make another couple of dollars from the sale.

Crash closed the register and lit up a cigarette. "So you found a bus pass laying in the street and decided to see how the ghetto folk live, or what?"

"I was, uh...downtown." I saw some movement out of the corner of my eye, and I glanced toward the candles, hoping Miss Mattie was there. Talking to her would calm me down. It wasn't her. It was the middle-aged woman, the one who looked totally out of place. And then I realized I couldn't expect to see much of Miss Mattie, not today. "I took some Auracel, actually."

"No kidding. Your pupils are gigantic."

Great. "So, uh, you do all that sage smudging and...stuff."

"Stuff."

"Y'know. Protective stuff. Spells."

He crushed out his cigarette and tucked his ash tray under the counter. "I prefer the term *rituals*."

"What can I do to protect my house?"

"What's wrong with your house? It feels fine to me. And you said there's no spirit activity."

The door opened and a middle-aged suburban couple edged in, eyes wide, trying to look everywhere at once. I'm not sure how I can spot a suburbanite from thirty paces; I just can. Crash watched with a tolerant smirk as they ogled his paraphernalia.

I glanced along the walls for telltale signs of spy equipment. If the FPMP had planted any, they'd had a dozen prime spots to choose from. The walls were covered with posters and signs, and the old plaster had been covered with paneling. The only way to spot a bug would be with one of those metal-detector-looking things. No doubt Jacob's gym buddies would swing by and show Crash how to use it. No doubt Crash would work out a sweaty, naked barter with them so he didn't have to pay them in cash.

"Did you see a bug?"

My eyes snapped to his.

"I think someone upstairs sprayed, 'cos they're all showing up down here. They usually have the decency to wait 'til I turn the lights out. I'd set off a roach bomb, but that shoots the Noble Eightfold Path straight down the crapper. You don't know any animal communicators who can convince 'em to get lost for me, do you?"

A Camp Hell scene popped into my head. Benign. Rhonda the Animal Psychic telling us the chickadee perched on the windowsill had thoughts that would make a truck driver blush. "I used to. Not anymore."

"Maybe I'll try one of those electronic things that's supposed to emit a deterrent force field."

"Like a GhosTV for insects."

"Oh. That again."

"Just because you've never found one doesn't mean they don't exist."

"I'm not giving you attitude because I think you dreamt it up." Crash gave the shoppers in his store a once-over, then leaned toward me and dropped his voice low. "I just think you're playing with fire if you start fucking around with technology that someone was willing to kidnap you to develop."

First the bug-scare, now the kidnapping. "Do you get a kick out of feeling my adrenaline spike?"

"I'd get a bigger kick out of feeling something else...." Crash's gaze slid from mine and focused over my shoulder on a murmured question. "Yeah? No, it's not dyed green. It's natural jade." He clucked his tongue. "Honestly...."

I looked back at the shoppers. The suburbanite woman had found the astrology section and was looking in earnest. Her husband looked like he was dying to leave. The goth girl wasn't actively stealing anything, and the middle-aged woman was pondering a Buddha statue.

"So, how do you stop remote viewers from looking at you?"

I'd aimed for a casual tone. Too bad I couldn't match it up with a casual emotion inside myself. Crash went serious again. "Is this just a vague idea you've got, or is someone watching you?"

"That's what I've heard."

Crash gave a low whistle. "You could start with the chakra cleanse...."

"That didn't work."

"Hey. You asked me for advice. Don't bite my head off."

I crossed my arms and stared down at the jewel-studded prayer statues in the Plexiglas case.

"Try another discipline if Vedic's not your bag. You could make up an affirmation, or do some transcendental meditation, or say a few Rosaries...or dust yourself with Get Away powder, light a Reversible candle and tie a bat's eye around your neck. How am I supposed to know what would keep the invisible eyes off you?"

"That's all stuff that amplifies talent. I want to back it off."

"No—you're thinking about it all wrong. You want to strengthen your own mojo so that you can bounce their energy back at them."

"Like a white balloon."

He smirked. "Like rubber and glue. Anything you spy on bounces off of me and sticks to you."

"Great. So that means if I'm on antipsyactives, I'm a sitting duck."

The store's door opened and shut. I glanced over my shoulder. Goth girl was gone. Crash took a good, hard look at the three remaining customers, then leaned in and spoke in my ear. "You mean to say you think someone's watching you right now? All the time?"

"I'm pretty sure of it."

"Look, this place isn't a fortress or anything, but I do take precautions to make sure the less ethical *botanicas* don't curse me out of business. I'd be surprised if your Remote Pen Pal could reach you here."

Maybe not. When I'd been tweaked on experimental psyactives, the ghosts hadn't followed me into the shop. Still, I couldn't very well stay there all night—actually, scratch that. All I'd have to do was ask. But I was positive it wouldn't be a very good idea.

"What can I do to shake off this Auracel?"

"How should I know? Chug some cranberry juice and sit in a sauna."

I got this idea. It wasn't like a flashback or anything, just something that I remembered. Something from Camp Hell. What I remembered was that props help me focus, but I didn't necessarily require them, not like a level two might. I don't need incense. I don't need prayers or affirmations or mantras. All I needed was a mental picture. I just had to visualize.

Probably from growing up in front of the TV set. But who cares? It was easier than having to rely on a bunch of meaningless words and sounds, or bizarre, hard-to-find ingredients. All I needed was to be able to picture something in my mind's eye.

I closed my eyes, and tried to shut out my immediate environment. That was easier said than done. Maybe I couldn't see the store, but I could smell the cigarettes and incense. And I could feel it, too. The middle-aged woman, shopping for Buddhas. The suburban couple who were so uncomfortable I could almost taste it.

Or maybe the problem was all the drugs in my system. Maybe I couldn't visualize because I was so fucking high.

"What have you got that's a psyactive?"

"I don't stock prescription drugs. Too risky. If I was raided...."

"No, not a prescription psyactive. I mean something like the High John the Conqueror bath salt. Do you have any more of that?"

"No offense, but I don't want you in my tub. Not right this second, anyway. I haven't cleaned it in months."

Normally, I would just sprinkle it all over myself. But it was working against Auracel. I figured that I should probably at least get it wet. "Can't I do it in the sink? How dirty can it be? I'll clean it out myself."

"If you're not a purist or anything, I can give you some High John soap. I think there are actual herbs and oils in it. At least, it smells that way to me."

It came in soap form? I was all for it. "Sure."

Crash brought me a bar of soap in a black and pink wrapper with a guy on the front that looked like the King of Diamonds. I sniffed it. It smelled pungent and strong, like herbs, but then again, so did everything else in the store. And all of that smelled like the incense that was smoldering on a bookshelf right next to my head. I gestured to the door behind his counter.

"Yeah," he said. "Go ahead."

I went in back. I had only been in Crash's apartment a few times before. I figured I was tempting fate if I got myself too close to his bed, which was in plain view from the bathroom. I decided to wash up in the kitchen sink instead. I hoped Crash didn't care if his dishes tasted like High John.

There were a few coffee cups and spoons in the kitchen sink, and some crumbs. I took the dishes out and put them on the countertop, among a bunch of big, red utility bills with "past due" stamped on them, which I pretended not to notice. I ran the water. He had no water pressure. He also had no spray nozzle. I splashed the water around until it got warm, and then I unwrapped the soap.

I scrubbed my hands and my face. The more I used the soap, the stronger it smelled. And not in a good way. I figured that meant it was working. When I was done, I turned off the water. I tried to visualize a protective wall around myself. I got nothing.

Stupid Auracel.

I ran the water again and took off my coat and shirt. I figured that I needed more contact with the High John if I expected it to do any good. I soaped up my neck and my chest, under my arms, my ribs and my stomach. I cupped water in my hand and tried to splash that off, but I didn't feel like it was getting clean. It was all slimy. Maybe that was OK. There would be more High John left on me to counteract the Auracel.

And then my eyes started to burn.

I couldn't find a towel. I pulled a pot holder off the wall instead, but a family of roaches, three big and a dozen small, scurried out from behind it and disappeared behind the stove.

I dropped the pot holder.

"What the hell are you doing in here? I thought you were just going to wash up. Fuckin-A! What the fuck happened to you?"

"My eyes—get me a towel!"

Crash pushed by me to get to the bathroom. He jammed a rough towel into my hands. I wiped soap out of my eyes.

"You look like you lost a fight with a lamprey. Hickey, hickey...bruise, bruise, bruise...bite. I thought that thing on your neck the other day was just a fluke. I guess not—looks like you get off on picking up a few souvenirs when you...get off."

I ran the towel over myself fast and pulled my shirt on, and did my best not to imagine what my pale, bony body must have looked like at the height of winter, fishbelly white and covered with marks in varying shades of pink, purple and red.

Crash was already gone by the time I crammed my head through the neckhole. He had his store to run.

I stood there, wet and uncomfortable, and stinking like High John the Conqueror soap, and tried again to visualize a protective sphere around myself. I even imagined a stream of light shining down into my pineal gland.

And felt a glimmer. Maybe.

There had to be some kind of tea I could drink, or some herb I could swallow—something that would attack the Auracel where it swam, in my bloodstream.

Common: mint, jasmine, cinnamon, roses. Specialized: mugwort, skullcap. Usable only in small amounts: wormwood.

I stared at my hand where it rested on Crash's cupboard door handle. Camp Hell. All that stuff had been on a test. Herbalism in theory and practice—that was the course. They didn't call them psyactives, not back then. Enhancements. That sounded so much more benign, less clinical.

I could see the test. It was a cinch, even though I'd been sneaking around with Stefan, and the night before was a blur of whippits, blowjobs, and less than two hours of sleep. They'd brought this stuff in the day before. I'd smelled it, touched it, sifted it through my fingers. I'd have to be as stupid as Einstein not to remember what it was.

Even now. Fourteen years later.

I swayed. My hand on the cupboard kept me upright. I could see the test paper as if it were right there in front of me, with the crumbs and the chipped coffee cups and the overdue notices and the roaches. And I saw what I'd written. Where I was supposed to fill in *salt* across a doorstep for protection, I'd written *flour*. According to me, cinnamon was poisonous.

I'd fucked it all up. On purpose.

I staggered out into the store to see if Crash had any mugwort. He was talking to the suburban couple, and he held his hand as if he were holding a cigarette, though he wasn't. But I'll bet he wished he was. The woman was trying to tell him that the statue she was holding had to be from China.

"It says it's from Thailand, right there...."

I grabbed him by the arm. "Where's your mugwort?"

"In a second."

I let go of him and turned away. I'd find it myself. Or maybe Miss Mattie would help me. Where was she? I was dying for some Valium. I didn't have any. I didn't have any Seconal, either. I hadn't brought any, only the single tab of Auracel, because there'd been a prison outing on my agenda that day, and I hadn't wanted to risk being strip-searched because the drug-sniffing K-9 caught wind of me. My weapon wasn't on me, either. Damn it. "I don't have my gun."

Crash's eyes cut to me. "Go lay down or something, okay? I'll close the store." Beside him, the suburban woman was looking at me funny. So was her husband.

"It's got to be here somewhere." I focused on the shelves, scanned them. I recognized some herbs, but others hadn't been in my Camp Hell herbal, and they were new to me. Cinquefoil. Tonka beans. Yarrow.

"What, your gun? I doubt it. Seriously, chill out. I've got some Stoli in the freezer. Have a shot, or five."

Stoli? As in vodka? Bingo—a psyactive.

I went in back and pulled open the cupboards. I found a coffee cup that looked relatively clean, but I rinsed it out anyway. The vodka was just about the only thing in the freezer, aside from a half-empty tray of ice cubes, a few bean burritos, and a bag of frozen peas. The bottle was frosty. It stuck to my fingertips. It was so cold that mist wafted up from its surface.

I poured some into the coffee cup and chugged it. Revolting. I shuddered and poured some more.

I heard some voices in the shop—raised, annoyed—and I had another few swallows. My throat burned. Warmth spread through my stomach.

I visualized the white light again, streaming down from the sky, or heaven, or wherever. Entering me through my fifth chakra.

Warmth zinged up my spine. My fingers and toes tingled. I felt like I was vibrating. I staggered.

I considered sitting on the floor, but it was so filthy I worried I might stick to the linoleum. I made my way through the bathroom, tripped over an enormous pile of combat boots, and fell into Crash's bed. I righted the vodka bottle before any more booze could spill out.

My cup was still in the kitchen. Fuck it. I took a long, cold pull right from the bottle, shuddered, and swallowed down the urge to puke.

White light. Blam. Take that, Auracel. I surrounded myself with an elastic skin of protection, like a big, psychic condom, and I wondered if maybe that was where the whole "white balloon" analogy started, an alternate word for someone too squeamish to talk about prophylactics. I didn't need a sphere with legroom; my protection could move with me, and that economy of space, that good, close proximity to my physical, astral and ethereal bodies, seemed to suck a whole lot less energy than keeping this big round ball floating around. I told myself to keep it going, and pictured a little faucet somewhere inside myself, set to a thin stream that would keep on flowing until I shut it off. I'd originally thought of that faucet all those years ago at Camp Hell, too—me and my incredibly literal visual brain. I'd never told a soul.

Another slug of vodka. I should probably stop, I knew, but I wondered if there was a permanent way to sever ties with the remote viewer, a way to drop off his radar so that he couldn't pick me back up the minute I was sober.

Black and White candle, Bat's Eye, Reversible. That was all Hoodoo lingo—I'd learned that, too. And *gris-gris* and *vèvès* and all the shit I'd seen in the zombie basement, I'd recognized that stuff right away. Voudoun. Even the silver Santeria charms. I just hadn't known it at the time.

I turned up my mental tap a little higher, channeled more mojo into the protective field, and coated the outside with a gleaming molten silver shell. Silver. Take that.

I sloshed more vodka onto my shirt, and wedged the bottle onto Crash's bedside table next to an ashtray that was about ready to erupt in a shower of butts and burnt matches. The vodka was half-gone. A lot of that was probably from spilling it. Though I'd drunk a good amount, too. Now I owed Crash a bottle of Stoli. It seemed like I always owed him something.

I flopped down on my back with my legs hanging over the side of the bed and looked up at the ceiling. Even the sheets smelled like cigarettes and incense. And maleness. Fuck, that was hot.

All I needed was for Crash to walk in and find me sniffing his sheets. Some things you can't downplay. But maybe if I wasn't obvious....

The room was spinny from the Auracel and the liquor. I rolled onto my side and pressed my cheek against the blankets, and sighed. Oh, yeah. A really hot smell.

Time lurched, as time tends to do when I've got too many pharmaceuticals warring in my system. I heard a laugh track and realized a TV was playing somewhere. The not-my-bed sensation was jarring. The mattress sagged beneath me, lumpy, soft and narrow. I whacked my hand against a stucco-plastered wall that took the skin off my knuckles. The smell hit me again, incense, cigarettes and musk. I hesitated with my eyes shut, afraid of what I'd see. At least my clothes were on, so whatever I'd gotten myself into, it couldn't be all that bad. I opened my eyes.

The sun was down, and a small, yellow reading lamp lit the room—barely. Jacob sat at the foot of Crash's bed with his elbows resting on his knees—watching me. When he saw me open my eyes, he looked away.

I sat up fast, as if I was guilty of something from the mere contact of my face with another man's sheets. Pain flared hot-white behind my eye like someone had stabbed it with an ice pick. Or maybe like something had burst. For real. I clapped my hands to my eye and keeled over. "Fuck."

"So. You're taking up drinking."

"It's not funny. God damn."

"Am I laughing?"

I peeked out from behind my hand. Jacob's gaze was focused on the wall. Not a good sign. "Listen. I know this probably looks bad. But there's a logical explanation."

"There always is." He pinched the bridge of his nose, looking incredibly fatigued, and sighed. "You could have left me a note this morning. I waited all day for you to touch base, and finally it's Crash who calls me and tells me to come pick up my wasted boyfriend."

Crash tattled on me? That was totally not fair.

I checked my internal faucet. Still on. I extended the silver condom to include Jacob. I don't know if it really did or not, since it was all just a prop that my visual cortex was creating. "I came here because I needed a psyactive. I found out the FPMP's tracking me with a remote viewer."

Hard to say if that bombshell broke through Jacob's hurt feelings. His face stayed the same.

"So, y'know, your P.I. friends from the gym wouldn't really be able to find that with a metal detector."

His gaze slid from the wall, to me. He looked distinctly not happy. "How strong is this remote viewer?"

"I have no idea."

"But you know they're watching you."

Did I? Did I know for a fact? Or was Roger Burke playing on my hard-earned paranoia to get me to recant my testimony? Jacob's eyes narrowed the second I thought of Roger. He'd figure it out, someday, somehow. Because that's what Jacob did. So I might as well tell him. "Roger Burke says they are."

Jacob swung around and faced the wall again. Muscles leapt in his jaw. The back of his neck flushed, and a vein throbbed at his temple. "Think, Vic. Just think. Why would Roger Burke give you information? Out of the kindness of his heart? No. He wants something."

"Well, I know, but...."

"And when were you planning on bringing me into the loop?"

"I'm telling you now."

Jacob rubbed his face with both hands, then clasped his fingers behind his head and turned it into a stretch. His long-sleeved black T-shirt looked like it was about to split a seam. "All right." His voice was calm, very calm. It didn't fool me. "Tell me. And if you leave anything out, you might as well sleep here tonight."

✦ SIXTEEN ✦

It wasn't that Jacob wasn't talking to me. Not exactly. He'd answer a direct question if I asked him, for instance. But I didn't trust myself to try and bring him around with chit-chat, not with the killer Auracel/vodka hangover and acid stomach from hell I was currently nursing.

We'd slept in the same bed after all, but none too close—and he'd left for work without saying goodbye. I considered calling in sick, but decided that if I ended up hurling, there'd be plenty of those green plastic kidney-shaped puke trays at LaSalle for me to aim at.

I ate a piece of toast in hopes of sopping up some stomach acid, but I passed on the coffee. Which was probably the cause of the caffeine-withdrawal headache that had spread over the top of my skull by the time I got to work.

I pulled into my usual parking spot at the Fifth, slid through a frozen puddle of God-knows-what, and scraped the bottom of my shoe against the threshold of the front door in an attempt to get the slime off the treads. I turned toward the stairwell that led to my second-floor office, and nearly collided with a uniformed officer, my height, and maybe thirty pounds beefier.

The FPMP guy.

"Agent Dreyfuss would like to speak to you," he said.

"Okay. I'll see what my schedule is and give him a...."

He held up a cell phone. "His secretary's on the line."

I took the phone. It was a different brand than mine, and it felt strange in my hand. I noticed that it was warm, and had to quell the urge to wipe my fingers against my pant leg. I turned away from the FPMP cop, as if that gave me any privacy at all, and headed toward the drinking fountain. "Bayne," I said into the strange cell phone.

"I'll connect you to Agent Dreyfuss." It was a woman's voice, cool and even. I'd spoken to her once before. Maybe. Hard to say for sure. She had the voice of a Midwestern newscaster. "Please hold."

I tried to imagine what Dreyfuss' secretary would look like and came up flat. He might be a super-secret federal agent, but I couldn't shake the image of him as a long-haired, neo-hippie pot dealer. Who'd then, in all seriousness, offered me reds. Even after he'd outed himself as the FPMP.

"Hello, Detective. Let's pretend I've inserted some obligatory friendly banter about the weather here. Frankly, I didn't notice what it was doing outside. I was too busy wondering if you'd finally decided to take me up on my offer."

"Not...really."

"Because I'm guessing it can't be much fun trudging through ghosts at LaSalle General. Am I right, or am I right?"

He had a direct line to my day job. Great.

"Of course it's full of ghosts," he said. "People die there every day. I mean, what do they expect you to find? It's like Warwick's got you searching for hay in a haystack."

"Thanks for your concern. I'm all misty-eyed over it."

"I guess I can't fault you for your attitude. The Police Academy teaches rookies to embrace their inner asshats, doesn't it? You never see many timid cops."

"If you're through with the lovefest, I've got a job to do."

"No you don't. A bunch of old ghosts? Zigler's got about a million files to pull and ponder. I told Warwick I could use you today."

"So we've stopped pretending that I've got a choice about this. Is that it?"

Dreyfuss laughed like he really enjoyed sparring with me. "You've always got a choice, Detective. You could tell me to go and soak my head, and troop over to LaSalle with Detective Zigler like we never had this conversation. You could pop in for a little afternoon delight at that psychic shop in Wicker Park you're always hovering around. Heck, you could even drain your savings account and jaunt off to Mexico City with Detective Marks, and pretend the FPMP never existed.

"Or you could do the smart thing, and let Officer Andy drive you to my office. 'Cos my staff medium says there's a cold spot in here. And it would be a very lucrative thing for you to explore that temperature drop in a little more detail."

That's it? He wanted me to scope out a ghost for him? I'd had visions of experimental drugs and tripped-out machinery, and wrist restraints, and maybe vivisection. Checking a room for ghosts seemed too damn simple.

Then again, who else could really do it but me?

"Lucrative...how?"

"Five big. Cash money. Not bad for a couple hours' work, wouldn't you say?"

My heart pounded in my throat. Had Roger Burke been encouraging me to do this thing for Dreyfuss, or trying to scare me in the opposite direction? I thought hard. Whether Burke had been trying to or not, he'd seriously freaked me out.

So I figured he was trying to keep me away from Con. And I did the opposite.

"Ten," I told him. After all, I didn't want to seem too enthusiastic.

I gave the phone back to good ol' officer "Andy," and he led me to his cruiser.

It'd been a few years since I had my own squad car. They were a lot nicer inside now, sleeker and more rounded—but smaller too, and I needed to tuck my elbows in to keep from brushing against "Andy."

I didn't talk, and either did he, which was good. I was too busy being hung over, and fuming at the way Dreyfuss had laid out every plan I could possibly think of. Except the "afternoon delight" contingency. Even the thought of Crash bent over that bed of his with his jeans pulled down and his naked, tattooed ass pointing right at me couldn't flush out the brainworm those two words had planted in my gray matter.

"Andy" took surface streets to the North Loop, where he slid into an underground parking garage I could probably drive by a dozen times without ever noticing. Heck, I'd probably still miss it now, if I came back to look for it.

Maybe there was a spell on it, or a ritual, or whatever you want to call it. Some psychic skin to make you look the other way. I turned up my internal faucet and strengthened my silver full-body condom, even though the effort nauseated me.

I followed "Andy" to the elevator. He waited for me to get in first. I imagined him shooting me in the back, my blood spraying against the mirrored back wall. But there was no gunshot. He came in behind me and pressed five, the top button, and the door closed.

No music piped into the elevator; the only sound was the quiet whoosh of the car sliding on cables. I imagined the elevator dropping. Five floors. It wouldn't be much, in the movies. But in real life? No doubt it would leave me a quadriplegic.

The elevator door opened. "Andy" stepped out, then sidestepped, so I'd have to fall into place beside him. Through my overcoat, I pressed my palm against the reassuring shape of my Glock. Nice to know there was no trust lost between "Andy" and me.

The Fifth Floor of the Nameless FPMP Building was the epitome of elegance that Stefan's high rise was trying (and failing) to be. Lights were low and cool. The desk cut a striking curve around an empty space punctuated by tall plants and a few classy pieces of wall-mounted and individually lit sculpture. I didn't have words for the paint colors. Orange, but not bright, sort of gold; a green, or maybe a gray, but bluish. Something else not quite black; a metal with hints of red.

Good thing I never wanted to be an interior designer. I'd need to learn a whole new language.

An Asian woman in an immaculate black suit looked up from behind the desk. She wore dark-framed glasses, which looked like they were only decorative, something to add to the severity of her suit. She stood and pushed open a door that looked like it was part of the paneling. "Follow me."

She led us into a comfortably large room. It wasn't a waiting room that a dentist or a car dealership might have; there wasn't a single dog-eared magazine to be found. Instead, a tea set rested on a silver tray—probably real silver, with two pots, a bowl of sugar cubes, a creamer, and a bowl of something that looked suspiciously like chocolate curls. Jeez.

"Agent Dreyfuss will be a few minutes," said the secretary. "Help yourself to coffee or tea. My name is Laura. If you need anything, let me know."

Asian-lady didn't look like a *Laura*, any more than the computer tech support guy in New Delhi struck me as a plausible *Jason*. But Laura spoke flawless English—she'd been the one patching me through to Dreyfuss all those times; I recognized her voice—so maybe Laura really was her name.

As much as anything there was real, and not just a slick veneer plastered over a scary group of ruthless spies.

I wished I could sink down into one of the deep leather chairs so I could stop trying to ignore the quiver in my knees, but "Andy" didn't sit, so neither would I.

Instead of traditional art, framed magazine covers decorated these walls, each one featuring a famous psych. I recognized Marie Saint Savon in her rustic, tweedy outfit, with her single gray braid hanging over one shoulder. I could name the other psychics, too. Uri Geller gazed out in a dramatically lit shot with one hand furled under his chin. Jeanne Dixon faced a 1960s press conference in a jaunty pillbox hat. Edgar Cayce smiled down at me in that reassuring way of his, as if to tell me that sometimes you just had to take things in stride.

Unfortunately, I'd already tried burying my head in the sand, and this was where I ended up.

The door hinges were so well-oiled, the floor so solidly anchored, that I didn't hear Constantine Dreyfuss until he sucked in a great big breath and let it out with a whoop. "It's cold out there, huh?"

I did my best not to look as if he'd just scared me half out of my skin. He stood just inside the waiting room door in a bunch of layered sweats, wiping his nose on the hem of his outermost sweatshirt. "Nothing like a good run to get the heart pumping."

Pretty much any other thing I could think of was preferable to a run. But I kept my mouth shut.

Dreyfuss turned to the tea set, fished a sugar cube out of the bowl with his fingers and popped it into his mouth. "So." It sounded like *Tho*, since he was talking around the sugar. "You need anything to get started? A beer maybe? A little...." He raised his fingertips to his mouth in a pot-smoking gesture, and made a puffing noise.

"Cripes—no. Where's your cold spot?"

"You don't beat around the bush, do you? Are you positive that you're a government employee?" He gave the sugar cube a few loud crunches, then swallowed. "You haven't even touched the java."

"I don't want any."

"You sure? It's pretty awesome." He poured himself a cup. The smell made my mouth water. I glared at him.

Dreyfuss took a sip, added some cream, took another, and then a long swallow, followed by an, "Ahh."

I tapped my foot.

"You sure you don't want any? What else've you got to do while we're waiting for the staff medium to join us?"

Oh, great. Their own guy was coming to keep tabs on me. What level, I wondered. And how pissed would he be that I'd been called in to double-check his work?

Dreyfuss sipped and sighed, and wandered past Marie Saint Savon's magazine cover. "Too bad Marie kicked the bucket," he said. "There's never been another medium like her, before or since."

I stared at a blank spot on the wall. Dreyfuss might be able to force me to work for him, but there was nothing that said I had to be buddy-buddy about it.

"You ever been to France, Detective? No, I imagine not. Wouldn't it be cool to visit her grave, get her take on the whole spirit world now that she's on the other side? I wonder if you'd need a translator."

"No one knows where she's buried." Sonofabitch, he'd baited me into a conversation. I reminded myself to stop talking. But I'd already made eye contact.

Dreyfuss was smiling. "Of course someone knows where she's buried. It's not as if she buried herself. I specialize in information, Detective. If you wanted to visit with Marie, I could make that happen."

"What I want is for the FPMP to leave me alone."

"I'm talking realistic wants here, not pie in the sky. As long as psychs exist, the FPMP—"

He stopped talking when the silent door swung open. I'm sure that whatever he was going to say, it would've been a crock of shit, anyway.

A guy stepped into the room, probably my age, but male pattern baldness had done a number on him and left him with only a ring of hair from ear to ear, so he looked older. And familiar.

He looked from Dreyfuss, to "Andy," to me, to Dreyfuss again, and gave a timid smile.

I knew that smile.

"Einstein?"

He spun around to face me and nearly overbalanced. "Why'd you call me that? No one's called me that in years."

My God. It was him. He'd been a thin, wimpy, soft-shouldered guy in his youth, and now he was a pudgy, bald, middle-aged guy. His eyes were the same, though. So sincere, you suspected you could make him cry by teasing him about his Velcro-fastened shoes...if only he was smart enough to know you were making fun of him.

"It's me. It's Vic. Victor Bayne."

Einstein blinked, and furrowed his brow.

"From Heliotrope Station. C'mon, man. There were only a few of us mediums. You and me, Faun and Darla."

His eyes went wide and he smacked himself in the forehead with his palm. "Hardcore Vic? You're kidding me!"

Shit.

Einstein rushed over and grabbed my hand. He pumped it up and down so vigorously, I almost forgot to be embarrassed about him dredging up that old name. Nowadays, the only thing "hardcore" about me was the DVD selection next to my bed.

"Wow, you look really good." He held on to my hand, but pushed me back to arm's length. "You've got all your hair and everything. And you're wearing a suit!"

From anyone other than Einstein, that would've been an insult. But he didn't really have the capacity to differentiate between one of Jacob's tailored suits and my bargain-rack specials. He just knew I had a job where I couldn't show up in jeans and high-tops.

"I'm a detective."

He gave his trademark giggle, heh-heh, and memories hit me in a rush. Stefan and me, imitating that goofy little laugh of his. Him going along with it—laughing right along with us, because at least it meant we were paying attention to him. That we knew he existed. "Whoa, that's so neat. Just like TV, huh?"

"We spend more time on paperwork than they do on TV." God damn. I was such a fucking prick when I was young. "I guess I should call you Richard."

"Richie. What about you?"

"Vic's fine."

He nodded. "I'll try to remember."

Yeah, me too.

I did end up having that cup of coffee. Or three. And not because Dreyfuss offered, but because it felt so good to see Richie. Of everyone at Camp Hell, I never would've thought he'd be someone I'd reconnect with. That it would feel so good to see him outside that razorwire fence, well-rested and well-fed. Well-paid, too, according to him. He told me he drove a Lexus, and had a vacation home in Michigan.

Constantine Dreyfuss didn't leave the room while we caught up. In a way, I was glad. It's not as if I would've thought he wasn't listening in anyway. "Andy" was a nonentity.

I reached for my coffee and my phone rang—Jacob's ring. I figured I'd let it go to voice mail, but both Richie and Dreyfuss gave me an "are you gonna get that?" look.

"I'll just take it in the, uh...." I pointed to the lobby.

"Of course," said Dreyfuss. He'd probably hear both my end of the conversation and Jacob's anyway, if not at that very moment, then later on in instant replay. But I guess we were keeping up the semblance of privacy.

I went through the soundless door and snapped open my phone. "Hey."

"Listen. I don't like the way things have been between us lately. Can we...." Jacob sighed, his breath distorted over the receiver. "I don't know. I don't know what to do. I've run out of ideas. I just want things to be good again."

I glanced around the lobby. It was empty, just me and the low lighting, and the giant swoop of the desk. "Me too."

I heard phones ringing in the background. I could picture Jacob at the Twelfth, near his battered desk, or maybe the industrial, double-decker coffee pot. "When are you coming home?" he said.

"I'm not sure. Not late, I don't think."

"Maybe we could go somewhere. A movie."

"Sure, whatever you want." My environment wasn't giving Jacob any clues as to my location. I suppose it sounded enough like a hospital, at least the quiet pocket of stillness you'd find here or there, that it didn't prompt him to ask. I figured it wasn't the best time to bring it up. "I'll try to call if I'm going to be too late."

I looked around again. Still nobody but me and the plants. And probably a giant electronic listening device—and maybe a psychic one, too. "I love you."

Heck, I was sure they'd already heard that from me, and worse.

"You too."

I disconnected, and stared at the phone for a second before I slipped it back into my pocket. Then I patted my gun again to assure myself that it was still there, and went back to see what Dreyfuss wanted me to do.

✦ SEVENTEEN ✦

I had to sign something before I could access the part of the building where the cold spot lived. It was only a single sheet of paper. Something about its brevity frightened me.

Signing it would bind me to complete confidentiality, the breech of which was a felony, and could be punishable by up to twenty years in federal prison. No doubt an ex-cop wouldn't last nearly that long. Which led me to wonder what Roger Burke would say if he could see me now, staring at this thing and trying to imprint the legal jargon on my shoddy memory.

We left "Andy" in the room with the framed magazine covers and went through a door in the opposite wall. Richie schlepped along beside me as if it was no big deal to work in such a top-top-secret facility. And I noted he wore loafers now, rather than gym shoes fastened with hook-and-loop tape.

"Did you ever get a handle on your talent?" he said.

"What do you mean?"

"I remember it was pretty strong sometimes—but wild, almost as many misses as hits."

I shrugged. Evidently the evasiveness I'd groomed for talking in front of Carolyn the Lie Detector was useful in more situations than just that; I couldn't say how much Dreyfuss knew about my capabilities. I scored plenty of hits on the force. But I never gave a lot of detail as to the mechanism by which I saw the ghosts. For all anyone knew, I was sensing and extrapolating, not seeing all the dead people as if they were right there in front of me.

And that "wildness" Richie was referring to was a bunch of false impressions I'd seeded through my time at Camp Hell to make sure my level tested no higher than Five. It was easier than you'd think. Point in the wrong direction, switch the gender around, mangle the method of death, that sort of thing.

I never repeated the ghosts verbatim, either. Didn't want anyone to know I heard specific words.

"They know more about mediumship now," said Richie. "They say electricity can make it confusing. Like the spirits are some kind of electricity themselves."

"Really."

"I felt the cold spot when someone backed into the wall and accidentally turned off the lights. D'you think that's why they used to do séances in the dark, back in old-fashioned times?"

"I dunno, Richie." I suspected he was referring to the Victorian table-rapping phenomenon. I didn't have the heart to tell him that electricity hadn't been around quite yet. At least, not in handy wall sockets.

Dreyfuss opened a conference room door for us, and I followed Richie in. A transparent man was seated at the table, but about one foot to the right, as if the furniture had moved, but he hadn't. He pushed the muzzle of a Beretta under his chin and fired. The recoil threw the weapon from his hand as the back of his head exploded. He disappeared, and reappeared again, seated at the table with his head intact and his Beretta in his hand. He wedged the muzzle under his chin.

I pretended I hadn't just seen that, and tried to figure out where to look so that I didn't have to watch it a dozen more times while I worked on getting us out of that room.

"I was gonna bring a candle," Richie said. He patted down the front of his sweater as if maybe he'd brought one along with him and just forgotten about it. "No windows. We won't be able to see when Agent Dreyfuss shuts off the electricity. We should have a candle."

"S'okay, I've got a flashlight."

"Electric?"

"Uh, no. Battery operated."

Richie smiled. "That should work. Shouldn't it? That's different from electricity, right?"

Crap, was it? I'd never taken any science beyond biology. "A flashlight's never interfered with my talent."

"I should have a flashlight." Richie looked at Dreyfuss. "Will you get me a flashlight?"

"No problem. Go get Andy's."

"No, I mean, my own. I want my own agency-issued flashlight."

Dreyfuss pointed at him and winked. "You got it, pal. No later than the end of the week."

Richie beamed, then went back into the lobby to divest "Andy" of his cop-flashlight.

"It's nice to see him gainfully employed," I said quietly as the door whispered shut behind him.

"I don't have any complaints. Except that I wish his talent were stronger. He's maybe a high Two, a Three on a good day if we shut down the electricity to the part of the building he's sniffing. Could you imagine how much lighter the workload would be for a Five? It's a salaried position. Sweep the building, call it clean, and you're done for the day."

Pretty sweet job. Except I'd be taking Richie's livelihood away from him. And I'd be working for a bunch of creeps. I pretended Dreyfuss hadn't just alluded to me working for him permanently, which meant I couldn't look at him—and I didn't want to look at the guy repeatedly blowing his own brains out at the conference table, either. I stared at the carpet instead.

Richie swung through the door and shone a huge magnum in my eyes. "Mine's bigger than yours. Heh-heh."

I forced a smile.

"I guess we're ready," Richie said. "Turn off the power."

Dreyfuss pressed a button on an intercom beside the door. "Laura? Cut the conference room power, please."

"I'll call maintenance."

Richie positioned himself in the far corner of the room with his hand outstretched. "This wasn't the spot, but I like to do the whole room, make sure I don't miss anything."

The guy with the Beretta blew his brains out again.

The lights cut out, and the magnum's beam cut a swath through the darkness, revealing chairs, a whiteboard, the sleeve of Dreyfuss' sweatsuit. I pulled out my pocket flashlight and cast my own beam. I kept it trained on Dreyfuss, and I wondered if they'd fault me for drawing my weapon.

Richie'd made it to the far wall. He turned around, and his flashlight beam spun. "If you wanna do the opposite side of the room, you can," he offered.

I trooped over to the opposite corner while Dreyfuss watched me with a look of immense satisfaction on his face.

"Does he have to be here? Because it's harder for me to work with all these people around, all these distractions."

Richie shone his flashlight in Dreyfuss' face. "Is that okay? It really would be better if you let us do this ourselves."

Dreyfuss held his hands up on either side of his shoulders. "I know when

I'm not wanted." He smiled when he said that, but obviously, he wasn't too thrilled.

His gaze lingered on me for a moment, and then he left. Richie pointed his flashlight beam directly at my eye. "Yeah, I think I used to have trouble doing this in front of other people, too. But then I got this job, and it got easier eventually."

I decided not to tell Richie that I'd been supporting myself with my talent for a few years now. Let him feel like he was the one with all the inside information and all the good tips.

I flashed a light toward the conference table. The suicide was still there. Blam. Richie's lights danced over the wall. "Now, this is where I felt it," he said. "It was really cold, right here."

Good thing Richie's light wasn't shining on me when I saw her. She startled me so badly that I jumped back. I aimed my flashlight beam where Richie was pointing. Yep. There she was. Doctor Chance.

Dead.

"I'm getting it again," Richie said. "It's definitely cold here, even colder than the time I told Dreyfuss. It must not matter that you're here with me. Probably because you're a medium too."

"Maybe so."

Doctor Chance had a bullet hole in the middle of her forehead, right where her third eye should have been. She crossed her arms over her chest, and looked around the room. She didn't seem very happy. She also didn't seem like a repeater.

"Richie, why don't you come over here? I thought I felt something in the corner."

Richie's flashlight beam bounced over the wall, shone through the suicide—blam—and then joined mine in a spot where absolutely nothing was actually happening. "Is this it?"

"Yeah, right here. Let me move so that you can see how it feels to you." I inched away from him, skirted my way around the suicide, and eased up to Doctor Chance. "I can see you," I whispered, and then I cleared my throat as if I'd just been standing there, making random noises.

Doctor Chance's eyes met mine. She smiled, in a grim sort of way. "So, they got you after all. I figured they would. You might have a few...personal problems. But you're still the strongest medium around. Anywhere."

I shook my head. The FPMP didn't "get" me, I was just scoping them out. I couldn't figure out how to say that and still make it sound like that was only clearing my throat. "Hey, Einstein, is there a bathroom around here?"

Richie aimed his flashlight beam on a door. "Sure, right there. You're not going to do coke in there or anything, are you?"

I took a couple steps towards the door, then shone my flashlight in his face. "Why would you say something like that?"

"Oh, I mean, I don't know. I just thought...you're so skinny and all. Sorry. I didn't mean anything by it. Really. It was a stupid thing to say."

"Don't worry about it, Richie." I made myself smile. "I could stand to gain a pound or two. But I'm not doing coke. I've got three cups of coffee raging through my system. That's all."

I trained my flashlight beam on the bullet hole in Chance's forehead, then swung it toward the bathroom. I almost held the door open for her, but then I realized that gesture would be totally unnecessary. Which gave me the creeps.

I tried to flick the light on, three, maybe four times. But then I realized they'd cut the power to this part of the building so that it was easier for us to see the ghosts. Creepier still.

I found the lock, locked it. I turned around, and there she was. I flinched.

"You should've just gone along with me," she said. "Everything would be different now. We'd have our etheric amplifier. We'd have all the money we could ever need. Why couldn't you set your inconsistent and totally useless values aside and help me out?"

Being dead never made anyone rational. Not if they weren't that way in life. "How did you get here? Did you die here?"

"In the hallway, actually. I was on my way for psychiatric evaluation outside the Cook County Medical Center, when the FPMP intercepted us and brought me to their headquarters. And now, here I am. For good. What an ending." She shook her head. "I'll bet I could've recruited a medium in the psych ward, too. It would've set me back a few years, until I got out, at least. But it could've worked."

"Look, I'm not working for these jokers. I mean, not permanently. What was I supposed to do? Tell them no?"

"Maybe you should leave the country. I'll bet they'd take you in France."

"The FPMP might be a federal agency, but I think they would follow me, even once I'm past the border. Especially since most mediums aren't quite... so...." I couldn't figure out how to say that I was the most amped-up medium I'd ever known. That wasn't something to brag about—especially in the heart of the FPMP—not if I wanted to keep psy researchers from handling my organs.

She tilted her head, the way she used to when she studied my blood test results. "I suppose they would follow. They have the money. They have the manpower."

"And they have remote viewers."

"You know about that, do you?"

Oh God. So it was true.

"Whatever you're doing to scramble them," she said, "I think you're on the right track. They have trouble seeing you."

"Trouble, how?"

"How would I know? Do I look like a remote viewer to you? They seem angry all the time, frustrated. You're hard to pin down. Now that you figured out not to say anything useful on your cell phone, they've got nothing to go on."

That sounded pretty promising.

"Except those reports they've been getting, every couple of days."

My stomach turned. "What reports?"

"Handwritten things. Faxed. I guess that leaves less of a paper trail for the sender than an e-mail might." She was right. All the sender would need to do was shred whatever they'd written, and there'd be no evidence on their end, not without a subpoena of their phone records. And all that paperwork would prove was that a fax was sent, not what it contained.

I wondered who I saw on a regular basis that had access to a fax machine. Then I wondered if we had one at home, and recalled that I'd noticed one of those all-in-ones when I was unpacking our office. But no, that was stupid. Jacob wouldn't go through the trouble of scanning our house for bugs, and then turn around and leak secrets about me behind my back. Unless it was some elaborate double-cross...Christ almighty. I was so sick of the whole thing that I was tempted to eat a bullet, except I knew it was a piss-poor solution that'd only leave me with no one to talk to but Doctor Chance, possibly for eternity.

"Can you look at the faxes, tell me where they're coming from? There has to be some identification on them, even if it's just a phone number."

"I could. But why should I? You never helped me."

I jammed my thumb into my eye. Ow. "There's got to be something you want. You wouldn't still be here if you didn't."

"Think you can bring down the FPMP?"

"I doubt it."

She laughed. "Me too. At least you're honest. Will it bring me any peace if you avenge me, if you tell someone that the FPMP grabbed me up and made sure I kept quiet about my amplifier...about you? I don't know. It's no fun being dead, Detective. On one hand, I'm free from my physical body and all the limitations that went with it. On the other hand, things get foggy at the strangest times, and I'm filled with urges and compulsions that make no sense. I always thought I'd be reincarnated once I was through with this life. So how do I make sense of...this?"

She had to have known that I was about the last person who had anything intelligent to say about the afterlife, but maybe it didn't matter. Maybe she was telling me because I was the only one who could listen.

"I really do have to pee," I said. Because I had no idea how she was supposed to make sense of being dead. Once she was gone, I felt around for cold spots and I channeled white light to make sure she wasn't lingering around invisibly, waiting for me to unzip my pants. Even with that much focus, I couldn't tell she was gone for sure, and it took me forever to relieve myself.

"I don't feel the cold spot no more," Richie said when I finally emerged from the bathroom. "Do you think it went away 'cos we were looking for it?"

I shone my flashlight at the suicide. Blam. The cold spot must've been Chance. "I dunno. I'm picking up a little something over here, now."

Richie walked over and stood in the spot where the skull fragments and brains had sprayed. "Where, here? I...I don't think I feel nothing. Do you?"

Click. Blam.

"Yeah. I get something."

Richie's face twisted up. "Violent? Sudden?"

"...maybe."

He nodded. Maybe he'd needed my permission to sense the repeater. Or maybe he couldn't feel it at all. Maybe only the ghosts with their personalities intact, spirits like Doctor Chance, registered on his afterlife radar.

Richie stuck his head out the door, and called Dreyfuss. "Okay, we're ready."

Dreyfuss strolled in. He'd been right outside the door the whole time. "Well? What's the verdict?"

Richie answered him. "Sudden death. Violent." He held his hand palm-down beside the suicide. "Gunshot, I think." Maybe Richie really could feel it. Maybe he'd just needed me to confirm his vague impressions.

Dreyfuss looked up at me. I had my flashlight trained on him. If he thought it was spooky, being alone, in the dark, with a couple of mediums, he didn't show it. He was the picture of nonchalance. "What do you think, Detective?"

"What he said."

Undoubtedly, Dreyfuss knew about the suicide. I'm guessing he could tell that I was holding back. But hopefully he couldn't figure out that now I had all those specifics, too.

Dreyfuss clapped his hands together. "Okay, then. We can't be having cold spots wreaking havoc on our state-of-the-art HVAC system. Let's get this mess cleaned up, shall we?"

✦ EIGHTEEN ✦

When Dreyfuss called his secretary, I had assumed he would tell her to turn the power back on. And then what? Send in the janitor? I don't know what I thought would happen, but whatever it was, it wasn't this.

A black guy in a khaki uniform wheeled in a cart. It was as full of boxes and bottles as a shelf in Crash's store. But more orderly, as if they had managed to institutionalize magic. The guy in khaki lit a white candle, and handed it to Richie. Richie took it and set it next to the suicide. I noticed he had unerringly selected the cardinal points. And then I was surprised that it had taken me fifteen years to remember learning that, when Richie, with his IQ of 80, had had access to this information all this time, in his conscious memory.

Our helper lit a circle of charcoal, and Richie took it by the holder and sprinkled some frankincense on. It smelled like every other resin, but lemony. And I was surprised I remembered that, too.

Richie put the censer on the table. He set it right in the spot where the Beretta kicked back, but I didn't say anything. The black guy knelt on one side, and Richie knelt on the other. They both folded their hands, and began to pray. Out loud.

"How can we who died to sin yet live in it? Or are you unaware that we who were baptized into Christ Jesus were baptized into His death? We were indeed buried with Him through baptism into death, so that, just as Christ was raised from the dead by the glory of the Father, we too might live in newness of life."

Seriously? That was it? That was how you are supposed to get rid of a repeater—by praying? The back of my neck prickled, and I caught Dreyfuss looking at me. He didn't look relaxed at all, not anymore. He looked eager. Hungry.

I turned toward Richie, to have somewhere to look other than at Dreyfuss' glittering eyes. There was a gentle glow around him that seemed like it was coming from the candles, only it wasn't. It was too steady, too uniform.

"For if we have grown into union with Him through a death like His, we shall also be united with Him in the resurrection."

The repeater aimed, pulled the trigger, and fired. His body jerked. But I could see the outline of the chair through him more clearly than I could before.

Richie was definitely glowing now, a soft, mellow, beautiful glow. I looked hard at his crown chakra, and when I really focused, I could see the faintest thread of white light flowing in.

"We know that Christ, raised from the dead, dies no more; death no longer has power over Him. As to His death, He died to sin once and for all; as to His life, He lives for God."

Was it working because Richie believed it? Or did the words have power? Or maybe a combination of both of those. Because Richie was obviously pulling on something, some sort of power, but who's to say that lots of people wouldn't have been able to do that, depending on the circumstance, or the level of their beliefs.

I realized that I had been pulling white light down harder than before, too. It must've been a reaction to seeing it flowing into Richie. I wanted some of that for myself. When I realized I had this energy tingling inside of me, I focused it outwards, and strengthened the silver condom.

"For the wages of sin is death, but the gift of God is eternal life in Christ Jesus our Lord."

The repeater was faint now, and it seemed like he was cycling more slowly. The pause was greater between the time his head exploded, and the next time he shoved the muzzle under his chin.

After maybe half an hour, the repeater grew faint, and finally disappeared. Dreyfuss spoke, so close to my ear that he startled me. "Pretty good show, huh? And you've got a front-row seat."

Damn. My poker-face needed work. I shrugged.

"It's way past lunchtime. You want a donut? I've got donuts in my office. I promise, they're clean."

"If it's all the same to you, I'd rather leave." And never come back.

Richie snuffed the candles in order, last to first, while his helper doused the area with a cloud of frankincense smoke.

Dreyfuss set a plain, white envelope on the conference table. "He's a lot more confident with you around. There's room on the team, Detective. And it'd be a win-win. You'd pick up those skills that didn't seem to take the first time around, when you trained."

"I have a job."

"It doesn't have to be full-time. I'm flexible—keep that in mind."

I promised myself I'd do no such thing, but I picked up the envelope. It felt heavy. I tucked it into my pocket, and gave my Glock yet another reassuring pat.

Dreyfuss went about getting the power restored, and Richie approached me with a mile-wide grin on his face. "Well, Vic, what do you think?"

"The room feels clean to me. You getting that, too?"

He nodded.

I clapped him on the shoulder, almost pulling away at the last minute, but forcing myself to follow through. He was the closest thing I had to a fraternity brother, after all. "Good work, man."

"Did I hear Dreyfuss trying to hire you?"

"I already have a job...."

"'Cos that would be so neat, to work with someone I know from the old days, from Heliotrope. And you get a company car, and a big, huge Christmas bonus."

That's what they were telling us, but my guess was that Richie might conveniently disappear if I accepted Dreyfuss' offer. Even though Sergeant Warwick and Betty had been reporting to the FPMP all these years, and even though I'd have to pass "Andy" in the hallway on a regular basis, I still felt a hell of a lot more comfortable at the Fifth than I could ever hope to feel at the FPMP. I patted Richie on the arm, more stiffly now, though I don't think he noticed. "I'll keep it in mind. Take care, all right?"

The stink of burning sage hit me on my front doorstep. I opened the door—the one that used to have the word *fuck* spray-painted on it, and now had a spot that was paler than the surrounding wood where we'd scrubbed it with acetone and mineral spirits—and a burnt cloud wafted out.

A motorized whine came from the main room, followed by the sound of pounding. I hung up my coat and poked my head out of the vestibule.

A haze of sage smoke hung near the ceiling. Crash and Jacob stood on either side of a high-set window, Crash on a stepladder and Jacob on a chair. Jacob held a cordless drill, and Crash was hammering nails into the windowsill. Once the nail was sunk, I cleared my throat.

Crash and Jacob both turned and looked. Jacob was unreadable. Crash smirked and held up a nail. "Hi ho, silver."

Well, I had asked him to protect me from the remote viewer. But I didn't mean tonight. "Do you have a fax machine?"

"Used to. It broke. I do it all online now. Why, you need to fax something?"

I hadn't really thought Crash was leaking information about me to Dreyfuss, but it was a relief to hear it, anyway. He glanced over my shoulder and I turned.

Carolyn came out of the kitchen with a smoking bundle of sage. Her hair was covered with a bandanna and she had a faint smudge of charcoal on her jaw. Never one to mince words like "hello," she said, "How reliable is your information about the remote viewer?"

"Reliable. And confirmed by a second...source."

"Seriously," said Crash. "Do you pigs always talk like a basic-cable crime reenactment, or do you just toss the lingo around for my benefit?"

I sat on the arm of the couch, because it felt less vulnerable than sitting all the way down, and glared at each of them in turn.

"Obviously, you resent us being involved in the situation," said Carolyn. "But if you're being monitored, then I'm sure Crash and I are, too—even if it's only because of our proximity to you."

Jacob was. Crash was. Dreyfuss had hinted as much. I didn't volunteer it. Carolyn? Undoubtedly, her too. "You're a Psych. I'm sure you had your very own file before you even met me."

"I'm not blaming you. I just wish you'd trust that we've all got the same goal."

"Do we? What do you want to get from all this?"

"Well, I...." She stopped, frowned. "I don't know." She thought, and the room went so quiet that the crackle of her smudge stick made me flinch. "It doesn't feel right that we should be followed and watched just because we're Psychs. It's a talent like any other talent. But I think that psychic abilities are considered to be somehow evil, at least subconsciously, by a certain segment of the population. I worry about what will happen to all of us if a spark of panic ever flares up."

Oh. Maybe we were all on the same page. Only Carolyn was able to articulate what she saw in her worst-case scenario a hell of a lot better than I ever could.

"So, what're you working on?" I asked.

"House blessing, protection. Wicca-fusion."

"What about...Christian?"

All three of them stared at me so hard that I squirmed. "I thought you were agnostic," said Jacob.

I shrugged. "I'm not really sure what I believe."

"That's the definition of *agnostic* to everyone but philosophy geeks," Crash said.

Oh. "It's just that, today, I saw this guy exorcise a repeater with some bible verses." Of course, as soon as I volunteered that, I had to explain where I was, and why, and pretty soon I'd told the three of them everything I knew about the FPMP. Which specifically went against the contract I'd signed for Dreyfuss.

I was only slightly concerned. We now had silver nails pounded into our thresholds and windowsills, after all. And I was sure that neither Jacob, Crash or Carolyn were the fax culprits. Pretty sure.

"Chance was murdered," Jacob sat down hard in the chair he'd been standing on, cupped his hand over his face, and squeezed his temples between his thumb and middle finger. "Shit."

I shifted and found an interesting speck on the coffee table to look at. Giving the three of them the FPMP's secrets was one thing; I'd also told them exactly how much I saw, right down to the glow that surrounded Richie. The Stiffs I'd worked with knew I could see and hear the dead—and even then, I usually downplayed the specifics—but I'd come clean about everything, right down to glowing Richie.

It was naïve of me to think it would feel better after I'd spilled my guts. I must've mistaken confession for puking. I was still ready to jump out of my own skin.

Crash stood up. "I need a cigarette." He walked out before I could tell him that he might as well stay inside. What was another cigarette's worth of smoke compared to the bucket of sage they'd already burned?

"Did you seriously think he was the one sending faxes about you?" Carolyn snapped.

Oh. Right. I'd asked him if he…oh, shit. "Well…no. I mean, I just had to check. I thought he'd own a fax machine, since he has a store.…" Okay, that sounded really lame. Carolyn narrowed her eyes, but she didn't tell me I was lying. So I guess it was also true. Lame, but true.

I decided it was in my best interest not to divulge that I'd also wondered if Jacob's inkjet printer was an all-in-one. "Listen, I'm gonna go talk to him.…"

Jacob's cop-look slipped. He was not thrilled—with my tactlessness, or with something else? Who knows?

I snagged my overcoat and went out front. Crash sat on the concrete stoop, huddled in his leather biker jacket. Thermal underwear poked through holes in the knees of his jeans. Fresh snow dusted his shoulders and sleeves, and glittered in the pale green spikes of his hair. He let out a long exhalation of smoke, and didn't look at me when I hovered beside him. "I should've done something mean to you when you were passed out in my bed, like sticking gum in your hair, or writing my name on your wiener in permanent marker. But I resisted the urge. 'Cos I'm such a sensitive guy."

Up and down the block, the streetlights flickered on, all except the one in front of the cannery. I stared at the dark glass globe. "I didn't really think the faxes came from you. I just...had to figure out who owned a fax machine."

"Police procedure or some such shit. Right?"

"Right," I answered, before I realized how thick the sarcasm was. I sighed and sat down.

He smoked, and he stared out at the street, and finally he said, "I know. You just piss me off to no end, is all."

I stopped myself from asking what he had to be pissed off about. Maybe the implication that he was the faxer, maybe the Stoli, maybe having to come out to SaverPlus on a cold and blustery night. Or maybe something else I'd done without even realizing it. "I'm trying to apologize, here."

"Oh, so you can just say and do anything you want—why, 'cos your life has been so hard? Get over yourself. Everyone has their own shit to deal with. Not just you."

Not everyone had the FPMP spying on them, but I wasn't going to point that out in a spot where someone with a really sensitive microphone might overhear us.

"Still..." said Crash. "You gotta wonder who you know that would be willing to sell you out—who'd be smart enough to pull it off."

"You're really not making me feel any better."

"And that's what you dig about me—I'm not gonna pull any punches when you ask for my opinion. So who do you think it is, really? Someone who hates you? Or someone who can be blackmailed or bought?"

"Jesus fucking Christ, can we not talk about this?"

"For someone who's supposedly open to the possibility that Christianity is legit, you're really disrespectful. Y'know that?"

I looked at him, finally, because I figured I'd better take aim before I backhanded him. He was watching me over the sleeve of his biker jacket. His eyes were laughing. Nothing like Jacob's eyes, which were always so serious lately. "Fuck you."

The corners of his eyes crinkled. "You're just disappointed that I didn't have my wicked way with you last night."

"That'll be the day."

"Baby Doll, you want it so bad I can practically feel your hard-on poking my thigh."

Nice image.

He scraped his cigarette out on the stair, then tossed the filter among a small cluster of identical butts on the sidewalk. "When I rock your world, I want to make sure you're awake to enjoy it."

The whole experience I'd had the day before felt surreal now, and not just because I'd been drunk and high. Crash's bed, even his whole apartment, was so like something I would have stumbled into ten years ago, before I had a mortgage, before I found the occasional gray hair to pluck out.

Crash stood and dusted off the seat of his jeans. "Hey," I said before he went inside.

He looked down at me.

I reached into my overcoat and took out the fat envelope from Dreyfuss. I wondered what Crash would normally charge for a whole-house smudging. The cost of a video camera, whatever that was. I could ask him, of course, but it seemed like it should have been one of those things that I knew intuitively. If I asked, he'd think I was even less savvy than he already did. And if I gave him too little, or too much, he'd get insulted.

The envelope held only hundreds. I guesstimated enough of them to cover the big, red past-due notices, the ones I'd seen, anyway. "For helping us out. With the house. We're lucky we've got an expert to turn to."

I've never been weird about money, but I didn't care for mixing business and pleasure, especially when I didn't know what the rules were supposed to be. I didn't quite look Crash in the eye as I handed him the folded bills, and he didn't quite look at me, either. "Okay, cool."

I guess nothing deflates a guy like a big handful of money that he can't afford to turn down.

It was late when Crash and Carolyn left, and no one suggested doing anything social, like ordering a pizza. They were probably already in the FPMP's Rolodex for being close to me, and a simple pizza wouldn't have made it any worse—but I had the feeling I wasn't going to crack open the dictionary and find myself under the heading for *popular* anytime soon.

I heard the water running in the kitchen, and found Jacob standing there, leaning against the countertop and staring at the wall. I came up beside him, and turned off the faucet. "I thought we were going to do something fun tonight. If this was your idea—"

"Don't. I'm not in the mood."

"Hey, don't make me the bad guy. What about the phone call today, when you said you wanted things to be good again? What was that? Just something that sounded promising at the moment?"

"You were at the FPMP."

"Yeah, I was. You knew I was considering it. And I couldn't very well announce it right there, not when the ink was still wet on the thing I'd signed that said I would keep it quiet. Give me at least that much credit. It's not all about keeping things from you. I came home and told you everything, didn't I? Sometimes I just need you to trust me. We're both on the same side, right?"

Jacob's gaze had moved from the wall to my eyes. I wanted to squirm. "You've got to start acting like it," he said.

✦ NINETEEN ✦

"I think I might have found something." Zigler consulted his notebook, then looked up at the room. "Nearly forty percent of the patients who died spent some time in this emergency partition."

I decided I didn't like the ER, not at all, and I was filled with gratitude about the fact that when I sprained my elbow, I had gotten to go to The Clinic, where they ushered me into a private room right away, and saw to me within a reasonable amount of time. And there wasn't a scary, toothless guy who smelled like vinegar sitting next to me, cursing up a blue streak. And there wasn't a little kid crying loud enough to shatter my eardrums. Don't get me wrong; I felt bad for the kid. Heck, the vinegar guy, too. But I wouldn't want to be sitting among them if I was in need of emergency medical care.

"Forty percent," I repeated. I wondered if that was statistically important, and decided it probably was. If not, Zig wouldn't have mentioned it. "And, uh, the other sixty percent?"

"Divided among seven other partitions."

Sixty divided by seven...or was that seven divided by sixty? Seven sixtieths? I sucked at fractions. Anyway, it was smaller than forty percent. Probably.

We approached the curtained-off area, and Zigler poked his head in. "Occupied," he told me. I peered over his shoulder. A middle-aged Asian woman was laying on a table, covered with a blue blanket that wasn't long enough to do her much good, unless she was only cold from the waist down. Zig backed out, and I scooted over so he didn't have to brush up against me. "So forty percent of the people who come through here die?"

Zigler looked at me funny. "No. Forty percent of the deaths came through this station."

As I struggled to see the difference, a pair of swinging doors clanged open, and a couple of paramedics steered in a collapsible gurney with an IV swinging back and forth like a bell on a kids' train ride at the amusement park. And I wondered when anyone had ever taken me to an amusement park, that I'd been able to come up with that association. But I didn't have too much time to wonder, because I noticed something else attached to the gurney that I'm guessing hadn't come from a kit in the ambulance.

It floated along behind the gurney to one side of the patient's head. It was dark, and semi-opaque, and it kept roiling around so that I couldn't really pin a particular shape on it. It was like smoke, kind of—smoke that didn't dissipate. And that looked somehow evil.

And totally connected with the patient on the gurney.

The paramedics hauled her into one of the safe partitions, and I lost sight of the thing.

"What is it?" Zigler asked me.

I pointed weakly. "There was a, um...." How much could I tell Zigler, really? That I'd seen something? He already knew I got visuals. Did he know I could see them like they were solid, corporeal things sometimes? That if I got close enough to this being, I could probably detail it down to each slithering, smoke-like coil? By now—yeah. He had to know. And he was a lot more accurate about recording my exact wording than Maurice had ever been. Damn it. "I kind of sense a...uh...I dunno. Hard to tell."

One of the paramedics left. The other hooked up with an ER doctor and started talking, giving a report of some kind, judging by the fact that the doctor was taking notes on a clipboard. They stood close and mirrored each other's body language while they spoke, like they knew each other all too well, and had seen too many sick things together to be formal anymore. The EMT rolled his eyes, and he and the doctor both shook their heads.

I took a few steps closer and tried to eavesdrop.

"You sense something with the patient?" Zig asked me.

I nodded.

"The patient was alive, though. Right? She was moving around. And speaking."

Actually, she'd been kinda swearing and muttering. I guess that qualified. Zig would probably always be somewhat concerned that a moving person might not actually be alive, since the zombie incident made such an impression on him. "It's not *on* her—more like it's around her."

Zigler approached the doctor, a stout black woman with gray-flecked hair, and talked to her in a low tone. Her manner did a 180, from the laid-back attitude she'd had with the paramedic, to a stiff, guarded, no-nonsense demeanor with Zig. I wondered why.

"If there hasn't been a criminal complaint, then there's no reason for you to be in the ER at all," the doctor told him.

"We're conducting an investigation...."

"If it doesn't involve my patient, then you've got no business being here. My patient isn't suspected of anything, is she? Your badge is green. You need to go back out in the lobby."

"But we...."

"I haven't got time for this. It's an emergency room. My patient is my priority. Understood?"

"But I...."

"I trust you won't make me call security, Officer?" The doctor stepped into the enclosure and yanked the curtain shut with a decisive snap.

Zig could've corrected her, told her he was a detective, not an officer. He didn't bother. I'm guessing he didn't think it would make any difference. Either did I. Zigler glanced down at his badge. "I'm going to put in for some better clearance."

"But maybe she's right. I don't really want to be in the way if they've got a bunch of spurting GSWs rolling through the door."

"There's a woman lying in the forty-percent partition. Just lying there. Nothing's spurting, no one's calling the crash cart. You think it's a problem if you go in there and look around?"

I tried to remember how big the security guards were. Once in a while, you come across a security guard who flunked out of the Police Academy, and he'd take extra care to be a complete and utter dick where authority overlapped. "I guess not. Once we get better badges."

Something tugged at my conscience as we walked out of the ER, though, and I couldn't ignore it. That thing, that supernatural whatever-it-was following the patient...what was I supposed to do about that?

Not that it was my problem. But it wasn't as if anyone else could help her out with it.

The paramedic who'd been talking to the doctor—before she went off on Zigler—was signing some paperwork at the intake desk. "Um, 'scuse me." I tried to look as unintimidating as I could, since Zigler's tough-cop act had put everyone off. Which meant that I slouched a little, and didn't make assertive eye-contact. And that all came naturally to me, anyway. "Y'know that patient, the woman you just brought in...is she gonna be okay?"

The paramedic was a forty-something Latino with a shaved head, fairly buff. "As much as she's ever okay," he said. He looked me over. I watched his shoulders relax underneath his reflective-trimmed uniform jacket. "Homeless schizo, falling-down drunk. She should probably be institutionalized. But they'll keep her 'til she dries out, and when she's more or less lucid, send her on her way. Happens all the time."

"You mean schizophrenic."

He gave me a "duh" look.

"She's been tested?"

"For what? Drugs?"

I ran my hand over the back of my neck. I was starting to sweat again. Damn it. Maybe The Clinic could give me some kind of salt pill to make me stop perspiring at the first sign of anything that reminded me of Camp Hell.

"Psych tests." I realized he might take the old meaning from that. Pre-eighties, *psych* only meant psychiatric. Nowadays, it could be either or, depending on the context. "Psychic," I clarified.

The "duh" look turned to a "yeah, right" expression. "I dunno. I just bring 'er in. Doctor Gillmore would be the one to ask about that."

I found Zigler waiting by the information desk. He had his green badge in his hand and he didn't look happy. The woman behind the desk was busy talking on a headset phone, and wasn't even looking in his general direction. "If you think there's something paranormal involved," he said, "then we should go through Warwick and get a warrant."

I'd had scads of warrants granted over the length of my career. I'd never been turned down. And maybe I could've pressed my talent more times than that—heck, I was sure I could've—but I was always too busy being evasive about what I actually saw to make a big stink about it and drag it in front of a judge.

"I sensed a presence," I admitted. "With that homeless woman. An...evil presence." I wished I could've thought of a word that with less moral connotations. Maybe Zig would frame it in copspeak for me.

Zigler glanced at the receptionist. She was still fielding calls on her headset. His voice dropped to a whisper. "You mean...possessed?"

"Uh, no. I don't think so." Unless that was how possessions happened. I'd had a ghost or two in my skin before, and I sure as hell hoped that wasn't how it all started, with a creepy black blob looking for a new body to tool around in.

Zigler was positive that whatever it was we needed to see, it was inside that ER. We headed back to the station to hash out a plan with Warwick to get us in there, and I signed some statements for the judge that said I "sensed" something on the premises. We'd changed the word *evil* to *supernatural*. It didn't look all that much better on paper.

Warwick tried to convince LaSalle General that we were guaranteed to get our warrant, and it would save us all a lot of time and taxpayer dollars if they just gave us an all-access badge. He reminded them that we were as qualified as any other emergency personnel, and that we wouldn't wander around and stick our hands under the defibrillator paddles.

Still, no luck.

I had an appointment with Stefan that afternoon, so I left Zig to fill out paperwork and went back home to find something less polyester to wear.

Except that I passed the street that would take me back to the cannery, and I kept on going. LaSalle Hospital loomed up ahead, a dark, uninviting pile of bricks.

It was nearly an hour, and a half dozen cups of coffee, before I crossed paths with Doctor Gillmore in the cafeteria. She looked mildly startled when I sat down beside her, and then when she recognized who I was, annoyed.

"I'm guessing you've heard of doctor-patient privilege," she said.

I took a sip of coffee, and then wished I hadn't. I was really tired of coffee. "Listen, I'm sorry if my partner was acting like a prick. He isn't, really." She should see a cop who had it in his mind to be a bully; compared to that, Zig was Captain Kangaroo. "We're just kinda stuck on this one thing.... Well, anyway, he thought he spotted something that might make a difference in our investigation."

"And what would that be? Your investigation."

Great. Since we'd established that Zig would do the talking, I didn't bother thinking about political ways to say what we were doing. "A death rate is... high."

"This is a hospital. People come here when they're sick and injured."

"There are other aspects involved."

"And you can't talk about them, because they're part of an ongoing investigation."

"That's right."

Doctor Gillmore gave me a meaningful look.

"Okay, I get it." I took another sip of coffee and had to swallow twice to get it down. I pushed the cup away. "But I was just wondering something about patient intake, something general."

She sized me up. "And what would that be?"

"People who come in seeing visions, hearing voices. Do they get a psychic ability test before they're given any psychiatric meds?"

Gillmore smiled—the first smile I'd seen from her—and shook her head wearily. "You're serious?"

"Um...yeah."

"Have you seen the psychic ability test?"

I looked around as if it might've appeared on the dessert kiosk. "Not lately."

She glanced at her watch. "I've been on for over fourteen hours. My plan was to eat, go home, and sleep."

"I, uh...I have shifts like that, too."

She assessed my face. I wondered if she had a touch of talent, or if she just knew how to read people. "I imagine you do, Detective." She wrapped her sandwich in a napkin and stuck it in her pocket. That seemed like something I would do, except I'd probably manage to fall on it while chasing a fleeing ghost down an icy alleyway. "Let me show you LaSalle's psychic abilities test, and you tell me how effective a diagnostic tool you think it is."

A couple of young doctors on their way to dinner—or maybe it was breakfast, for them—saw Gillmore and me walking side by side, and gave us a long stare. No hostility, but plenty of curiosity. "You been a doctor long?"

"Eighteen years next month. Is this relevant to your case—the one you're not going to tell me anything about?"

"No. I was just curious." I glanced at her pocket. Her sandwich was still okay. "Scrubs. Seems like they used to be...blue."

"Blue. Navy. Turquoise. You name it. Blue, blue and more blue. Good riddance, I say. I hate blue."

I think if I were unattached, and straight, I would've asked her out to dinner. Her sandwich would keep.

We came to a locked door. She swiped it with a keycard and led me into an administrative section. The walls were the same bright white, the floors the same speckled linoleum. But there were framed prints on the wall of slightly faded flowers. Someone had at least tried to make it less soulless. The hallway smelled strongly of hazelnut coffee and microwave popcorn. "At least they didn't burn it this time," Gillmore muttered.

We turned off the hall into a small office. "We're short on space, so I share with the night supervisor. Don't touch anything. He hates it when people move things."

She gestured to a chair and I sat. It was uncomfortable. "Let's see, now. Where'd I put that...." She stared up at the shelves above her desk. They were so packed with books and three-ring binders that they were starting to sag in the middle. "Oh. Right. Here it is. Ready to see how psychic you are, Detective?"

Was it dickish of me not to clue her in? "I just want to see the test itself. That's all."

She pulled a cardboard box from a shelf, and a sprinkling of dust bunnies drifted out behind it. She hefted a stack of books from her desk and set it on the floor with utmost care. Her officemate's, I took it.

"All right, what do we have here? A pair of dice. But where's the Candyland? Where's the Chutes and Ladders? Guess there is none. Just this."

She pulled a tri-fold board out of the box and stood it up between us. "Don't peek."

"I, um....You really don't have to administer.... I just wanted to see it."

She rattled the dice. "Call it, Detective."

"Four. Listen, I'm not a precog. They test for that on the force."

"The more you talk, the longer this will take. Call it."

She did four more throws, and then moved on to the cards. There were circles, squares, triangles, and crosses. That's it. She showed me one of the cards before we started. It had the words *circulo* and *cercle* printed on the back.

"What about the colors?" I asked her.

"They're all the same. Black and white."

I named five random shapes for her as she flipped over the cards. "But if there are no colors, there's a one in four chance that I'd get that right," I told her.

"Detective, do you know how they analyze the results of psychic ability tests where both color and shape are used?"

I suspected one of the U of C residents tried to explain it to me, once. But I probably had my pants down and wasn't paying much attention.

"Of course, if this were computerized, it would be easier to score...."

"But TKs and computers don't mix, so you'd get a false read. Some other psychics do funky things to electricity, too."

"And do you know how likely it is we'd get a telekinetic wheeled through that door, complaining that he was hearing things, seeing things?"

"I'm not all that good with...statistics."

She slapped the deck of cards down and stared at me hard. "Have you ever met a telekinetic, Detective?"

A mental image of Movie Mike twitching in his wheelchair sprang to mind. Sweat rolled from the crook of my knee down my calf, where the top of my sock soaked it up. "Why do you ask?"

"TKs are rare. Exceedingly rare. I'd guess there are no more than a dozen in the entire country. That's one in twenty-five million. And yet, the AMA voted that the psychic screening must not be electronic, because of the possibility that a telekinetic will cause a false negative."

I spotted a box of tissues on the desk and took one, despite Doctor Gillmore's warning not to touch anything. She was too busy scribbling on a score-card to notice.

"What about the mediumship test?" I said.

"That's the only part of the exam they've taken any pains to make legiti-mate." She took a smaller box from inside the kit and handed it to me. It was silver. Just like Show and Tell. "If you got any hits on the clairsentient portion, I'd need to get someone else to administer this section, someone who'd never seen the key."

"But I pretty much bombed."

"Not entirely. You got a *four* right. But everything else was incorrect, so the single hit won't classify you as a clairsentient."

I opened the silver box and pulled out a bone fragment. "This is human, isn't it? They wouldn't test mediums with animal bones."

"No, they wouldn't. But you're thinking like a cop. Not a medium."

I didn't know about that. I hadn't been doped up on Neurozamine and stuck in a room with a corpse to prepare me for the Police Academy, that was for sure.

"Tell me who that bone belonged to, Detective. Age, gender, cause of death."

"I have no idea."

"You could guess."

I snapped the box shut and handed it back to her. "That's a lousy test. The only way you'd know if someone was a medium or not is to have a more power-ful medium confirming their findings."

And I'd never met a medium who saw more than I did. So how did they rate me? They must have just...guessed; that was all I could figure.

"This is human bone," she assured me.

"Maybe so. But it doesn't mean its previous owner is floating around in your office waiting to read his memoirs to the next talented medium who opens that box."

Doctor Gillmore glanced down at her papers. "A real medium would be able to tell me something."

I dug my I.D. out. My CPD badge is on the front, but I poked behind it and pulled out a little paper card. It had been printed off on a laser printer—not even a plastic card, because they make so few of them every year—insanely forgeable, if you even knew what they looked like. Most people never had occa-sion to see one. I'm thinking maybe Doctor Gillmore, as an ER shift supervisor, might have.

I placed the card on the desk facing her.

She picked it up, brows knit, and read. "Is this some kind of joke?"

I wish.

"Doc, I'm a PsyCop. And your patient, the homeless lady? She's not crazy."

"She's...what? Possessed?"

Why was that the first idea that popped into everyone's head? "No, not possessed. But something ugly's following her."

Doctor Gillmore folded up the tagboard screen and put the cards away. She kept the instructions and my test scores out of the box. "You scored average on this test," she said. "Did you do that on purpose?"

I shook my head. "The bone's just a bone. And all that other stuff? I'm not precog or clairvoyant. But there's no way you'd know that by this test. You didn't take enough readings to score me. This test took five minutes." I thought back to the earnest U of C residents and their flash cards. "You need to do an hour's worth, at least. And with better cards. Some clairvoyants only hit on the colors."

Doctor Gillmore tapped on the directions. "I followed these to the letter. And you see how effective it was? It scored a fifth-level certified psychic as NP. You think I don't know how a real test is done? We haven't got the time or the manpower to administer and score them manually." She looked around the crowded little office. "We haven't even got suitable conditions or equipment."

She turned the testing directions around in her hands and frowned at them. "How does the federal government test for mediums?"

"There are some hot spots where other mediums generally agree they sense something, and we'd be taken there, see what we came up with. Usually there's documentation of a death in that location, so the tester might be able to compare the medium's impressions with a photo, or a report. It's...more of an essay question than a multiple choice."

Gillmore nodded. "That's too bad. Because if there were any way to make this test work, even if it was flawed, you can bet I wouldn't let it gather dust on my shelf."

✦ TWENTY ✦

I was half an hour late for my appointment. Stefan's secretary was waiting for me, and motioned me right in.

"Are you running a tab, or anything? I should pay you today."

Stefan looked up from his desk. He was head to toe in black today, and I suspect he may have penciled his eyebrows to make them more imposing. "Should I have Carissa open up a claim with your health insurance? Or are you still convinced you're being watched?"

"I am. And besides, my permanent record is already a mile long. I'll pay in cash."

Stefan checked his day planner, tapped some numbers into a calculator with the eraser end of a shiny black pencil, and named me a four-digit figure. Dang. Good thing I had a pocket full of hundreds. I'd been thinking I could surprise Jacob with a vacation, or maybe a new upstairs bathroom to smooth things over a little between us, give us something to be happy about. Make things good again.

If I wanted to pursue the regressions, my plans for a bathroom remodel would need to be downgraded to a new air freshener.

Stefan sat back in his huge leather chair. It creaked beneath his weight. He stared down his nose at me, and said, "How are things?"

"Things are..." I shrugged. I'd never really told him very much about my current situation, other than the fact that I was having panic attacks, and that I conveniently forgot a hell of a lot of stuff. "Things are kind of...stressful."

"And the Valium—you're not taking it every day, are you?"

"No...I know it's addictive." I couldn't remember the last time I took a Valium. I was too worried about the FPMP catching me off guard. I needed to be sure I had an edge. That I wasn't high on Auracel. Or drunk.

"Anything unusual going on at work?"

"I don't know, work's okay. I'm at this hospital. It's thick with ghosts. But nothing I can't handle." Work was fine. Really. Except for Officer "Andy." But I doubted there was anything Stefan could say to make me feel better about the FPMP following me around, spying on me, siccing a remote viewer on my pathetic life. "I'm remembering more. I think maybe it's good that we're doing these regressions. I think maybe I'm ready to remember."

"Is there anything in particular you want me to focus on in today's session?"

Probably, but no doubt I couldn't articulate it. "This is going to sound crazy, but the stuff I'm remembering, everything except for being locked in a room with a dead body, well...how can I say it? It's not too bad. You and me, we had some fun."

Stefan watched me intently. There was a deep vertical crease between his brows. "At times. I suppose."

"The kitchen raids. The whippits." The sex, of course. I didn't say that. It felt too awkward. "A lot of that wasn't any worse than any other kid our age would have gone through in a dorm."

"At first. Before Krimski."

Another huge jolt of memory rocked me. My throat closed up, and I started to sweat all over.

"Inhale, slowly, and then let it out. You're safe here." Stefan's voice was close now. He seated himself in the chair across from the hypnosis couch. I hadn't even seen him cross the room. "Inhale—two, three, four. Good. Relax."

It started as a memory. Krimski's face. In his forties, slim, a full head of hair, gray at the temples. Maybe handsome, once, but now etched with deep lines at the sides of his mouth, across the forehead. Eyes deep set, never missed anything.

Stefan spoke again. "Show and Tell day again? I hope they brought donuts."

We sat in the smoking lounge, even though I didn't smoke, with our legs dangling out the window. I had on zip-up combat boots so scuffed that the toe was separating from the sole. Stefan wore black creepers with leopardskin tops and silver buckles. We both kicked our heels against the brick building.

The wings of Heliotrope Station formed an "L" shape, and we could see the cafeteria from our perch. One floor down, at a ninety-degree angle, a bunch of kids who were about our age, but much less jaded, set their gear up on the lunchroom tables. A branch of the University of Chicago Medical School sent a select group of med students over every month. Every month, they set up their little plastic barriers and engaged us all in a very tedious guessing game. Some of them were very earnest. Some of them were quite obviously scared.

And sometimes, some of them were kind of hot, and would let me and Stefan double-team them. I never trusted myself to pick those out, of course. I let my empathic boyfriend do it.

Stefan exhaled, and a veil of smoke clouded my view for a moment, before the wind snatched it away. "Do you think one of these days they'll get bored with Show and Tell and maybe play ping-pong on those tables instead?"

None of the students really did it for me today. I guess that would make it easier for me to focus on the game and act slightly psychic, but not too much. "Anything is better than one more minute in a classroom with Faun Windsong. I swear to God, she asks the most retarded questions just to hear herself talk. Blah, blah, blah. And The Nun? She just lets her keep going."

The medium facilitator, Miss Maxwell, used to be a Catholic nun. That's what we heard anyway. Once a nun, always a nun. Even if she was excommunicated for talking to dead people.

"Foosball." Stefan took a long drag of his cigarette. He exhaled through his nose. "Now, that would be something. I'd show up for that completely sober."

"There you are," said a familiar voice from the doorway.

Stefan raised one eyebrow and smirked. He took a long, deep drag deliberately slow. I rolled my eyes. Einstein.

"They're gonna start any minute. They're setting up the tables."

"We can see it from here," I said in a monotone.

Einstein came up and peeked over my shoulder. I think his puny brain couldn't grasp the shape of the buildings, and he'd never realized you could see the West Wing from the lounge. He stared for several drags of Stefan's cigarette, getting his bearings. And then he laughed. "Heh-heh."

Stefan and I both immediately imitated his laugh. In unison.

"Movie Mike says that if he gets a hot chick, he's gonna try really hard today and send something flying across the table."

Stefan's lip curled. "I'll keep my eye on him. If I'm lucky, I'll get to see his head split open and his brains ooze out."

"Heh-heh."

Einstein left, because for him, the thought of being late for Show and Tell was as inconceivable as skipping a meal.

"What did Movie Mike do now?" I asked Stefan.

"The little douchebag was passing by me in the lunch room, and he told me to suck in my gut." Stefan smiled as he said it. Which struck me as menacing.

"And then what?"

Stefan pressed his lips together in an attempt to stop smiling, but he couldn't suppress it. He shrugged gleefully.

I prodded him with my shoulder. "Come on, man, tell me."

Stefan put his lips against my ear. "I made him shit himself."

I flinched. "You can do that?"

"I didn't mean to. I was actually trying to make him vomit in front of Pretty Pretty Paula. Sending him vibes about how sick he felt, how his stomach was churning." Stefan clapped his palm over his mouth and his whole body shook with laughter. He knuckled a tear from his eye, took a final drag from the cigarette, and flicked it out the window. "Oh, the smell...."

"Come on," I said. Because I couldn't figure out how to act like I thought it was funny. Mike should have known better than to get himself on Stefan's bad side, but still. "You don't want to miss Show and Tell."

We acted like we were taking our time because we were both so cool, but eventually we followed Einstein downstairs. I didn't mind Show and Tell, and I think Stefan didn't either. Even if there wasn't anyone new to cruise, it was the only time we ever saw each other during training. I would watch him, glancing at me over the table divider, giving me coy eyeliner looks. I dug it. Even if he did scare me a little.

The telepaths and the empaths had multiple stations dedicated to testing them. Because there were only four mediums, we got one table that we had to share. Faun was there already, handling the personal effects of some recently deceased unfortunate. It was a stupid test. The med school had never snagged anything important enough to bring a ghost along with it. I wondered what their paperwork said about any of us mediums. A bunch of blanks?

Dead Darla scowled at me from her post by a shy-looking med student who looked like he might be convinced to accessorize his black turtleneck with some silver skull jewelry. She'd dated someone briefly since my arrival, but gay or not, I'd picked Stefan over her, and she'd never forgiven me.

Einstein was talking away. He could go on and on. I wasn't listening at the time, but now, from my strange half-here and half-there perspective, I could tune in on his words.

"And Director Sanchez is moving to Miami, and the new director will be here today. Some Polack name. Heh-heh."

"Maybe you should challenge him to a game of screwing in light bulbs."

Einstein thought about it for a second. "Heh-heh."

I caught Stefan's eye. He gave me a long look, up and down. I slouched harder against the wall, and angled my hips. I dug my thumbs into the pockets of my Levi's, and framed my package with both hands. A naughty smile flickered over his expression, quickly hidden as he guessed yet another color from a series of obscenely bright cards. He was reading the presenter, and not the cards, since he was no precog. But I guess he still got a lot of them right, once he got a feel for the person holding the deck.

On the opposite side of the room, one of the med students opened up a gigantic box of donuts. I watched Stefan look up from his test. Not that he'd heard it or smelled it or had any reason to have seen it. But I guess a room full of people give off a certain vibe when the donuts show up.

Einstein ran over to take first pick. I had a stomach full of institutional pancakes, and wasn't ready to add more starch to my body at the moment. Faun Windsong finished up, and Dead Darla was still hovering around her med student. That left me. I sat down across from a nervous girl who looked like maybe she'd had skin problems once, and never gotten back her confidence.

She pulled out a metal box and set it on the table. There was no divider between us, not like the tables where the telepaths and empaths and precogs tried to guess colors and shapes. She probably would have been more comfortable if there were. She folded her hands in her lap and tried not to fidget.

I pulled a string of pearls from the silver box. Silver. I noticed that now, I hadn't thought much about it then. There was nothing supernatural about the pearls. Nobody appeared when I handled them. Nobody whispered in my ear. Even so, there were certain things that were expected of us. "I think the energy is female. Maybe a mother, or a grandmother. Or...like a mother. To someone." One of the things they expected was that we wouldn't neglect the obvious.

Once I'd finished sorting through all the trinkets and giving the med student answers I'd pulled out of my ass, I turned to head over to the donuts. Because, of course, that's where Stefan would be.

Only, he wasn't.

Einstein was there, with a long john in one hand and a cruller in the other. Faun Windsong broke a bagel into a dozen small pieces, which she did to fool herself into thinking that she was eating less, and whined about the lack of low-fat cream cheese.

But no Stefan.

I felt a presence beside me, not in a psychic way. More in a something-is-blotting-out-the-sun way. A guy in blue scrubs stood beside me, over two hundred pounds of solid muscle. Some new orderly. There was a handful of regulars, but the other ones came and went; I had a hard time keeping track of them. "Are you getting a donut, or not?"

I almost said, "What's it to you?" Except that I didn't care for the look in his eye, and while I didn't think I was in danger of getting punched in the head, it didn't mean that I wanted to make an enemy among the staff. After all, people can find all kinds of ways to get back at you if they're looking for revenge. They can "accidentally" crash a cart into your door while you're trying to sleep. They can spit in your food. With that in mind, I just shook my head.

"Then let's go." He stared at me until I fell into step beside him and the two of us left the cafeteria.

I was curious, but not overly so. Heliotrope Station might be boring, but at least it wasn't full of crazy people like the CCMHC. But the closer we got to Administration, the more uneasy I felt. I wondered if maybe I wasn't performing well enough to stay. If that were the case, would they give me some kind of warning? Or would they just kick me out and leave me on the street to fend for myself? Shit, what if I had to go get a real job?

The new orderly lead me up to Sanchez' door. Only it wasn't Sanchez' anymore, not if Einstein had been up on his gossip, and he probably was. He might be stupid, but his short-term memory was okay. "Wait here." The orderly stood beside me with his hands loose at his sides. He stared straight ahead. I wished I had taken a donut. It might be the last free meal I got in a while.

In a couple minutes, Sanchez' door opened. Another new orderly came out, leading one of the precogs, a black kid named Big Larry who never really liked me because I never bothered to hide the fact that I checked out guys' asses. And yet I felt a certain kind of solidarity with him, because he and I were psychics. And these other guys could have been professional wrestlers. I tried to catch Big Larry's eye. "Hey," I said.

Big Larry was dark-skinned. I'll never forget the way his eyes looked, with the whites showing all around. He didn't say a word.

Did Big Larry have something to worry about? I'd always thought he was pretty accurate. "Go on," said the gigantic orderly. I didn't see any way out of it, so I took a deep breath, and I stepped into the office.

✦ TWENTY-ONE ✦

What I remembered most about Sanchez's office, not that I made a habit of hanging out in there, was that there were stacks and stacks of papers and manila files everywhere. Lots of chairs too, maybe five, and you could only sit in two of them, because all the others functioned as some sort of elaborate filing system.

Now, not only were all the teetering stacks of paper gone, but the chairs were, too. All but the single, imposing modern-day throne behind the desk. And that one wasn't even being sat in.

Krimski stood behind Sanchez' old desk. He wore an immaculate pinstriped gray suit, double-breasted, with a black tie that was thin enough to look modern, but wide enough to keep it from being too edgy. Now, from my vantage point on Stefan's hypnosis couch, I saw the faintest impression of a holster on his left side. Back then, I wouldn't have noticed unless he whipped out the gun and pummeled me with it.

"Mister Bayne, is it? I see you have the distinction of being the highest level medium."

"I think Faun Windsong might call you on that."

He went on as if I hadn't said a word. "As a courtesy, I'm letting you know that certain policy changes are in effect, immediately."

My brain scrambled. Courtesy—good. Policy changes—probably not so good.

"As outlined on page fifty-eight, paragraph four of your intake agreement, we will continue testing the psyactive and anti-psyactive properties of certain substances. Unfortunately, nicotine skews the results. Cigarette distribution will be ceased, and the smoking lounge is closed."

Cigarettes were one of the main commodities at Heliotrope Station, just like they had been at the CCMHC. That, and maybe sexual favors—which I personally liked to save for recreational use. Though I guess some people felt that way about their smokes.

Besides that, it was just plain rude to close up the smoking lounge, whether or not we had anything to smoke once we were in there.

I opened my mouth to suggest as much, but Krimski started talking before I figured out what to say. I guess he'd had practice. Big Larry. Maybe Stefan, too.

"Your file says you've been having sexual relations with your fellow residents. What you do in your own time makes no difference to me. But when you're within these walls, you're on my time."

My mouth worked. They put stuff like that in my file?

"Fraternization, between staff and residents, and among the residents themselves, ends now. After focus groups, residents will return to their rooms and remain there, unless they are called upon for testing."

"You mean, like solitary confinement?"

"Hardly. The program is in danger of being shut down. The telepaths can't see anything, the TKs can't move anything, and the mediums don't get anything but the vaguest impressions. Heliotrope Station isn't a social club, Mister Bayne. It's a training facility. And we will train you."

I really, really didn't want to be the star pupil in the medium department. I'd need to be sure to do even worse next time I was tested. And if I did get thrown out for underperforming, at least I'd be able to get laid without someone documenting it in my goddamn file.

"Mister Brown will show you back to your room." I had been there nearly four months—it's not as if I didn't know where my room was. And I don't think that was the point. I turned toward Brown, because I would rather walk beside him then have him start grabbing me, when some motion in the far corner of the room caught my eye.

A bunch of meaningless highlights resolved themselves into a figure, transparent, but recognizable enough. I knew Director Sanchez by his bald spot. It was shaped like an hourglass, big on the crown, wide across the forehead, and a tiny bridge of hair that tried to connect from ear to ear over the top of his head. His face was not so recognizable. It was swollen and bloated, and his eyes looked ready to pop out of his skull. A length of wire was wrapped around his neck so tightly I was worried it would act like a cheese cutter and lop the whole thing right off.

I stumbled, and I looked at my boot. But I don't think Krimski was convinced that the carpet was what had distracted me. Sanchez had died there. And I knew it. And he knew I knew it.

That night I picked a hole the size of a La-Z-Boy in the plaster of the wall in my room, not that I thought I could escape through it or anything, but just because I was bored, and antsy, and of course second-guessing my decision to hop ship from the CCMHC to come to Heliotrope Station at all.

Because logically, once I'd tested as a Psych, couldn't the medical center have just let me out?

I hadn't wasted much time thinking it through. Heliotrope Station promised a cutting-edge career in Psych work. I was twenty-three, and I'd only made it halfway through the tenth grade. Heliotrope seemed like a logical choice, especially since it was residential, and I wouldn't have to worry about finding somewhere to live and coming up with rent month after month.

I slept, eventually, but it couldn't have been more than a couple of hours. "Wake up." I opened my eyes to an orderly shouting in my face. Not Mister Brown. But another new guy. As if all the orderlies we knew (and loved to make fun of) had been replaced by a soulless bunch of thugs.

I was escorted to the medical wing. "I'll be late for class," I told the dried-up guy in the nurse's office. He wasn't the nurse. He looked vaguely like a monkey. If Stefan were there, he'd crack a joke. But Stefan wasn't there.

"You won't be attending focus group today," said monkey man—the man with the rainbow of pills and the pointy syringes. "Today, we'll be testing the effect of a new medication on mediums."

"Breathe deeply, and focus on my voice." I'd know Stefan's voice anywhere. But he wasn't there. Hadn't been there. Shit. My sense of time was all screwy.

"You're centered, you're relaxed. As I count down to one, you find yourself becoming more and more alert. Ten. Nine. Safe and relaxed. Eight."

Hypnosis couch, right. My breathing was fast, like it could tip into hyperventilation at any second. The back of my shirt was soaked with sweat.

"Four. Feel your hands resting on your thighs. Feel the soles of your feet on the floor. Three."

What if I opened my eyes, and I was still in the nurse's office? The last fourteen years would turn out to be a big, drug-induced nightmare. Seriously, what if? Would I do anything different? God, I'd like to think so.

"One. Open your eyes, feeling completely refreshed."

"If this is what refreshed feels like, I'd hate to get a taste of the exhaustion around here."

"You were talking about Einstein."

"Richie. Yeah. I saw him. He's doing okay."

"And Krimski. You said he was in Sanchez' office."

"I did? What do I say during these regression things, anyway? Do you record them?"

"Of course not," he snapped. "I would've told you if I was recording them."

"Okay, okay, I just wondered what I said." Because it would've been really awkward if I just came out and said that I used to pose for him with my crotch sticking out. I suspected he knew, given his empathic ability. But putting actual words on it made it sound so pathetic.

"You don't say very much, which is pretty typical of my patients with PTSD. You'll tell me where you are, who you're with, maybe what you're doing. And only if I ask you. All the sights, the sounds, the subtle nuance, that's something that you keep to yourself."

So, the crotch thing. I'm guessing I didn't say that.

"The big talkers are the suburban ladies with way too much money and way too much time on their hands. They go on and on—they're narcissistic that way."

"But you can imagine all this stuff, can't you? You were there."

"Yes. I was. That's probably the only reason I get half of the things you're talking about."

"When you reminded me about Krimski, I slipped back into one of the memories from before, from the first regression we did. When they tested Neurozamine on me."

"It's not uncommon to revisit a traumatic event at various points. It's your way of trying to make sense of things."

Various snappy comebacks occurred to me, but none of them seemed worth saying. "So, when did we start sneaking into the kitchen? Before Krimski, or after?" .

"Before. Don't you remember that lock? I could pop it with a sharpened comb. The cafeteria was more like an all-you-can-eat buffet back then, until he got that lock fixed and hired all those disgustingly muscular orderlies." Stefan stroked the soul patch under his lower lip. "When you think about it, Heliotrope Station was more like a cheap vacation package back then. Especially the classes. Those were like sitting through timeshare presentations."

"The classes...we had a nun, and she was actually pretty nice. But then she was gone. And the classes were gone. And they called them focus groups instead."

Stefan's chair creaked as he resettled his bulk in it. "How devastated would you be if I suggested that not only were you traumatized by the meds, and the invasion of privacy, and the restriction of your activities—but you also miss what Heliotrope Station might have been, if the management never changed over?"

"They would have folded. Krimski told me as much, when I met him."

Stefan raised his eyebrows and pursed his lips. "Did he?"

"I don't think I'm mourning what Camp Hell might have been. I think it's more that I'm baffled that I went in there voluntarily. I mean, no one twisted my arm. Right?"

"We were all there voluntarily. If you've been telling yourself differently, it's probably a harmless little fantasy that's been helping you deal with your experience."

"Now you're making it sound like maybe I am crazy."

"We don't use the word *crazy* around here. We prefer *coping mechanism*."

I grabbed a tissue from a holder next to the hypnosis couch, which had probably been placed there for the suburban ladies who were moved to tears by the experiences of their regressions, and I used it to wipe off my forehead and upper lip. I wondered how coherent I'd been when I was reliving the experience of Stefan telling me about what he'd done to Movie Mike. And I suspected that Stefan was more interested in my regressions than he'd been letting on. How could he not be? He played a starring role in the tawdriest scenes.

I asked him, "What did Krimski say to you the first time you got called into his office?"

Stefan twirled his chin hairs and his gaze went far away. "No smoking. No fraternization. And that they'd finally start taking advantage of the section in our intake papers that said we'd consented to be human guinea pigs. I think I got hung up on the no-sex, no-smoking part of the lecture and didn't realize how bad everything else would actually get."

"And he didn't say anything about your performance."

"Why would he?"

I shrugged. I'm sure Stefan felt my anxiety, but its causes were so poorly thought-out that I don't think either of us could have articulated what I was struggling with.

"Did you ever try anything with him?" I asked. "You know, like *Boo-Hoo-You?*" I think that the other residents suspected one of the high-level empaths was behind the unexplained bursts of tears that punctuated our days, at least some of the time, but I don't think they ever pinpointed Stefan. Not definitively.

"Believe you me, I would've done all that, and worse. Remember, I never got a read on him. He had an emotional suit of armor—kind of like Jacob."

Time stopped for a second. I tried to process. But it was like eating pudding with chopsticks. "What?"

"What do you call them, Stiffies? That's what Krimski felt like."

"Stiffs," I said, too distracted to bother to make fun of his Freudian slip. "Seriously, you couldn't read Jacob?"

"You didn't know that?"

I wiped my face with the tissue, which was disintegrating in my hand. "How would I know? I don't read live people, only dead ones."

"When I push hard enough with my talent, other people give. But not Krimski. Never Krimski."

Or Jacob. Holy shit. Stiffs were supposed to balance Psychs, but as far as I knew, everyone just saw them as being psychically neutral. Heck, NP, or non-psychic, was an interchangeable term for Stiff—old-fashioned, but more politically correct. They were a neutral gray in a world of black and white.

But what if they weren't really gray? What if they were silver?

And there wasn't any way to test it...because a test would bounce right off a genuine Stiff.

"Where are you right now?" Stefan asked.

"I'm here. I'm just thinking."

"Okay. Let's talk about it. That's what you're paying me for."

I studied Stefan's face. I'd been through hell and back with him, but he'd had thousands of experiences since then, too. He was Steven Russeau now. And whatever new idea my inadequate brain was trying to piece together, it seemed too personal to drag out, half-formed and naked, and show him.

"I'm gonna go home," I said. I glanced at my watch. It was after seven. I could be home by eight if I didn't run into a traffic snag. "Jacob and me...things have been kinda...bumpy...lately. I really want to see him."

Stefan gave a careless shrug. "I don't know how you do the whole relationship thing. It's so complicated, so much work. I'd much rather keep things casual. It's more fun to just date."

I glanced back at the hypnosis couch as I stood. Luckily, my sportcoat had stopped me from leaving a giant sweat mark behind. "What about Fernando? Don't you love him?"

"We have a good time together. It doesn't mean I want to marry him."

On my way to the elevator I thought about Stefan's attitude. Or more accurately, what it said about me, that his unwillingness to get involved with someone made me sad. I flipped open my phone and hit a memory dial.

"Sticks and Stones."

"Hey, it's me. Listen, I was just wondering, as an empath, could you...you know. Could you get a read from Jacob?"

"Newsflash, I'm working here."

Okay, so it was pretty tacky of me to ask Jacob's last boyfriend how he felt psychically. But who else could I ask? "I mean, as a Stiff, was he different from other people? Was he harder to read sometimes?"

"I bet you're trying to pull something over on him. Don't drag me into the middle of it. Honesty is the best policy, sappy but true."

"No, nothing like that." The elevator door opened. I stepped on, and my phone connection got staticky. "I was just wondering if he felt different."

"Well, sure he does. All those hours in the gym pay off."

I almost said "Jesus," but then I remembered him saying I was disrespect-ful, and I turned it into a brief sigh. "You know what, never mind. I'm sorry I asked."

"*Hasta la vista*," he said, and hung up.

I stepped off the elevator into the lobby, and saw the plate glass windows were dark. There was a handful of people wandering inside against the crappy weather, some of them poking at their PDAs, some of them on the phone. When one figure in black peeled itself off the wall and came at me, I nearly reached for my weapon, figuring it for the FPMP. But it wasn't Officer "Andy." It was Jacob.

"Jesus, you scared the shit—"

He grabbed me by the shoulders and stared into my eyes. "Are you okay? You're soaked."

"Yeah, I'm..." the feel of his hands, even through my overcoat, made me giddy with relief. I felt my whole body relax. And I thought about my internal faucet, my protective barrier, and I wondered if my proximity to Jacob made it stronger. "I'm sick of this. I want to be able to stop worrying. It's like we're always worried about something—like we're always looking around to see who's watching us."

Even in the lobby of Stefan's building we were the center of attention, whether or not anyone else was spying for the FPMP. Because everyone else was a conservative businessman, and none of them were currently engaged in a big, gay, personal melodrama.

Jacob slid his hand up my shoulder and cradled my cheek. So intimate, so public. And I leaned into his touch, even turned my head to brush a kiss across the inside of his wrist.

"Let's go somewhere," he said.

"Where?"

"Anywhere. It doesn't matter. At least for tonight. Let's just drive."

✦ TWENTY-TWO ✦

"Just driving" would have been a heck of a lot nicer in Jacob's roomy Crown Victoria. But he'd taken a cab downtown, so he tilted up my steering wheel, pushed my seat back as far as it would go, and made do. We hopped on the expressway and drove. Jacob was at the wheel. I stared out the passenger window.

We headed south, through good neighborhoods and bad ones, then good ones again. In about an hour, we crossed the border to Indiana, where the gas prices dropped by a dime, and old signs for fireworks, half-covered by snow, periodically appeared alongside the road.

Jacob chose a small motel at random and paid for a room with cash. The desk clerk and the other clientele were all black, but although they took a good long look at us, a couple of gay white guys clearly out of their element, they didn't seem inclined to give us any hassle.

I peeled off my overcoat, jacket and holster, and threw them on the bed. "I'm remembering so much, but I can't make sense out of it. It's too much. All at the same time. All jumbled up. And what sucks is that I'm not even so sure what I'm freaking out about anymore."

"Seeing you like this? It kills me. I swear, it's like somebody sticks a knife in my gut and gives it a good, hard twist."

"Seeing me like what?"

"Is it possible for you to remember these things without completely reliving them? It seems like you're doing everything the hard way. I wish you could go easy on yourself, just for once."

I stripped off my shirt. It was rank. I threw it on the floor, went into the bathroom, and ran the water. I unwrapped one of those little bars of soap. My skin was blotchy across the stomach, where I hadn't rinsed off the High John the Conqueror well enough and my skin had reacted poorly to it.

Jacob came over and leaned against the doorway with his arms crossed. He had done that the day I met him in Maurice's basement, while I was trying to swallow a pill that was stuck on my tongue. See, I was able to have a pleasant memory. And maybe not everything that happened in a basement was traumatic. Not always.

I wasn't eager to put my clothes back on until they'd had a trip to the cleaners, so while I took a shower, Jacob ran out and got me some sweats from one of the half-dozen strip malls we'd passed. I noted a smaller shopping bag inside the large one that held a new bottle of lube, too. It was reassuring to know that Jacob thought lube might come into play that night, given the roller coaster ride that our life had turned into.

We stretched out side by side in the strange bed with sheets that smelled like bleach, and we stared at each other in the dim, yellow light of the bedside lamp.

"Don't be mad at me for protecting our house." Jacob brushed a strand of hair off my forehead. "I just want us to be safe. I want us to be happy."

"I'm not mad." He did make me feel safe. And happy. Just looking at him made me feel like my heart was so big that my body couldn't contain it. He was decisive, and Type A, and I had known that from the beginning. That was what I liked about him.

I covered his hand with mine, and he leaned in for a slow, easy kiss. When I opened my eyes afterward, he was watching me. "You need to know who's sending those faxes. And I think Doctor Chance is the one who can tell you."

I thought about spotting Sanchez, dead, in the corner of his office. And how Krimski knew that I'd spotted him. "Yeah? What if the whole reason they brought me in was because they were testing me to see if I could find her?"

"What if it was? They probably think she's gone now, because Richie performed the ceremony on that repeater."

Maybe so. He'd said it was sudden, violent. A gunshot—I remembered he'd said gunshot, not suicide, and he didn't name a gender. They could've thought he meant Chance.

Jacob rolled me onto my back and straddled my hips. He sank his elbows into the hard, unfamiliar mattress on either side of my head, cupped his chin in hands, and stared down at me. Breathing was a challenge, with all his weight on me like that. And I felt good. Safe.

"Do you want to keep going?" I asked him. "Just drive—anywhere? I've got money."

His dark eyes softened, and a wistful smile tugged at the corner of his mouth. "I would, if I thought it would work. I like hearing you say it, though."

"Like" being Jacob's shorthand for the growing bulge pressing into my hipbone. "So if you won't let me run away with you...why are we here?"

Jacob brushed my hair back again, then kissed my temple, my eyebrow. "Everything in our house reminds me of the FPMP. All of our stuff is a potential hiding place for a bug. I just wanted to be alone with you, only you, even if it was for a single night."

I slipped my arms around his back and pressed him against me tighter. He felt even bigger than usual, as if he'd been working out his frustration about the unrelenting surveillance with extra bench presses. "Then we'll have to make a choice." I really never expected me to be the one to say it. "Whether we live with the FPMP watching us and accept that there isn't shit we can do about it, or we cut the cords, and we go."

Jacob traced his finger along the top of my ear, and I shivered. "Where would we go?" he asked.

I drew a blank. Because mostly I was thinking that I could totally feel the shape of his cock. And I wondered if I should grind myself against it. "France?"

Jacob's mouth brushed mine. His goatee tickled my chin. "I don't speak French."

Neither did I. "Mexico?"

"I doubt we'd be any better off. They have their own brand of corruption in Mexico."

Jacob shifted, and grunted when my stiffening cock slid into place beside his, bulge against bulge. I gave in to my urge to hump him, and his breath hissed in.

"I've been thinking about Crash," I said. Actually, I'd been thinking of something Stefan said, but it was all connected.

Jacob rolled off me and pulled me against him, chest to chest, with my leg locked between his. "Okay."

"Now that you're not mad at each other anymore, it's obvious that you're close. Good friends. And even though I want to smack him sometimes—really hard—I think I can say the same for him and me. And I'm sure we'd have a blast if we took him to bed with us."

I trailed off to gather my thoughts, lapsing into silence long enough that Jacob had to prompt me. "But...?"

But I wasn't in it for the "fun." At least not the way Stefan had talked about it, him and Fernando. "Having a three-way with Crash is something I would've done in a heartbeat when I was younger. And I'm figuring out that I don't really like myself, not the way I was back then. Especially seeing it through my eyes... now. I'm not that guy anymore. And I don't want to act like him."

"I'm sure Crash will be devastated. And then he'll find a dozen other men who'll be more than happy to take his mind off us."

"A dozen? Seriously?" I twitched my hips, and our hard-ons rubbed. "You think they'll be hot?"

Jacob's mouth covered mine, and I felt him smile. "There's hot, and then there's hot."

I turned my head aside so I didn't laugh directly into his mouth. "Yeah, right."

He trailed his fingertip over my lower lip, down my chin. "What can I say? I'm a sucker for blue eyes."

Jacob took advantage of the moment I was completely blown away by the notion that he was after anything other than my Psych talents. He snuck a hand down the front of my sweatpants, and then the waistband of my new boxers, which were still sharply creased from the package. It seemed like everything here was squeaky clean and new, or at least freshly-scrubbed. What a nice change.

Jacob gripped my cock loosely, and stroked the underside of the head with his thumb. My cock swelled until it was good and stiff. He nuzzled my wet hair out of my ear, then teased me with his tongue, in and out, like a preview of what my ass could expect.

I arched into his touch. I realized I'd been holding my breath, and sucked in air in one big, loud gasp. He moaned in my ear, and pressed his stiffening cock against my hipbone. I wedged my hand in between us and grabbed his balls, right through his jeans. I caressed them and he flexed into my hand.

"I noticed you bought something besides the clothes," I said.

"It's amazing what you can find at SaverPlus these days." He gripped me harder and started stroking. I used to think Jacob squeezed just a little too much when he handled my cock. But now my inner masochist was totally into it.

"So are you gonna just beat me off, or do you plan to break in the new lube?"

"That's what you want?" he said, in his low, hot porno-voice. His nuts shifted in my hand. I traced my thumb over the root of his shaft. He felt ready to bust out of his jeans.

"Yeah."

He tongued my ear again, hot and wet. "Tell me."

Damn it all, did I have to? I sounded like a moron in bed. But I was still loopy from the blue-eyed comment, so I gave it a shot. "Grease up that thick, hard meat of yours and fuck me with it."

Jacob's breath caught. "Suck it first," he whispered. Needy. Hot.

I undid his jeans and peeled them open. His cock was ruddy and hard, thick with veins. I did my first slow lick right up the middle with the flat of my tongue. My mouth filled with salty cock-taste. I curled my tongue over the head and wet it with my spit, letting Jacob feel the heat and wetness, but not sucking, not yet.

Jacob held onto my head two-handed, fingers in my hair, pressed against my scalp. I let my lips drag against the head while I licked it all over, down one side, back up, and down the other. I eased up to the slit, and stroked the saltiness out with the very tip of my tongue. Jacob's fingers tightened on my scalp, and he shuddered.

I wrapped my lips around the head, and Jacob groaned. He wanted to thrust, I could tell, but instead he held himself still. He probably wanted to jam my face down over the whole massive girth of it. I reached into my new sweats and gave myself a few quick pulls at the thought of it.

One inch, then another. I worked my way down slowly, until my jaw was stretched to capacity, and I felt the tickle of his pubes on my lips. And then I started to suck.

Jacob gave a moan that probably carried back to the motel office, and his fingers clenched in my hair. "So good," he said, the words nearly lost in all the sexy noises.

I started to move my head, up and down, really deliberate, while I kept up the suction. I set a rhythm that made my jaw ache. I ignored the pain and focused on Jacob's breathing.

"Maybe we should go away." Jacob's grip had loosened, and he stroked my hair while I blew him. "Canada. Buy a little place out in the middle of nowhere and hide out."

Canada, huh? They spoke English there, mostly. And we could gay-marry and everything.

Holy crap, had I actually thought that? I pulled off of Jacob's cock with a big, wet smack. He stroked my cheek with his knuckles, and stared down at me with an expression so comically tender that I could swear he'd just read my mind.

"Straddle me," he said. "I want you on top. I want to watch you ride my dick."

Well, maybe he hadn't. Not exactly.

I pushed out of my sweatpants, opened up the squirt-top of the lube and punctured the foil safety barrier with my car keys. Jacob's clothes were all out of place—shirt hitched up under his arms and pants bunched down around his thighs—and he'd swung his feet over the side of the bed to take off his socks. I gave the lube a sniff while he finished stripping, since it wasn't our usual type. No odor. I worked a drop between my thumb and forefinger, and admired the chiseled lines of his abs as he pulled his shirt over his head. He was more pumped up. I'd never expected muscles to do much for me; after all, his gym-buddies had left me flat. But more of Jacob to love? I could get into that.

He stretched out on the bed and tucked an arm under his head, and his biceps bulged so big that I wondered if he could even bend his arm comfortably. "You're looking...ripped."

He glanced down at his insanely cut body and then back up at me. He grinned. "I didn't think you noticed things like that."

"I might be a head-case, but I'm not blind." I climbed onto his legs, low on his thighs, and jerked off his veiny cock while he and I both watched the shiny purple head appear and disappear from the tunnel of my fingers. My saliva on it grew sticky, so I squeezed some lube over Jacob's cockhead and smoothed it around with my palm. Instant glide. Jacob's breath caught.

"You're not a head-case." He was struggling to sound normal, but he'd said it between clenched teeth. I squeezed harder, and the sides of his ass dimpled as his body reacted. His breath huffed out.

I wasn't going to argue about it, not now. I knew I wasn't schizophrenic, but all my time in institutions had left a mark on me, no two ways about it. I let go of Jacob's cock and climbed him. His thighs were bigger now, too. There was less space between us when I straddled him.

I crooked a leg to line him up, and then I settled back down with the tip of his cock pressing at me just so. A push, even a shallow one, and he'd be inside me. I always dug that moment. Almost there. But not yet.

Jacob stared up at me like I had a riddle in my face that he hadn't quite pieced together. "What?" I said.

He shook his head.

"You feel amazing," I told him. I bore down, almost imperceptibly, and Jacob and I both held our breath. He reached up and put his hands on my shoulders. He wanted to press—oh yes—and impale me on his cock. But he didn't. He just rested them there. And I closed my eyes and enjoyed the just-about-to-be-fucked sensation for one more selfish moment before I eased down and buried him inside me.

His hands roamed down my chest. He slipped them around my waist and encouraged me to fuck myself on him. I flexed, and we both gasped again at the feel of him inside me. I put my palms flat on his chest and pushed myself up straighter, figuring I could force myself to let him watch me, since he'd asked for it and all. His eyes lingered somewhere around my collarbone. Hickeys. Or bite marks. Both, probably.

I sat up tall, held on to his hips, and felt the length of him right up my ass, so stiff, so good. I moved faster, and my cock slapped down against the rock-hard curve of his abs. I left it to beat itself against him for now, and just focused on the thickness of him stretching my hole.

He tilted up in a half-crunch and the veins in his neck and shoulders bulged even more prominently. The reading lamp cast a roadmap of shadows over the landscape of his arms and chest. He ran his fingertips along a dusting of bruises on my thighs. "These probably shouldn't turn me on...."

"Why not?" I ground my body all the way down, clutched his hips, and pushed myself back up so I could repeat the move, feel it over and over again. "We both get off on it. What does it matter?"

He laid himself back down and gave over to being ridden. I leaned in only enough to reach his nipples, and I squeezed them in time with the motions of my hips. Up, a hard pinch...down, release. So that something was always peaking, and something else was always ebbing.

Jacob clutched my thighs and flexed his body, adding a little thrust each time I came down. Eventually, the constant in and out—and the breathing and the noises and the half-coherent dirty talk—brought on that old familiar ache. I let up on Jacob's nipples and touched myself two-handed, stroking my cock with one hand and my balls with the other.

"Yes," he said, and the word wavered, like maybe he would've added something, but he was too far gone to have more than a three-letter vocabulary.

I stared down at him, left off my balls, and let that hand trail up my body, pinch a nipple out for him. Stiff. I glanced down at it. Pink, too. A dusting of hair around it, and bruises, and bites. I smiled at him, and tweaked it harder. His breathing picked up and his body tensed. Veins bulged everywhere.

Just him, and just me. I thought we were pretty good together when that was all we had to worry about. I thought about the bugs and the cell phones and the remote viewer, and I opened up the allegorical tap inside me, let the white light flow down and cover Jacob and me in silver. So it was just us, no one but us.

Jacob grunted, and his stomach did that amazing rolling twitch that it did when he was just on the verge. I beat my own cock hard and fucked myself on him even harder. His back arched, and he came. A couple of strokes and I felt it, slick and hot, and I tightened up my ass to see if I could actually feel the throb of him shooting that load in me.

Jacob made a strangled sound and his grip on my thighs heightened to the point of pain. That's what tipped me. I tensed, and I shot, and I closed my eyes and laughed, 'cos it felt like I was coming white light.

✦ TWENTY-THREE ✦

Normally, I'd swing off and hit the shower. But I needed a second to gather myself up. I was sprawled with my face in Jacob's chest hair and I felt like I'd just come back from an out-of-body experience. Jacob was breathing so hard that I rose and fell on his ribcage as if he was wearing me.

He let go of my thighs and I flinched. "I'm sorry," he whispered.

"Are you kidding? Why do you think I shot so hard? Damn."

He folded his arms around me and I breathed in the tang of new sweat and sex, and to a lesser extent, the smell of hotel soap.

"When you look for those faxes, I wish I could come with you," Jacob said.

"Where? The FPMP?" I don't know what he thought he could accomplish there. Maybe getting between me and whoever might do to me what they did to Doctor Chance. Unless, of course, they had a telepath or an empath squinting at me from behind a peephole. Maybe then I'd agree to use him as a human shield. I peeled myself off Jacob's torso and sat up on his thighs. "Say...does Carolyn ever have trouble reading you?"

"Sometimes. She has her off-days."

"What about Crash? Could you ever decide not to share your mood with him?"

"I can't say I've ever understood in any great detail what Crash can and can't do...with his talent." A smirk. I imagined that aside from his talent, Crash did plenty. Good thing we could joke about it. "So I couldn't say."

"It's just that I've got this idea...and I dunno, it doesn't jibe with any kind of Psych research I've ever heard of."

Jacob got his elbows under him and pushed up from the bed. He was alert. Me? I managed to not topple off onto the floor. "Go on."

"I think you do something to block people. Psychs. But not just in the run-of-the-mill way that the Department made it out to be when they thought up the Psych and Stiff teams. I mean, I think you can control it and choose who to let in, and who to keep out."

"I scored average, completely average, on every test there is. A lack of talent isn't a talent itself."

"But what if you're looking at it wrong, because it can't be measured—because who's gonna measure it, and with what? I took a Psych test today, and you know what? It sucked."

And then it occurred to me, if he administered a card-flipping exercises to a bona fide telepath, a high-level, super-accurate seer, he could theoretically block the transmission, and then his ability—if you could call it that—could be measured and recorded. Even more accurately than mine.

Jacob swung his feet over the side of the bed and headed for the bathroom. "I think you just want to shore up my ego."

Oh, like that was necessary. I refrained from saying it out loud. "Jacob, do you know how strong Stefan is?"

Water ran in the bathroom. Jacob came out mopping his stomach with a hand towel. "How strong?"

"He's so empathic that not only can he tell what you're feeling, but he can twist your feelings around into anything else he wants."

Jacob stared down at the wad of damp towel in his hand, weighing it like he was probably weighing his words. "Pretty ballsy of you to date someone who can force you to love him. If he's as good as you say he is."

"He wouldn't have needed to do anything like that—he just happened to be my type. At the time. When I was twenty-three."

"And so he uses this talent of his, and he helps you with your panic when you're doing regressions, right?" He glanced down at my sweat-stained clothes. "Or am I missing something?"

"What you're missing is my point. What I'm trying to tell you—if you would stop being jealous for ten seconds—is that Stefan couldn't read you."

He glanced up at me. His eyes narrowed. "Why not?"

"He just couldn't. He says he's met other people that way, too. Psych-resistant."

Jacob stared at me, hard.

"They don't have a test for that," I said. "I know—I've taken every test in existence a dozen times or more. The tests haven't changed in the last fifteen years—or if anything, they've gotten sloppier. They can't test you for blocking."

Jacob stared for another several seconds. Then the corner of his mouth twitched. "Are you calling me a block?"

I shouldered my way past him, went into the bathroom and turned on the shower. "Fine, don't believe me. I never know what I'm talking about. Why should I start now?"

"It's a pretty big concept you're asking me to wrap my head around. Cut me some slack." Jacob stepped into the shower and pulled me against him, back to front. His wet hands moved over chest and stomach, up and down, brushing my hips, my groin—more to touch me than to wash away the stickiness.

I leaned back against him. His stroking hands had me half-hard, but I'd just had a pretty sweet orgasm, so there was no sense of urgency there. "Not a block. That's a lousy choice of words. A shield—how about that?"

"You're serious."

"Cripes, why else would I bring it up?"

Jacob pulled away and stepped out of the shower. He left a trail of water across the floor.

"Where'd you go?" I turned off the tap and wrapped a towel around my waist. I found Jacob naked and dripping by the bed with his cell phone in his hand. "Who are you calling?"

"Lisa."

"Hold on."

Jacob paused with his wet thumb hovering over one of the buttons.

"We both promised her we'd lay off the *si-no*," I said. "And even though you want to verify the existence of some mysterious seventh talent so bad you can taste it, just remember. Anything we say on a cell phone, we might as well go announce it to the FPMP."

The sinews in his jaw leapt as he ground his molars.

I realized that at some point we'd started yelling. I lowered my voice to talking-level. "I know it would be a big deal."

"If it were true," he added. Which was what I'd been thinking, but it sounded pretty harsh.

"If I'm right."

Stefan had seemed pretty damn sure there was something up with Jacob. He had no reason to lie to me. What would be the point? He could reach into my head and tweak my reactions if he didn't like the way things were going. So there was no reason for him to make it up.

I'd always assumed that Stefan never used his talent on me, other than obvious stuff that he couldn't block—tasting my willingness to do something risqué, or getting hit with my anxiety.

I would like to think that he never went into my head and rearranged things to his liking. But unless I asked him—in front of Carolyn—I'd never be sure he hadn't.

My stomach prickled. Drying semen and a High John the Conqueror rash weren't a very pleasant combination. "Leave Lisa out of it," I said. "Play Q & A with Carolyn tomorrow and see if you can block her. She's a sturdy level two. If you can shut out Stefan, you should be able to turn it on and off for her, no problem."

I went back into the bathroom and started the shower again. I wished I had something a little higher quality than the cheap sliver of soap that had come with the room, but I'd have to make do. I soaped myself up.

Jacob cast a massive shadow on the shower curtain. "If I was able to block Carolyn, don't you think it would've happened by now?"

"How should I know? Maybe you never really tried." Or maybe he needed to be giving off his "don't fuck with me" vibe while the poor, unsuspecting Psych was trying to read him. "That thing you do, I'll bet that's you, flexing your shield muscles."

Jacob stepped back into the shower and took the soap from me. He ran it over my back, and I leaned into the touch of his strong hands. "What thing?"

"You know. Laser-beam eyes."

Jacob cupped water in his palm, and smoothed his hands over my shoulder blades until our wet skin squeaked together. He kissed me at the top of the spine, and the hairs on my forearms stood at attention. "We'll talk about it later," he said. "I want to test it out, first. Make sure I'm not getting my hopes up for nothing."

✦ TWENTY-FOUR ✦

Doctor Gillmore glanced down at the new red badge that dangled from my la-pel. Full access to anywhere in the hospital I cared to go, thanks to the judge who'd pushed the paperwork through. Even a magnetic strip to swipe through electronic door locks. "Barring unusual weather," she said, "the ER activity typ-ically follows a bell curve. The middle of the week is fairly calm."

Someone in one of the partitions was howling in pain, and someone else was crying. I'd hardly call it calm.

"It might have been helpful for me to know the nature of your investigation before you obtained your subpoena." She gave Zig a withering look.

Even though I wasn't normally the talkative one, I said, "We need to keep an eye on partition number eight."

"I trust you'll stay out of my way?"

I gave her a hard look. She gave it right back, then looked down at her clipboard and went back to work. Zig and I stood outside the eighth partition. Inside, a preschooler cried a blue streak while his mother murmured to him in Spanish.

"What do we do?" Zigler asked. "Do we wait for it to empty out, or do we go in while there are patients inside?"

I opened the curtain a couple of inches and peeked inside. The mother couldn't have even been twenty years old. The baby was red-faced and covered in snot. *"Habla usted inglés?"* I asked her. I had to raise my voice to be heard over her wailing kid.

She gave me a really annoyed look, but she nodded. I wondered if I looked like a Child Welfare agent in my blue polyester sportcoat. Probably. I slipped my badge out of my pocket halfway. "Listen, I'm a cop, and my partner and me, we're taking a look at this hospital. Do you mind if I look around this...room?" If you could even call it that, with its gray fabric walls that allowed every last scream and moan to carry straight through. There was room enough for an exam table, a small desk, a crash cart and an IV stand.

The girl must've taken me at my word—I'm told I come off pretty honest when I do actually engage someone in conversation—and she shrugged. "Whatever."

It didn't seem like there was really enough room in the partition for anything that nasty to be inside. That thing following the homeless lady around, though? That didn't look like anything I'd want hovering around when my resistance was low.

I looked at the single chair, and the howling kid, and the glaring mom. "Um...thanks."

Doctor Gillmore was busy stitching up a guy who'd dropped a circular saw on himself at a construction site. I stood with my hands in my pockets and stared at the wall, and Zigler jotted down the fact that I'd seen nothing in partition number eight in his notepad.

"So, you're still here," Gillmore said. She snapped off her latex-free gloves just like I did when I was glad to leave a crime scene. "I take it you haven't found what you're looking for."

"Your patient yesterday...any chance I could talk to her?" Not that I really wanted to see that thing that was hovering around behind her, but I didn't have any other bright ideas.

"That's up to you. You'll have to find her, first."

"She was released," Zigler said, more of statement than a question.

"Her blood alcohol content was nearly .18 when she was admitted. Once she'd slept it off, there was nothing I could do to hold her."

Crap.

"Well, what's her name?" I asked. "Where can I find her?"

Doctor Gillmore looped her arm though mine and pulled me down to speak to me close. "Your warrant says you can search the ER—not the patient records. I can't give you her name, not without a warrant."

"Seriously? I mean, you can't just happen to say it to yourself...you know, in passing?"

She gave me that look again.

"I'm trying to help her," I said.

"And I'm making sure that I give her the same respect that I'd give someone with top-notch health insurance. Patient information is confidential unless your warrant says otherwise."

"That whole conversation we had yesterday—didn't it mean anything to you?"

"Of course it did. Look, if I see her again, I'll give her your card."

"Right. Like she's gonna follow up on that."

"I tell her there's something in it for her? Maybe she will."

I stared at Gillmore, hoping that she might cave in. She stared right back. An ER nurse hovered to one side with something for her to sign. I decided I didn't want to keep her from patching people up just for the sake of a staring contest, so I dug out a couple of business cards and handed them over. "You keep one, too. In case you see her again, and just happen to accidentally dial my phone number and tell me to drop by for some coffee."

She pocketed the business cards, gave me a "yeah, right" expression, then turned toward the nurse and went on with her work.

Zigler and I decided that a trip to the cafeteria was in order, since we weren't doing anything in the ER that we'd struggled so hard to obtain clearance for except potentially keeping someone from a timely blood transfusion by blundering between them and the staff.

Besides, it was really loud in there.

Zigler stirred his coffee with a thin plastic stirrer. I took an individually wrapped plastic spoon instead. I had a lot of sugar to dissolve in the bottom of my cup. "So you didn't see anything out of the ordinary in partition eight?" he said.

"What, you think my story's going to change when I get some caffeine in me?" I sipped. It needed another sugar. I'd stayed up way too late the night before.

"You didn't go all the way in. You stayed in the entryway."

If there was a ghost in there, it's not like I had to be standing on top of it to get a reading. Was that what it meant, to be fifth level? I'd never seen a definitive list of what various level mediums could or couldn't do—maybe because ghosts weren't like flash cards. They weren't just circles or squares, red or blue or yellow. "That kid in there...I didn't wanna be slimed, okay?"

"We'll go back later. Take another look."

I stared at his notepad from my seat across the table. I couldn't read it upside down, but Zig was staring at it like it was some kind of talisman. He reminded me of Jacob, smart and bullheaded, and unwilling to stop chewing at something when he thought he was right. I wondered if Zigler was a shield, too. Or just an average guy.

"What about the homeless lady?" I asked him.

"What about her? Did you get a good look at her?"

Not really. She'd been on a gurney, covered with a blanket. I couldn't have pegged either her height or her weight, and the homeless are notoriously difficult to pin ages on. Besides, my eyes had been on the cloudy black thing more than on her. I shrugged. "I guess not."

"We could canvas, try to find her, but with no name and no description other than the fact that she was brought in by EMTs yesterday, it'll be nothing but a waste of time, and we both know it."

Time in which we could be watching the same repeaters doing the same shit, over and over and over. I pinched the bridge of my nose and reminded my internal faucet that I'd like the remote viewer watching me to eat shit and die.

"What was that blood alcohol content again?" I asked Zig.

He glanced at his pad. "Point one eight."

I gave a low whistle. No wonder she was on wheels. Walking's a challenge at point one five. "What I don't get is how she ever got hooked on drinking at all."

"I don't follow you."

"Cause and effect. Let's say she's got some mediumship talent. She senses something paranormal. She doesn't like it. And every time she hits the bottle to try and get away from it, things only amp up. We might be stupid, but our bodies aren't. Eventually she'd have to figure out that booze is a psyactive."

"No it's not."

Zigler and I both stared at one other like we'd each sprouted a second head. "It is," I said finally. Because I have such snappy comebacks.

"You trained, what, fifteen years ago? You must be working off old research. If anything, alcohol has a neutral to negative effect on talent. The results are similar to motor skills tests. Alcohol eventually dampens down psychic talent, if you consume it at a high enough level."

Okay, if I kept on denying that booze was an antipsyactive, he'd only start rattling off actual figures: rates and percentages and all that meaningless BS.

I let him think that he'd had the final say on the matter, and I stewed on it. And I really had to bite my tongue to keep from telling him that at the moment, he reminded me an awful lot of Jacob, since that'd probably give him the willies. "I'll be right back," I said, and I made a beeline for the restroom.

It was clean enough, and luckily, empty. I ducked into a stall and dialed my cell.

"Sticks and Stones."

"Oh good, you're there."

"Well, I tried setting out a tip jar and letting everyone use the honor system so they could shop here whether I was around or not, but that didn't really work out so hot."

I sighed before I could stop myself. One of these days I'd be prepared for a conversation with Crash. I just wasn't sure when that'd be. "Alcohol," I said. "Is it a psyactive or not?"

Silence on his end. Or, more accurately, breathing, and the sound of a radio playing in the background, and a cash register. I wondered if maybe we were experiencing some kind of cell phone weirdness where I could hear him, but not the other way around, when finally he answered. "So that's what the other night was all about. Which effect were you aiming for? I thought you were asking me about uppers."

"I...was."

"So why'd you go all frat party on me?"

"You told me to. You told me there was a bottle of vodka in your freezer."

"Well, yeah. Because you were freaking out. I thought a stiff shot or two would calm you down. I didn't think you'd drink half the bottle and pass out in my bed."

I sighed again. Damn it. "Could we not go into detail on the phone? Just answer me. Alcohol. Psyactive?"

"No, not really. Not anywhere I've ever read."

But it was. It had to be. Lisa told me so, and Lisa's always right. "Okay, thanks." I hit disconnect before Crash could provide any additional detail about my proudest moments to the FPMP wiretappers. I called Lisa, figuring she might be willing to talk about it since it was more of a Psych-school question than a *si-no*, but I got her voice mail and hung up.

Zig and I went back to see if the Haunted Partition was between patients yet. Unfortunately, Doctor Gillmore's assessment about mid-week ER traffic didn't pan out, and every time someone was wheeled out of there, the second it was wiped down, someone else was carted, carried or dragged in.

"Take one more look," Zig said. "The guy in there now, he's just laying there. He won't mind."

"He's unconscious...."

"Like I said."

I peeked through the curtain. It was a middle-aged Caucasian, hefty. Very still, but his heart rate monitor seemed to be beeping regularly. Gillmore was waiting for some test results, and meanwhile, she'd gone to check someone else. I had five minutes, maybe more. But I still didn't care to go snooping around an unconscious guy. "With my luck, I'll knock his IV out."

"There's a clear path, right there. Come on. I really think there's something about this partition."

The waiting room was packed, and it didn't look like the exam areas would empty out anytime that day, so I figured I'd just go in there again, look around, and then Zig and I could try Plan B. Or whatever letter we were on at that point.

I looked both ways to make sure there weren't any medical personnel running toward the partition, and I slipped in. The fabric walls did nothing to block out the sounds of the room beyond. If anything, it was worse being inside the enclosure and hearing all the noise without being able to see the source. I reminded myself that when I heard ghostly voices, the sound wasn't being processed by my actual ears, and I did my best to listen.

Nothing.

I squeezed past the heart monitor and the fabric wall, and slipped behind the exam table. It was a tight fit. A bigger guy wouldn't have managed. Still nothing. I could tell Zig there was nothing to see.

As I touched the exam table to avoid tripping over an extension cord, a chill raced up my arm. I touched the stainless steel surface to make sure the table wasn't just positioned under a weird vent, but no. The table itself wasn't cold. I looked around. Nothing. I squinted, hard. Still nothing. Damn it.

I managed to ease out without pulling the guy's plug or knocking anything down, and I told Zig, "Okay, maybe. But I'm not getting much. A cold spot."

"Really?" He seemed awfully pleased with himself. "You're sure."

"I said there was a cold spot."

"No visual. No verbal."

Like I'd be able to hear squat with all the beeping and rattling and crying and screaming. "What do you want me to say?"

Zig grabbed me by the arm—the first time he'd ever touched me—and hauled me over to the opening of the partition. "Show me where, exactly."

More touching from the other side, this time a shove from a no-nonsense nurse who barked, "Excuse me," and then gave me a filthy look. She looked at a chart on the foot of the exam table, then shot a syringe into a shunt on the IV.

I backed off. "We can't do this while there's a patient in there."

"We can't afford not to do it." Zig stepped in close and lowered his voice. "Forty percent. What if he dies because we didn't get a better look at that cold spot?"

"Not the stats again."

"Why can't you see it? Does that mean it's weak?"

I shook my head.

"Or maybe that it's strong," he said, too damn stubborn to give it a rest, "and it's making itself invisible to you on purpose?"

"It's a cold spot, Zigler. How the fuck am I supposed to know?"

A passing nurse glanced at us, then looked away quickly. Zig stared at me, pop-eyed and stunned. Once he got over his surprise, his expression hardened. "How you got certified at level five is beyond me."

✦ TWENTY-FIVE ✦

I left Zigler with his damned notepad and went in the hallway to cool off. The whole conversation about alcohol was still bugging me. I would've assumed Zig had read a bad article or had his wires crossed, what with all the papers and journals he tries to keep up with. But Crash was a Psych himself. And he'd actually agreed with a cop's opinion for a change.

I was wearing a groove in the linoleum by pacing back and forth in front of a water fountain when a hospital security guard approached. He was as tall as me, and a lot wider. Great. Now I'd have to deal with some flunked-out cop who thought he could prove himself by kicking a PsyCop out of the hospital. "What?" I snapped.

He held out a cell phone. "Agent Dreyfuss wants to talk to you."

A chill ran through me that had nothing to do with cold spots. I'd been at LaSalle less than two weeks, and already the FPMP had maneuvered their own men into place. Suddenly I felt like a real moron for biting Zig's head off. With the FPMP breathing down my neck, I needed all the friends I could get.

I held the stranger's phone to my ear, careful not to press it against my cheek. "Hello?"

"Detective Bayne?" asked a calm, female voice. The Asian secretary, what was her name? Something really white. Lauren? Laura. "I'll connect you to Agent Dreyfuss."

There were a couple of clicks, and then the man himself came on. "You're still at LaSalle looking for hay, huh?" he asked me. "How's that going for you?"

"Fine," I lied.

"Good. Glad to hear it. How's about an afternoon of coffee, conversation, and minimal chances of being stuck with a hepatitis-laced needle?"

I'd rather take my chances with the needle stick. But Jacob was eager for me to talk to Doctor Chance, so I figured I should take Dreyfuss up on his offer—although I probably shouldn't act so excited about it. "I dunno," I said, and I wondered what I could ask him for that wouldn't seem out of character. He'd materialized ten grand like it was nothing. More cash? It would make for a good escape fund. "I might need...cab fare."

"You drove with Zigler, I suppose. Well, I'm sure Ben would be happy to play chauffeur. Just say the word."

Oh, great. I'd just succeeded in setting myself up for a really awkward car ride. "I mean, I'm short on cash," I clarified. So smooth.

Dreyfuss thought about that for a second, then had a hearty laugh at my expense, which made me feel like even more of a dope. "Understood, Detective. Take care of some more of these cold spots, and there'll be a nice envelope waiting for you at the end of your shift."

Ben creeped me out less than Officer "Andy," but only slightly less. I searched for some details to remember about the turnoff to the FPMP underground lot, but there wasn't much to take note of. I finally settled on a lamppost across the street, then glanced in the sideview mirror and counted back. Four from the last intersection. That would have to do.

We went up the elevator, and Laura looked up from the big, curved desk. "Hello, Detective. Can I get you anything to drink?"

"I'm fine." I wasn't. Lately I'd been sweating at the drop of a hat, but the inside of my mouth was bone dry at the first sign of stress. I felt in my pocket for a piece of gum, and my hand brushed my holster through my sportcoat. I was carrying again, and no one seemed very worried about it. Which worried me.

Laura showed me into the waiting room where Dreyfuss was hovering around the coffee service. "Having your house fumigated?" he asked me.

My stomach clenched up. What was he talking about now? Bugs? I was so sick of games. "Not that I know of. Why—should I?"

"Ha ha, that's a good one. I was just curious where you spent the night. I suppose you're welcome to sleep wherever you want. We're all adults here. It's a free country."

Was it? I jammed a stick of gum into my mouth and fought a wave of anxiety-induced nausea.

"If you're keen on a little vacation, I could set you up with a couple of first-class tickets. Where are you looking to go?"

I wondered if the remote viewer cued him in to the "let's go to Canada" conversation I'd had...or rather, that Jacob had with me, when his dick was stuffed down my throat. I chewed my gum harder, and noted that my jaw ached. It would give me great satisfaction to stick that gumwad under the rim of some expensive piece of furniture when Dreyfuss wasn't looking, but that would only be inviting a clairsentient to come along and use it to get a bead on me.

"No travel plans at the moment," I said. "Y'know. New house and all."

"Well. You need anything, you know who to call." He smiled. His teeth were very white, and very even, at odds with his shoulder-length hair that looked like it needed a good combing, and probably a trim. "You really wowed me on your last visit. I think it's time I initiate you into the inner circle."

"How many babies will you need to sacrifice?"

"You're too much! C'mon, let's mosey on into my office."

We went down a short hall and through another doorway. Whether this was actually his office, or whether it was some kind of test, there was really no way for me to know. It occurred to me, just as he pushed the door open, that I might find something behind it with Camp Hell associations. Something like an empty desk. Or something like....

Ghosts.

Movement flickered on either side of me in my peripheral vision, and the cold felt like I had just opened the big beer cooler at the corner store. I expected my breath to puff out of me in a visible cloud. It didn't, of course. But it felt like it should have.

Dreyfuss said, "I thought it might take a few more visits to bring you around to my way of thinking. What was it that made you change your mind?"

Crap. Why did he have to keep talking to me? The more he chatted, the more obvious it would be that I was uncomfortable—incredibly fucking uncomfortable. "Richie looked pretty good," I said. Which was the truth. He did look good. He seemed genuinely happy, too. "I figured if he was okay with the FPMP, then I might want to reconsider. Not that I've made up my mind yet, or anything. Where is Richie, anyway? You didn't send him swimming in the Chicago River in concrete shoes when I said I would come over today, did you?"

"Richie's fine, just fine. He's working in the basement today. Should we go down and say hello, just to put your mind at ease?"

The basement—did he engineer that on purpose? And how dangerous would it be for me to tell him to fuck off? "Uh, no. That's fine. Just checking."

Dreyfuss walked over to his desk and bent across it. He pushed a button on his phone. "Laura? You want to dial Richie's cell for me and put him on?"

"Of course, Agent."

The thing flickering in the peripheral vision on my left resolved itself into a repeater getting shot. Bullets took him in the thigh, the hip, the shoulder. That last one spun him around, and he sprayed blood. I turned and tried to find somewhere else to look. I think I looked casual enough. Another repeater ducked a bullet only to catch one in the throat. Great. I really wanted to see that.

My eyes went to Dreyfuss. He had on jeans and a T-shirt today, and a loose hooded sweatshirt, unzipped and hanging open. No gun. Not unless he had an ankle holster—and who wears ankle holsters anymore? They're practically impossible to reach, and you'll probably get kicked in the face while you're trying.

"Richie says there's a cold spot in here. I have him bless the room every Monday, but according to him, they still stick around. Now, I've got no way of checking up on him, but it seems to me that if he was trying to make himself look good, he'd tell me the problem was all gone. What's your take on that?"

"Richie is honest to a fault." He also didn't have the mental capacity to cook up an elaborate scheme. Or even a very simple scheme.

"True. But I'm not talking about Richie. What do you think of the cold spots?"

"I'm surprised you don't put on an extra sweater when you come in." I hadn't meant to be quite so honest. But at least I didn't tell him I could see them.

I think it worked to my advantage, saying something before I had considered it carefully, or really, at all. Dreyfuss broke into a smile. But before he could try to milk any more information from me, his intercom beeped. "Sir? Richie is on the line."

"Thank you, Laura." The sound quality changed, with a slight hiss indicating connection to a cell phone that was at two bars or less. "How're you doing, Richie?"

"Hello, Agent Dreyfuss. Do you need me to come upstairs?"

"Victor Bayne is here, and he just wanted to say hello."

Dreyfuss prompted me with his eyes. "Hello, Richie," I said.

"Hi, Vic! You should have come earlier. They had lasagna for lunch. You like lasagna, don't you?"

"Yeah, it's fine. Listen, the cold spots in Agent Dreyfuss' office—you've been working on them?"

"Yeah, what a pain. I try to clean them out every Monday, but then they're back again the next time I check. You think you can do anything about it? You will try, won't you? I get so tired of doing the same thing over and over, you know?"

Richie's bald-faced honesty was painful to hear. Anyone else would be worried that I was out for their job, but not him. He just wanted the problem solved. He might not be able to see or hear what I did, but when you thought about it, he was probably the best damned medium that Dreyfuss could hope to have.

"I won't keep you," I said. "I just wanted to say hi."

"We should get together sometime. But not Saturday. I'm in a bowling league. Unless you bowl. Do you bowl?"

I tried to imagine Richie slinging a 20-pound ball down a lane and had to stop myself from smiling. It felt too vulnerable to let Dreyfuss see me smile.

"Uh, no. Some other time, then."

"So, these cold spots," Dreyfuss said, once he turned off the intercom. "You read any more into them?"

I debated how much to tell him. We both knew damn well that I saw more than I was willing to say. But there had to be some way of making it seem like I was telling him almost as much as I knew. I figured I would feed him a little more information and see how he took it.

"This one over here." I reached out as if I would touch the repeater who'd gotten spun around by the bullets, but I stopped just short of it. "I feel...impact." I touched my thigh where the bullet hit the repeater. Theatrical. Not like me. Did Dreyfuss know that? Not unless he had video cameras on me, or the remote viewer was incredibly descriptive. And if the remote viewer really was that good, I imagine they would have him spying on Castro, or Donald Trump, or Bill Gates...or anyone but me. I touched my hip, absently, the way Crash touched his stomach when he was reading other people's feelings.

"I see." He saw, all right. He saw that I could tell someone was gunned down here once upon a time. I wished I had toned down the theatrics. "Can you take care of it?"

"You mean exorcise it? I wouldn't even know where to begin."

"I could have Richie assist you."

"No, I don't think so. Bible verses? You've got to believe in that stuff for it to work for you. I'm what you might call a skeptic."

"The FPMP doesn't endorse any particular religious affiliation. You need different gear? I'll get it. I'll even order it from your friend. Tell him to mark it up if he wants—I won't quibble on the price. What do you need? Voudoun? High magic? Say the word, and it's here."

I wanted to tell him that unless Richie eventually wore the repeaters down by visiting them every single Monday, he was stuck with them, and their bullet holes, and their blood spray. And, in fact, that I hoped they seriously creeped him out.

But then I surprised myself. "Get me the latest information on exorcism, and I'll see what I can do."

"Done, and done. Laura will have it couriered to your place tonight. I'd assume that's where you'll be, anyway."

I didn't dignify the remark about my hotel stay with a response. "Unless there's anything else, I'll be on my way."

"Report back here in the morning. LaSalle can wait. I'll send a car for you."

"I can drive."

"What about your cab fare?"

"I haven't done anything for you today."

"Your blue-collar ethic is refreshing. Psychics don't get paid for results, Detective. They get paid for their time. Because until somebody invents a Geiger counter that tells them whether the Psychs have produced any measurable effects, who's to say if any work has been done or not?"

I thought of Doctor Chance and her GhosTV, and had to force myself to keep from rubbing goosebumps off my arms. "If I could just use the john before I go."

Dreyfuss pointed through yet another repeater, a gunshot victim just like the others, and indicated a door. "Use my private powder room. It's got a solid gold toilet and a roll of hundred dollar bills to wipe your ass with."

I must have been giving him a Richie-look.

"Just kidding—but there is a bidet. Pretty swanky."

I really didn't want to spend any amount of time in the same room where he shot water up his bunghole. But I needed to talk to Chance. "Just make sure you turn off the video cameras before I piss."

"Do you seriously think I would plant mechanical eyes in my own crapper? I gotta draw the line somewhere."

Given how many people had been gunned down in his office, I wasn't planning on entrusting myself to his line-drawing skills any more than I had to.

I locked the bathroom door and looked around. Dreyfuss was right. It was pretty swanky, and there were no paranormal film loops of people getting shot to death, either. I focused on white light and my third eye, and tried to suck in as much power as I could. Then I thought about Doctor Chance, and hoped that my *need* to talk to her would override the fact that I really didn't *want* to.

Hopefully, Chance would sense me reaching out to her, and respond. That's how it was with those Victorian table-rappers, right? They held séances and summoned spirits. They were mostly hoaxes, so I guess that didn't count. Still, you had to wonder if maybe the occasional spiritualist was legit.

I turned the water on and watched it run. "Doctor Chance," I whispered, low. Because Dreyfuss had told me he wouldn't be filming me in the bathroom, but I didn't recall him saying it wasn't bugged. "Are you there? Can you hear me?"

Maybe Dreyfuss' office was out of range. Did I need to get back into that boardroom? I supposed it was possible. I'd need to lie, maybe say that I saw something that I wanted to check out. What? A trail of bloody footprints? I was weighing the likelihood that Dreyfuss would fall for the footprint ruse when Chance's reflection appeared in the mirror beside me.

I couldn't help it. I jumped.

"I would think you'd be more difficult to startle," she said.

"Shh, he's right out there."

She glanced over her shoulder, which gave me a gruesome new angle to see into the bullet hole in her forehead. "Then you'd better keep your voice down. But it's not as if he can hear me."

True. "How did you know I was here? Did you feel me trying to contact you?"

She looked puzzled. "I don't know. I just came here on impulse. What else have I got to do with my time but check up on the people who work here?"

"So you do know what they're up to."

"Keep your voice down." She crossed her arms and looked peevish. "I might."

"I need to know where those faxes are coming from. Have there been any more?"

"Yesterday, actually. Assuming that my sense of time passing is in any way accurate. Which it probably isn't."

My voice shook with the effort of keeping it quiet. "Who was it from?" I said carefully.

"Don't know. I didn't get a good look at it before Dreyfuss shredded it. It was the same handwriting though—I could see that much."

She had to be yanking my chain. She was a ghost, for Christ's sake. If she wanted to see the fax, she could have appeared beside it before it hit the shredder. "Okay...is there anything I can do to help you remember more clearly?"

"Are you trying to bribe me?"

"If that's what it takes."

"What could you possibly do for me? I'm dead."

Maybe Chance thought that death was a huge barrier, but I'd dealt with enough dead people to know they could be motivated. "What about your amplifier? Tell me where you hid the prototypes and I'll take up where you left off. I'll make sure everyone knows it was you who started it all."

She stared at me, thinking. That was good. She didn't shoot the idea down, not right off.

"It worked, you know," I told her. "In the hotel room—I made it work."

"Damn it." She whirled around and disappeared through the wall.

I waited for a long time for her to come back. The water ran. I wondered how long it'd been. Agent Dreyfuss was right there on the other side of the door. *Damn it* was right.

I peed—furtively, because I didn't know who was watching—just in case there was some kind of sensor in the toilet that would monitor whether I'd used it or not. And then I could've kicked myself. Because if the toilet was monitored, I bet it could analyze my urine for drugs. Sonofa....

"Roger Burke knows where the amplifiers are."

I buttoned my fly, fast.

"Roger's not keen on telling me much." I washed my hands. Actual towels hung beside the sink. I looked around for a paper towel dispenser, or even one of those blow-dry things. There was none.

"You've spoken to him? How is he?"

"His usual charming self." I patted my hands against the towel without moving it from its bar. Then I finished by wiping them on my pant legs. "Trying to get me to do a 180 on my testimony to reduce his sentence. Guess you can't blame a guy for trying."

"You can do that?"

Hadn't it occurred to her? Maybe not. She didn't work in law enforcement like Roger and me. "I don't think anyone would buy it. How can I just walk in there and say I had it all wrong when I testified?"

"But I gave you Amytal Sodium. Several doses. Can't you tell them you were confused? It's not unheard of for it to do strange things to your memory."

And my memory was turning out to be a hell of a lot patchier than I thought. "I don't know."

"I know you're angry at me because we weren't straightforward with you about the amplifier," she said. Nice understatement. "But don't leave Roger in prison, not if something you do or say can get him out. I'll stick to that fax machine, I swear I will, and I'll make sure I find out who's sending them. How about that?"

I'd now been washing my hands for, what? Ten minutes? I'm sure that didn't seem suspicious at all. I debated whether or not I should make some vomiting noises to explain my absence. "And the amplifiers," I said. "Tell me where they are. I know there are two more left. I want to get to one before Roger does."

"I won't—not until you change your testimony."

The thought of lying under oath, shuffling my story around to get a guilty bastard off, sat hard and cold in the pit of my stomach. But every time I turned around, the deck was stacked higher in its favor.

"Someone you're in regular contact with is reporting to Dreyfuss," she said. "Can you really afford not to know who it is?"

And there it was. The tipping point. Fuck.

"Then keep your eye on the fax machine," I told her. "I can't guarantee whether they'll believe me or not, but I'll recant."

✦ TWENTY-SIX ✦

My land line wasn't bugged—the gym monkeys had told me so. And if the line wasn't secure at the other end of my phone call, well, that was the FBI's problem. All the digging and delving I'd been doing with Stefan over the past couple of weeks had really paid off. I gave an Oscar-worthy account of going under, flashing back to the Bed and Breakfast, and realizing that Roger had no idea that he was kidnapping me. I framed Chance as the mastermind. She'd been the one to shoot me full of Amytal, after all. And evidently they already thought she was crazy, since she'd been on her way to psychiatric evaluation when she was scooped up and killed.

Although the agent's stray comment about the good doctor being "at large" made the queasiness I'd been fighting crank up several more notches. The FBI didn't know Chance was dead, and I did. What the fuck was the world coming to?

I pulled something out of the fridge and ate it for dinner without tasting it, then forgot what it was as soon as my plate was in the dishwasher. A cascade of lies filtered through my brain as I went through the motions of cutting, chewing, swallowing. And with every lie, I reminded myself that I was going to have to tell Jacob what I'd done, that I'd spun a story that might get a murderer off, all in the interest of figuring out who was whispering behind my back to the FPMP.

Jacob burst through the door and grabbed me up from the couch by my upper arms. He mashed me into his chest. His wool overcoat smelled like winter. "I don't want to get too excited," he said, "but Carolyn thinks I might be able to block her."

I tried to shake off the disappointment I'd been wallowing in and be happy—

because he was on the verge of something big, and maybe he was the happiest guy in the world. And because I'd finally given *him* something for a change. That made me feel a little bit better. "You're sure."

"No completely. But there's definitely...something. I wish I had more Psychs to practice with and work out the details."

"Who else could you test it out on? Lisa? Crash?"

"I was thinking of that precog PsyCop on the west side. I put a call in to his precinct."

"I know you're excited and all—and I am too—but do you really want to show a stranger what you can do?"

Jacob slung his coat over the back of the couch and sat down beside me. "I hadn't given it any thought. I just wanted to know...."

"Yeah. I get it. But once the cat's out of the bag, there's no turning back." I should know. Telling someone about a single fucking car crash put me on a roller coaster that took me through two institutions and the Police Academy. I took Jacob's hand and held it between both of mine in my lap. "Maybe you could practice with Lisa, see how it works over the phone."

"You think it would?"

"I dunno. What if you're the reason the remote viewer has trouble keeping tabs on us?"

"There has to be some way we can test it...."

We both flinched at the sound of our doorbell. It was an industrial buzz that could wake the dead, and we hadn't yet gotten around to replacing it with something that wasn't designed to be heard over the noise of heavy machinery.

My holster was lying on the coffee table. I pocketed my gun before the two of us went to the front door.

A guy in a baseball cap with "Fleet Delivery" embroidered above the bill stood on our doorstep with a huge banker box in his hands. "Victor Bayne?" He had an Eastern European accent, and he managed to give my last name two syllables. And then I remembered that Dreyfuss promised he'd send me something that passed for Psych research these days.

"...yeah."

"Where you want I put this?"

If he was an FPMP spy, he had a really good disguise. Particularly the five-day B.O. he was working on. I backed away from the door and into Jacob, who gave in once I pressed on him, and backed away, too.

I signed the clipboard, Jacob tipped the guy a five, and then we both stared down at the box on our vestibule floor. "I went and saw Dreyfuss today."

Jacob gave the box a meaningful look, then hustled me into the bathroom and turned on the radio. "Go on."

"I talked to Doctor Chance, like you wanted me to."

"Can she figure out where the faxes are coming from?"

"Maybe. She said she'd try."

"You think she really will?"

I massaged the back of my neck. My phone call to the FBI had left me feeling battered and sore. "She's not doing it for me." I sighed, hoping that some new air in my lungs would make me feel a little bit cleaner. It didn't. "I had to recant my testimony to try to get Burke off."

"When?"

"Today. I did it already. It's done."

I snuck a look at him to see if I'd managed to kill all the joy that he'd been basking in over his newfound talent. His eyebrows were drawn down, and the crease between them was deep. He was thinking hard.

"You think what you told the Feds was plausible?"

"Maybe. Chance coached me. Said that Amytal could have affected my memories. Plus, I figured that my sessions with Stefan were dredging up so much buried shit, who's to say that one of those things wasn't my night in the hotel room with the GhosTV?"

"And Roger Burke has no way of knowing that Chance talked you into it. Right?"

Weird. I'd been so caught up in Chance that I hadn't thought much about him. "I don't see how he could."

"Good. Let him know, and make it sound like it was all him. He promised to give you the FPMP. See what he's got. Now what about this box?"

"It's psych research," I said. "I was trying to figure out what the FPMP had that I would want...and it was the best I could come up with."

I followed Jacob back into the vestibule where the box sat on the floor, looking mundane. He picked it up and hauled it into the main room. He set it on the dining room table and gave it his best interrogation-look. He ran his hand over the top of the box, then broke the seal and carefully lifted the cover.

For just a second, I imagined a flash, and a detonation. But no, a bomb wouldn't make any sense. Dreyfuss needed me to clean up his repeaters. And besides, a bomb would be too hard to cover up. It'd be a bitch to keep a big explosion on a residential, inner-city street out of the news. Anthrax, or maybe ricin? That seemed a little more like the FPMP's style.

Jacob lifted some bound reports out of the box. Still, nothing exploded. "Keith and Manny say that books are the perfect hiding place for transmitters."

It never fucking ended. "Do you want them to come over and scan the box?"

"I want to be able to speak freely with you."

"Fine. Whatever. Just...don't invite them to hang around for beers or anything. I don't feel very sociable at the moment."

"In and out." Jacob picked up the top report and thumbed through it. "And assuming that they're clean...I can't wait to read these."

I peeked into the open box while Jacob called his friends on the land line. Reports. Dozens of them. Books, too. With catchy titles like *Statistical Analysis of Precognitive Subjects, Levels 3 - 4*. I glazed over before I'd read beyond the title.

Jacob, on the other hand, was raring to go. He even put on a pot of coffee. It was going to be a long night—but at least he and I were on the same page.

Manny, or Keith, who's to say which was which, dropped by with the big metal detector and gave the scary box an all-clear. Then Jacob and I settled in to do some serious reading.

The most relevant book I found in the stack was less than a hundred pages long, hardbound with a plain cover stamped *Paranormal Eradication: A Modern Approach to Exorcism*. No thumping bedframes or pea soup vomit in this one. Six case studies of modern exorcism, each one more bone-dry than the last. I skimmed.

"Says here they use a different scale of ability in Japan," Jacob said without looking up from the report he'd been working his way through. "No levels. More like X-Y axis personality profiles."

I had no idea what that meant. "Uh huh."

"Kind of makes you wonder how accurate the Western seven-level, six-talent classification system really is."

A draft snuck through a window in need of tuckpointing and hit me on the back of the neck, and I realized I'd just broken into a sweat. I shrugged off my flannel shirt and let it fall beside me on the floor, but even so, my armpits and the crooks of my knees felt clammy and wet.

I stared down at the page, which looked like nothing more than a gray blur of ink and paper now, and told myself to get it together. It was just Jacob, and just a passing observation. Nothing to be scared of.

Sweat beaded my upper lip. I went to the bathroom and splashed my face, blotted it dry. I gave myself a hard look in the mirror, and reminded myself that Jacob had only remarked on something I'd been thinking myself for a hell of a long time. That's all.

I coaxed myself out of the bathroom and found Jacob still engrossed in the report. "D'you maybe want to take a look at this exorcism book for me? I think I need a cheat sheet."

And just like that, Jacob switched gears, started plowing through the insanely dull exorcism book so that I didn't have to. I felt a little bad. But mostly relieved.

I'm not sure how far into the reading-bee I dozed off. Once I thought about it, I recalled moving over to the recliner when the dining room chair and I realized that neither one of us had enough padding to extend our acquaintance beyond an hour or so. And then I started rubbing my eyes, and decided it would be a good idea to rest them. Just for a minute or two.

I woke up to Jacob running the backs of his fingers down my cheek. Everything was dark except a light shining out of the loft from our bedroom. But even in the mostly-dark, I could see him smiling at me. "You coming to bed, or do you want me to leave you here?"

It was a great recliner, but I'm more of a side-sleeper. And besides, my back feels naked without Jacob curled against it.

Jacob tried to give me a crash course in exorcism while I ate my corn flakes, but even with him explaining it to me from the point of view of various religious disciplines, I still found my mind drifting to my day's to-do list, and my eyes drifting to the vee of his unbuttoned dress shirt, where a few of his chest hairs beckoned from the top of his crewneck undershirt.

I did gather this much: different religions and different disciplines each approached exorcism in their own special way—and supposedly all of these methods worked, to some extent, depending on the strength of the practitioner, and the stubbornness of the paranormal infestation.

Which all seems like common sense, when you think about it. But my common sense wasn't telling me which method would work for me. It only told me that I'd feel like a phony if I cracked open a bible like Richie, or swore by the sword of Saint Barbara like Miss Mattie. So that meant I had to figure it out for myself.

I called the Fifth and took a personal day while Jacob got ready for work with one hand and one eye on a psy-manual. "When do you have to give these back?" he asked me.

"I dunno." I was sure the FPMP kept multiple copies. "Maybe never."

Jacob swung by me where I brooded beside the coffee pot and gave me a mouthwash-flavored kiss. "You're sure you don't want me to go downtown with you?"

"They won't let both of us in to see Burke," I said, which I knew that he knew. "You weren't involved in his case. And it's not like we're his family."

"Don't go there, mister." Jacob kissed me again, then ran his fingertips down my forearm. "There's creepy, and then there's creepy."

I watched the vestibule door as Jacob left, heard his Crown Vic's engine turn over, and then settle into a low purr as the car pulled away. I felt very, very alone without Jacob there, but free to flex my talent, too.

I could think of a few things that amped up my talent. The GhosTV was the most high-tech, but I wouldn't be able to get my hands on one of those until I coaxed their location out of Doctor Chance. Alcohol was an option, but everyone insisted it wasn't really a psyactive after all—and besides, it wouldn't be a good idea for me to show up at the prison smelling like a brewery. And there was High John the Conqueror, which came in bath salt or soap form. And which I still had a rash from, thank you very much.

If only I had a practice ghost to exorcise. I could hunt down Tiffany, the dead girl in the alleyway, but it seemed rude to exorcise someone I knew. I'd rather start on a repeater, but all the repeaters I could think of were in such public places that I'd probably get carted off to the loony bin for trying to erase them.

I glanced at the clock. I needed to get moving. Preparing for an exorcism wasn't like studying for a test. I'd have to wait and try it on the real deal once I was faced with an actual ghost. I drove downtown, parked in an outrageously-priced lot, and locked my gun in my glovebox so I didn't have to deal with checking it in at the desk. And then I headed in to the Metropolitan Correctional building to give Roger Burke the "good" news.

The wheels of injustice would take a few days to grind into motion, but for now there was a scarred plastic tabletop between me and my buddy in orange. As much as he needed me to recant, I think that on some level, it disgusted the ex-cop in him that I'd done it. Sure, he'd been punching two time clocks: the Buffalo PD's and the FPMP's, but in his heart of hearts, I doubted he saw himself as a dirty cop. Not if he actually got both jobs done.

Burke sat with his shackled hands folded in his lap and his head high, glaring at me as I wrote on the notepad I hardly ever used. "Here's the structure," he said, taking no pains to talk slowly enough for me to get everything down. "Headquarters in D.C., but most of the work done in the regional branches. New York, Chicago, Seattle, Vegas and L.A.—those are the cities with their own branches."

Vegas? Shit. Maybe the Joneses weren't hiding in plain sight quite as well as they thought, after all.

Iowa, Minnesota and Wisconsin had one poor sap trying to keep tabs on all the Psychs spread over all those miles of rolling cornfields, not to mention Minneapolis-St. Paul, Milwaukee, and Des Moines. Missouri's director was in the doghouse for the kidnapping debacle—the very same one that had put Roger, and me, in this piss-and-disinfectant-smelling meeting room in the MCC.

Burke gave me the names of each and every one. They were all men—no big surprise there. They were probably all white, too. And each and every one in the Midwest answered to Dreyfuss.

"Why'd you start off by giving me the name of the top guy?" I asked. I didn't necessarily expect an honest answer, but I might get some insight into the way Roger Burke ticked.

"You think this is some kind of poker game? Every day I'm in this place is another day I could get shanked with a sharpened pen. Besides, if there's a bigger mindfuck than Dreyfuss, I've never met him."

Seeing as how Dreyfuss' office was my very next stop, the confirmation of my suspicions about him made me feel oh so much better.

Then he started in on the addresses. He knew them all by heart, and he was able to spit them all out without any hesitation. Even the Chicago office. And that one checked out, as far as I knew. The street, the number, it all looked right to me.

"So what do you suggest I do with all these names, other than shove them up my ass?"

"You'd probably enjoy that." His mean smile was back. "I gave you what I promised. If you can't figure out what to do with it, that's your problem, not mine."

I'd suspected he would say something like that. The worst part about it was that it was true. Still, Burke had always thought he could run mental circles around me—and when you think about it, he could. But if he had a weakness, it was that he was in love with how smart he was. "So the FPMP is everywhere. What does that mean for me? What do they even do?" I considered baiting him, implying that maybe he'd always been too low on the ladder to know. But I figured that was laying it on a little thick.

"You've seen what they do. They watch."

"Why? Why the hell should they care about what I'm doing?"

His nasty little smile widened. "What do you think would happen if foreign intelligence pinpointed you as the next Marie Saint Savon?"

I imagined myself having a long chat with Lenin inside his glass coffin. Through a translator, of course. "They would...try to hire me?"

Burke laughed. It was an ugly little bark, a perfect match to his smile. "Okay, Boy Scout. You go right on thinking that."

Was that so farfetched? After all, the first thing Dreyfuss had me do once I'd returned his call was to clean up the board room. Roger gloated, and I stared him right in the eye. Finally, when he realized I wasn't going to prompt him, he let me in on his little joke. "Why should they risk bringing a double agent into their inner sanctums? Much quicker to put a bullet through your head and be done with it."

"But how would that...?"

"Where do you think all the remote viewers go? To the Bahamas?"

I swallowed hard, and did my best not to lose my corn flakes all over that graffiti-covered tabletop. "So all those creepy cops who aren't really cops—and Dreyfuss, too—you're saying that they're actually looking out for me? That they've been protecting me this whole time?"

Burke's smile reached his eyes. He really was enjoying our little talk.

"Give me the locations of Doctor Chance's transmitters," I said. I felt exhausted. My voice was small and dry, as if the volume had run out.

"Now why would I want to do that? I might need a favor from you someday. It wouldn't be very smart of me to give away that information for free."

I stood up. I had gotten my names and my addresses, and that was all I could expect to get from Roger Burke. Maybe Dreyfuss was the biggest mindfuck he knew. I guess it takes one to know one. I'd tell him to look in the mirror, but he'd probably take it as a compliment.

"Pleasure doing business with you, Detective."

I was all out of witty replies. I made for the door.

"One more thing."

I looked over at my shoulder at him. Maybe he'd tell me what it would take to get the locations of the GhosTVs from him. And maybe it would be a price I'd be willing to pay. I had no doubt it would cost me dearly, but maybe it was something I could part with. "The transmitters?"

"You wish." He gloated. "No. Of course not. But there was one name I neglected to give you."

I wanted to wipe that smile off his face so bad that when I clenched my fist, it ached to punch him. "Watch it, asshole. There's nothing stopping me from calling the FBI and saying that I was confused about being confused."

He did a *que sera sera* shrug. "You keep on tarnishing your reputation, eventually you won't have anything left to polish. But that's up to you. See, the reason I can't give you that final name is that I don't know it."

I stared. Because I knew he hated it when I stared at him.

"The assassin," he said, once he'd gotten sick of my staring. "No one knows who he is." He raised one hand to his forehead and mimicked shooting a bullet—straight into the spot where Chance had gotten plugged. The other hand, shackled, came with it. But even that didn't ruin the effect. "The FPMP, Detective Bayne, is like a mean, crazy dog. He'll make the crackheads think twice about pissing in your front yard. But keep your eye on him, or the second your back is turned, he'll maul you."

✦ TWENTY-SEVEN ✦

My phone rang while I was on my way to the Chicago branch of the FPMP, whose official address was recorded in a little book that I'd locked in my glovebox once I'd taken my gun out. I checked the number to decide whether or not I should answer. It was Zigler's cell.

"Hello?"

"Where are you? I've been trying to get ahold of you all morning."

"I called in," I said. I decided not to tell him that my phone had been in a locker at Metropolitan Correctional when he'd left his message.

"I know you're dealing with that therapist and whatnot," he said. Whatnot. What a bizarre way of telling me he was doing his best not to pry. "But I got Gillmore to agree to keep the cold-spot partition clear for the morning so you could look at it." He lowered his voice. "And she's pretty pissed that you're not here."

Well, crap. I'd wanted some exorcism practice away from Dreyfuss' prying eyes, and there it was. I tried to remember if I'd promised Dreyfuss one way or the other that I'd be in today. He must've know that I'd called in to the Fifth. "Okay Zig, I'll, uh...." What equipment did I need for an exorcism? "I'll be there."

I could stop by Crash's store, but between getting on and off the expressway, explaining to him what I was trying to do, looking around for Miss Mattie, and fending off his friskiness, it would add another half hour to my trip. At least.

Instead, I swung by a convenience store that was between the exit ramp and the hospital. Their selection of herbs and spices was lousy. Then again, what did I expect them to have in stock? Rue? Mugwort? I thought back to the botched exam where I'd recommended scattering flour for protection. Black pepper—that was supposed to be good stuff. And salt. They had both of those, in a couple of cardboard tubes printed with onions, tomatoes and lettuce, one with an S and another a P, shrinkwrapped together. I was about to leave with my salt and pepper when I spotted a shaker of cinnamon sugar. Plain cinnamon would have been better. But I doubted that a little extra sugar would stop it from working.

I got to LaSalle before eleven. Patients inside two of the emergency partitions were trying to hack up their own lungs, but I suppose that gut-wrenching coughing is par for the course for snowy, damp Chicago springtime. I spotted Zigler before I saw Gillmore. Good. I thought that Gillmore liked me, more or less, even though I was a fifth level psych—but it freaked her out a little, too. And also, I was nosing around her emergency room and probably getting in the way, even though I supposedly knew what I was doing.

Zig had been writing on his notepad. Or at least pretending to, so that he looked like he had something to do while he waited for me to show up. Probably actually writing. Maybe. "Good, you came."

I scratched the back of my neck, which I realized was some kind of tell that advertised that I was nervous. I stuffed my hand in my pocket. "Yeah, sorry. I kind of have a lot going on."

"What do you need me to do?"

Zigler's role in this whole thing had never occurred to me. What did I need him to do? And more importantly, what could he do? He was a Stiff, just like Jacob—but did that mean he had the ability to put the kibosh on psychic phenomena, or was he just perfectly, absolutely average?

And if he was like Jacob, would he think I was nuts if I asked him to picture a remote viewer spying on me, and to change that bastard's mental channel? I don't think so. Zig took psychic stuff very seriously.

"Why don't you run interference? That will buy me some time."

Zigler nodded and planted himself beside the partition opening. I went in. The enclosure spooked me, but not because of the cold spot. It was the stainless steel table, the defibrillator in the corner, the rolling cart with drawers full of tongue depressors and syringes and latex gloves. I hated that shit. I would always hate that shit.

I pulled three bottles of spices out of my overcoat pocket, and I set them on the exam table. Salt, pepper, cinnamon-sugar. I was glad Zigler was outside. I couldn't imagine how anyone could look at my pathetic ritual supplies and not laugh, even Zigler.

I had no idea what to do, but I figured I wouldn't make anything worse if I winged it. I took off my overcoat. There was nowhere to hang it, so I rolled it up and placed it on the exam table. I held out my hands and walked slowly up one side of the table, then back, then up the other. I thought I had felt a cold spot in back. I lingered there. Maybe—hard to tell.

My spices sat there next to my coat, and now even I thought they'd been a stupid idea. If I bought pepper at Sticks and Stones, it probably would have been harvested with all the rest of the pepper, but at least the people who purchased it, imported and shipped it would have done so with an intent. And that intent, if it was tangible at all, would affect the vibration. This pepper? A dollar ninety-nine and a little cardboard shaker jar? It was made for picnics, not exorcisms.

And then I looked at the cinnamon-sugar. Cripes—what was I thinking? And I wasn't even high.

I couldn't tell anymore if my hand was cold from the paranormal cold spot, or if it had just gotten that way because I'd been holding it out in front of me so long.

I looked at my stupid spices again. Salt for protection, cinnamon to enhance psychic ability, and pepper to drive away evil. I figured I should start with the cinnamon.

My first impulse was to snort it. I'm guessing I picked that up prior to my Camp Hell training, and that it wasn't my most effective course of action. I took some into my hand, and I sniffed it—but not too close. Yet. Smelled like cinnamon. Come on, I told myself. Think.

Or rather, visualize. White light. Third eye. Internal faucet. Okay, I could do that much. I smelled the cinnamon, and I imagined myself full of white light. I think I felt something. Something more than the desire for a piece of toast—though that was there, too. My eyes were closed. I'm not sure when that happened. I opened them. The cramped enclosure that stunk of germicide and gleamed with stainless steel had a soft glow. It did. It wasn't just wishful thinking on my part.

I wondered what I was supposed to do with the spoonful of cinnamon-sugar now. I didn't see a garbage can. It didn't seem right to drop it on the floor. I stuck my hand in my pocket and shook it off.

The palm of my hand felt sticky, and cinnamon darkened the creases. I wiped my hand against the side of my jacket and hoped the material was dark enough to hide it. Still sticky. I wiped it again. I felt a little tug, kind of like when you walk through a spiderweb, and I realized I had been busy fooling around with the sugar on my hand while my psychic faucet was turned on high. I looked up, and staggered back. Something was visible where the cold spot had been. Something moving.

Not moving like a person, though. And ghosts like that, who moved wrong, really creeped me out. I backed toward the door, toward Zig—who might even be able to help me fend off the creepy crawlies if he was anything like Jacob. I watched the thing move, floating, undulating, and I couldn't make heads or tails of it. Or any other feature, for that matter. It looked like something that might grow up from the floor of the ocean. Were we in a low spot, someplace that used to be underwater? And if so, what the hell used to live there that would leave a ghost behind it that looked like that?

Several minutes passed while I stood there and stared at the thing. All the exorcism texts I'd read the night before blended together in my mind, shuffled like a deck of cards, a phrase here, a phrase there, but nothing that made any sense with the phrases before or after it. It was all just a bunch of meaningless static now.

I called Jacob. He had read more than I had. He probably even remembered what it all meant. But his phone went right to voice mail, and I figured he was probably in court, which meant he could be hours. My phone was sticky with sugar. I snapped it shut and tucked it into my breast pocket.

The ghostly sea creature grew fainter. I focused on it, and it grew brighter again. At least it seemed to be stuck in one place. Something that can't chase you isn't quite as scary as the stuff that can. I took a couple of steps forward and tried to figure out what I was looking at. My shoe brushed against the convenience store bag, and I remembered my salt and pepper. I didn't actually remember what I had meant to do with them, not now that I was actually staring at a supernatural being, but I remembered that they were there.

I peeled a plastic safety seal from the pepper, screwed off the top, and sniffed it. I coughed, and my eyes teared. I wiped the tears away with my sticky cinnamon hand. Not yet, something told me—some tiny part of my brain that remembered my focus groups at Camp Hell. Always begin with salt.

Too bad I hadn't thought of that before I broke out the cinnamon sugar. I opened up the salt, said a silent apology to whoever had to sweep the floors, and laid down a salt circle around the perimeter of the enclosure.

I looked down at the salt, and considered it. It didn't feel like anything to me. What was missing?

I thought about Miss Mattie telling me to feel God's love shining down from heaven. And in a more secular recollection, I recalled one of the Camp Hell trainers telling me to activate the herbs.

White light, faucet, silver full-body condom. Check. Then I imagined some of the white light shooting out from my fingertips, superhero style. I imagined the salt circle lighting up like I had just dropped a match on a circle of gasoline.

Three things.

One, I reenacted too many fake Evel Knievel stunts when I was in first grade.

Two, it occurred to me that the ghostly sea creature was not a sea creature at all. It was a flame.

Three, everything was glowing now, as if I was in an overexposed eighties New Wave video. I don't think it was really glowing, of course. It was just my very literal brain letting me know that my activation had actually done something. The same way Richie had, when he'd been praying over that suicide.

Now it was safe to break out the pepper. I could snort a little more cinnamon-sugar too, if I was really set on it. But it didn't seem like I needed to. You know how sometimes if a little is good, a lot must be better? Talent isn't like that. It's more like the vodka in Crash's freezer. Some is good. But beyond a certain point, it can be too much.

I eased toward the flame with the pepper shaker held two-handed against my chest. The pepper wasn't activated yet. All I had to do was think about it, flow some of that white light into it, and then it felt warm to my touch, as if I was holding a hot cup of coffee.

I took a couple more steps, and then looked at the ghostly thing. Yup. It was definitely a flame.

I thought harder about the pepper. The cardboard shaker felt hot, really hot, like the coated paper might actually start smoldering. Damn it. I wished I had a ritual, an incantation of some sort that would make it feel like I was actually doing something, and not just flinging spices around and making an ass of myself. But Miss Mattie's method didn't ring true for me, and neither did Richie's.

"This isn't your place anymore," I whispered. "You're on another plane now. Move along." I stabbed the pepper shaker out in front of me, hoping for some distance. I felt lame beyond belief. But I did it.

It flickered. But it was a flame, and that's what flames do.

I dug the top of the pepper shaker off with my thumbnail and poured a mound of it into my palm. I realized that I'd never had any clue how strong black pepper smells when I was sprinkling it over my mashed potatoes. My eyes watered hard, and I held it away from my face.

"This is a hospital," I explained to the ghost flame. "People come here to get better. And you...well, it looks like you're not helping."

The flame didn't talk. It just...remained where it was. On fire.

"So here's the deal. You gotta go. Today."

It sat there. Flaming.

I intended to follow that up with a very official-sounding "now," only I was overwhelmed by the smell of the pepper before I got the word out. A sneeze ripped through me instead, a massive convulsion that threatened to turn me inside out, and caused me to spray spit, pepper, and white light all over the back of the enclosure.

The flame shot high, like some invisible hand had cranked up the etheric gas burner, and a heartbeat later, dwindled to nothing as if it had used up all the oxygen in its final, bright moment.

My sticky hand was covered with pepper. And so was the back half of the enclosure. I sneezed again. My eyes burned. I wiped my nose on my upper arm, then sneezed a third and final time.

"Do you need anything?" Zigler called through the fabric wall.

I spotted a box of tissues. "No. I'm good." I wiped my nose, and my face, and my cinnamon hand. I didn't bother with my suitcoat—that would only call attention to any sticky spots by highlighting them with paper lint. "Actually, I think I'm done."

The curtain opened a few inches and Zigler's face appeared in the gap. "The cold spot's gone?"

I held my hand over the spot where the ghost flame had flickered. I closed my eyes, sucked some extra white light into myself, and I focused. Nope. Nothing. All clean.

Except that tiny shiver.

Damn. I opened my eyes and looked. There was a hole in the floor, maybe two inches in diameter, edges charred black all around, and through it, movement. "C'mere a minute," I told Zig.

He squeezed into the enclosure.

"Notice anything funny about the floor back there?"

Zigler edged by me and looked. "There's some sort of granular residue on the floor."

I rolled my eyes. "Salt, pepper, and cinnamon." I refrained from adding that the cinnamon was in a shaker with sugar, and that I'd found it on the same shelf as the syrup and the toaster pastries. "Other than that?"

"It's a little damp. Don't tell me I'm looking where you just sneezed."

"Probably. Nothing else?"

He straightened up. His knees popped. "You want to give me a hint?"

"A hole in the floor that you can see through, all the way down to the level below. You don't see that?"

"Hm. That's different." Zigler checked again, as if he might have missed it. "No hole." He juggled a few filled notepads, and then he nodded to himself and frowned. "We're above the old coal cellar."

As in, the basement. Oh boy.

My phone rang in the elevator on the way down. The caller I.D. read *Unavailable*. "Bayne," I said.

"Detective?" A pleasant female voice. Laura. "Agent Dreyfuss would like to speak to you."

I sighed. "Yeah, sure. Put him on." The elevator doors opened. Zig and I stepped into the basement lobby. There was a giant urn with a fake plastic tree inside. I think the moss that covered the base of the trunk was real, though. Someone had stuck a wad of gum in it.

Laura patched Dreyfuss through. "You do know that it's okay to ditch Sergeant Warwick's assignments to work on mine," he said, "don't you? He won't harbor any hard feelings. Cross my heart."

"It's, uh...." I wished there was a place I could sit. There wasn't. I followed Zig down a series of corridors that got smaller and dingier the farther we went. "I need to do more research. Richie's a pro, but I can't work the way he works."

"Right, you never bought the whole heaven and hell bit either. I can respect that. What about the reading material I sent over?"

"It was...." I sighed. I couldn't think of a word to describe it. "There was a lot of it."

"I tried to be thorough."

I noticed. The banker box had been fifty pounds of thorough. "Was there something I missed?" he asked me.

"Plain English would've been nice."

"No kidding. Do you think you've got a book in you, Detective? Because really, the market's ripe for a text on mediumship that hasn't been soaked in technical terms in an attempt to make it sound legitimately scientific. You'd need to publish under a pen name, of course, to keep some right-wing religious kook from gunning you down in the SaverPlus parking lot. But still—I think the world could use a definitive work on spirits."

"No. I don't think so." I wondered if he knew I'd recanted my testimony on Roger Burke. He had to.

Zig stopped in front of a security door and ran his high-level pass through a card reader. The door clicked open.

On the off-chance that it hadn't yet filtered back to Dreyfuss that Burke's lawyer had enough to spring him once the judge got around to looking at his case, I figured I should sneak back and pump whatever information I could from Doctor Chance before I found myself banned from the FPMP headquarters. Whatever was haunting LaSalle had been there for years. One more day wouldn't hurt it.

Zigler opened a dented steel door and stepped into a room. I followed. "I guess I could stop by and...Jesus Christ."

The room was on fire.

✦ TWENTY-EIGHT ✦

"I gotta go," I said. I closed the phone with numb fingers and slipped it into my pocket.

"You sense something?" Zig asked.

Saying that I sensed something in that room was so far beyond an understatement that I needed a whole new word for it. Ghost flames licked the walls, and spirit soot darkened the ceiling.

Old cardboard crates were stacked high on a pallet, boxes for shipping hospital equipment. They obscured the room, and the ghost flame danced on them, lighting them without casting any shadows.

"What is it?" Zig said. "You're white as a sheet."

Spirit was so thick in the room that it was just as real as the physical to my eyes. Maybe more. I shuffled my feet to keep from tripping over a piece of rubble that I couldn't see because the ghost flames blotted it out. "This is it," I said.

"What? What is it?" Zigler sounded scared—which rattled me, because he wasn't the one who was supposed to be scared. He couldn't see the weird world that happened in the same space as the one we were trying to live in, that poked through every time I thought I'd gotten a handle on things.

I rounded an eight-foot stack of boxes and banged my shin against some spare ductwork that was piled against the side wall. The noise it made was huge, and hollow, and disproportionately startling. "Fuckshitsonofa...."

A figure stood in the center of all the flames. It whirled to face me. My hand went to my gun. Stupid. And then to my pocket. Cinnamon sugar. Oh, fuck me.

The temperature plummeted. "What is it?" Zig barked. Ductwork rattled as he approached.

"Fire."

"Fire? My God, I can see your breath."

I took that as a cue to start shivering, partly from the cold, and partly from the look on the ghost's face.

She was young, I think. Or skinny and flat-chested, at least. The old-fashioned hospital gown didn't offer me any clues, and her face...her face was twisted to the point where she could've been eighteen or forty-eight and I wouldn't have known the difference.

Her mouth dropped open like she was screaming, but no sound came out. She disappeared and reappeared in almost the same spot, and the shape of her mouth changed. Still open, but like it was a glimpse of a different scream on a different day. She flickered. A new scream, still silent, framed by twin tear tracks. Another flicker—more of a strobe. She was closer now, mouth open so wide I could see the dark, mercury-laced fillings that covered her molars. Another strobe—fuck, she'd nearly appeared inside my left arm. I staggered back.

My hand went for my gun again. Damn it. Wrong world. I should probably talk to it. See if it was a full ghost or just a repeater. But sonofabitch, I was scared.

"G-girl. Woman, I mean. Caucasian. Um. Age...fuck, I dunno."

"Vic. Maybe we shouldn't...."

I took a deep breath, and I held it, because I realized my breathing had gone fast and shallow, and was leaving smokelike puffs in front of me in the air. I wanted to look at Zig, show him I'd heard him, but the freaky ghost stuttered all over like a film loop hopping forward in a projector, and when she reappeared, her face was right in front of mine, mouth open in a silent scream, glassy eyes huge, jittering, riveted on my face.

I bolted.

The ductwork rolled out of its stack with a thunderclap clatter.

I ran all the way to the security door and pulled. It didn't budge. I kept pulling, as if that would make any difference, until I felt Zigler's hands on my shoulders, dragging me off the door.

Once I was out of the way, he swiped his key card, and we ran until we got to the elevators.

A janitor watched with mild interest as we both tried to catch our breath. I turned away so he couldn't see the terror on my face. Zig and me, we were the PsyCops. We weren't supposed to cut and run.

Zig motioned for the janitor to go ahead and take the elevator. Once he was out of the way, and the two of us were alone, he bent his head close to mine, and he spoke. "What the fuck was that?"

A small, distant part of me thought it was funny that he'd finally dropped the F-bomb in my company. But mostly I was still shitting myself. "I...I...."

"You know what? If it's that bad, maybe I don't want to know."

I chafed my upper arms through my sportcoat. My sprained elbow gave an ugly twinge. "It's...she...."

"Maybe I don't want to do this."

I stopped trying to figure out where to begin and looked at Zig. "What?"

"You heard me. Maybe it's not worth it."

My toes felt numb. I stamped my feet. "Really? I mean, uh, what're you saying?"

"I told myself those zombies were the worst thing I was ever going to see. I told myself it was a fluke, and it could never happen again—that the chances of anyone else having both the twisted idea to do something like that and the ability to carry it off were as unlikely as lightning striking the same guy twice. And I told myself that if I could handle that, I could handle anything."

"You did. I mean, you can."

"Victor, back there in that basement, when the zombies were...were...*moving* around on those tables.... Twitching? And dead? You didn't even blink."

"This is nothing like those zombies."

"No shit. Because this time, you're scared—beyond scared. You're terrified. And whatever's got *you* scared? I don't want any part of it."

The elevator door opened, and we both flinched. A guy wheeled a cartful of hospital linens by us, and we both stood there awkwardly until the sound of the squeaky wheels died away.

"It was, um...a ghost woman. In a fire."

Zig didn't move to write it down.

"She was pretty...intense. Messed up. Like maybe there was something really wrong with her, even before she died. And, uh, I dunno. She's right underneath the spot where the mortality rate is sky-high, right?"

"I *saw* your breath."

I looked down at my shoes. "Yeah."

We stood there without saying anything for a good minute or two, and then Zig said, "I'm not doing this."

The elevator opened. It sat in front of us, empty, as if the building agreed with Zig. Nothing more to see here. Move along.

He took the building up on its offer, and walked toward the elevator. "Look, sleep on it before you do anything stupid," I said, because I remembered how he'd sounded when he told me that the only time his kids ever cared about his career was the day he got the call that he'd beat out a thousand other candidates for the PsyCop job. "Warwick doesn't need to know. I've got a whole stack of cutting-edge Psych research at home. Let me do some of the work. I'll figure out our next move, for once."

I glanced at him. He was focusing hard on the floor. He nodded.

"Give me your security pass," I said. I was worried he'd turn it in to the front office to reassure himself that he didn't have to come back.

Zig handed it over, shook his head, and looked pointedly at anywhere else but me.

✦ TWENTY-NINE ✦

I called ahead, and Stefan's secretary managed to cram me into his schedule. I had a feeling there were some people out there who were developing unhealthy attachments to nicotine gum because of me.

If I'd played the name-that-vest game while I was waiting to see Stefan, I would've lost. He wasn't wearing one. He was head-to-toe black in a turtleneck and jeans, with a chunky silver necklace that looked tribal, maybe African. Since there was no special place for a pocket watch, he'd opted for a silver Rolex. I guess smoking cessation and work productivity were pretty good business, after all.

He tipped back in his chair, laced his fingers over his stomach, and stared down his nose at me. "How is work?"

"Work is, uh...." I hung my overcoat on the coat tree and looked down at myself. My entire right side was streaked with cinnamon sugar. Damn. I wouldn't have thought it would show up so vividly on the navy. "Shit. Work is messy. Which is kinda why I'm here." I took off the blazer and hung it up beside the overcoat. "See, I need to remember this one training session, and so I was hoping we could aim for—"

"What...is...that?"

I wondered what else I'd managed to spill on myself. I held up my arms and walked around in a little circle, which I realized, as I was doing it, was completely lame. "Where?"

"Strapped to your body."

I had to take another good look at myself to realize that he'd been talking about my holster. "You mean my Glock?"

"You brought a *gun* into my office?"

"Well...yeah. It's my service weapon. I came here straight from work."

"And you've had it on you all along? Every time?"

Cripes. Stefan wouldn't be the first person to get weird about the gun. I'd had a short-term boyfriend whose morbid fixation with it had caused me to permanently misplace his phone number. "You want cinnamon all over your couch? I'll put my coat on so you don't have to look at it."

"No. I don't think it's the sight of the gun that's bothering me. Just the thought of you having it."

"What's that supposed to mean? You think I'm gonna shoot you?"

I'd been aiming for sarcasm. But Stefan's eyes cut down to the gun, and his laugh came a fraction of a second too late.

"I've got the FPMP following me around, and I'm not going anywhere without it. You'll just have to deal."

"Fine. Not another word." He planted himself in the chair across from the hypnosis couch, and muttered, "Good lord." Which, technically, was two more words. But I didn't want to waste my hour bickering with him.

I thought about Einstein and Faun Windsong and Dead Darla as Stefan counted me back. If Einstein could exorcise a spirit, then it should be a piece of cake for me. I'd known this, once. Those pictures that you look at, where you can shift your focus and a pretty lady looking at herself in a mirror becomes a skull? It was like that. I'd have to shift my focus, and whatever had been holding me back would fall away. I'd be able to see.

I lost present-day Stefan around four, which seemed strange to me. I'd been diving down at seven or eight, sinking far, fast. But this time felt different to me. I hadn't landed in a mediumship training session, which was where I'd been aiming. And I kept a stronger link to my present self than I had in my previous regressions.

The orderlies had just sprung me from the green room, and every time I looked at a light source and then moved my head, an orange tracer would trail behind. It was kind of like acid, though unfortunately, without the rock concert.

I think I'd been awake for about a day and a half. I'd touched dozens of personal effects, from a teddy bear to a wallet, to a wig. An actual wig—short, no-nonsense, dark blonde. I'd laughed at that when the silver box rotated into the room on the lazy Susan that connected me to the research area on the other side of the mirrored wall. Because how morbid could you get, stealing a dead woman's wig and dumping it in the lap of a Psych who was pumped full of drugs. And how stupid would it be if I actually stooped to saying, "I sense a female presence," because...duh. It was either that or a trannie.

Every time I put that dumb wig into the slot to return it and get the next object, it revolved right back around. Because I'd laughed at it, I realized. It was the first reaction I'd shown them in months, and they thought I'd gotten a read.

But there was no read to get. It was just a dead woman's wig. That's all.

The orderly had a wheelchair ready to bring me back to my room, but I told him I wanted to walk. It was an instinct I'd picked up at the loony bin, not to let the other residents see I was weak. Besides, the chair reminded me too much of Movie Mike, who'd supposedly been going to rehab, but now, rumor had it, would never walk again. His vision of himself as a Chess King model? Gone.

I looked up at the lights and a bunch of cool afterimages dragged down the hall. My keeper—I'd given up on learning their names—grabbed me by the upper arm so hard it hurt. His hand was big enough to close around my biceps. "C'mon, space cadet. Your room's this way."

I turned in the direction he was pulling me, and my hair fell into my eyes. They'd taken away our plastic safety razors a week after Krimski came on board. My scalp had gotten caught in the cheap electric razor I'd been given for my face, and the 'hawk was too much trouble to keep up with the tiny manicure scissors. So I just wore my hair long and uncombed. It was the best rebellion I could manufacture without any access to proper haircutting tools. And besides, I looked pretty tough scowling through my hair.

The orderly dragged me to my room and tossed me onto the bed. The overhead light made a shape that looked like a caterpillar, and I watched that crawl around on the ceiling for a while. But the sound of papers shuffling distracted me, and when I stopped tracking the caterpillar, I found the stupid orderly had never left.

He stood by the barred window, where my texts and notebooks were spread over the shelf above the radiator. And he had my red notebook in his hand—the one I'd been using to write a note to Stefan.

"What the fuck?" I said. "Get out of my room."

He glanced up at me and gave me an unpleasant smile. And his eyes—goddamn, he had the blond-haired, blue-eyed, reptilian look of Roger Burke, combined with the gym rat physique of Jacob's private investigator pals. No wonder I ran across someone every now and then who seemed to rub me wrong for no reason at all. And to top it off, he had a mullet.

"Don't go through my shit," I said. "I'll tell Krimski." Who probably wouldn't do a damn thing about it...but what else could I say?

"Krimski wanted me to check up on you."

"Bullshit. You're just an orderly."

He licked his thumb and leafed through some more. I tried to take notes during focus group, but always seemed to end up doodling anarchy symbols over three-quarters of the page instead. I wondered if Big Blond Hockey Hair was anywhere near the note. Damn it. The whole staff knew I was queer anyway, but I didn't want to let anyone in on that particular fantasy but the guy I'd intended to give it to.

He paused in the doorway that led to my institutional half-bath, and read. Probably focus group notes, since he didn't seem particularly interested. "The wig," he said, without bothering to look me in the face. "Is that supposed to mean something? 'See if Mister Bayne will tell you about the wig,' that's what he said."

I looked up at the ceiling again. The caterpillar returned. "You can take that wig, pass it back and forth, and take turns shoving it up your asses."

He laughed. "What are you trying to prove, anyway? You should see your file, big black marks all over it, 'will not cooperate,' and 'conceals information,' scribbled in the margins. You think you're some kind of badass because you don't tell them what they want to hear?"

Well, yes.

No.

Not exactly. I held back because I didn't trust them. Because a ghost had told me to be careful, and it seemed to me that he hadn't had any reason to lie to me.

I tore my eyes away from the light-caterpillar and found the orderly reading my notebook a little more closely. I swung my feet over the side of the bed and grabbed the thing out of his hands. I was actually an inch or so taller than him, if I stood up straight. His arms were as big around as my thighs. But I was taller.

"Don't go through my stuff."

"Tell me about the wig, and I'll leave you alone."

"Leave me alone, or I'll tell Krimski you're harassing me. And he can always find more goons—but where's he gonna get another medium?"

Mullet-head rolled his eyes and walked out. He left the door open, just to irk me, I imagine. I clambered over my bed and off the other side so I was facing the door, and tracers exploded everywhere. The entire wall was filled with light caterpillars that squiggled down from the ceiling. It took me three tries, but I found the handle, pulled the door shut, then ran over to the bed and flipped through the notebook so hard that the pages bent and tore.

Lecture. Lecture. Lesson. Essay. Doodles. And then I found it—the note that contained the fantasy that featured me, Stefan, a couple of med students from U of C, and a case of aerosol whipped cream. A page and a half of my most intimate thoughts. It had taken me nearly twenty minutes to get it down.

I tore it out of the notebook, ripped it into tiny little pieces, and flushed it down the toilet.

I was pissed.

Those notes were the only way for Stefan and me to be together anymore. We disappeared into various labs for days at a time, and emerged woozy or puking, or semi-conscious. The only time we actually saw each other was in the cafeteria. We couldn't just leave, run off to the smoking lounge, or the basement stairwell by the pop machine, and get a few quick strokes in. And we'd tried— in the men's room, which was as far away as we were allowed to go. I'd earned myself an embarrassing "no fraternization" lecture, and Stefan got locked in his room for three days straight.

I thought about writing a secret confession that I actually had the psychic ability to kill people from a distance, so that the goons who went through my shit could find it and think twice about being such dickheads. But I got a few words into it, then covered it up with a bunch of spiral caterpillars, and decided it was more fun to lie in bed and watch the lights perform.

The rattling of my door handle pulled me from a light doze. I clenched up inside, figuring that Mister Mullet had decided to take another stab at me, and wishing there was some way I really could make his head explode.

A large figure slipped into the room, but the shape was all wrong for the orderly. Black on black, and teased-out hair. My God. Stefan.

I jumped out of bed and pulled him against me. He felt big and solid. "What're you doing?" I whispered. "How'd you get here?"

He cupped my face in both hands and stroked my hair. It was a lot longer than the last time he'd touched me which was, when? A month ago? Maybe two. "I wanted to see you. A lucky break with only one douchebag on duty, a well-placed *Boo-Hoo-You*, and here I am."

I wondered who'd retreated into the bathroom to cry uncontrollably over nothing at all. I hoped it was Hockey Hair. It probably wasn't, since Stefan and I were housed in two completely different sections. But it was fun to imagine that jerk sobbing like a little girl, anyway.

I touched Stefan's lips. Black. Probably permanent marker, since his make-up had long ago run out, and it was doubtful that Krimski would send one of his goons out shopping for us. "You shouldn't have come here," I said. "You'll get in so much trouble."

"Not if I don't get caught." He pressed his mouth into mine. He tasted like mint. But in a weird way, I missed the flavor of cigarette smoke—not because it was tasty, by any stretch of the imagination, but because it reminded me of our honeymoon months, where we could get away with nearly anything—even though, at the time, we hadn't realized it.

I guess if we had, it wouldn't seem quite so bittersweet now.

I felt myself sway against him. I tightened my arms around his neck, and he guided me toward the bed. "I'm so high right now," I told him.

"Any good?"

"Not too bad."

Stefan bent me back over the narrow bed, then sank down between my legs. I eased my fingers into his hair. It felt floppy now, without hairspray to hold it up. "I gotta get out of here," I told him.

"Why now?" He undid my jeans, pulled them down, then paused to unzip my combat boots and work them off, too.

"These fucking orderlies...I hate them. And I hate the sessions. And Faun Windsong. I hate not being able to go where I want, do what I want. Maybe I won't get certified into a good job after all, but it's getting to the point where I don't fucking care—I'll go flip burgers somewhere instead. Whatever testing they've got on me so far, that'll be enough to keep the guys with the butterfly nets from coming after me. I just feel like I can't even breathe without someone jotting down a note in my fucking file about it."

Stefan's tongue was on me, and the psyactives in my bloodstream didn't stop my body from snapping to attention. Then again, I was a twenty-four-year-old kid, and they'd need to be some pretty potent drugs to keep me from rising to the occasion.

"I wrote you a note," I told him as I pushed into his mouth, "but they're going through my notebooks, now. So I tore it up."

"Mm." He couldn't really give me a more detailed response without stopping what he was doing, and it'd been so long since anyone had touched me, except to shove a needle in my arm, or to steer me down the hall when I was pumped full of experiments. I'd rather he kept going than to shore up the conversation.

Stefan slipped his hands underneath the hem of my T-shirt and ran his fingers over my ribs. He loved my ribs, said he'd never actually seen his own, other than in the X-ray that was taken for the admission physical. His hands moved higher and his fingers fixed on my nipples. I squirmed and clutched his hair with one hand, held my dick steady for him with the other. His lips brushed my fingers with each downstroke. I peered down past the bunched-up wad of my T-shirt to look at them, black with permanent marker, and I felt the peak start to creep up on me.

"I'm close," I said, once he'd sucked me to that sharp-edged point where there was no turning back. He stopped sucking and switched to his hand. He pumped fast, and trailed black-lipped kisses over my heaving stomach. I held him against me with both my hands tangled in his hair, and I struggled to keep quiet while I came so hard, it felt more like pain than release.

✦ THIRTY ✦

Stefan and I barely fit on my bed together, but if we held on tight, we managed. "Why do you think they're giving you such a hard time?" he asked me. "When I do what they tell me to do, they leave me alone."

"Yeah. But you test well. You can tell them what color card the subject is looking at. And how it makes him feel."

He stroked my long hair, and held my face against his chest. "How come you don't?"

"I don't what?"

"Test well. It doesn't make any sense. You told me you spotted the haunted grave right away during that field trip, remember? Before Faun Windsong, even."

"Well, yeah. But that's 'cos a ghost was there. All the stuff they're giving me to look at and touch? It's empty. Nobody's home. I think the people who get reads off dead people's trinkets? They're a little bit clairvoyant—and I'm not. I'll spot a ghost in two seconds if there is a ghost to see. But I can't do shit with their possessions."

Stefan kissed the top of my head. "What were they testing today that's got you flying so high in the sky?"

"Enhancements."

"And even then...?"

"Even then. Nothing. Because there was nothing to see." I slipped a hand between his legs. He was wearing silky drawstring pants, black with gray skulls on them, and no underwear, judging by the feel.

Stefan slipped his hand into mine and wove our fingers together. "No, not now. We don't have time."

"Really? How come?"

"I feel them in the hall, confused. They'll probably come around and do an unscheduled check on everyone within the next few minutes."

"I'll be fast. I can make you come in two minutes."

"I can do that myself. I never get to see you anymore—I'd rather talk to you."

That had to be the most romantic thing anyone had ever said to me, and I went all gooshy inside.

"Maybe if you try to test better," he said, "you can get certified and get out of here. I heard they've started placing the Psychs with good track records."

I had a track record, but it was the opposite of good. And anyway, I didn't actually believe we'd get out—because how could they replace us? Now that that psychic abilities were no longer a one-way ticket to the nuthouse, who would be stupid enough to sign away all their civil liberties, and their medical rights, on top of it?

"What're you gonna do when you get out?" I said.

"Me? I don't know. I haven't thought about it."

Either had I. "We should get an apartment, in Boystown. Paint the walls black."

"It has to have a bathtub," he said. "If I never see another shower in my life, it'll be too soon."

"And windows that open. Without bars on them."

"And a pizza place next door. Or Chinese takeout. Or a bakery. All three."

"Or a record store." I'd had a record collection, once upon a time. Not extensive, but hard-to-find pressings of bands who'd never made the top forty. I wondered where they'd ended up. Probably in a garage sale at my last foster home. I could find those albums again. And Stefan and me, we could mingle our record collections.

"So there wasn't anything you could've told them tonight to get them off your case?" he asked me.

"Like what?"

"I dunno. You didn't even get a little glimmer? Not from anything?"

I watched the lazy Susan revolve in my mind's eye. "Nope. Nothing. They thought I did, though. I opened the box and—get this—there's a wig inside. A fucking dead lady's wig. I think I laughed. I mean, who wouldn't? And when I put the wig back in the slot, it just came rolling back out again. Over and over. It was funny, for maybe fifteen minutes." I really hated to admit that sometimes I lost my ability to find humor in the absurdity of it all. "But they kept showing me that wig...for maybe, I dunno...twelve hours."

Stefan clasped me against his chest tighter.

"D'you think they take shifts?" I told him. "Krimski would have to pay 'em overtime if they watched me for more than eight hours."

"I don't know. Focus on the sound of my voice. Feel your feet on the floor, and your body where it rests against the couch."

What? That didn't make any sense. I wondered if Camp Hell's funding had been cut, like Krimski had told me it would if nobody started to perform, or if now they could afford to pay the psy-goons overtime to watch me while I stared at a dead woman's wig for twelve hours straight.

"Five, you're breathing, you're relaxed. You're firmly anchored in your body, and you're tuning in to the present."

Jesus. I was in Stefan's office. My holster felt clammy against my side. I was hungry. What with the fire ghost and the emergency regression, I hadn't eaten since breakfast.

And I was a little...excited. Oh God. Did it show? I had a boner, it had to show. Unless it just looked like my pants were bulging, the way cheap dress slacks sometimes do...except that wouldn't slip by Stefan. He was an empath. If I was turned on, he'd totally know. Shit.

"Two, you're refreshed, and you're centered, and you're fully awake. Did you hear me, Victor? You're fully awake."

"I heard you."

"All right, then. One. Open your eyes."

I opened my eyes, half-expecting to find Stefan with teased black hair and permanent marker on his lips. But, no. It was present-day Stefan, with his black turtleneck and his pointy sideburns. I looked away.

"Want to talk about what you just saw?"

Where he sucked me off? And we talked about moving in together, and then a month later I disappeared into the Police Academy without so much as a *Thank you, ma'am?* No, not really. I slid down to the opposite side of the couch so I could get up without fear of prodding him with a really inopportune hard-on.

"I'm starving. I need to eat."

"I have a diet shake in the fridge. You can drink it if you're having a low blood sugar headrush."

I tried to pull on my blazer, realized it was inside-out, then shook out the sleeve and yanked the thing on, spraying cinnamon sugar. "No thanks." I glanced at the windows, planning to say that it was late, that Jacob was expecting me, that I should get home...and I realized that the windows were all dark. I looked at the wall clock. It was nearly nine. "Is that right? It's nine o'clock?"

"You were so eager to locate this particular training session, it seemed like I shouldn't bring you out until you were ready."

"Oh God." I flipped open my phone, which had been in my overcoat, set to vibrate. A message from Zigler. One from Jacob. And one from Unavailable.

"Really, have the shake. And you can tell me what you're so upset about. Because the regressions are only half of the healing process. You've got to make sense of them."

"Look...thanks. For everything. Really. But I gotta go." I slapped a few hundred dollars on Stefan's desk without counting it, and I drove like a madman all the way home.

In a way, it was good that a half-hour drive separated me from Jacob. I felt like I'd just cheated on him—without meaning to, of course. All I'd wanted was to figure out how to exorcise an evil spirit. I'd gotten a fourteen-year-old blow-job from Stefan instead.

Stefan's countdown had been exactly the same as always. I'd been aiming for exorcism. So why jump back to a moment with my pants around my knees? Why now?

I parked in front of Jacob's Crown Vic, slammed the car door, jammed my hands deep in my pockets, and crunched up the rock-salted walkway. I wondered if I could activate a twenty pound bag of sidewalk salt to make it that much harder for remote viewers to spy on Jacob and me. And I suspected that I could.

Jacob thundered down the stairs from our loft as I hung up my overcoat in the foyer. He skidded to a stop in the doorway and looked at me, all smiles. I was trying to figure out what to do with my sportcoat.

"Did you put a donut in your pocket again?" he asked me.

"I've just had one sorry-assed day." I dropped the jacket on the floor. He picked it up and draped it over his arm, and followed me into the kitchen.

I opened the fridge, dug around for a minute, and found a few cold pieces of pizza wrapped in foil. I unwrapped a piece and ate it while I leaned over the sink so that I didn't have to wash a plate. Jacob stood beside me and watched.

I swallowed the last corner of crust, which I usually throw out, but I was starving, so I didn't. Then I turned on the tap, drank a few swallows of water to move the ball of congealed cheese and dough stuck in my esophagus down towards my stomach. I wiped my mouth with the back of my hand, and I turned to face Jacob.

He looked like a kid on Christmas morning, trying hard not to smile, and failing miserably.

"What?" I asked.

"Did you get my message?"

"No, I...." I was busy avoiding my messages, because I didn't want to hear the one from the FPMP. "I thought I'd just focus on getting home before sunrise."

Jacob grabbed me by the biceps and pulled me up against his chest. He put his mouth to my ear, and whispered, "You were right."

Really? No, seriously. Really? "About what?"

"I can do this thing...it's like...." Whatever it was like, it left him speechless. He got his arms around me and crushed me against his rock-solid body. He squeezed all the air out of me, and I let myself dangle against him, because maybe if Jacob was this happy, some little corner of the world was still okay. He kissed me, clashing teeth with me in his impatience, and his hands roamed up and down my back. One hand traced the lines of my holster, the other one grabbed my ass hard. He broke the kiss, then pressed his mouth to my ear again. "I have a talent. For sure."

I almost asked if he was sure he was really, really sure, even though I'd been the one who suggested that he might. Because now, when I saw his reaction to it, I realized that if I'd been wrong, he'd be devastated.

But he seemed positive, and that gave me hope. I spoke with the last of the breath in my lungs, a little croak. "So, what can you...do?"

"I can shut down other Psychs' talents."

He was so sure, in fact, that he said "other" Psychs, as if he was positive that he could count himself among our number. "Who did you test this with?"

"Don't worry—just Carolyn and Crash. But Carolyn's telepathy is accurate enough that after we practiced it, she could tell when I was blocking her and when I wasn't. She said it was like I'd flipped the light switch off."

"You've been together for years. How is it she's never noticed before?"

"I never did it with her. It's a very conscious thing I need to do to activate it. A mental shift."

Like the beautiful woman in the mirror who turns into a skull. "Oh. I get it."

"And even Crash could feel it." Jacob smirked. "He says I used to do 'that thing' to him whenever we argued—so he just figured the blank sensation he'd pick up was the way he registered my anger."

Two Psychs for two. I was guessing that if we wanted to broadcast to the whole world over our cell phones, we could call Lisa and verify that she couldn't answer a *si-no* that Jacob asked while he was actively blocking her. But I didn't think we needed to go there.

Jacob hustled me into the main room, where the books and reports from Dreyfuss covered the dining room table. They were all open, weighted down with knick-knacks, unopened cans of protein drink, even the TV remote. The pages bristled with colored sticky notes. Jacob circled the table once, then picked out a report that looked like it had been printed out on a dot-matrix printer and then photocopied through about twelve generations. "Here. Listen to this."

He read: "The talent of the psychic partner will be balanced by the absence of talent in the non-psychic partner, and care must be taken in the selection of the NP. The candidate should score neutral in every category, over a minimum of five separate testing days. Further, he should prove resistant to clairsentient probing."

"What's that?"

"It's the original PsyCop proposal. And look."

He thrust the document at me. The paragraph he'd been reading seemed to have some kind of printer malfunction toward the bottom. The last sentence was hardly more than a light pattern of dots. The only reason it read as a sentence to me at all was because Jacob had deciphered it. "Shitty copy."

"But that's not all." Jacob pulled our current PsyCop handbook from the pile. He'd highlighted a section bright orange. The paragraph was the same, word for word. But the last line was missing.

I dragged a chair out and sat down hard. My gun dug into my ribs. "All right—that's interesting and all. But I don't think it's earth-shattering. Everyone knows that Stiffs are harder to influence and possess, and that they're supposed to balance out Psychs."

"Because the balance is mentioned again later on in the proposal. But the key thing here in the testing is resistance to clairsentients, not the neutral scores in everything else. And the part that really mattered, that's the portion of the test that was never instituted."

"Why does it not surprise me that a Psych test evolved into half-assedness? Wait, scratch that. I know why. I took a modern test at LaSalle, and I scored as NP."

"How could someone test for a medium unless they had a ghost in their kit?" Jacob said.

I took up the line of reasoning. "And how could they test for a psychic shield unless they had a reliable Psych hanging around for him to shut down?"

Jacob pulled up a chair, rotated it so it faced me, sat down, and pulled my hand into his lap. He worked my fingers and palm in his strong, warm hands, and stared into my face so earnestly I thought one of us was going to start blubbering. I'm not sure who.

"Zigler tried to quit," I said.

"Quit what?"

"Quit being a PsyCop."

Jacob stroked my hand with his thumb. "What happened?"

"I found something at LaSalle." I swallowed hard. "In the basement. Fuck, it was one of the worst ghosts I'd ever seen. It lit up the whole room with ghost-fire." I shuddered. "And Zig...he read my expression, I guess. He figured that if I was spooked, he didn't want any part of it."

Jacob gave a low whistle. "I didn't see that coming. So what would you expect him to do?"

"Well, he...." I stopped, and thought. What *had* I expected from him?

"What could either of you do?"

"I could get rid of it."

Jacob stared me in the eye.

"Exorcise it," I said. Even though it had been obvious what I'd meant, it seemed like it was important that I use the technical term, even though it meant admitting that I knew what I was doing, sometimes.

Jacob sat back and stroked his goatee. "You're serious. I thought you'd been studying up to get rid of repeaters."

I stared down at the sea of books, and the words all ran together. "If Einstein could do it, Richie, I mean—the guy's a level three, if even that—then I should be able to do it, too. I saw him fade a suicide out of existence with a few Hail Marys. So if there's a big, nasty, psycho fire-ghost in the hospital, and its negative vibes are killing patients, I've got to at least try to flush it out."

Mind you, I was fully aware that my own logic didn't quite jibe with the advice I'd once given Lisa. I'd told her that she wasn't responsible for eradicating every last evil in the world, just because she had the gift of *si-no*.

Maybe the fire ghost was out of my league, and if so, it didn't seem too bright to put myself in danger, if I could walk away instead.

On the other hand, it was actually my case. My job.

"I'll help you," Jacob said.

I wanted to say no. It wasn't his responsibility, it was mine. And he didn't see that spirit, *feel* it deep down in his core, get a sense of how twisted and wrong it actually was. I wanted to tell him that, but I didn't. Because it wouldn't have made any difference. Jacob had something to prove—to himself, to me. And he intended to prove it.

✦ THIRTY-ONE ✦

Jacob emerged from our basement with cobwebs in his hair, and a battered, red spiral-bound notebook in his hand. I took the notebook from him and flipped it open. Anarchy symbols. My handwriting from when I was twenty-four looked different than it did now. Neater. And I pressed harder back then, too, leaving impressions of my writing on the page beneath. I still left my o's open on top and crossed my t's crooked and to the right, but now I had a looser, easier scrawl that didn't eat into the pages below.

I flipped toward the center of the notebook, wondering if some of the notes covered up impressions of the sex fantasy I'd written for Stefan fourteen years ago. Forensics could probably scan the book and recover it from the impressions I'd left in the paper. I might've been blushing a little, but if Jacob noticed, he probably chalked it up to the excitement of the ghost hunt.

"I think candles would help," I said. Because although I was primarily visual, I remembered how the cinnamon sugar had turbocharged my powers, and I though a few basic props were in order if I was going to pay another visit to that scary-assed ghost. "Salt, too. And..." I was being facetious with this last part, "do we have any rue?"

"Crash left a bag of supplies here when he did the house blessing."

Lo and behold, we did indeed have rue. And charcoal, with Crash's signature resin, copal, to burn on top of it. We had sage smudge sticks and a Baggie of fuzzy green stuff that I couldn't quite place until I dipped my fingers into it and felt it. Mugwort. Drinkable, as an infusion. Supposedly grants prophetic dreams—in other words, a natural psyactive. A half-dozen white candles, too, tied in a bundle with a red ribbon. Red and white. Protection. And if I shifted my vision while I looked at them, they seemed to give off a subtle glow, even unlit. I figured they'd been activated by Crash.

There was even a prepackaged container of "Double Cross" incense. It looked like it was manufactured by the same company that made the High John soap, the one that had given me a rash. I set that aside. Instinctively, I trusted more in simple ingredients that I activated myself than I did in factory-made blends. Or maybe that wasn't instinct talking at all. Maybe it was training.

"This ghost looked pretty strong," I said, "and I'm thinking it's had its hooks sunk into LaSalle for fifty, maybe sixty, years now. We need to be careful."

Jacob nodded.

"So...boil some water. It's tea time."

While Jacob got the mugwort started, I scooped some sidewalk salt out of the bag in the vestibule, funneled white light into it until it glowed, then scattered it around our downstairs bathroom. I put an incense burner full of smoldering copal on the countertop, and I burned one of the activated white candles.

The room felt right.

I hung a clean suit on the hook inside the bathroom door while I showered, so the smoke and the steam and the protective vibes could permeate it while I washed the stink of the day, both physical and spiritual, from my body.

Jacob came in with our tea while I was soaping up for the fifth time. He put the cups beside the sink and started to strip.

"Uh-uh, we shower separately," I told him. "You've got to save your mojo. You'll need it."

He slid the shower door open a crack and leaned against the pastel-colored tiles. "You're serious?"

"Dead serious."

He nodded. We could take a tumble anytime. But big, juicy exorcisms were harder to come by.

Once we were clean and centered, suited up in clothes that smelled like Crash's store, and sloshing with bland mugwort tea, we climbed into Jacob's car and headed toward LaSalle.

I gave him Zig's security card, and the staff didn't bother to check the name on it against Jacob's badge. They knew the police had been scouring the building all week, and we looked like cops. We might not have smelled like cops. But we looked the part.

My heart pounded in my throat as the elevator doors closed, and the car started to sink. "I feel like I'm buzzing," Jacob whispered.

I shifted my focus. I did, too. "Imagine a stream of white light flowing into your pineal gland...your third eye."

"I know what the pineal gland is." I looked at Jacob—he had a mile-wide grin on. I glanced down. And a hard-on. If we came out of things in one piece, I'd be in for a wild ride once we got home.

"Picture yourself full of white light."

"My God," he said. "I'm really buzzing. For real."

I touched his hand, and static electricity crackled between us, connecting us with a bright, brief, visible spark. It was real, all right.

The elevator doors whooshed open. The basement lobby was empty, except for the potted plastic tree and its wad of gum, which had been joined by a crunched-up drinking straw wrapper.

I was about to steer Jacob toward the old coal cellar, but he was a step ahead of me. I took a couple of long strides to catch up and get a good look at his face. Definitely in the zone—laser beam eyes. He was looking at the world with his perception shifted, and he made a beeline toward the supernatural activity without any help from me.

He stopped in front of the safety door and tugged on it. "Locked," I told him. I pulled out my red security card and slid it through the card reader. The door clicked open, and Jacob shouldered me aside and went through first.

"Maybe I should go ahead," I suggested to his back, "because you won't be able to see it."

"It got all up in your face, right?"

"Yeah, but—"

"Then I go first."

He'd been listening, back in the car, when I described the fire ghost. I know he had. Because the second you say the word *ghost*, Jacob's there, a hundred and ten percent—so he knew the spirit was freaky enough to send Bob Zigler packing. I was tempted to tell him that he wouldn't be able to bench-press it into submission, but when Jacob set his sights on something, there wasn't any talking him down. So instead I streamed some more white light into my pineal gland, and I gathered it up inside myself until my fingertips tingled, and I hoped that when the blowout came, I'd survive it.

Jacob strode by the dented steel door, and then stopped, cocked his head, turned back to the door and put his fingertips, spread wide, against it. "This is it, isn't it?"

I nodded. "How do you know?"

"I can tell. I can feel it."

I pulled a bundle of candles from my overcoat, and consulted a tiny compass that we'd plucked from my dashboard. I was happy to see it put to good use; it had certainly never helped me when I got lost driving somewhere. I held it up and saw a ball with lines and letters bobbing under a crosshair. "I can't read this fucking thing."

Jacob took it from me and studied it for a moment. "North," he said. He pointed back in the direction we'd come from. He took a few paces and turned. "The walls run in cardinal directions."

Walls in Chicago often did; that was the way the streets had been laid out.

"You sure you don't want me to set the candles?"

Richie's assistant had helped him set the candles, but I had the impression that I'd build a better ritual if I did it myself. I shook my head. "You're here. That's enough."

Jacob opened the door and flipped on the light. The ductwork I'd crashed into on my way out of there had rolled out of its pile. It covered the floor now, like a galvanized steel obstacle course. Silent ghostfire licked the walls all around us. "She's two-thirds of the way to the back wall, past that stack of boxes," I whispered. I wasn't sure why I was whispering. I had no doubt that the fire ghost knew we were there.

Jacob took a ceramic ash tray that we'd cleaned in salt water from his pocket, put a black charcoal puck in the middle, then took a lighter to it. The ridge around the edge of the charcoal flamed briefly, then went out, sending a thin line of physical smoke up toward the ceiling. It smoldered for a moment, and then sparked bright orange. It gave a pop and sparked again, and pretty soon a web of twinkling orange sparks coursed through the briquette as the saltpeter mixed in the charcoal caught and ignited. Once the ridge around the charcoal turned gray, Jacob took out our Baggie of copal.

"Activate it first," I whispered, and placed my hand over his. I felt a jolt, and almost jerked back. I steeled myself against it—if we sent that charcoal flying into the heap of corrugated cardboard, we might burn the whole building down.

When I took my hand from the copal, the resin was glowing red. "Do you see that?"

"See what?"

"It's glowing."

Jacob scowled. "No. But I swear to God, it's vibrating."

I searched for a word. "Visual, verbal, what's it called? The sense of movement."

"Kinesthetic."

"There you go. That must be how your brain interprets sixth-sensory vibes."

Jacob stared into my eyes with a look that was full of wonder. Earlier, he'd figured out he could tell Carolyn a gigantic whopper without getting caught if he shielded from her first. But this? This was Major League Psych.

"Dump it on," I told him, "and then we'll do the sage."

We activated the sage together, and now that I was ready for the jolt, it felt more controlled. When my hand touched Jacob's, the white light around us flared bright. The sage continued to glow, even after the light around our hands faded. "It's ready," I said.

The makeshift censer billowed smoke that stunk to high heaven when we added the sage. I waved the smoke out of my eyes, and the fine hairs on the backs of my hands stood up. "Shit. It's awake." I pulled out the activated salt and scattered it in front of me.

Jacob backed away from me with the censer, and his gaze went to the boxes. "What now? The candles?"

I lit one, and held it out in front of me like a crucifix. It went out. Damn it. I started stepping over fallen ductwork and realized that my chances of getting past the wall of boxes with my candle lit had been slim to none, anyway. I jerked my head toward the boxes, and Jacob followed me there, surefooted, with the incense.

Ghost flames ringed the empty space beyond the box wall, burning low, maybe a couple of feet high. The crazy fire ghost stood in the center with her head slumped, as if she'd been a bad girl and was too ashamed to look up and meet anybody's eyes. Her matted hair covered her face, and her hospital gown hung, stiff and still.

She moved, though, blips and stutters, now a couple inches closer, now a foot away. Now rotated so I saw her in perfect profile—knobby knees, spine slouched, pointy, upturned breasts. Now with her back to us, hospital gown tied sloppy, backs of her legs streaked with something dark, blood, or maybe feces.

Jacob grabbed me by the forearm and I got a white-light jolt. "Set the candles."

"She's, um...." I pointed to the general area of spots where she strobed in and out of sight.

"I know. I feel her. Set the candles."

My hands shook as I tried to light the first candle, and my breath streamed out of me in a big, white plume. I glanced up. The ghost was still in the same general spot, maybe three yards away from us. I drew a mental circle around her, found north according to the walls, and moved to set my first lit candle on the floor. Then Faun Windsong's voice popped into my head, unbidden, parroting back some ancient wisdom about starting your circle in the east, "like the sunrise."

Thanks, Faun.

I set the candle.

The temperature plunged. My teeth started to chatter.

Jacob had been squinting in the direction of the ghost, but the sound of my molars knocking drew his gaze to me. "I can see your breath."

Not his. Just mine. Cripes.

"White light, Vic. Center yourself."

I sucked in a gout of energy just as the flames leapt high. Fire ghost started strobing faster—here, there, appearing and disappearing. Always in the same pose. Just standing, head down.

I lit the second candle from the first and set it in the south. I pulled a third candle from my pocket and moved to light it from the second.

Her face filled my vision—mouth gaping. I fell back, and she was on me. No sound. Just the sight of her face. And now, close, closer than ever before. Close enough to see her lips were cracked, and white gunk was built up in the corners of her mouth, and her tongue, her horrible tongue, was coated, pale and furred.

"No." Jacob had stepped into the circle I'd been trying to create and stretched his hand toward the ghost. "Get off him."

The lank mats of her hair flopped over her thin shoulders as she swung around to look at Jacob when she realized that he could see her, too. In a sense.

"She's coming at you."

Jacob closed his eyes and cocked his head, and left his hand out there as if he was asking her to dance. "She's in pain," he said.

"You don't get it," I yelled over the roar of ghostfire in my ears. And I don't think he did. Because Jacob, fucking Jacob, he thinks he's indestructible. I sucked white light.

The fire ghost strobed, and strobed again, and I threw a white balloon around Jacob as if it was a fastball. She slammed into my barrier and shattered. Ghostfire dropped to the floor in a shower of sparks, then coalesced again in the center of the room, in the shape of a woman, mouth open, eyes wide and jittering.

"What did you just do?" Jacob snapped.

"She was barreling toward you—"

"I know. I felt her."

I picked up the south candle, set it right side up, and lit it. My breath vapor froze to my eyelashes, and the ice crystals acted like a dozen tiny prisms that cast sparkles around everything I saw. "But you can't see how horrible—"

"I don't care. Listen to me. She's in pain."

I glanced up. A bunch of expressions snapped over her face in rapid succession—scream, sob, rictus grin—shifting fast from one to another in stop-motion cuts. I sidled around the circle and planted a third candle at the western point. She blipped in front of me, scream-mouthed, and I dropped the candle. She flickered back again to the center.

Jacob took a couple steps forward.

"Stay out of the circle, would you?"

He planted his hands on his hips and glared. My hands were so cold it took me five tries to light the wick. His staring didn't help. Once the flame took, I ran in a crouch to north point and set down the final candle.

The temperature dropped so low that each inhalation felt like knives in my lungs.

"Can she hear me when I talk?" Jacob said.

"I don't know." My eyes watered, and the tears froze to my cheeks. "Ask her."

"Miss? Ma'am?"

Shit, he was serious.

"You need to remain calm, and listen to me. You're in the wrong place. Do you understand me?"

She blipped and flickered like crazy, but after a few seconds, it seemed that she'd rotated to face Jacob. Mostly. Every few strobes, she faced me to make sure she kept tabs on what I was doing, too. But the majority of her appearances faced Jacob.

"The only thing here for you is suffering," Jacob told her in his most reasonable tone of voice. "You need to pass over. Let it go."

The ghostfire dimmed against my sacred circle, in the way stars dim when streetlights flicker on. But the ghost woman still seemed pretty damn solid.

"Can you channel any healing energy toward her?" Jacob asked.

"Do I look like a healer to you?"

"At least try. White light—whatever you want to call it."

What did he expect from me? If he wanted a healer, he should have stuck with Crash. I drew down more white light anyway, because I suspected that if I just said I did without actually trying, Jacob would be able to feel whether I'd made the attempt or not.

Once I was topped off with white light as far as I could fill myself, I jogged the last few steps toward the east point of the circle, where Jacob faced off with the fire ghost.

"We're here to help you," he murmured.

"Um. Hey. I don't exactly know how to change my settings to 'heal.'"

Jacob clucked his tongue and grabbed me by the arm, presumably to demonstrate what I should do. Pressure changed in the room so sharply I thought I'd end up with a case of the bends, and the white light surged through me, and into him.

He let go of my arm like he'd just grabbed a live wire. He hadn't sucked out all my juice, but he'd made off with a good portion of it. He spread his arms wide, and a benevolent glow surrounded him.

"All right," I said. My head was spinning. I locked my knees to keep myself from kissing the concrete. "You grabbed the energy, you heal her."

He looked at me, wide-eyed and open-armed.

I was miffed he'd taken the white light I'd been hoarding all night, accidentally or not. "Go on. Do it."

Jacob was too far into the zone to argue with me. He turned toward the center of the circle, and he focused. The white glow that surrounded him reached out toward the fire ghost. It surrounded both of them. If the white light ran like a faucet inside me, it rose from Jacob like a gentle morning mist.

Fire ghost's strobing slowed. She stared at Jacob with a look of both agony and bewilderment. I started to look away, but forced myself to keep my eyes on her—and when I did, when I made myself really, really look, I saw the chain around her neck.

✦ THIRTY-TWO ✦

"Shit."

Jacob's white light wavered. "What?"

"She's chained here."

"Restrained? Like a straightjacket?"

"No, literally chained—like a dog. Like some sick fuck hid her down here." For sex...or torture? Or both. "Goddammitall."

"Who?"

"I don't know who. She's not talking. Wouldn't I have said something if she was talking? Maybe she can't talk. Maybe she never could."

Jacob's eyebrows drew down and the veins in his neck bulged. His white light glowed steady. The fire ghost clawed at the chain—a choke chain—and I saw the red gouge around her neck where it sat, and the fingermarks where she'd tried to pry it off. And maybe she could have. If she'd been sane, or at least mentally competent. If she'd realized that all she needed to do was stop pulling.

"Tell her to stop pulling," I said.

"What?"

"She doesn't like me, she likes you. She'll listen to you. It's a choke chain, and the harder she pulls on it, the tighter it gets."

Jacob's focus narrowed to a pinpoint, and he looked at her so hard, I would've bet money that he could see her, too. "Don't worry, Miss. I'm here to help you. I need you to calm down."

Fire ghost stared at Jacob, mouth open, tongue working.

"She's listening," I whispered.

"It's a trick chain," Jacob told her. "Step back and it will loosen. Stop pulling, and you can slip out."

She flickered, doubtful. Her hands went to her throat.

I spotted a hospital band around her wrist, an old-fashioned thing that looked like it'd been through an industrial typewriter. "Jacob," I said. His name left my mouth in a visible stream. "I think I can get an I.D."

"Miss? My partner's going to approach. I need you to stay calm. I'm here to help. We're both here to help."

I stepped inside the circle I'd created, and the spirit-cold fell away so suddenly that at first I thought it had actually plummeted more, sub-zero and capable of singeing my fingers and toes with frostbite. But no. The burn I felt was an actual burn, and smoke seared my lungs when I took a breath.

The ghostfire that looked blue from the outside glowed red from where I stood. And the scenery shifted, too. The ductwork and corrugated boxes had turned into coal bins and shovels, and big, hulking, black furnaces with fire glowing behind closed grates.

"Look, lady, it'll all be over soon. You want me to get you out of here? Just stay still for a second. Okay?"

It cost me to say even that much. Tears ran down my face and I gagged on the thick, charred air. I read the bracelet, got a first initial, last name, and a date. M. Connoley — Ward 5, April 12, 1949. That narrowed things down. Under that, just before she blinked back a few steps, I caught a glimpse of a word, ...*hizophren....* I'd had no idea the medical profession had even diagnosed schizophrenia way back when. But it explained a lot.

I staggered back out of the circle, choking on my own breath. "Connoley," I told Jacob. "And Ward 5, whatever that means. Probably the psych ward."

"Miss Connoley," he said in his most velvety, it's-all-gonna-be-okay voice. At the sound of her name, she stared at him like he'd just whacked her with a tire iron to get her attention. "Listen to me carefully. What I need you to do is step back two paces, then reach around to the back of the chain and loosen the part where the links pass through one another."

Jacob sent her more white light, bathed her with it, and she stood there for a long moment, just staring at him. I figured she'd been hypnotized by his voice, his face, his smooth white light. But then her face twisted up as she struggled against herself, and she stepped back.

The last expression that flickered across her face was surprise.

And then she was gone.

The ghostfire dwindled and disappeared. The air pressure changed again, and my eardrums flexed painfully until I worked my jaw and made them pop. I swayed, and Jacob's hand was on my shoulder.

"We did it," he said. Pleased. Proud, even. But not surprised, not really—in the way people who think they're capable of anything are never too shocked when it all shakes out in the end.

I swatted his hand from my shoulder. "You stole my light."

"I didn't mean to," he said, totally earnest.

I picked up the candle at my feet. When I stood up, Jacob pressed into my back. I blew the candle out.

"The white light," he said, "it felt like warmth to me. Vibration. You see it as light?"

I sighed. I wanted to snap at him, that greedy light stealer. But it was his big day, his first triumph as a non-NP. So who was I to rain on his parade? "Yeah. It's all a big TV show for me. Sights and sounds."

He pressed his forehead against the back of my head and breathed into my hair. "And the temperature drop?"

"Dunno. It's a ghost thing. Always has been."

"Can spirits hear your thoughts? Did I need to speak to Connoley aloud, or could I have communicated mind to mind?"

Since when did I have all the answers? Or any at all, for that matter. "I don't know. I've never been able to Vulcan Mind Meld with 'em, but that doesn't mean it's not possible. Carolyn hears thoughts, right? Maybe there's a medium out there who's got a touch of telepathy." And maybe a different medium actually could get a reading off a dead person's possessions, if the medium's talent came through a clairvoyant-looking route. Who knows?

Jacob took me by the shoulder and maneuvered me around to face him. Our lips brushed. Mine were cold, his warm. He touched my cheek. His hand was trembling.

"You okay?" I asked him.

He smiled against my mouth. "Yeah. More than okay." He cupped the back of my head and put an end to our conversation with a long, deep kiss.

"Detective Bayne?" I wondered if Betty was using her normal tone of voice, or if she was especially chipper. Hard to tell. "Sergeant Warwick wants to see you before you go to LaSalle General this morning."

I tallied up my mental scorecard and decided that the chances of me getting called on the carpet for something I'd screwed up were exponentially higher than anything else: a pat on the back, a harmless question, or a couple free tickets to a Bulls game. And yet, Betty wasn't doing that thing with her eyes—the thing that said, "be careful—he's in a mood."

"Like, uh, now?"

She glanced back at his office as if to see if he was listening in, and then nodded.

I wouldn't even get to talk to Zigler, tell him that we'd sent the fire ghost on to wherever it was that tormented, crazy spirits went when they were done haunting the spot they'd died in.

I brushed some bagel crumbs off the front of my sportcoat, waited for Betty to buzz Warwick and give me a nod, and went in.

Ted Warwick was scowling at his computer. He didn't use a mouse, just the touchpad. I watched his blunt cop-finger stroking the plastic square as he scrolled something on his screen. I couldn't really gauge how irritated he was. His face had a few permanent lines on it that tended to be misleading.

"Sit down, Bayne."

And again, that could be either good or bad. I straightened my tie, and I sat.

Warwick closed his laptop, and sighed. "I need advance notice if you plan to venture out with Detective Marks in any official capacity."

I can't imagine how blank I must've looked. Scratch that, I can. Pretty blank.

Warwick looked at me hard. He didn't seem angry, exactly. Just really, really focused. He stared at me for a second, then swiveled in his chair and pulled a sheet of paper off his inkjet printer. He slid it in front of me.

It was a candid photo, slightly dark. A three-quarter view of Jacob striding by in a black suit and overcoat filled most of the frame. My God. He was so hot.

And there, just behind him, was me. I don't photograph well. I was opening my mouth to talk. But it was definitely me.

"Cameraphone," Warwick said. "One of the nurses snapped a shot of Marks so she could show her girlfriends."

"This was taken last night," I said. "How did you end up with it?"

"I'm getting phone calls and e-mails about you left and right. This one came from D.C., though. So I figured it was time to lay down some ground rules."

I wanted to balk. I've never been good with rules. But I couldn't get over the fact that Warwick wasn't angry with me. Warwick was always angry. He'd been angry with me since day one. So naturally I was curious about what had changed.

Warwick slid me a card. "Cell phone, home phone. Call me half an hour before you and Marks go ghost hunting."

I took a pen out of my pocket and wrote, very small, on the back of the card, *Is FPMP watching?* I rotated the card so it faced Warwick. "And this is your e-mail," I said, "right?" He squinted at it, then met my eye, and very deliberately, nodded.

I jabbed my finger at the card, because damn it, I was so fucking sick of being monitored. "This one bounces sometimes. Don't you have another one?"

He looked at me hard.

"'Cos I had this Psych research article I wanted to send you. So we could talk about it." I was so not smooth.

But I guess I was good enough.

"Okay," Warwick said. He wrote out *Evidence Rm.* in small block letters. "Try this one."

I'd been in the evidence room a time or two, but to be honest, I'd usually let my Stiff deal with the evidence, same as the paperwork. The long, stuffy, rambling room was floor-to-ceiling with boxes and bags, and oddball oversized pieces of furniture, cars, and even architecture. I stared down at a hunk of banister and tried to imagine the tech sawing it off the staircase.

There was also a distinct hum in the air. The west wall was covered in electrical breakers and archaic conduits that looked like a blatant code violation, even to my untrained eye.

"Too much interference," said Warwick, his gruff voice quiet and close. I hadn't even heard him approach. "They can't hear us through the static."

I turned and looked Ted Warwick over. He looked like a cop to me, big and muscular, with a few extra pounds and additional folds of skin that'll sneak up on you in your sixties, but still, someone you wouldn't pick a fight with in a bar. He had a cop face. Cop eyes. And so I'd always assumed that was exactly what he was: a cop.

Then again, so was Roger Burke, technically.

"Will I be in the doghouse if I ask who you work for?" I said.

Warwick turned toward a shelf, picked up an evidence bag, held it at arm's length to read the faded label, then set it back on the shelf. "No," he said. He shook his head. "It's probably better for you to hear it from me, and not cobble together some half-assed theory."

He turned toward me, stuffed his hands awkwardly in his pockets, and said, "I work here. Period. But if I wanted a PsyCop, I had to play ball. With…them."

"Okay. I'll buy that." I wondered if he'd known back then that adding a medium to his roster would buy him a building full of bugs and a bunch of double agents on his force. But I'm not sure it mattered. Whatever Warwick thought he was getting into, it's what he ended up with that counted. "But this paperwork you're funneling to them, the way their goons show up when I'm at a crime scene...you could've given me a heads-up."

"It wouldn't have changed a thing." Warwick picked up the same evidence bag he'd already looked at, turned it over a couple of times, and put it back again. "Here's what I can tell you. You do your job, keep a low profile, and do the odd side-job for them, and they're not gonna bother you. That's what you want. Ain't it?"

I wanted to argue, but when he put it that way, maybe it was.

"You and Marks meeting up," he made a broad gesture, as if it could encompass Jacob in his absence, "all of a sudden, you stood the chance of popping up on everyone's radar. I wouldn't go so far as to call Marks a celebrity...but people recognize him. They remember his face. People hear the word *PsyCop*, the first guy they think of is Marks."

That was true.

"They start connecting him and you...." He stuffed his hand back into his pocket and shrugged.

I thought about the way we approached the media at the Fifth. Warwick himself always spoke to the press, and he never named names. It was always "investigators" who would be following up, or collecting evidence, or combing the scene. Jacob's sergeant, on the other hand, recognized him as the public relations dream that he was, and stuck him front and center every time they so much as nabbed a peeping Tom. Which meant that while the Twelfth got the enthusiastic community policing program, and the new parking lot, and even the good softball team T-shirts, the Fifth got nothing.

"Is it worth it?" I asked.

Warwick looked up at the ceiling. My eyes followed his. Ductwork. He rocked on his heels, and weighed his reply so long that I thought he might not even answer me. But when he did start to talk, it all came out in a long rush.

"I wanted a medium. My sister's kid, her oldest son...he was a medium. We always knew, see? 'Cos he could talk to my mother, who passed when he was just a baby. We all thought he was making it up. He seen her picture, maybe. Heard us talking about her.

"But then he recited the birthdates of all her brothers and sisters, nine of 'em.... None of us knew any of them dates. My brother-in-law, he went down to City Hall, looked 'em up. It took him the better part of a day, but he did. And each and every one of 'em was right."

Warwick gazed at the ductwork. I tried hard to breathe normally, but I was fighting off a lump in my throat. Because how could I help but compare this other guy's experience to mine? What if I had someone to confide in, an actual family member, someone who wasn't itching to ship me off so that they could wash their hands of me? Everything would've played out differently. Everything.

"Uncle Lou?" Warwick said. His voice startled me. "His first name was really Leslie. The kid even knew that. I asked my cousins. They said he never went by it, not since he started the first grade.

"Once we figured out the kid was for real—and believe me, I was a beat cop on the south side, and I looked for every other explanation I could think of—we had him keep quiet about it. And little Alex, he was a good kid. He never told nobody."

I couldn't look Warwick in the eye, not while he told this story. Because I could tell it wasn't gonna end well. If it did, Alex would be the one with the gun and the shield. Not me. I stared hard at the humming conduits.

"Until they came up with those Psych screenings. Alex was twenty. And we brought him in to be tested."

Cripes. He was a year younger than me.

Warwick was quiet for a long while. I looked at him, finally, and found him staring at the evidence bags with a red flush over his cheeks and neck. "Did he train?" I asked.

Warwick nodded.

"Heliotrope Station?"

He nodded again.

Jesus.

Maybe Camp Hell was the part of my life I'd managed to repress, and maybe I was sweating buckets lately, and popping Valiums while I tried to sort it all out. But I realized something. At least when Camp Hell recruited me from the Cook County Mental Health Center, I was already fairly jaded.

Imagine if I'd thought the world was a fairly decent place? They would've flayed me alive.

"He didn't last long," Warwick said. "Slit his wrists after three months. That's what they told me, anyway." He pinched the bridge of his nose, and gave a heavy, world-weary sigh. "I viewed the body but...who's to say what really happened?"

"He tested too high," I blurted out.

I'd meant to comfort him. Warwick was a cop; he'd want the truth. Wouldn't he? But when his eyes snapped to mine, and I felt the full intensity of his gaze, I wished I'd kept my mouth shut. "Alex died before you even signed up," he said. "You got no way of knowing that."

I didn't add anything else. We both knew that I did.

Warwick shook his head and turned on his heel. "I wanted a medium, I got one. End of story."

I had to take long steps to keep up with him, and even so, I barely caught what he was saying because he was so busy walking away from me. "Sarge," I said. "Hold on."

He stopped with his hand on the doorknob and looked. I could tell his patience was running on fumes—and that maybe I'd get a better answer later, once he'd shed a tear or two for Alex in the privacy of a restroom stall. But then again, maybe I wouldn't. Maybe we'd never speak of any of this again. After all, that was the way he handled anything problematic, by pretending it wasn't happening. Right?

"Why me?"

He stared.

"I'm sure you saw everyone's files. Faun Windsong was almost as strong. Maybe even a level four. Me? My talent's stronger, but I know my file was full of black marks, and it had 'queer' written all over it."

Warwick considered. "The gay thing? Technically, it's a sexual harassment lawsuit waiting to happen if anyone hassles you over it. And you always had enough sense to downplay your...lifestyle. So I didn't worry about it. The rest of the file?" He thought about it. "I been on the force longer than you been alive. What your record said to me was that you knew how to take care of yourself." He shrugged. "So far, I been right about that."

He opened the door. A rush of air drifted in from the hallway, cool and clean in contrast with the sour stuffiness of the evidence room. "Faun Windsong," he said, so low I almost didn't hear it. "Now there's the most annoying interview I ever did."

✦ THIRTY-THREE ✦

I sat down hard at my desk and stared across it at Zigler. He was typing something up on his ancient desktop, and it was a good enough excuse for him to not have to look me in the eye. So he ditched a scene with a crazy ghost in it. In my eyes, that made him more of a pragmatist than a coward. But Zig seemed to be having a little trouble swallowing the way things had gone down in the basement at LaSalle.

"You talked to Warwick a long time," he said.

I nodded, then realized he was still not looking at me, and followed it up with an affirmative grunt.

Zig typed. The keys made sticky plastic sounds. Elsewhere on the second floor, a half dozen conversations rose and fell and a couple of phones rang.

"Anything I need to know about?" he said.

"Huh?"

"Come on, Vic. Stop playing around. What did Warwick say?"

"Oh." He'd said so many things that I hadn't even processed them all. But nothing that pertained to Zigler. "Nothing. Not about what happened yesterday, anyway."

Zigler's typing stopped.

"I, uh...I didn't mention anything to him," I said. "So, y'know. It's all good."

Finally he looked me in the eye. "It isn't 'all good.' We've still got a thing in the basement at LaSalle. What'll happen with that?"

"Oh." I scratched the back of my neck. "I kinda went back and...dealt with it."

"You went back." Zig thought about that. "Alone?"

"Jacob...helped."

Zig sat back so hard his chair wheezed. "You and Marks took care of it."

He seemed so baffled by that idea, I almost felt sorry for him. "Jacob's into stuff like...that."

He shook his head. "Jesus."

"I guess we could check out the repeaters now. But my guess is that they're all tied to that ghost in the coal cellar. She was restrained down there, a fire started—heck, maybe she started it herself—and a bunch of people died, including her. A few of those people left repeaters behind. She left a full-blown spirit."

Zig was nodding at my explanation, but he still looked stunned. "So you worked with Marks."

"Unofficially. I mean, I think it's not exactly smiled upon by either Warwick or Owens." Or the FPMP, or whoever else was keeping tabs on me. "How do you even fill out a time card for that?" I joked.

My attempt at lightening up the mood fell flat. "He's a better NP, I imagine."

"Working with Jacob is like being chased by a bulldozer. If he were my Stiff, I'd be used up and burnt out by now." I didn't mention that Jacob technically wasn't NP, either. I figured it was safest to keep it our little secret, even though it meant that I couldn't complain about him stealing my white light.

Zigler looked doubtful—as if I could make something like that up just to spare his feelings. "Trust me," I said. "On the job, Jacob's a shark. Carolyn Brinkman can handle that. Me?" I pushed a paper clip along the edge of my desk blotter. "I've got enough to worry about without keeping one eye on my partner, too."

Zig nodded slowly. "So. If we head back to LaSalle, are we still going to see your breath in the coal cellar?"

"Nope. It's clean. Other than all the boxes and ductwork I knocked over, anyway."

My phone rang and vibrated, and Zigler went back to his typing when I flipped it open to take Jacob's call. "Hello?"

"Last night was amazing."

"Uh huh. I was just telling Zig about that."

"You know what would've made it even better?"

I could imagine. "Well, it was kinda late." I was running on three hours' sleep as it was.

"I want to do it again."

I reminded myself that I should be happy for him. He actually *wanted* to be a Psych. "Yeah, uh, sure. I imagine something will crop up." Given that I was surrounded by death, I was fairly confident we'd find more ghosts to play with. Hopefully, they'd be nice, safe repeaters.

"Don't work too late," he said. His tone of voice suggested that he'd make it worth my while.

We disconnected, and I looked at my messages. "This message you left me after all the fun we had at LaSalle yesterday," I said to Zigler. "Do I need to listen to it?"

His cheeks flushed. "I'd prefer if you didn't."

"You got it." I hit erase.

There was yesterday's unplayed message from Jacob, telling me I was right. He didn't go into any details, but the tone of his voice made me smile, even though I knew now that it would lead to white light theft, and who knows what else, down the road. I saved it. That left one more message—the one from Unavailable.

Even though I expected Dreyfuss' voice, he still managed to surprise me. "Here I am," he said, "in a swanky building overlooking the river, and there you are, in a musty old basement. Does that make any sense to you, Detective? Because you're the one with the skills. Shouldn't you be able to cash in on them?

"Look, I don't expect you to be crazy about me. But let's be practical. We can help each other out, so why shouldn't we?

"I'm really keen on getting those cold spots taken care of, dig it? So here's a little something that might light a fire under you.

"A certain someone's come into possession of a *Get Out of Jail Free* card. Rumor has it that he flies the coop at noon tomorrow. So consider yourself forewarned. And think about how much easier life would be if you got a heads-up on some of the nastier curve balls Fate's throwing at you, before they nail you in the head.

"You want to play ball on the winning team for a change? You know where to find me."

My blood turned to ice in my veins. I looked up at the clock. "Zig? Can you get me to the MCC in forty minutes?"

"This time of day? We'd need a cruiser, and we'd have to run the siren all the way downtown."

I jumped up from my desk, flew past Betty, and took the stairs down two at a time. I spotted Officer "Andy" at one of the interchangeable desks where the patrolmen work. He was filling out some forms for an earnest-looking Hispanic guy who was nodding a lot, and had the look of someone who didn't speak very much English. "Andy's" partner was at the opposite end of the station, hovering around the coffee pot. I skidded to a stop beside "Andy." He looked at me, startled.

"Give me your cruiser."

"Andy" stared at me for a second. His Adam's apple bobbed. Then, lo and behold, he unhooked his keyring from his belt and handed it over without a word.

Zigler caught up with me at the front door. I tossed him "Andy's" keys. "Let's go."

The way Zig handled that squad car was a thing of beauty. The speed, and the whoop of the siren, and the precision with which he wove in and out of traffic, all of that combined into a steady buildup of adrenaline. I was charging. And Roger Burke was at the end of that charge.

Not that I was sure I knew what to do once I got there. But at least I'd make it on time.

"So," Zig said. "You planning to tell me what this big emergency is? Who've you been checking on at Metropolitan Correctional?"

I glanced at Zig, and tried to get a feel for whether I should tell him or not. Warwick wasn't snitching on me, I was pretty sure about that—unless he was the world's greatest actor, and that thing about his nephew was a script the FPMP had put together for him to gain my trust. But I doubted that. The blotches on Warwick's neck never lied.

Zig, though? Even if my gut instincts were totally worthless, I'd met his family, his kids. And that, alone, made me want to trust him.

I took a deep breath and steeled myself. "It's Roger Burke."

Zigler huffed out a sound of disgust. "What about him? Is he being sentenced today? You trying to make it there, see if you can get the judge to add a few more decades to his time?"

"About that...."

My phone rang.

I checked caller I.D.—Russeau and Kline. "Sorry, Zig. I need to, uh...." I hit the talk button. "Hello?"

Stefan's voice was velvety and calm. "You left in a hurry last night."

Did I? The main thing I remembered about the night before was exorcising the fire ghost with Jacob, who glowed even more brightly than she did. I thought back to our appointment, and the regression. That's right: I'd been a little squeamish about that blowjob. And I didn't really want to go into it in a closed car with Zigler.

"Is that a siren?" Stefan asked.

"Yeah. I'm at work."

"I'm concerned about your job. I picked up a fair amount of anxiety from you when I brought it up yesterday."

Again, yesterday seemed like ten years ago, and I tried to imagine what might've been bothering me about work. Zig had just tried to walk off the case. And I was scared of the fire ghost—who wouldn't have been? But other than that, work hadn't really been an issue. "No," I said. "I don't think so."

"Are you sure? Sometimes anxiety feels generalized, when it's actually got a specific cause. Think back. Did anything unusual happen yesterday?"

A driver in the right lane panicked when she saw our lights, and swerved like crazy onto the shoulder. My heart pounded in my throat. "Now's really not a good time."

"Are you driving?"

"No."

"Then what's the harm in it? Tell me something you did yesterday."

Zigler swung toward the off-ramp. I checked the time. Fifteen minutes to get to Metropolitan Correctional. "Look, I'm sorry, but I really am busy. I'll call you back."

"Will you?"

"Why wouldn't I?"

Traffic snarled up at the bottom of the ramp as some drivers tried to move to the right, and others tooled along, oblivious to the siren.

"Stress is a leading cause of poor performance at work. I just feel that unburdening yourself of some of these things you carry around can only help you out in the long run."

"I'll call you back. I promise. Swear to God, I'm right in the middle of something."

"Riding in a car. If it's not work that's got you tied up in knots, maybe it's your lover. What's going on with him lately?"

"Jacob? We're fine. Things are...." I glanced over at Zig, who looked like he was trying his best not to hear me, and failing miserably. "They're fine."

Metropolitan Correctional loomed up ahead. We had eight minutes to spare, so Zig cut the lights and the siren. I made a circular motion to indicate he should go around the block, and luckily he was quick enough on the uptake to understand what it was supposed to mean.

"He hasn't said or done anything out of the ordinary lately?" Stefan prompted.

"I'm sorry," I said. "I gotta go. I'm sorry." I fought down the urge to apologize for repeating myself, disconnected the phone, and turned it off.

Zigler cleared his throat. "You want me to park, or...?"

"Go around. I want to see who's here."

There were civilians outside the doors, and a couple of uniforms. Was that unusual? Maybe so. Every time I'd gone to see Burke, the outside had been clear. But it was nearly noon. Maybe some people worked nearby and were taking their lunch breaks. Still...I didn't trust myself to tell the difference between an office worker and a reporter, not in the middle of winter where everyone's wrapped up in a coat.

"I don't mean to pry," said Zig, once we'd turned a corner and the front of the prison was out of sight. "But was that your therapist?"

I gave a small, humorless laugh. I supposed that label was as good as any. "Yeah."

Another two turns, and we approached the front of the building again. "Hope you don't mind me saying, but he seems kind of pushy."

"I guess. We've known each other a long time. He doesn't feel like he needs to beat around the bush for the sake of being polite. Pull over here."

Zig pulled the cruiser into a bike lane.

"You want me to come along?"

I did. But I didn't want to get him into trouble if things went south. "Nah. It's better if you wait in the car."

"If you want the number of the doctor I'm seeing, she's pretty good. She's got a lighter touch. Easy to talk to."

"Really. It's okay."

Zig held his hands up in surrender. I got out of the cruiser, sized up the people milling around the prison entrance, and opened my overcoat and jacket so I could draw my sidearm if I had to. Not that I thought I'd actually need to shoot anyone. But just in case.

I walked with my head down and wished I had a pair of sunglasses on me. That cameraphone shot of Jacob and me had me spooked. Heck, everything that'd happened since Burke had told me about the FPMP had me spooked.

One of the uniforms approached a couple of civilians and told them to move along. I should show him my badge, introduce myself. Hide behind him, if necessary. But between Burke, and "Andy," and whoever was sending those fucking faxes to Dreyfuss, I just didn't know who to trust anymore.

So I didn't think it was Warwick leaking information about me, and I didn't think it was Zigler. Who else did I see with any regularity? Betty? She was the keeper of the personnel files. But I couldn't see that she had access to much else. Heck, she hadn't even figured out that I was queer. Which I'd actually discussed with Warwick earlier, without even meaning to.

Okay, so none of them. And "Andy" probably couldn't do much more than report on my general movements, given that he needed to actually perform his police job to maintain his cover.

I didn't socialize with any of my neighbors, and I didn't have any friends, other than Crash. Okay, that was beyond sad.

Stefan would probably spin some kind of psychiatric mumbo-jumbo out of my inability to make friends. I'm sure my lack of personal connections was indicative of an inferiority complex, or trust issues, or some other failing in my personality makeup.

I felt exhausted even thinking about how that conversation might go. I made a mental note to steer the discussion in a new direction if the topic of friends ever came up. There had to be some way to shift topics. Work, for instance. He always acted so curious about what was happening at....

Jesus. Jesus fucking Christ.

No.

Not Stefan. Not him. God damn it, anyone but him.

My fists clenched up so hard that my fingernails cut into my palms. I struggled to catch my breath for so long that in an attempt to keep myself from blacking out, I ended up crouched like a guy who'd just run a marathon.

"Sir, we're gonna need you to clear the area."

Black polyester pants and a heavy belt hung with gun, flashlight and pepper spray filled my vision. I straightened up, and somehow, managed to breathe. And even to talk normally.

"Detective Bayne, Fifth Precinct," I said. I pulled my badge.

The uniform glanced at it, and then at my holster, and for whatever reason, decided not to make anything out of the fact that I was having a panic attack. Either that, or he figured I'd just run the last couple of blocks. "Officer Collins, Twenty-Third. You here for the ex-PsyCop's release?"

I figured I couldn't claim that I'd just happened to run by in search of a deli. I nodded.

"They're over there, on the other side of the van," he said.

They? I knew I should probably ask, but that would blow whatever credibility I'd stumbled upon. "Thanks," I said instead, and walked toward the van as if that was exactly where I'd been headed all along.

A cluster of businessmen on cell phones approached on my left, and I stepped up the pace to blend in with their pack while I scoped out the van. More people in suits, some of them in sunglasses. Plainclothes officers? FPMP goons? No, probably not FPMP. You'd never spot them. They looked like Roger Burke, and Jennifer Chance, and Constantine Dreyfuss, and Officer "Andy," who I'd only spotted because I felt paranoid that day, and I noticed he was looking at me a little too hard.

One of the suits near the van turned, and I realized I'd seen him before. Caucasian. Middle-aged, but fit, on the muscular side. I detached from the crowd, backed up to the building, and pretended to take a phone call, holding the phone as naturally as I could while I shielded my face with my hand.

I waited for another group of civilians to walk by, and I risked another look at the suits behind the van while the people passed between us.

I knew that guy. Damn it. Think.

There was a gap in the crowd, and I turned toward the wall. I wondered if I should actually talk to my phone, or if that would make it even more obvious that the thing was really off. I settled for nodding.

A couple of women in business suits and bright white sneakers passed by, and I risked another glance behind the van. I totally knew that guy. But I'd never connect the dots, not now, not when I was in a tailspin and the whole world felt like it was crashing down around my....

FBI. That's it. He was one of the agents who'd met up with me in Missouri after they nailed Roger Burke. Shit. I hadn't counted on anyone having met me before. And of all people, him. Was he the one who'd been on the receiving end of my phony recant? Or was it his partner? Or did it even matter?

Lying had become such a way of life for me that I couldn't figure out why I felt like such a heel for spinning the story that would set Burke free. It made no sense. Swearing under oath? What was an oath to someone who couldn't even picture God? But the fact that I'd recanted gnawed at me anyway, deep down in my guts.

I put some distance between me and the Feds to try and avoid being spotted, which suddenly seemed way more important than getting a look at that smug, smiling bastard when he emerged from those bulletproof doors.

The front of the building was a nightmare for anyone trying to hide, which I imagine was no mistake. The only shelter anywhere near the door was that van, and of course, I needed to hide from the agents who were hiding there.

I approached a Plexiglas bus shelter that was farther away than I would've liked, and more transparent, too. But it was better than nothing.

Maybe if I positioned my head directly behind one of the torn, faded handbills, I could keep my eye on the proceedings.

There was a civilian in the shelter, a businesswoman. I would've preferred my very own spot, but there was nowhere else for me to lurk. I hunched into the far corner and tore a corner off a poster so I could see the doors, and I hoped the bus would come soon so I could be alone.

I had to crane my neck to see the doors, but I had a pretty good view of the feds. One minute they were relaxed—for Feds—and the next they were coiled for action, tapping earpieces and talking to their Bluetooth mics.

Crap. I couldn't see. A group of uniforms appeared at the doorway, and a guy with a handheld video camera.

A bus wheezed up on its deafening pneumatic brakes, and it blotted out what little sunlight filtered through the El tracks. The bus door opened. I expected the businesswoman to get on, but she didn't. I glanced at the bus driver. He was staring at me, annoyed. I shook my head, and he closed the door and rolled away.

I knew why I didn't get on, but what about the businesswoman? I looked at her, and froze.

Not only was she staring at me—I'll assume for the same reason I'd looked at her—but I knew her. She was more familiar than the Fed, even. It was Laura, Dreyfuss' secretary, in head-to-toe shades of designer gray.

I really, really wanted to pretend I hadn't noticed her and just go on with my snooping, but that option had evaporated the second our eyes met. "Dreyfuss couldn't be bothered to do his own spying?" I said.

"Why are you here, Detective?"

"Why?" It seemed pretty obvious to me. "I have a little history with Roger. I guess I just...needed to see what he'd do next." Besides, her boss had been the one to give me the heads-up, so wasn't it obvious? Or was it? That had been the first time Dreyfuss had ever dialed me directly.

"You should go home," she told me. "It's not safe." She gave the silky gray scarf around her neck an extra wrap and strode past me, out of the bus shelter, and past the FBI agents who were all hopped up on red alert. I'm sure they saw her. But an unremarkable Asian woman? Not worth their notice.

Laura slid between a couple of parked cars, and then I lost sight of her.

One of the uniforms got into a standoff with the video camera guy. The cop was body-blocking, a lot like Jacob does when he's trying to get his way, and the guy had the poor judgment to give him a shove. Three officers converged and spun the guy's face to the wall, the video camera bounced off the concrete, leaving a few shards of plastic behind, and a set of cuffs snapped on the cameraman's wrists faster than you can say "dislocated shoulder."

The cops dragged the cameraman toward a squad car. Speaking of which.... Was Zig still around? I assumed so. I'd had him park. I bet his cruiser would offer a better vantage point than the stupid Plexi bus shelter. But I suspected my "I'm just a guy on the phone" act had worn thin, and I didn't want to risk drawing attention to myself by marching past the Feds yet again.

I checked the street. It looked like typical South Loop traffic, slowish, stop-

and-go. I could squeeze between the parked cars and the moving vehicles without too much fear of losing a limb. Bike messengers did it every day.

Once I actually tried it, I had no idea how they managed. My heart was already in my throat from the whole who's-who that seemed to be going on in front of Metropolitan Correctional. Add moving cars brushing against my right side to the mix. The sideview of a gigantic SUV clipped me in the shoulder. Damn it. I passed the FBI van and squeezed through the other side. Zig was about ten cars back. I could do it.

There was a scuffle behind me, and I glanced back over my shoulder just in time to see Roger Burke emerge, flanked by a couple of lawyer-looking white guys in suits and a half-dozen security guards. They turned toward the sedan I was currently standing directly in front of. So much for camouflaging myself.

I wouldn't say Roger was smiling, not exactly. His eyes were wide and his lips were pulled back from his straight, white teeth, but he looked more dazed than anything. Manic.

I was trying to fix that fucked-up expression in my mind's eye—probably so I could sort it out later—when the red hole appeared in the center of his forehead.

The report of the gun probably happened at roughly the same time, or even slightly before. But my brain registered the sight of the bullet hole before I heard it. Or maybe my sixth sense was ever so slightly precognitive, and I could see gunshot wounds before they happened, but not far enough in advance that I could actually do anything about them.

Not that I would've thrown myself in front of Roger Burke and taken a bullet for him, anyway.

Car doors flew open, and men in suits streamed all around me. Seems I wasn't the only one who'd decided that a parked car was the only logical place to hide.

"Vic." My arm was on fire. I didn't realize that stupid SUV had hit it so hard until someone grabbed it. Zigler. "Get in the car."

"Wait."

I looked at the swarm around the spot where Roger Burke had gone down. And there he was, standing in the middle of it with that bullet hole in his forehead, security guards ducking through his spirit to get to his rapidly cooling corpse.

His wide eyes went wider still, and his head snapped up to meet my gaze.

"Vic, come on." Zigler pulled my arm harder.

Roger Burke cocked his index finger and thumb into a gun shape, and mimed the shot that had killed him.

He'd done that before—shackled, so that his other hand had dragged along behind the first. Back in the visiting room, when he'd told me about the assassin.

I nodded. I couldn't think of a more fitting way for him to go.

I started to turn away, but then Roger waved at me to get my attention. I looked, grudgingly, because I've always hated that habit of his, feeding information out slowly so that he can have the last word.

He put his fingers to the outer corners of his eyes and pulled back.

If we were playing charades in a schoolyard, I'd interpret that as "Chinese." But that couldn't be right.

"Get in the car," Zig barked, and I flinched. He'd never used his bossy cop voice on me before, and it was pretty darned effective. I climbed in.

He'd double-parked next to the sedan, and traffic behind him started to clog the street. Zig drove to the end of the block, then pulled into a bus lane and parked. "What did you see?"

Burke. Gun. Chinese. "I'm not sure."

"You had to be seeing something. Otherwise you would've had the sense to get your ass out of the direct line of fire."

"Oh." He was getting pretty good at reading me. And he'd just sworn, which meant he was pissed. "Uh...yeah."

Gun. Chinese. The only Asian I even knew was...Laura.

I'd always heard that secretaries run the show, but this was a little much. Laura, the assassin?

Or was that really so crazy after all? It would've put her in the perfect spot to keep tabs on Dreyfuss. Shit. I'd drunk half a pot of coffee brewed by an assassin. My fingers and toes felt numb, and I was shivering. I aimed the heater vent toward my face and pressed my whole body back into the seat. "His spirit stuck around, but I was too far away to hear anything."

Zigler grunted. "Doesn't matter. I'm sure whatever he said would've been a lie."

✦ THIRTY-FOUR ✦

I gave a statement in the FBI van. There wasn't much to say. I'd been looking at Roger Burke, and the shot had come from behind me. Somewhere out in the street, or maybe across it. Maybe from wherever Laura had ducked off to while the Feds had their eyes on Metropolitan Correctional's front door.

I didn't mention Laura, even when they asked me if I had noticed anything unusual or relevant that I wanted to add. Maybe I could've said something in passing...but how could I, without invoking the name of the FPMP?

The last thing Laura had told me was to be careful. And I took that advice to heart.

They took my card and told me they'd be in touch if they needed anything else, but even though it was a different agent who took my statement than the one who'd been on the receiving end of the fake recant, I didn't think they'd base their investigation on anything I had to say, not unless it was corroborated by someone reliable.

Zigler might've seen more from his vantage point on the street, or maybe not, given that he was busy keeping an eye on me. The Feds split us up before I could ask. Given my track record, I guess I didn't blame them.

Despite my heavy overcoat, I was chilled through and through, and my teeth started knocking together while I waited for Zigler to give his statement. The cruiser was locked, and he had the keys. And it wasn't as if the lobby of Metropolitan Correctional was anywhere I could kill an hour while I waited for Zig.

I stared up at the gray sky between the El tracks, and I guesstimated the distance to Russeau and Kline. Seven city blocks? If that. It would be easier to block Stefan's number from my cell phone and drop off his radar for another fifteen years, but I knew if I weaseled my way out like that, the unfinished business between us would eat away at me. I needed to look him in the eye, and tell him that I knew.

Cold turned to numbness as I made my way to the big beige skyscraper. By the time I got to the elevator, I couldn't feel my feet anymore. I think it was only partially the cold. Mostly, it was nerves.

Carissa looked up when I walked into the waiting room of Russeau and Kline. "Detective...Bayne is it? I don't think you're in the schedule today."

I walked by her, figuring the chances of her being able to physically prevent me from walking into his office were pretty slim. After all, how many secretaries moonlighted as assassins? Probably not as many as you'd think.

Stefan stood as I burst into the room. Or I tried to burst, anyway. The door had a pneumatic closer at the top, and the best I could do was cause it to bump into the circular rubber doorstop on the wall.

He was at his hypnosis chair, and a woman in a sweater suit with an artsy necklace on sat across from him on the couch, head lolling. She sniffed and stopped talking as if she sensed my presence despite her hypnosis, but then resumed whatever she was saying. Evidently, her subconscious had decided that I really wasn't a threat. I couldn't quite make out the words. It was as if she was speaking in tongues, or maybe twin-language.

Stefan marched up to me like he was ready to bite my head off, but then he stopped maybe a yard away. I can only guess at what he might've thought: that I was coming in for my panic attacks, maybe—or that I had the sudden urge to uncover yet another buried memory.

I had no doubt that if that was the presumption he'd been working under, his sixth sense had cleared it all up for him and let him know, in no uncertain terms, that I was pissed.

"Not now," he whispered, and jerked his head to indicate his patient.

I glanced at her. She mumbled something, smiled, then mumbled some more.

"Don't worry." I tried to whisper back, but I was so mad that I spat the "D" out. "This won't take long."

He put his hands on his hips. I struggled to keep myself from poking him in the chest. "I don't know what's worse," I hissed. "You passing yourself off as some kind of therapist and then running to Dreyfuss with everything I say, or back then, all those years ago, when you and me, we actually had something."

He held up his hands as if they'd ward me off. "Before you fly off the handle...."

"You told Krimski about the wig!"

His eyes went wide. I guess I'd gotten more out of the regressions than he'd bargained for.

"You won't show mama the carpet," the patient on the couch blurted out in a sudden burst of clarity. Then she resumed her bizarre mumbling.

"It was stupid of you not to," Stefan whispered. "What on earth were you hoping to accomplish by lying about it? It was a wig. That's all. A fucking wig."

"I told them I couldn't read anything from it. They kept sending it back anyway."

"But you didn't explain that whole thing about objects and clairsentients. You never told them anything about anything, and it was always so obvious that you knew. You held back because you were stubborn, end of story."

I though of the Joneses and their cheeseball Vegas act, and the fourth-level medium who'd bought it in Florida, and all the remote viewers who'd been sucked into the Bermuda Triangle without the benefit of a Caribbean cruise. And I wondered if maybe Stefan had never actually figured out it was entirely possible to be *too* psychic.

"If that's why you think I was holding back, then they must've been grading you on a bell curve to give you a level five."

Stefan scowled. I'd never impugned his ability. I'd never dared. After all, he could very well make me shit myself.

"It's not as if I can read you now," he said. "You're nothing but angry. But back then? I guess I would've said you were scared."

"And still, you gave away secrets—my secrets—behind my back."

From the couch, the hypnotized woman muttered, "No, Mama. It was like that when I got home."

"What the fuck is her problem?" I snapped.

Stefan rolled his eyes. "Bulimic. Weird relationship with her mother." He turned his back to her and steered me toward the wall, as if was just the two of us, alone, in the room. "Vic, if I didn't tell Krimski about the wig, the next time they took you into the green room, the twelve-hour wig-fest would've seemed fun in comparison. I didn't tell them anything new. I confirmed what you'd already told them: that there was nothing to see."

My anger ratcheted down, but I couldn't determine if it was because he was using that smooth baritone voice on me, speaking in that well-modulated, calm and controlled way that would lower the blood pressure of anyone within twenty paces of him, or if he was using his talent on me, stroking me internally and telling me that everything was perfectly fine, nothing to get worked up about... or if maybe I simply believed him.

I tried to rally my self-righteous anger. "You make it sound like you were doing it for my sake—but here's what I don't get. You had to know how pissed I'd be if I found out. You could've let me in on it from the start. We could've fed them what we wanted them to hear together."

"And have a precog tattle on me?" He shrugged, disgusted. "It wasn't as if there were any decent options for me to choose from. I did what I thought was best."

The woman on the couch picked up the tissue box, tore the cardboard side off it, and stuffed it into her mouth.

"Aren't you going to stop her?"

Stefan glanced disdainfully in her direction, and said, "Dietary fiber."

I told myself to stay focused. Stay mad. "That was then. What about now?"

"What about now?"

"I know about the faxes."

His expression shifted subtly. Hardened. "Fine. So you know. I'm surprised it's taken you this long to figure it out, considering what you supposedly do for a living. What do you think I tell them? About your Valium and your panic attacks and your terrifying boyfriend who's harder to read than the coat rack in the corner? No. I tell them where you had lunch. I make note of what you're wearing. I mention what you've done at work...which they can just as easily pick up by monitoring your workplace. And, by the way, they do. But I give them that very same information, and they think they've got a secret window into your psyche. And maybe they stop digging so hard."

I stared him in the eye, and I tried to figure out whether or not I believed him. He could've been telling me the truth. My guess was that he'd given me some truthful reasons, but probably not all of them. Only the ones that would paint him as less of a Judas.

The hypnotized woman started gagging.

"Good lord," Stefan said. He took a few steps toward the hypnosis couch. "You're in a safe place, Eloise, where no one can hurt you, and most of all, no one is judging you."

Right.

His voice was like velvet. But once the eye contact had been broken, I realized that, yeah, I was still mad. So not only did Stefan have the balls to try to make me think he'd been spying on me for my own good, but then he was reaching into my head with a spoonful of sugar and trying to tweak my emotions to make me swallow down all of his flattering half-truths.

Stefan was a certified fifth-level empath. And if he was anywhere as proficient at his talent as I was at mine, then arguing with him was like trying to bail out the Titanic.

I heard the splatter of vomit as I slipped out Stefan's office door. I hoped at least part of it had hit him.

✦ THIRTY-FIVE ✦

Zigler needed to make his noontime call to Nancy, but I wasn't ready to stop what I was doing just yet. If I turned my head and tilted it, I could still see a pale sliver of white where the suicide nurse's cap disappeared into the wall. Except she wasn't really a suicide nurse. She'd jumped to escape the fire that started in the coal cellar in 1949. I'm guessing she didn't make it, judging by the repeater she left behind.

"Go ahead," I told Zig. "I'm gonna give this one a few more passes."

I'd discovered I was perfectly able to do my own exorcisms—even without Jacob beside me, glowing with the white light he'd pilfered. I'd been watching Zig pretty hard ever since we discovered Jacob's talent, and my guess was that Bob Zigler was NP through and through.

I didn't mention it to Zig, of course. He felt bad enough for bailing on the fire ghost, and I wanted to make sure he stuck around for the long haul because, psychic or not, he was a good guy to have at my back as long as zombies and crazy fire ghosts weren't involved. Not only had he been willing to step in front of a shooter to haul me into the cruiser—he'd also cooked up the idea to rig a box of exorcism tools to look like an evidence kit, so I could act like I was dusting for prints while I spread powdered herbs. He couldn't figure out a way to pass candles off as forensic gear, but a luminol bottle filled with Florida Water worked just as well.

The zombies and crazy fire ghosts? They were the exception rather than the norm. But a day didn't go by where I didn't spot a repeater somewhere.

I sucked some white light, spritzed the not-suicide nurse with my flowery luminol, and gave her ghost a mental shove toward the spirit realm. It was the twentieth time I'd done it, and the mental effort combined with the smell of the

Florida Water was making me giddy.

But when I looked hard at the spot where she'd been disappearing into the wall—over and over for roughly sixty years—and saw that she was finally gone, I felt like I'd really accomplished something good.

I turned to leave, and found Doctor Gillmore standing in the doorway. "How's the shoulder?" she said.

I rotated it. It hurt. But now I was in the hit-by-a-car-and-lived-to-tell-about-it club. If sideview mirrors counted. And judging by the way my shoulder felt, I'd say they did. "Stiff. Sore."

"Hold it out. I'll check your range of motion, see if it's any better than it was last week."

I was glad she didn't have me strip down first. Jacob had added a fresh new series of toothmarks to my belly. I chewed on my lower lip and tried not to look too smug about it.

Gillmore pressed my arm back.

"Ow."

"You're taking aspirin?"

Sure. Wait, no. "I uh...I meant to."

"I can't write you a prescription for anything stronger, not with your other meds. But I could call your clinic and give them a recommendation." If the phone number of The Clinic was even listed. Maybe it had to be, in case a psych turned up unconscious in Gillmore's ER.

I decided not to think about that, since I could feel my sweat glands gearing up for another good soak. "No, that's okay. Aspirin's fine. Things just slip my mind sometimes when I've got a lot going on."

She pressed my arm up, then back, then rotated it. "Mm hm. Better. But don't knock the aspirin. Anti-inflammatories are your friends."

"Okay. I'll leave a bottle in my car." Gillmore sank her thumb into my shoulder and I did my best not to wince. "So, what about that homeless lady? What was her name?"

"I never told you."

Damn. I'd thought I was so smooth. "But you'll give her my card if you see her, right? And tell her I'll buy her dinner."

She nodded like maybe she was just humoring me, but I suspected she would at least try.

Gillmore turned toward the door, and then paused. She put her hands in the pockets of her white lab coat. She spoke slowly, in a voice that was a lot softer than her usual ultra-authoritative tone. "I did track down a couple of Miss Connoley's nieces," she said. "In case you need to tell them how she died."

"Oh." I scratched my head. "I dunno. I think she's at rest now. I mean, I know she is. If I go to her family and start dragging skeletons out of the closet, it'll turn into a whole...thing."

"And they'll wonder why she was confined in the coal cellar, and not safe in her bed."

In the mental ward, which I'm guessing wasn't all fun and games, either. Not back then. "Maybe you're the one who needs to know," I said.

She shook her head. "Who would do something like that?"

"Never underestimate the twistedness of a guy with screwed-up urges. My boyfriend works sex crimes...." That had just come rolling right out. Gillmore glanced at me, but didn't seem terribly blown away by the revelation that I was queer. "He sees stuff like this, and worse, day in and day out. I don't think he asks why anymore. He just puts an end to it."

Doctor Gillmore sat on the edge of the bed, laced her fingers together on her lap, and sighed hard. "But what about the hospital administration—where were they in all of this? Didn't anyone notice she was gone? Didn't anyone look for her?"

Maybe, maybe not. Crazy people are kind of invisible that way. "It was too long ago. We'll never know." And even if we could figure out who was responsible, I was sure he was long dead. I think Gillmore wanted an explanation. She wanted justice. Sometimes things don't work out that way.

⚡⚡⚡⚡⚡

It was nearly a week before Jacob and I had a day off that coincided. We parked his Crown Vic in the lot of a small industrial park that hadn't seen much use in the past several years. A few enterprising weeds had sprung up in the cracks where the snow had recently melted, though the bigger drifts that fell in the shade of the building were still lying across the asphalt in pollution-specked white ridges.

Jacob looked the squat brick building up and down. "That's not it," I said. I pointed between a couple of corrugated metal machine sheds. "Over there. I, uh...I think." I looked up at the sky, as if I could find a landmark there. "Kinda hard to say."

"Let's take a look."

Jacob marched on ahead, and I followed, placing my feet in his footprints where he'd punched through the crust of old snow.

We walked to the back of the property, which ended in a chain link fence. I looked at the top, and tried to imagine the razorwire looping through. That was fifteen years ago. There wasn't anything left to protect now, so the old fencing had probably gone the way of the Camp Hell building itself.

"Need a leg up?" he said.

I stared at the eight-foot fence. "Can't you just lean on it and knock part of it down?"

Jacob raised an eyebrow.

"The last time I went over a fence, I sprained my elbow. And since then, my other arm got hit by a car."

He gave me a sharky smile. "Come on. I'll give you a good push. You'll only have to worry about your landing."

I had no doubt Jacob could throw me over the fence like a big, gangly football if he wanted to. And also, since I'd brought him this far, there was no turning back now. Jacob's a pretty patient guy. But there were some areas where his self-control had clear limits.

Camp Hell was one of those areas.

I pitched the exorcism kit I was carrying over the top of the fence. "Fine. Give me a boost."

My arms said ow, and ow, but I managed to make my way over without damaging any other part of my body. And even though my elbow was still smarting, the sight of Jacob scaling the fence in his form-fitting black jeans and leather jacket was enough to dull the pain.

I picked up my exorcism kit, and Jacob pressed his hand against the small of my back. "What do you think? Was this it?"

I stared at the empty lot. It had no street address of its own. Instead, it was tucked away in the middle of a bunch of other properties, mostly industrial, or maybe storage. Patches of ground were covered in snow. Others had last year's brown husks of weeds poking through. I tried to picture the building itself, and then just a few details. The reflective black glass doors. The view of the parking lot from the smoking lounge. But everything was different now.

I shook my head. "I dunno. It's changed too much."

Jacob slipped his arm around my waist. "It's okay."

"For me it is. But I've got to make sure Warwick's nephew is gone. You know?"

He nodded. "All right."

We walked carefully. The ground changed, from old asphalt to old concrete, and then, to dirt—fill dirt thick with pebbles and stones. There had been a building there once. But whoever tore it down had done a thorough job of it.

"Spirit activity?" Jacob asked.

"Nope. Sorry to disappoint you."

"I'm that obvious, huh?"

I decided there was no good way to answer that. Instead, I reached over and stroked the back of Jacob's neck where his hairline ended, just over the collar of his leather jacket. He shivered, and gave me a dark-eyed look that told me he'd be happy to throw me down and add a few more marks to my collection.

I felt myself smile back at him. Even though I was possibly standing smack on top of the corpse of Camp Hell.

His gaze went to my mouth, and he brushed his lips over mine. I pressed my forehead against his, and funneled white light into the two of us. I couldn't say if he was glowing or not, given that we were standing outside under a pale gray overcast sky. But I suspected that he was.

We stood there together, quiet, glowing. And then Jacob's gaze shifted to something over my shoulder. "How about that red roof?" he said. "You remember that?"

I turned to looked at the squat, industrial skyline at my back. Gray, gray, brown, tan, gray.... Red. A burst of color in a sea of neutrals. It did indeed tug at my memory since, after all, I really am a visual kind of guy. I held on to Jacob's sleeve, gave his forearm a squeeze, and stared.

The red roof. I'd been able to see it from the classroom where I'd spent so many hours in focus groups with Faun Windsong, and Dead Darla, and Richie. I stepped onto the packed fill dirt and walked toward the red roof, pulling Jacob along behind me. I stopped right under my old classroom.

"Yeah," I said. "This is the spot."

"You okay?"

Surprisingly, the sureness that Camp Hell used to be there didn't send me into a panicky cold sweat. "I'm okay."

I walked forward, Jacob right behind me, and did my best to pick out the perimeter of the building. There were areas I'd only been to a few times, mostly the storage spaces, or the administrative wing. But there were others where there wasn't much else to do but stare out the window and wonder what kind of life could possibly be out there for a freak like me.

I saw a tree, a papery white birch among a straggling of neglected maples, or maybe oaks, which look the same to me once the leaves have dropped. And I realized that I remembered that tree with its pale, smooth trunk, the odd one out among all the other trees that were dark and gnarled. I'd seen the birch from a window in the stairwell behind the pop machines.

"The basement was over here," I said. I pointed at a patch of ground, and tried to envision myself walking down a flight of stairs, turning, and going down another. A steel door. A hallway. Here: a drinking fountain. A fire extinguisher.

A pair of doors. Men's room. Ladies' room.

I'd retraced the steps. All at ground-level, of course, but my vision was shifted inward. I stood in the spot where the repeater slipped and fell, and cracked her head open on the sink. I looked for her, but didn't see her. Maybe she was still there, but buried under twenty feet of backfill, slipping and falling for all eternity. I hoped not.

"I don't really see anything," I said. "But I think I want to clear the area. Just in case."

Jacob pulled the dashboard compass out of his pocket and consulted it. He squatted beside me, and cleared away a stubborn mound of snow that had clung to a bit of rubble. He jerked his hand back and a bead of blood welled on his fingertip, bright red, like the red roof. "Broken glass," he said.

I squatted beside him and pushed the snow away more carefully. The stump of a prayer candle had cemented itself into the fill dirt, but the glass holder had cracked from the cold. The base was held together with white wax, but the sides had fallen away, all but the sharp point that had drawn blood on Jacob. "Maybe this is why the area's clean," he said. He sucked the blood off his fingertip, then wiped his finger on his black jeans. "Due north. Another medium got here first."

We looked more carefully, and found the remnant of a candle on the east point. The others were long gone. Whoever'd cleaned house had done it a long time ago.

"You think it was Richie?" Jacob asked. "You said he used prayer candles in his exorcisms, right? And he would've known about this spot."

"I dunno. I don't think it matters. If I call him and ask, I'll need to make up some excuse why I can't go bowling with him, and...."

Though I had no great love of bowling, the real reason I wouldn't call Richie was that he was employed by the FPMP, albeit in a more transparent capacity than Stefan. Since I preferred to keep my pineal gland bullet-free, I'd decided to step back and let the FPMP go about its business with no further help from me.

Dreyfuss had stopped calling me after I'd watched Roger Burke buy it. I wondered if Laura had told him she'd seen me at the scene of Burke's shooting, or if he'd gathered it from his sources at the Fifth Precinct. Or the FBI. Or if I'd been spotted by his stupid remote viewer.

I touched Jacob's knee and fed him some more white light. If we weren't willing to slip off to an uninhabited desert island, then we'd need to keep ourselves glowing white, go back to doing our jobs, and make as few waves as possible. I felt a deep pang of loss at the realization that someone else was going to end up with the two remaining GhosTVs...heck, maybe they'd even get junked without anyone ever knowing what they really were, since the gigantic tubes were so heavy and archaic in the age of flat-screen, high-definition everything. But I couldn't risk visiting Chance again. There were too many ghosts full of bullet holes in Dreyfuss' office. I wasn't about to add myself to their number.

"I'm not saying you shouldn't perform an additional exorcism," Jacob offered. "Just to be safe."

I met Jacob's eye and suppressed a smile. He'd like that. "I'm pretty sure it's clean."

"One hundred percent sure?"

I rolled my eyes and gave his knee a squeeze. "Yeah. Sorry."

I stood, and my knees popped. Jacob followed, and his didn't. He planted his hands on his hips and squinted toward the edge of the property line. "The aftermath of that fire in LaSalle lasted for decades," he said. "But there's nothing left of Camp Hell but an empty lot. Go figure."

"Doctor Gillmore thinks the admin at LaSalle swept the fire under the carpet. Records from 1949 are nowhere to be found, even though some of the files date back to the Second World War. The Tribune buried the fire on page five with some vague mention that the number of 'casualties' was unclear, and some big rah-rah spin about how they were going to remodel. So the best we can figure is that money changed hands somewhere to cover it up."

I poked some broken glass with the toe of my sneaker, and added, "I imagine Camp Hell's coverup involved a lot more than just money."

Jacob gazed longingly at a point between the north and east candle where the exorcism had happened without him. "I don't think it would hurt anything to go over this spot one more time. I'm sure you're a lot stronger than whoever else they've got on their payroll."

I laughed, a short, sharp burst that surprised me, surprised both of us.

Jacob smiled tentatively. "What is it?"

I stared at the spot where Warwick's nephew had warned me never to tell anyone what I could do, and then I slid my hand into Jacob's and pulled him close. He slipped his other arm around me and held me. I kissed him, and tried to clear my mind of everything but him and me. I looked deep into his eyes, and tried to determine if I was ready to let him in on the one thing I'd been carrying with me since my first round of psychic testing.

He stared back at me like a man who'd fallen for me, hard. And that part inside me, the one that usually tells me to run, or to shut up, or to play along and make myself invisible and hopefully whatever I'm dealing with will just go away? That part of me said, *Yes. Tell him.*

"I've got more talent than everyone on their payroll put together," I said. Jacob squeezed me tighter. His eyes never moved from mine. "I'm so far beyond level five it's not even funny."

Jacob held me so hard I was worried he might crack a rib, and he crushed his mouth to mine, filled my mouth with his tongue. I felt his fingers dig into my back, even through my jean jacket and two sweatshirts. His hand roved downward, and he took a good handful of my ass, and squeezed. I pressed my crotch against his thigh and enjoyed being manhandled.

Jacob kissed me until I thought we'd both pass out from lack of air, then he tore his mouth from mine and pressed his wet lips to my ear. "You have no idea what that does to me."

I was fairly sure I did. But I still liked hearing him say it.